THE
MAN WHO
PLAYED
TRAINS

THE
MAN WHO
PLAYED
TRAINS

RICHARD WHITTLE

urbanepublications.com

First published in Great Britain in 2017
by Urbane Publications Ltd
Suite 3, Brown Europe House, 33/34 Gleaming Wood Drive,
Chatham, Kent ME5 8RZ
Copyright © Richard Whittle, 2017

A CIP catalogue record for this book is available
from the British Library.

ISBN 978-1-911331-03-2
MOBI 978-1-911331-05-6
EPUB 978-1-911331-04-9

Design and Typeset by Michelle Morgan

Cover by The Invisible Man

Printed and bound by CPI Group (UK) Ltd, Croydon, CR0 4YY

urbanepublications.com

CHAPTER ONE

THE PICTURES IN SPARGO'S HEAD come to him in the no-man's-land between sleeping and waking. Though they are not dreams they have the way of dreams, occasionally frightening and always nonsensical. People, if those he sees in his visions are indeed human, are corpse-like and pale. Landscapes and skies – when there are landscapes and skies – are dull and drab, they are never in colour.

Years ago Spargo described to his mother the creatures he saw. Dead people, he called them. Morag, in all other aspects of young Spargo's life a devoted parent who righted wrongs and made bad things good, had seemed peculiarly indifferent to his problem. Nightmares, he'd called them, a word picked up from school and which seemed to apply. Imaginings, his mother corrected, and attempted to explain them away by saying he was a growing boy – as if this information was new to him and made everything right.

That his mother dismissed so readily the greatest problem Spargo had encountered in his life affected him deeply. Nevertheless, he did what she said and tried hard to forget. Months later, when she asked him if the pictures still troubled him he lied to her. Said he no longer saw them.

Many years later, while relaxing on his bed in university hall, Spargo considered how convenient it would be if there was a device that could project films on to the ceiling. His thoughts strayed to projectors and then to his old school, to the projector and cans of film the head teacher hired each Christmas for the annual school treat. These films, Spargo realised, were the first moving pictures he'd seen.

Kilcreg, Spargo's home village, tucked away in the far north-east of Scotland, was too small to warrant its own cinema. Television –

black and white – had become commonplace in cities and towns but in Kilcreg it was unknown. When the mast that finally brought television signals to that part of the Scottish coast was erected high on a hill above the village, every Kilcreg resident turned out to watch. That was in the nineteen-sixties. John Spargo, in his final year at university, missed the great day.

While staring at the ceiling it occurred to Spargo that his imaginings might stem from those early films. He and his friends had watched four such movie marathons, reel after reel of Saturday morning cinema serials that, over the years, amounted to around twenty hours of black and white movie stock. Dredging his memories he recalled skeletons, luminous horses and headless ghosts. That he had forgotten about these until that day made his hypothesis even more valid. Isn't that what you do with your worst fears? Don't you banish them to dark corners of your mind?

If this explanation didn't quite exorcise Spargo's ghosts it certainly disabled them. For his remaining years at university the no man's land of near sleep held no fears.

His decision to become a mining engineer surprised nobody. His late father had been manager of the long-defunct Kilcreg Mine, an underground mine that until the late nineteen-thirties had been a one-man-and-a-dog operation producing small amounts of tungsten, a vital ingredient of steel. The increasing likelihood of war with Germany triggered massive investment in Kilcreg by the Government's Ministry of Mines. The first change they made was to recruit Cornish engineer Samuel Spargo to expand operations and make it all work.

That John Spargo graduated with first-class honours from London's Royal School of Mines came as no surprise either, such was his dedication to his subject of choice. Back then, finding a job in his chosen profession was easy. Metal mining was booming, investment was strong.

Work meant moving overseas. After leaving London Spargo joined the ranks of engineers recruited by the Zambian copper mines. Within a few days of starting work at he encountered an old school friend, Stuart Campbell, at the bottom of the mine's new McLaren shaft at Roan Antelope Mine. Unlike Spargo, who had lived in the mine manager's spacious detached house in Kilcreg, the Campbell family occupied the very last semi in the village's only street, a stone-built two-up and two-down overlooking the small harbour. A month after Kilcreg Mine closed the Campbell family upped-sticks and left. The same might have happened to Spargo, had his father not died.

The two young men rekindled their friendship. Over subsequent weeks and many beers they swapped memories – of school, of Kilcreg, of the old tungsten mine. During one of these sessions Spargo steered the conversation around to their school's Christmas films. Not only did Stuart remember them, he remembered their titles and everything about them. What is more, he insisted that none of the films they watched at school were in the least bit frightening.

The dismissal of the school movies as the cause of Spargo's imaginings did him no good at all. Campbell had, unknowingly, demolished at a single stroke the barriers Spargo built to keep out his demons. A barrier that even now, in late middle age, he hadn't quite managed to rebuild.

The news that Morag was in hospital came from Jessica, Spargo's daughter. It came as a shock to him because though his mother was well past what she often referred to as her allotted span – the three-score-and-ten years she reached healthily and then romped past as if still in her sixties, she was remarkably fit and well.

'Inverness,' Jez said, her voice shaky but firm. 'Raigmore Hospital. They want you there, Dad. It sounds bad...'

Luck rather than good timing took Spargo north out of Edinburgh on unusually clear roads. Deep in thought he approached the Forth Road Bridge with his mind on his mother, trying to recall when he'd last made the trip. Kilcreg was, dependent on traffic, two hours beyond Inverness, in total a five hour drive on roads not made for high speeds.

He had visited Morag at Christmas and then again in March, a weekend stay to replace a gutter that fell in the snow, a gutter the local handyman hadn't managed to repair because he was too old to climb ladders. By the time Spargo was well into the journey he was admitting to himself it was seven months since he'd last seen his mother, seven long months since he'd swept the dead woodlice from between the same sheets he had slept in at Christmas – short flicks of his hand that sent the tiny grey balls bowling across the spare bedroom.

He had phoned Raigmore before leaving and they'd used the same words to him as they had used to Jez. He had quizzed them the same way he had quizzed her, learning only that his mother was brought in by ambulance and her condition was serious.

As far back as Spargo could remember his mother's hair had been tied back in a bun. Now, laid on her back in her hospital bed, her hair had been let loose by nurses, combed out straight to frame her face like twin pillars. Tidied for him, perhaps, an attempt to make bad things look less bad. Her eyes were closed, not tightly but peacefully. Her arms were on top of the bedclothes, resembling, he thought, a brass rubbing on the tomb of a medieval knight.

He was drifting again, fantasising. In truth the woman in the hospital bed looked nothing like his mother; her right eye was hidden behind a puffy bruised cheek and the skin around her other eye had yellowed. A sterile pad, taped to her forehead, had loosened to reveal twin tracks of tight stitches running back through her scalp.

He had not gone in. He had frozen in the doorway of the one-bed room.

'I had no idea...' he mumbled. 'No idea it was so bad...'

The nurse who led him there didn't hear him, she was no longer there. Glancing back along the corridor he saw her returning, no longer alone, attempting to keep up with a woman a head and shoulders taller than her who walked with long strides, her legs flicking the edges of her unbuttoned white coat as she walked. A stethoscope, the medical badge of office, poked up from a side pocket.

'Mr Spargo? John Spargo?'

Spargo nodded. By the time the doctor reached him he still hadn't moved.

'Mr Spargo... how much do you know?'

He frowned. Fought for words and failed. The doctor waited. Stared impatiently.

'We have done all we can for your mother,' she said. 'I have to say it's a miracle she survived at all.'

'I had no idea,' Spargo repeated, this time to listeners. 'No idea it was so bad.'

The nurse remained patiently in the corridor while the doctor eased herself past Spargo. Once in the room the doctor beckoned Spargo. Flicked impatient fingers.

'Come in properly, Mr Spargo...'

Using the doctor as a shield he moved close to the bed, his legs, like his voice, under his control again. He noticed for the first time his mother's right arm was bandaged from wrist to shoulder.

'I don't understand,' he said. 'The injuries. Did she fall?'

Had it not been for the fact that for the last thirty years his mother had lived in a bungalow he would have sworn she had fallen downstairs. Or if not stairs, then perhaps the stone step outside the back door. Had she tripped going out to the garden? The stones bordering the flower bed were lethal. Years ago he'd turned some of them over to bury their fang-like points. It was his fault she was here. He should have moved the lot.

The doctor wore glasses, frameless but for a thin strip of bright steel along the top of the lenses. When she looked at him she peered over them as if looking over a garden fence. Looked judgemental.

'Have you spoken to the police?'

'Police? No. The hospital called my daughter, they said Morag was here. I drove here straight away. It took almost five hours.'

What was meant as an apology sounded more like a complaint. The judgemental stare intensified. This time it was accompanied by furrowed, puzzled brows.

'The police have not spoken to you?'

'Why the police?'

'Your mother was attacked in her home, Mr Spargo. You should have been told.'

Spargo opened his mouth. Closed it again and took time to find words. 'Mugged? Is that it? Is that what you're saying?'

'Not exactly. I understand someone broke into her house. Your mother was beaten. Beaten viciously and deliberately.'

Spargo pinched his wrist. Nothing changed. Never in his worst nightmares – and he knew about nightmares – had things been this bad.

The nurse slid a chair up close to the bed, put her hands on Spargo's shoulders and guided him down onto it. The paper cup she slipped into his hand some time later was hot and it hurt his fingers but he hardly noticed. For most of the next hour he sipped dutifully at a sugary liquid that might well have been tea, all the time staring at his mother, this stranger in surgical dressings. He tried, in vain, to edit-out the bruises, the swellings and the outrageous colours.

It was as well the police hadn't told Spargo what had happened to his mother. During his journey from Edinburgh he had driven too fast on a road well-known for fatalities. Had he known the facts he would have driven even faster, risking his life and the lives of others for no purpose. Because, at three minutes to midnight, his mother died.

CHAPTER TWO

'MR MITCHELL HAS BEEN TOLD about your mother, Mr Spargo. That she died, I mean. He is still at Kilcreg but he's due back at first light. It's a bad business.'

Spargo gave a nod, an acceptance of sorts. Flicking back his cuff he stared down at his watch. First light? When the hell was first light? Seven o'clock? Eight?

'Who is Mitchell?'

'Detective Sergeant Mitchell. He's dealing with it.'

Spargo had driven from Raigmore on the outskirts of Inverness to a police station in town, a brand new building well hidden in back streets. In the dark it had taken him half an hour to find the place – time to work out what to say to police who had neglected to call him and explain what had happened. By the time he found the police station, parked in one of the many vacant slots and walked in through the front doors to the officer at the desk, he had lost what little confidence he'd had.

'The doctor at Raigmore said my mother was attacked,' Spargo grunted. 'I want to know what happened. I want to know why I wasn't told.'

'I don't know any details, Mr Spargo. Best you wait for the DS. I'll get word to him that you called.'

Spargo, again in the cold, eased himself into his car, pulled the door closed and sat lost in thought, only thinking to start the car's engine when he started to shiver. Once the car was warm he reclined the seat and lay back, thinking and dozing. Only when the buzz of his mobile phone woke him did he realised he had slept. He fumbled in the dark for it.

'Spargo...'

'Dad? Where are you? You said you would call me!'

He had been dreading Jez phoning him. He hadn't the guts to phone her, not last night. He moistened dry lips with his tongue.

'She didn't make it,' he mumbled. Realising how pathetic he sounded he sat up straight and turned off the engine. 'I'm sorry, love,' he said. 'Gran died last night, just before twelve.'

He hoped she wouldn't ask questions. Hoped she would accept her grandmother's death in the same way he had accepted the news of her hospitalisation. Morag was an old lady. Old people got ill. Sometimes they died.

'She had a good life,' Jez said. 'We knew it might happen soon.'

Jez, always practical. If she believed her grandmother had died a natural death then that suited him, for now.

'The doctor said she had a stroke,' he said. 'A massive one. They really didn't expect her to recover.' Not just economical with the truth but blatant lies. Later she would give him hell. For now he could live with that.

The morning sun rose suddenly, lighting the dark undersides of dense cloud with a brilliant orange glow. Then, in the manner of a reversed sunset, it started to fade as the sun rose higher until it was obscured by cloud. Spargo, oblivious to dawn's fine display, realised he could now see his car clock. He stared at it absently, unaware he was counting the seconds between the clock's passing minutes, expecting its digits to change when every time he reached sixty. Got it wrong every time.

At five to seven he tugged his collar high against cold wind and walked to the police station's glass doors. The constable he had spoken to in the early hours had been replaced by a stocky, surly sergeant with deep-set eyes. Spargo faced him squarely and said who he was. Didn't have a chance to say more before a voice interrupted him.

'John Spargo?'

The voice came from behind him. He turned, took in the man's square face, thick eyebrows and dark hair that greyed at the sides. Mitchell – he assumed it was Mitchell – was about forty years old and fit and lean. Somehow, Spargo wasn't sure how, the man didn't fit his image of a detective. Too dapper and darty, too small. He readied himself for a handshake. It didn't come.

'Detective Sergeant Mitchell... I'm sorry to hear about your mother.'

Spargo gave a sharp nod. 'I want to know what happened to her.'

'Don't we all.'

It wasn't the answer he expected. He wanted explanations, not sharp comments. He considered pressing the man for information but thought better of it.

Twelve hours in coveralls had reordered the creases in Mitchell's suit. It had the appearance of having been stored overnight in a bin bag. Though he wore a tie it was undone, hanging like a halter around a drooped-open, unbuttoned collar. He had taken the trouble to comb his hair and its neatness was at odds with his dark-rimmed eyes and a day's growth of stubble.

Spargo stroked his own chin and wondered if he looked the same. It didn't take detective training to see he'd spent the night in his car.

'Forgive my bluntness Mr Spargo. I know your mother didn't regain consciousness. I have been told you were with her when she died.'

Spargo didn't respond. He wanted to ask why the police hadn't had someone there in case she came round. Perhaps they knew there was no chance she would. Mitchell, Spargo thought, was inspecting him as if he were a suspect, his eyes darting from his hair to his ears, his nose and his chin. From there they went down his clothes to his shoes. It seemed very personal. A whole body scan.

'No, she didn't regain consciousness.' Spargo said. 'The doctor said she was attacked. I want to know why I wasn't told... why my daughter wasn't told.'

Mitchell stayed looking down, his manner thoughtful. 'Things don't always go to plan.' If it was meant as an apology for poor communications then it was short lived. 'I know this is a bad time for you,' he continued, 'but I want you to come to Kilcreg with me.' He looked up from the floor and into Spargo's eyes. 'I need you there. There are things only you can explain to me.'

'Kilcreg? You mean now?'

Mitchell nodded, started to speak but interrupted his own flow by wagging a finger, first at Spargo and then to some distant, unseen point.

'There's a cloakroom. You want to clean yourself up or something?'

Then, mindless of his offer, Mitchell ushered Spargo outside. Spargo took a couple of steps towards his car. Mitchell walked the other way. Spargo called to him.

'Will you go first? Shall I follow you?'

'No, I want you with me, how else can I talk to you?'

Mitchell's car was moving before Spargo fastened his seat belt, down the lane from the station and out to the road. Mitchell stayed quiet. Spargo wanted to initiate a conversation but decided Mitchell's attentions were better directed towards manoeuvring through traffic.

The sun, Spargo noticed as they took Kessock Bridge at an uncomfortably fast speed, had now vanished completely. The day was darker now than it was an hour ago and the Black Isle, the land to the north of the bridge, was living up to its name.

Most of the traffic came towards them, early starters heading south for Inverness and beyond. The few that drove north were overtaken by Mitchell, at speed. His car was grey with no markings, an omission Spargo considered unfortunate because if there was ever a man who needed flashing blue lights, it was Mitchell. He drove mechanically, as if programmed to travel fast come what may. Spargo gave his seat belt a subconscious, tightening tug. Still Mitchell said nothing. Perhaps tiredness and events of the night conspired against conversation. They were twenty minutes into the journey before Mitchell spoke.

'Did your mother keep valuables in her house?'

'A few personal treasures. Nothing you'd call valuable. Don't suppose they'd fetch much. Is that why she was attacked? Robbery?'

'What do you mean by personal treasures?'

'Old jewellery. A couple of hundred pounds worth of odds and sods. Did they take it?'

'Did who take it?'

Spargo was tempted to ask who the hell Mitchell thought he meant.

'Whoever attacked my mother.'

'Not as far as we can tell.'

'There's a DVD player I bought her last year. And the TV, of course.'

'They're still there. What else?'

Spargo shrugged. 'Nothing. Certainly nothing worth beating an old lady to death for.'

No, he didn't mean that. Nothing in this world was worth beating an old lady for. He had hoped Mitchell would start at the beginning and tell all. The way it looking, it wasn't going to happen.

'I need to know what happened,' Spargo said. 'I'm not expecting miracles. I don't expect you to tell me who did it.'

'What have you been told?'

'Nothing. Nothing at all. Yesterday I went out and forgot to take my mobile with me. When I got home I found a message from my daughter on the house phone. When I spoke to her she said someone had called her to say my mother had been taken to Raigmore. She wasn't told anything about an attack.'

Mitchell took time to answer. 'That was my fault,' he murmured, so quietly Spargo hardly heard. 'The hospital was told not to mention it. They gave your daughter my mobile number. You or she could have called me.'

'Nobody gave her any numbers.'

Mitchell kept his gaze straight ahead, his eyes on the road as he overtook vehicles.

'I didn't know that.'

'Who found her, Rosie?'

'Who is Rosie?'

Rose Munro had lived in the cottage next door to his mother's for as long as he could remember. It was a stone-built bungalow with a small garden at the front and a larger one at the back, almost a mirror image of his mother's place. Both had always-open gates and short drives that were little more than parking spaces, each terminating at one-car, prefabricated garages. The drives were separated by a low chain-link fence on concrete posts and the side doors of the houses faced each other. It was a sociable, small village thing.

'You mean Mrs Munro? No, she's not there. It was the postman.'

Spargo's mind drifted to a story he had read long ago, a Father Brown mystery, by Chesterton, if he remembered correctly. The postman did it. He simply walked in and out of a house. Murdered a man and nobody really noticed him. Spargo bit his lip, angry to be bothered by such trivia.

He waited for more from Mitchell. Nothing came. The man was negotiating a tight bend, down through the gears and then up through them rapidly.

'And?' Spargo asked.

'He – that's the postman – said the door was open. The side door, that is. Did your mother always use the side door, never the front?'

'The postman always came to the side door. Years ago my mother used the front door for visitors, but now the only ones she gets are her neighbours. The front door is blocked off with a bookcase. She can't use it.'

Mitchell nodded. Said nothing. Spargo continued:

'There can't be more than a handful of people left. The village is dying.' Bad choice of word. He bit his lip again. 'Sometimes the postman gets invited in for tea. Stops for a chat.'

'People still do that? Really? Who else calls at the house?'

Spargo went quiet. 'Different now,' he murmured. 'There was a milkman once. And a baker. And a man who sold groceries, he had a small bus, a green thing, a corner shop on wheels with the bus windows painted over. Don't think he comes now.'

'So how did your mother manage? She hasn't got a car. I'm told there's no bus.'

'An old couple a few doors down drive her to the shops once a fortnight. Drove her…'

'Mr and Mrs Dundonald?'

'You've spoken to them?'

'We've spoken to everyone. That's except for Mrs Munro. She is away at her daughter's, apparently. Up north somewhere.'

There wasn't much further north anyone could go. Spargo wondered where he meant. Thurso? The Orkney Isles?

'You still haven't told me what happened.'

'She was attacked, Mr Spargo. I'm sure you were told. You must have seen her injuries.'

'Was there more than one attacker?'

'I can't say.'

'Can't? Won't?'

'Can't, not yet. As I said, the side door was open. The postman saw your mother on the kitchen floor. His mobile didn't work so he used the house phone to call an ambulance. We're investigating the possibility she opened the door to her attacker.'

'More likely her attacker just wandered in. Kilcreg's the ass-end of the world, there's no reason for anyone to go there. You don't get walk-in thefts.'

'Are you saying anyone could walk in to any house there?'

'Yes, during the day,' Spargo said. 'Not that easy though, is it?'

Spargo turned his head and looked at Mitchell. He noticed the growth of stubble on the man's chin and cheeks. Then, as he'd done in the police station, he raised a hand to his own chin. It felt rough. He was usually clean-shaven and the stubble made him feel grubby.

'What do you mean, not easy?'

'You've seen Kilcreg, it's at the end of a valley, surrounded by high moorland. The harbour is the only low bit. Each side of it there are sea cliffs. Unless you are a hiker or boatman the only way in is via the road across the moor, you've driven it, you know what it's like. The hillside behind my mother's cottage is open land with hardly a tree in sight, there's nowhere to hide. It's easy to see people coming.'

'That's assuming there is someone to see them. The place isn't exactly buzzing. What about the end of the road, the turning circle? I saw paths there. Where do they lead, along the beach?'

'One of the paths goes to the old jetty. There's no real beach, just boulders and collapsed cliffs. Didn't you go there? Haven't you seen it?'

'I haven't had time to go sightseeing. What about the lane across the road from your mother's cottage? Where does that go?'

'You mean the path beside the old school?'

The school, left to rot when it closed in the nineteen sixties. At some point it had been robbed of slates, its roof timbers and then its stone. The stubby short walls that remained gave it the appearance of a partly restored Roman villa.

'So that's what that ruin is,' Mitchell said. 'I did wonder. So where does the path go?'

'Up the hillside to the old chapel and graveyard. The chapel's a ruin and the graveyard's disused. Apart from that there's nothing but mile after mile of heather. That side of the valley isn't a good place to watch the house from.'

More silence from Mitchell. Then:

'When did you last see your mother?'

Father, it should be, Spargo thought. When did you last see your father? – the painting, the Cromwell soldier and the boy. He checked himself. His mind was taking side-roads. Anything to avoid the real issue.

'Well?' Mitchell said. 'Mr Spargo? When did you last see her?'

Guilt, now. Kilcreg isn't the easiest place to get to and it wasn't as if he hadn't offered to move his mother to Edinburgh years ago. If she'd agreed to move he would have seen her more often and this wouldn't have happened. He took a deep breath and let it out with a sigh. He knew he was blaming her for his shortcomings. Now was not the time for untruths and excuses.

'Too long ago,' he confessed. 'Months. Seven, I think.'

'How long has she lived at Kilcreg?'

'Since she was married. That's most of her life. Nineteen thirty seven. Maybe thirty eight.'

What was, to Spargo, beginning to sound suspiciously like an interrogation, terminated abruptly when Mitchell jammed on the brakes. What had been a fairly wide road narrowed suddenly. Though there was little traffic, the cars that came towards them travelled fast, middle-aged boy racers on autopilot, late for work. That Mitchell had been awake for more than twenty-four hours was clear from the way he overreacted to approaching cars. He jerked upright, as if stirred from sleep. Touched the brake pedal unnecessarily.

'Why does a place like Kilcreg exist?' he asked, the car up to speed again. 'There's nothing there. Just a few houses.'

'It was a fishing village. Rose Munro can remember when most of the older locals had boats.'

The white wooden signpost at the fork in the road, the one pointing to Kilcreg, had been there as long as Spargo could remember. They turned there, onto a tarred road that soon narrowed to become a single track across moorland, constrained between ditches holding brown peaty water. Spargo knew from unfortunate experience that at least once a year the road became impassable due to deep snow, sometimes for days. Posts to guide snowploughs stuck up at regular intervals like red and white javelins. These, and the occasional signs marking passing bays, far outnumbered trees. It was no surprise to Spargo that for the last fifteen minutes they had seen no other vehicles. Chances were they would get to Kilcreg without seeing a single car, animal, bird or human being.

Spargo's mind drifted. When he was young there was a snowplough in his father's yard, a massive beast with wheels taller than he was. Memories of it came easily and played in his head like a video – the huge plough with its twin engines screaming, grinding its way up the hill out of Kilcreg, flinging snow back to the sky.

He could see snow now. Way off to the north stood the granite dome of Stac Dubh, snow-capped as it often was, its upper slopes indistinguishable from its shrouding, low cloud.

Though the Kilcreg road ran straight for miles it undulated violently, as if over the years long lengths of it had sunk into bog. Spargo knew from experience that if you took the humps too fast then your car left the ground.

Mitchell slowed down. He had learned that too.

Not long now. They had started the winding descent from the moor. The Craig Burn came in from the left and the road followed it down, its tumbling, peaty brown waters obscured by thin mist. The burn changed with the years. The turbulent melt-waters that roared off the moor after late winter thaws scoured out its bed and rearranged boulders. Many of the short bushy trees growing near the water's edge were torn out by torrents, they never grew tall.

A sharp curse from Mitchell plucked Spargo from dreams. A van with police markings laboured uphill from Kilcreg, taking up road space. Mitchell braked; jammed the car in reverse; backed into a passing bay.

'Surprised this road hasn't been widened,' he grunted, 'seeing as it's the only way in.'

Spargo nodded absently but didn't agree. Couldn't see much point in widening a road that led nowhere.

Ahead, through a gap in the hills, two shades of grey met at a hazy horizon. The steep hillsides that framed the view of this distant sea and sky were as bleak as the high moor itself. As if aware of their own vulnerability, the few trees whose roots gripped the thin soil of the valley shrank into themselves like bonsai, their streamlined, seagull-winged branches pointing inland, as if attempting to hide from the sea gales.

The van gone, Mitchell descended the hill slowly, taking bends carefully. One more bend and they would see Kilcreg – two short rows of houses on a straight, narrow road. At the inland end of the valley, the end from which they approached, the road clung to the right-hand hillside. On the left side, the ground dropped sharply to a floor of green fields. At some time in their lives these fields had been fruitful, fertilised every year by seaweed dragged up from the beach. Now they lay neglected, barren but for swathes of bright moss and dark reeds. Barely discernible squares and rectangles disturbed their regularity. Traces of things that had been.

Kilcreg changed little with the seasons. The few firs on the hillsides stayed their own shade of deep green, as did the reeds in the once-ploughed flat land. Spargo recalled how his daughter once remarked that the main difference between the seasons in Kilcreg was that all times of the year except for two months of summer, smoke rose from chimneys. Today there would be smoke.

Nothing could have prepared Spargo for what he saw when Mitchell's car rounded the last bend. He had never seen more than a handful of cars in Kilcreg but today there were dozens. The approach to the village was littered with vehicles, cars crammed on verges, vans jamming the road. Police vehicles far outnumbered houses. Harsh fluorescent yellows and blues outshone Kilcreg's drab greys and greens. Disturbed the peace.

Escapism crept in again: Spargo, being driven to the dentist by his father, wanting to be somewhere else, praying the journey would never end. In the same way he didn't want to go to the dentist all those years ago he didn't want to go to Kilcreg now, didn't want to face what had happened there. He wished, for at least the fifth time since leaving Inverness, that he had refused to come.

He looked away. To his left, beyond the fields, the hillside rose up to heather-clad moor. At the foot of the slope, about as far from the road as it was possible to get, stood a large detached house of grey stone. It was the first and the largest house in Kilcreg and it was away from the others, isolated from them by a sea of rough grass. Like a child's painting it had a door in the middle and four windows, not quite in each corner. Long before Spargo was born an extension had been added to the left side of the building that had messed up the symmetry.

'An only child,' Spargo said absently, nodding towards the house. 'We used to live there. My father was manager of the mine.'

Mitchell glanced left. He saw no mine to have been manager of, only a large stone house with boarded-up windows and a hole in the roof where one of the chimneys had fallen through.

'I didn't know that.'

'The waste ground to the left of the house was the mine's plant yard. The mine itself was up on the high moor.' He nodded, indicating a track climbing high through a cleft in the hill.

'I thought you said fishing?' Mitchell said. 'I didn't know there was any mining around here. Can't have been coal, not this far north.'

'It started as a copper mine in the early nineteen-hundreds, a one-man-and-a-dog thing. Then someone realised some of the stuff they'd been throwing away was wolframite.'

'Wolframite? That's valuable?'

'It's one of the main ores of tungsten, a key component of steel. It strengthens it. In the last war it was a strategic metal, they didn't have enough of the stuff and because of the U-boats they couldn't import it. The government must have guessed war was likely because back in the mid-nineteen-thirties the Ministry of Mines moved in and sunk a shaft. Well, my father did. It made access to the mine easier. The old entrance was high in the cliffs, above the beach.'

'You learn something new every day,' Mitchell muttered. 'So that's why your mother was here. Didn't think Spargo was a Scots name.'

'My father came from Cornwall, my mother from Aberdeen. Not sure how they met.'

'A neighbour told me your father died years ago.'

'Back in the nineteen fifties. I was a boy. After the war the mine stayed open for a while but it couldn't compete with cheap imports. My father died within a few months of the mine closing. Died of a broken heart, the romantics said. The death certificate said cancer.'

Ahead, Kilcreg was grimly busy. Figures in coveralls moved slowly and solemnly, stooping and probing, searching through gardens and inspecting the street. A chequered-topped van blocked the road, its driver shuffling back and forth in a twenty-point turn. Mitchell braked, stopped his car in the road and came to life suddenly, muttering incessantly, holding the car on the clutch and drumming fingers on the wheel. A small van bounced out of a space on the grass verge and like a dog chasing a stick Mitchell jerked the car into the space, its wheels slipping and gripping and scattering stones.

The first house in the row – the furthest house from the sea, apart from the old mine house – was no longer the place Spargo knew but a quarantined cottage, sealed from the world by strands of striped tape. The stuff seemed to be everywhere and it spun in the breeze, blue words that rotated, mesmerising him, transporting him to a film set unreal and unnerving, his mother's house commandeered for the day by a film crew and actors.

Mitchell leapt from the car and came round to Spargo, opened his door for him and held it with both hands. Spargo stayed put. Knew he shouldn't have come.

Mitchell waited. Lost patience.

'I need you inside. You are no use to me out here.'

CHAPTER THREE

SPARGO'S MOTHER DISLIKED the word bungalow and had always referred to her house as a cottage. Spargo, since becoming a resident of Edinburgh, considered her place more suited to the suburbs of that city than to the wilds of Kilcreg. The building was chunky. It sat comfortably behind a low stone wall and a short but wide garden.

At the front of the house a shadowy, rain-foiling alcove sheltered a typically Scottish, double front door. To the left of the alcove stood the wide, curtained bay window of his mother's sitting room. The only difference between this house and the one owned by Rose Munro was that hers had a frog-eye dormer window in the roof overlooking what had been the school. Whether it was original or had been added later Spargo did not know. Nor did he care, not today.

Gravel crunched underfoot as he followed Mitchell down the side of the house. Surely his mother had heard her assailant approaching? Not that it would have mattered because everyone in Kilcreg knew everyone else. In this part of the world there were no strangers.

Mitchell reached the side door, stepped up on the tiled step and turned to Spargo. Instead of speaking he took hold of Spargo's cuff and guided him to the open door the way a father might guide a toddler.

Spargo allowed himself to be led. No matter he had never lived in this house, as he entered the kitchen the smells from his childhood came to him, an ironmonger's odour of bleach, hard soap and a faint smell of mothballs. He had modernised the kitchen twenty years ago, removing the deep stone sink that stood in one corner and installing a shiny new stainless one under the window so when using it his mother could see the back garden and the hillside beyond. He also bought her a new refrigerator, a freezer and a new stove.

'Why on earth do I need a freezer?' he murmured, remembering her words. Mitchell stopped and stared. Spargo shook his head. 'Nothing,' he mumbled.

The kitchen was unexpectedly tidy. The floor was clean. A cup and saucer on the drainer had been rinsed out and left to dry. Spargo moved to the middle of the room, involuntarily because Mitchell had moved there and was still gripping his cuff.

Spargo had supposed there would be something on the floor, if not blood then a movie-style chalked outline of his mother's body. There was nothing. The only sign something had happened there was a dusting of dark powder on the stainless steel drainer.

'Did her attacker panic and hit her?' he asked. They were brave words. He wanted simple explanations. Wanted it minimised.

Mitchell shook his head. 'That doesn't fit. Not the way I see it.'

Spargo wanted to know how Mitchell saw it, but there wouldn't be more. Letting go of Spargo's cuff the man turned on his heel and walked to the hall, his eyes moving constantly as if following a fly: floor to ceiling, ceiling to wall, wall to Spargo and then the front door – or where the front door would be if it wasn't blocked by a bookcase. Spargo made a pointless mental note of it all, as if anticipating being quizzed on everything he saw. He wondered why Mitchell had asked him about the postman using the back door, when he must have seen that the front door was blocked. Didn't want to ask.

'We've been through the place,' Mitchell said, his gaze steady on Spargo. 'Nothing seems to have been taken. I want you to check everything. I want you to tell me if there is anything missing, out of place or unusual. Check the bedrooms first. We are still working in the sitting room.'

There was nothing out of place in his mother's bedroom, nor in the spare room. He stared at the bed he last slept in seven months ago and wondered if there would be more dead woodlice between the sheets. He admitted to himself their presence in the bed was his own fault. Whenever he stayed he always told his mother not to remake the bed because he would soon be back. Where did the woodlice come from, anyway? Did their presence mean there was rotten wood somewhere, or did they just come in out of the cold? If so he could hardly blame them. Not at Kilcreg. Not with those winters.

Mitchell's voice brought him back.

'Mr Spargo… the sitting room… you can check it now.'

Spargo paused in the room's doorway, blocking it. A man and a woman in white coveralls excused themselves with low grunts as they eased past him into the hall. Spargo felt Mitchell's hand on his back, propelling him gently in to the room. Déjà vu.

'Go right in, Mr Spargo.'

Spargo looked at the television, the DVD player and the stereo.

'You've cleaned up,' he said.

'No. Only the kitchen. This is how it was in here.'

'It's not right.'

Mitchell raised his eyebrows. 'Tell me?'

'It's not right,' he repeated. 'It's too clean. My mother's eyesight wasn't good. She didn't notice how dusty things became.'

'Maybe someone cleaned for her.'

'Nobody cleaned for her.'

Spargo stood still and took it all in. No dust on the floorboards. No dust – apart from fingerprint powder – on the places you'd expect it to be, the TV screen, the DVD player, the mirror on the wall above the old fireplace – a fireplace blocked off for years behind a panel of painted plywood. No dust at all. Only brush-swipes of the powder.

He tried to get his head around what he was seeing. The fingerprint powder had been dusted on to spotlessly clean surfaces. Had the police found fingerprints? He didn't think so.

'Did your mother have any work done recently? Any repairs? Plumbing or building work?'

'Why?'

'Please answer my question.'

She'd had nothing done. Her pension was small. When things needed doing he did them for her or arranged for them to be done. He paid for them.

'No. She would have said.'

The floorboards in the room were painted in black gloss, covered partly by two rectangular rugs. Spargo watched Mitchell crouch near the wall and run his hand over the boards. He stood again. Showed Spargo his fingers.

'Fine sawdust,' he said. 'Just a trace. At first we thought the place was cleaned to remove fingerprints. Now we believe it was done to remove traces of sawdust. Many of the floorboards have been cut and lifted. Not just in here, in all the rooms except the kitchen.'

'The kitchen floor is concrete. It's covered with vinyl.'

'So we discovered. They removed this, too.' he said, walking to the boarded-up fireplace. 'The nails holding this panel have been removed and hammered back. The paint on their heads is damaged. Would your mother…?'

'No, not my mother. I meant what I said.'

'So why would anyone want to remove it? Why would they lift floorboards?' he looked at Spargo as if expecting an answer but Spargo just shrugged. 'We spent half the night lifting them,' he added. 'There's nothing underneath.'

'That doesn't surprise me. I've been under them. The space there is small. There's just enough room for cables and pipes.'

'Under? You? Why?'

'Had the boards up years ago. Rewired the whole place with new cables. Put in extra sockets.'

'What about the attic, has anyone been up there recently?'

'Not since I rewired. My mother didn't store junk. My father used to say that if something was ready for the attic it was ready for the tip. I haven't been up there for years but I'm sure it's empty.'

'It is, we checked. But somebody's been up there. Would your mother have had any reason to?'

'She wasn't much of a one for ladders.'

'I don't mean her. A builder or a neighbour?'

'She would have told me.'

His father's oak veneered roll-top bureau stood beside the fireplace. He went to it, grasped the two varnished wood handles on its roll-front lid and then released them suddenly, as if burned. He looked back at Mitchell. Mitchell nodded and Spargo held them again. The lid was a wooden-slat shutter running in a groove cut in the desk's sides. It snaked up and over as he lifted it, vanishing behind the small drawers and cubby-holes at the back of the desk. As it rattled and rolled out of sight he felt the same strange satisfaction he had always felt when he opened it.

He slid out each drawer in turn and upended each one, ploughing his fingers through things he had seen many times, long ago: glass marbles and golf tees; a leather tip from a snooker cue and keys to locks long-gone; a small metal wheel from a Hornby train; pen nibs and pencil stubs. One stub was the stump of an indelible pencil and he wondered if they still made them. Probably not. Now there are permanent markers.

All sparked memories. He was aware, between flickers of childhood images, that Mitchell was speaking but the words meant nothing to him, they were part of another world, a world harsh and unreal. He went to pull out the last drawer but didn't quite make it before his feelings overpowered him. Elbowing Mitchell aside he stumbled through the kitchen and out to cold air.

The weather changed suddenly, the way it does at Kilcreg. Thin icy drizzle crept in from the sea and drenched everything, Spargo included. Leaning heavily on the back wall of the cottage he breathed deeply, hoping that by doing so the nausea would leave him. Instead he felt dizzy.

A lone fir with gnarled branches high on the hill was the last thing to be swallowed by mist. The tree, that to Spargo was the same size and shape it had always been, vanished into steamy wisps only to reappear in its entirety for no more than two seconds. Then it went again, as if snatched from the sky.

He became aware of Mitchell standing beside him, looking around in that way of his, at the asbestos sheet roof of the garage, at the eaves of the house and the gutter, the rainwater downpipe, the water butt, and the stumps of cabbages in the vegetable plot that lay in the shelter of the garage wall. Finally at the mossy gravel path at his feet.

'Could the attacker have got the wrong person?' Spargo asked. 'The wrong house?'

Mitchell jerked his head to face Spargo. He raised one eyebrow independently of the other, something Spargo had often tried, but always failed, to do. It reminded him now of a Victorian automaton or ventriloquist's dummy. He had seen something like it long ago, in black and white, probably. That actor, Dirk Bogarde.

'Are you suggesting there is somewhere in Kilcreg worth burgling?'

Spargo tried hard to concentrate. Maybe Mitchell thought there was a moneyed recluse tucked away somewhere, either that or it was tongue-in-cheek humour. For once in his life Spargo didn't know. Couldn't tell.

'Most of the folk here are retired,' he said. 'Don't suppose they have much. No closet millionaires.'

'What did your mother do?'

'Do?'

'Did she work?'

She worked, yes. Worked like hell. Worked non-stop. 'She was a wife and mother. When I was a boy most mothers stayed home and looked after the house and kids.'

It sounded medieval and he remembered how it was. Morag baked her own cakes and sometimes the bread, did the washing by hand, tended the garden and grew vegetables throughout the year. There was more than enough food for the three of them and he remembered how boring their food was in winter, the potatoes and cabbages, the turnips, sprouts and swedes. In summer there would be tomatoes and lettuces brought by the van man, never any fancy stuff like asparagus, aubergines or courgettes. There were wild strawberries the size of his fingertips, and blackberries from hedges. When he got home from school each day – to the mine house, not this one – the beds were made and the house, unlike him, was spotless. By the time he had done his chores, cleaned his boots, brought in logs for the fire and washed himself, his tea would be ready. When his father came home from work all would be cleared away. Including him.

'So she never worked?'

'She never stopped working. When she was young she helped in a shop in Aberdeen. When she married and came here she worked at the mine in what they called the counting house, she did the accounts and helped with clerical work. The counting house was way over the moor at the mine and she walked there and back every day, up the track you saw when we came down the hill.'

'And that's all?'

'All? As I said, she never stopped. It was a busy life. What I suppose I'm saying is that even though she was the mine manager's wife she didn't have much. The mine was small, it employed no more than twenty or thirty men – mainly men – even in wartime. There are no gold bars hidden away, Detective Sergeant. There was no money here. A few pounds at the most.'

'We found twenty pounds and fifty pence in a tin in her bedroom.'

Spargo ignored him. He turned to face the man. Confronted the inquiring eyes.

'What I really don't understand is why nobody heard anything. Surely my mother cried out?'

Mitchell turned away. Gazed up into the mist. 'She couldn't cry out,' he mumbled, almost inaudibly. 'Whoever did this taped up her mouth.'

Spargo threw back his head and looked up to where the sky should have been. Drizzle drenched his face, ran down his forehead and flushed away tears. Then Mitchell's hand was there, clamped onto his shoulder.

'Come, Mr Spargo. It's time to go.'

CHAPTER FOUR

THE PLANE MIDGE ROLLO WAITED FOR in a coffee shop at Edinburgh Airport landed five minutes ahead of schedule. Midge had been there for two hours, not because he had expected the plane to be early – at the time he arrived it was still on the runway at Heathrow – but because he had no idea how long it would take him to get to the airport in the blue bus from Edinburgh's Waverley Station.

Rollo had spent the first hour of his wait staring at the baggage carousels, fascinated by bags that appeared, vanished and then reappeared until finally their owners heaved them off the endless belt with either too little strength or with much more strength than was needed. The second hour passed more quickly. He spent the time reading – for the third time at least – a thirty year old dog-eared copy of Readers Digest he'd stuffed in his pocket before leaving home.

Now Midge was on a blue bus again. He was returning to the city, upstairs in the front seat because that was where he thought Mr Luis, as a first-time visitor to Scotland's capital city, would prefer to sit.

Mr Luis is Mafia, of that Midge is sure. Never mind that the man is Spanish and not Italian, these Latins are all the same with their family ties and their loyalties. Like himself, he supposed. Or on second thoughts maybe not, as there wasn't much family loyalty in the Rollo household, not since his mum shopped his dad to the police when he gave her that kicking. Since he was five he had lived with his Nan.

Apart from himself and his grandmother the family were losers, he knew that. In his teens he had idolised elder brother Robbie but then things had changed. Only a complete bampot would park his car – his own car – on double yellows while he did over the Co-op.

Photographed at the kerb, it was, by the parking attendant who gave it a ticket.

As the airport bus trundled towards town Midge did the travel guide thing. Pointed out places of interest.

'Edinburgh Zoo,' he said with a flourish. Then, almost immediately, he swivelled around, jabbing a finger in the opposite direction. 'Wheelhouse, the tyre place,' he said. 'And that's new place that fills printer cartridges.' As if they were national monuments.

Though Mr Luis seemed to ignore him, Midge knew he was taking it all in. He had already established the man was not much of a talker. Uncongenial, Midge decided.

Despite his rudimentary education Midge knew such words; when he was twelve his Nan bought a suitcase at a car boot sale. It was heavy, packed with old Readers Digests. Because it was so heavy, and as she only wanted the case, she upended it over the first litter bin they came to and dumped all the books. Midge had argued with her and then, ignoring her protestations, he refilled the case, carried it home for her and stored every single book under his bed in his room. It wasn't long before he discovered a page in the Digests about increasing your word power. That night, and almost every other night since that distant day, he studied them under his blankets, by torchlight.

Mr Luis had, in fact, said only two things since they'd met in Arrivals. 'Mister Rollo, I presume…' like when that Stanley guy discovered Livingstone. Then: 'Mister Midge Rollo?'

Midge had been told Mr Luis would be wearing a black leather jacket and a white, open-necked shirt; also that he was tanned, had combed-back black hair, and was medium height. He would be easy to spot, his caller had said. At least five men from the flight matched that description, and none of them was Mr Luis.

Midge didn't find Mr Luis, Mr Luis found Midge, he came up behind him and tapped him on the shoulder. Gave him a fright.

Mr Luis pronounced Mister like Meester. Sinister, the way a Mexican bandit might say it. Didn't look sinister though, not upstairs on the bus. If anything he looked a wee bit camp with his knees tight together and his hands clasped in his lap. To Midge this was part of the man's cover, a certain coolness Midge would have been happy to emulate – and may have done had the rolled-up Argos bag he carried not kept slipping from his lap.

'It is not convenient you do not have a car, Mister Rollo.'

Midge, lost in the double negatives, gave a nod and a grin: 'My idea,' he said. 'Taking the bus. Not so conspicuous. Clever, eh?'

Not so much clever, as necessary. A pick-up from the airport and then a drive into town to do the man's bidding – the first job he'd had for months – and he had screwed up. He didn't have his car on the road. Hadn't taxed or insured it and he daren't drive without, not the number of times he got stopped by the police. For most jobs he got part-payment up front. Always used notes, sealed in a registered envelope.

For this job he'd got nothing, not yet. Three hours' notice meant a shortage of funds, and a shortage of funds meant the blue bus, reliable and cheap. Not what Mr Luis would expect, perhaps.

The bus pulled up outside Waverley and Midge stepped down. Looking hesitantly at the taxis in the rank across the road he considered explaining his temporary financial predicament to Mr Luis and then ask him to pay the fare. A man like Mr Luis would have wads of notes. And hopefully pounds, not some foreign stuff. He started towards the taxis. Felt a steel grip on his arm.

'We shall walk, Mr Rollo.'

Mitch's jaw dropped. Seeking reasons why walking would not be a good thing he looked up at the sky and considered telling Mr Luis that the smart bird who did the TV weather had said it would snow. The blue sky and wispy white cloud overhead made it unlikely.

'Walk, Mister Rollo. One foot in front of the other, like so.' The man looked both ways and took brisk steps into the road. 'I have studied a street guide. The house we are going to is near Tollcross. Do you know that place?'

Mouth still open, Midge nodded. 'It's fucking miles!'

'According to my guide it is approximately one-and-a-half kilometres. If we walk at a reasonable pace the journey will take us twenty minutes.'

Mr Luis raised an arm, slipped back his cuff to reveal a white gold Rolex. Midge had shifted a few fakes in his time. This one was real.

'We have time,' Mr Luis said. 'And Mr Rollo...'

'What?'

'... from now on you will refrain from using any vulgar language in my presence.'

Midge's jaw dropped again. The only person ever to tell him not to swear was his grandmother. And he'd learned most of his obscenities from her.

Mr Luis was ahead of him, heading for Cockburn Street. Midge scurried after him. Caught him up. Together they started the long flog up the hill towards High Street. Cockburn Street is not the steepest road in the city but it is a close contender.

The climb left Midge short of breath and he lagged behind, the carrier bag bumping his knee. Things would be easier if he could get rid of it. With great effort he caught up with Mr Luis and brandished the bag, opening it as he spoke.

'I was told to get this for you.'

Mr Luis stopped. Using a gloved hand he pulled the top of the bag towards him and looked in. Recoiled as if from a bad smell.

'Did you carry this into the airport?'

Midge nodded. Couldn't make out from the man's expression whether he was pleased or annoyed. He was certainly surprised.

To Midge, still on twenty a day despite having cut down, walking up Cockburn Street was like scaling the Eiger's North Face. Effing steep, he told himself, choosing his thoughts carefully in case Mr Luis could read minds.

Walking several steps behind Mr Luis seemed right somehow. He had seen it on the movies, the way a minder stays back and keeps an eye on his man. Because that's what he was, Mr Luis's minder. The man on the phone said he was up for a serious job with good money, the opportunity to get up there with the big boys. Why else would he have been told to find a gun?

'Royal Mile,' Mitch said as he struggled into High Street. 'Edinburgh Castle at the top, Holyrood Palace at the bottom where they're building a new Parliament.' With so little breath to spare for talking the same time as walking, he stopped. Called after Mr Luis, 'Apologies... wee bit knackered.'

Mr Luis, street guide open, negotiated Edinburgh as if he had been born there. Midge, trailing behind as they passed the pale stone of the National Museum, observed the man from a distance. The description he had been given could not have been more wrong. Mr Luis wasn't wearing a jacket but a long leather coat. He wasn't of moderate height but was short, an inch or two shorter than himself and with a long body and short legs. His leather heels clicked as he took short, determined steps. He looked, Midge realised, rather like that Poirot bloke on the box. But thinner.

They walked on. Turning right into Teviot Place he remembered he hadn't been pointing out landmarks.

'Royal Infirmary,' Midge proclaimed. 'Knocking it down. Building new flats.'

'Lauriston Gardens,' Mr Luis said, a short time later, street guide still open and fingers tapping the page. 'We turn left here, I think.'

'For Tollcross we keep walking.'

Mr Luis ignored him and Midge followed. Wondered how much further he could go at this pace before he dropped dead. Tall houses of Lauriston Place soon gave way to Bruntsfield Links – close-mown grass extending eastwards to even more close-mown grass.

'We go here, I think,' Mr Luis said, indicating a gap in the railings, heading for it and passing through it to the moist grass of the Links.

Midge followed dutifully, avoiding mud and leaves. Grass was not his thing. One thing he did know for certain was The Links was the world's oldest golf course. Probably. Reputedly.

Mr Luis stopped. Looking back at the long Victorian terrace overlooking the parkland he stopped and opened his street guide, this time taking from between its pages a small scrap of paper that he handed to Midge.

'These houses are apartments, are they not? Many people live in them. Locate number twenty. Walk to the door and read the names beside the doorbells.'

'The names?'

'The names, Mr Rollo. The names written on the bell pushes. You can do that, possibly?'

Though the question may have been a slur on Midge's education or upbringing he shrugged it off. Mr Luis was foreign. He was also a client, no doubt one that was paying handsomely. Crossing the road as instructed Midge stared at the flights of stone steps. Reading the names would mean going up them. Ascending them.

He supposed that if he was challenged he could say he was delivering pizzas, though as he was empty-handed it might not sound convincing. Lost, then. Lost and wanting directions. Nobody can prove you're not lost.

He found number twenty and placed a foot on the first step. Still unable to read the labels he went right up. Sure he wouldn't be able to remember all of the names he went through his pockets, found a chocolate wrapper and a stub of blunt pencil and wrote down each name: Mackie, Robinson, James & Brown. Morrison, Somerton, and Jessica Spargo.

CHAPTER FIVE

THOUGH IT IS TOO DARK TO SEE THE MAN, Theo is sure he is an officer. The car that brought him here was large, he could tell from the sound of the engine. A Mercedes Benz, perhaps, a military staff car. He'd heard the slam of the driver's door and the trot-trot of boots, he'd seen the silhouette of the car's uniformed driver as it passed in front of masked headlights. Then there was the salute, of course – heard but not seen – a sharp scuff of grit as the driver attempted, but failed, to click heels on the railway yard's clinker.

In his private little guessing game Theo has cheated. Even without the salute the car had to be military, for who else in these troubled times can get petrol? And he is prepared to go further; the man holds high rank; who but a high-ranker would be dropped off in absolute silence? Also, the man is most likely in uniform, because most people are these days.

The guessing game Theo plays has a purpose. A high-ranker dropped off at the station means a train is due. Why else would such a man dismiss his driver?

With no such foreknowledge Theo arrived in dull daylight eight hours ago in the hope trains would come. There have been four so far. The first engine pulled tank wagons transporting fuel. The second had open trucks carrying timber and coal, also closed wagons containing who knows what. Maybe munitions. Maybe food. The third and fourth came later, shapes in the dark that passed by at speed.

The oil lamps hanging on the slender iron posts along the platform have not been lit for years. What would otherwise be absolute blackness is broken only by a vertical sliver of yellow light from the station's small signal box. Twisted blackout curtains, perhaps. Theo looks skywards. His navigation skills tell him that up there, behind dense cloud, is a full moon.

So why would a high ranker wait here rather than Hanover or Braunschweig? Why choose a halt, a railway station where milk trains stop every morning at a god-awful hour and where cattle are loaded for market?

Sounds break the silence. The stranger is walking, not in boots but with a slow rhythmic step in shoes tipped with steel. Theo listens, hearing the sound fade as the man walks away. Hears it stop, restart, then get louder. The man is pacing to keep warm – an officer with a desk job maybe, a man unused to such cold. And there is something else, a fault in the man's step, an almost imperceptible, lazy-leg drag. Theo listens intently for the tap of a stick. There is none.

There was a time when Theo would have walked to the man, struck up a conversation and perhaps shared a smoke but you don't do that now. It would be just his luck to come face-to-face with an immaculately dressed Schutzstaffel colonel. The very last person you want to meet when you are dressed in a shabby leather jacket without military markings is a high ranking SS man.

As if it matters in the dark, Theo reaches up with one hand and adjusts his cap. At least he still has one.

The first hint of an approaching train comes as a barely perceptible, high-pitched squeal. At first Theo mistakes it for the noise that lives in his head, the sharp, constant hiss put there by engines. Or pressure. Or gunfire. Or any number of things that conspire to destroy hearing.

The track sings loudly now, a thousand feint bells with sharp, intermixed tones. Theo turns towards the sounds and detects, in the night sky, a feint red glow. He waits and watches. Soon the glow sharpens. Becomes an incandescent plume lighting up the whole sky. Two plumes, he tells himself; twin pillars of bright sparks from two chimneys. Two locomotives, burning bad coal. Night trains are such easy targets, so thank god for the clouds. Tonight there will be no bombs.

Theo waits nervously, wondering if the train is for passengers and if it will stop. He relaxes only when the steam that drives these things is cut back. The towers of sparks vanish; the brakes tighten on steel with long, painful groans. Then, almost unexpectedly, the noise is upon him, two hundred tons of steel pulling god-knows-what.

Way down the platform a hand lamp is swinging, a red light for the locos to head for. Bright burning coals in open fireboxes flash eerie orange glows as they pass buildings and railings, porters' barrows and the glass bowls of the oil lamps.

Fireships that slip silently alongside.

For a few seconds there is silence, broken only by a slow rhythmic pumping of the engines. Then, suddenly, the slam of a single door, and raised voices; window blinds move; faces peer out but there is nothing to be seen. Theo, overtired, comes to life quickly, heaves his bag to his shoulder and moves to the train. Searching for a seat he walks beside carriages and hauls himself up, opens carriage doors but sees no spaces. Though this is a main line these are not main line coaches. They have no corridors. There is nowhere to stand.

A railwayman shouts. Further down the train a carriage door hangs open. Theo heads for it and just as gets there the train starts to move. Strong arms reach out and haul him inside, arms that belong to a women. He mumbles his thanks. Gives a quick smile that in the dark goes unseen. He stands for a while and recovers his breath. Only then does he realise he is in a corridor, not a compartment.

Only two of the lamps in the corridor are lit. The outer windows are obscured with thick paper, pasted on, and the windows of the compartments have their blackout blinds down. These days most train corridors are packed tight with travellers and baggage, often soldiers, sailors and airmen on leave. This corridor is remarkably clear and he works his way down it, sliding doors open and peering inside. That none of the passengers look back at him does not surprise him. People don't do that, not now.

Unable to find a seat Theo dumps his kitbag on the floor and sits down on it. He is considering whether or not to light his pipe when a man in railway uniform and forage cap beckons to him. Tells him there is an empty seat in the next carriage.

Theo has checked all the compartments. He knows there were no seats. He even remembers the passengers in the one he is led to – the men in their suits, the woman with the smartly-dressed boy. The seat next to the woman is unoccupied; he wonders if he simply missed it.

The train is up to speed and rocking gently. The passengers in the compartment move their feet grudgingly as Theo shuffles in with his kitbag held high. To make space for it on the overhead rack he shoves other bags aside and heaves it up. The compartment is over hot and stuffy so he shrugs off his leather jacket, bundles it up and adds it, with his naval cap, to the pile. Finally, as a concession to smartness, he tugs down the hem of his naval tunic and straightens his neckerchief.

His clothes might not be smart but at least they are clean. He had hoped for a new uniform for his shore leave but there was no chance of that. Naval stores at Bremen, the port where he docked, had been flattened by bombs. He senses passengers sneaking looks, their eyes on his blue serge tunic and the twin stripes on each cuff, stripes now more dirty yellow than gold. Just a naval lieutenant. Nothing too grand.

The train changes tracks with a judder and Theo, uncharacteristically off-balance, drops clumsily into his seat space. The woman beside him shuffles as if to give space, somehow managing to take up more than before. That the seat is warm surprises him. He wonders if the railwayman himself vacated he seat and if so, why. While attempting to make himself comfortable he glances surreptitiously around him, moving only his eyes. His fellow passengers are waxen faced dummies, all with closed eyes, corpses in a crypt now with standing room only.

The compartments, like the corridors, are dimly lit. The only evidence there were once reading lamps on the walls is the small ragged screw holes that once held brass fittings. Fittings removed, no doubt melted down to make cartridge and shell-cases. Where is the brass now, he wonders? At the bottom of the Atlantic? In a field on the Russian Front? And the Allies, where are they now? Rumour has it they are already in France and Belgium. Rumour also has it the Soviets have reached Warsaw. Nobody is sure. And anyway, who can you believe?

The train moves slowly now. When the locomotives change speed the carriages vibrate and make the passengers nervous. They glance at the door, the floor, the roof of the compartment or its blind-covered windows. Theo hardly notices. He is used to such things. He is also used to bad air like he breathes now. Despite these things he struggles to stay awake; like the others he is lulled by the beat of the engines and the song of the wheels; like the others his head droops forwards. Slowly, very slowly, he drifts into sleep.

He wakes to the sound of voices. Some way down the corridor a compartment door slides open. Like him, his fellow passengers are awake. Like him, they recognise the sounds of a spot check on papers. He hears two voices. Two officials. Shrugging off sleep he gropes in his tunic for a white canvas envelope with his pass book and permit to travel. Others in the compartment fumble through pockets and bags. The woman stands clumsily, reaching up to tug at a brown leather bag. Fumbling with it, it slips off the rack and falls on to Theo. He looks up at the woman and smiles. It is not returned.

As the woman sits down the compartment door opens. Two men, one a uniformed railway policeman and the other wearing a raincoat, step inside and study faces. Theo moves mechanically, opens his naval passbook to his photograph and unfolds his travel permit. Tucking the permit in his passbook as a marker, he holds it out. He knows the drill: leave the passbook closed or the travel permit folded and you are insolent, they will be taken from you and thrown back in your face. Present both documents wide open and they wonder why you don't want them to see other pages.

There are more of these rules: be casual but not too casual; let them see your face clearly but don't look them in the eye unless they speak to you; show no interest whatever in what they do to others. And never, ever, smile.

Ignoring other passengers the man in the raincoat elbows the policeman aside and takes Theo's papers, glances at them and hands them back. Then, one by one and much more thoroughly, he checks those of the other passengers.

The last to be checked is an elderly man sitting opposite Theo, a man around sixty with long grey hair. The man in the raincoat glances several times from the man to the photograph.

'You are Helmut Sauer. You travel to Berlin.'

The man nods. He seems to shrink into his seat as if wishing it would swallow him. His eyes are wide, his hands tremble.

'Your bags, which are they?'

Without moving his head the man swivels his eyes upwards as if trying to see through his own head. The policeman swaps places with Raincoat, lifts two identical suitcases from the rack and drags them to the corridor. Without saying a word the passenger stands and leaves. As the compartment door slides shut Theo's fellow passengers, who have watched events unfold without apparent interest, glance surreptitiously at one other as if linked by a bond. Nobody speaks.

Theo dozes, his thoughts drifting to events that have so changed his life. He has no wish to dwell on them but he has no choice, they have become part of him. At quiet times like this they haunt him.

The train travels smoothly; it runs on straight track and the two locomotives are well matched – though every so often something gets out of sync and sets up vibrations, a regular drumming that unnerves the others but comforts Theo, reminding him of his boat, the sounds it makes when it break surface and the diesels start up.

He hears something else now, something familiar. The purposeful tap-tap of steel-tipped shoes hesitates at a nearby compartment and then continues. Theo stares at the door. Watches as it slides open. Watches as a tall, slim, middle-aged man steps inside. It is the man from the platform, of that, Theo is sure. What surprises Theo is that though the man has the bearing of an officer he is not wearing uniform but a finely woven grey woollen suit. When he turns to slide the door closed his right leg moves in an unnatural manner, doesn't turn as it should. To close the door he places the briefcase he is carries on the floor, transfers his folded raincoat from one arm to the other arm, slides the door closed and then reverses the process, raincoat to other arm, briefcase picked up.

All, including Theo, watch with expressions of feigned disinterest. A man of such an age, so smartly dressed in times of hardship, is a man to be reckoned with, a man who must be bad news. All of them know that if Helmut Sauer returns to claim his seat – an eventuality they consider most unlikely – then he will have to fight his own battles.

The man has his back to Theo. As he turns around all heads snap back. Eyes look down. Or up. Or anywhere but at the man. Feet shuffle, legs pull back.

'Kapitänleutnant...?'

Theo looks up. The man is looking down at him. He has made no attempt to lift his briefcase and coat to the luggage rack, it is a task requiring two hands. Theo stands smartly, takes the man's case and slips it on to the rack. He takes the coat and the Homburg hat, both passed to him awkwardly. Still looking at Theo the man sits down, taps his arm and smiles briefly. Theo nods. There is no need to explain. Too many have been crippled by wars, both this and the last. Avoiding the man's eyes Theo sits again. All strangers are bad news, especially those that smile.

Theo, reflecting on what just happened, gazes absently up at the man's belongings. The man came directly to this compartment, he opened no other doors. The window blinds are down in this and the others, he could not have seen the vacant seat. Theo ponders, concluding there is no mystery. The man was told about the space by an attendant, just like he was.

The stranger is one of the lucky ones. Losing an arm is a mere personal setback in a war that takes thousands of lives week by week. That Theo has survived unscathed after almost five years of war is something he dwells upon often. Something he cannot explain.

For the first two years of the war things went well for the navy. Then fortunes changed and in a single month they lost forty U-boats. Friends gone forever. Somehow he survived this hell and with survival came a reputation he didn't much care for – a reputation that he was one of the favoured few. A survivor. A commander men want to serve under.

On his last mission his luck failed him. His boat was caught on the surface and shot-up by a Wellington bomber – six crewmen dead and four wounded. They patched up the hull and limped back to Bremen, one diesel gone and a ballast tank holed. Four days ago – five, now – he brought her limping down the Weser with her deck tilting so steeply it couldn't be walked on. He berthed her, without assistance from tugs, in the bombed-out dockyards, slipping her gently between the shattered shells of what had been, until a few days previously, two newly commissioned U-boats.

It is four years since the Party men came to his town. They pestered his colleagues – his fellow mining engineers – attempting to sweet talk them into believing their future lay not in the Harz Mountain mines of their motherland, but in the iron mines of Lorrain.

For Theo, recently married to Erika and living in his parents' cramped house, a transfer to France had its attractions – if only because of the promise of more spacious accommodation. And, luxury of luxuries, the possibly of a lavatory inside the house instead of the communal one in the yard.

There were other attractions. When Theo left mining school the Hartz mines were small affairs, run privately. Then the government took over production and put in its own men. At first all went well, they replaced old machinery, increased production and improved safety. Then the military established vast camps to accommodate what were said to be new miners. Most turned out to be conscripted Poles who knew nothing about mines.

The promise of France lost its allure when his father, a mining engineer like himself, remarked over dinner that his mining engineer colleagues had become prison warders. In France it was worse, he said. The Schutzstaffel – the SS – ran the French mines with slave labour. It was, Theo's father insisted, time his son left mining for good.

Theo took his father's advice. A snap decision took him into the navy, the Kriegsmarine. Another snap decision, taken by someone else, assigned him to the U-boat school at Wilhelmshaven.

The train carriage shudders. Buffers clank. The train draws slowly to a stop and then, as if unsure what it should be doing, eases forwards and stops again. Theo remembers another train, the train that took him from Erica when he left home for Wilhelmshaven – how she ran along the platform in the cold and the rain, managing to stay beside his carriage window until she could run no more. And the letters she sent to him, he remembers those too, they are all safe in his kitbag. One letter, his favourite, both surprised him and shocked him. Erica wrote, in very few words, that she was expecting their child.

At the outbreak of war Theo's brother, a miner, joined the regular army. His wife Matti followed him from posting to posting, dragging her two children from Hanover to Berlin and finally to Hamburg.

When he was posted to the Eastern Front Matti couldn't follow him. And when they told her he'd been taken prisoner she believed them, they hadn't the guts to tell her the Soviets took no prisoners.

A few months after the birth of Peter, Theo's son, Erica left home with him and travelled to Hamburg. The reason, she explained in a letter Theo received five weeks later, was that she felt duty bound to help support Matti, to comfort her and help her look after her boys. The news disturbed him. It was common knowledge that Hamburg, with its shipyards, docks and railways, suffered nightly, devastating bombing raids.

These memories bring guilt. What Theo did not know when he received the letter was that Erika was already dead. If he had gone to France like the Party men wanted, Erica might have gone with him, she would still be alive.

The train moves again and then jerks to a stop. The boy in the corner lifts the blind, peeks around it, then drops it abruptly when the woman slaps his arm. The train creeps again. Continues to creep.

All eyes but the stranger's are on the woman as she stands up, reaches for a string bag, bunches its neck in her fist and drags it down. She takes from it a long sharp blade and a bundle of muslin she unrolls on her lap. Using the knife she pares off thin slices of sausage and lays each one neatly on a slab of dark bread. She attempts to fold the slab over to encapsulate the meat, but before she does it the boy takes it from her, rips at it with his teeth and chews it, quickly and noisily.

The boy is nine or ten, much older than Peter. Without turning his head Theo wonders, as he watches the boy, what Peter does all day on his grandparents' farm. And, worryingly, how long he will be safe there, now the enemy has reached Belgium.

Theo has seen Peter only once. On his first week's leave he took a train to Munich, hitched a lift south to Ingolstadt and then walked to the farm – three days to get there, one day with Peter and three days to get back – a single day spent with his own flesh and blood, a three year old child who screamed when he held him.

It is right Erika's parents should have Peter. Without them the boy would be lost. Before Theo heard what had happened to Erica they had travelled to Hamburg, found Peter in an orphanage and taken him with them, back to their farm. Trouble is, both grandparents are old. Arthur is arthritic; Barbara is unwell.

Theo tilts his head back and looks up at his kitbag. It is as if he can see through the canvas to the letter from Barbara, the small, neat writing telling him Erica was dead and Peter had been dug out of rubble. He asks himself the question he has asked many times: what kind of husband leaves his wife to the mercy of bombing raids? What kind of man puts his child through such hell? The answer he denies himself is simple. Most husbands. Most fathers. He blinks hard as if to stem tears but there are none, not now, not after the things he has seen.

The smart-suited stranger takes spectacles from his jacket, puts them on and looks straight at Theo. Theo looks away, his eyes dare not dwell. His split-second glance fleshed out a man in his mid-forties, possibly younger, with close-cropped hair that has already turned grey; there are no rings on his fingers; on the wrist of the arm that never moves is a gold watch with a wide leather strap. He has already noticed the man's shoes are old but well-made and that they shine. Theo's deduction that the man holds high rank was right. Who else would dare stare at him so blatantly?

The train travels steadily at a reasonable speed. Theo, sandwiched between the woman and an old man who snores, drifts gradually into sleep. When he wakes some hours later there is daylight. The window blinds have been raised to a cold, misty dawn.

'Elbe-Havel Canal,' the stranger says to nobody in particular and with a nod towards the window. His words are well-pronounced with no trace of an accent. 'Brandenburg very soon…' he says.

All look away. Gratuitous geography lessons from smartly dressed strangers are unwelcome.

'Potsdam first, then Berlin,' he adds, directing his revelations towards an unreceptive Theo. 'Two more hours, my friend.'

Theo nods. Nobody speaks. The train varies its speed for a while and then stops. Fifteen minutes later it still hasn't moved and the stranger, glancing at his watch for the third time in so many minutes, stands up, leaves his coat and his luggage and steps into the corridor.

He soon returns.

'I fear the news is not good. Our train is unable to enter Berlin and will terminate at Potsdam.'

The other passengers ask questions the man is unable, or unwilling, to answer. There will be other trains, he says, and there will be trucks, or buses. And in any case, Potsdam is only twelve kilometres from Berlin, a distance that can be walked in a few hours.

Theo sighs audibly. His trip is jinxed.

As the train approaches Potsdam the corridor comes alive. Passengers, preparing to alight, drag cases and bags to the doors. The boy in Theo's compartment clambers on to the seat and reaches for his mother's suitcase but it is too heavy for him, it slips to the floor and spills open. The woman goes to strike him but all eyes are upon her and she stays her hand. The boy scoops up the spilled clothes. Crams them back in the case. Fastens the catches.

Three of the compartment's occupants have moved into to the corridor. Finally Theo stands up, reaches for his bag and places it on the floor. He does the same with the stranger's and it earns him gratitude. Also, it gets him the man's unwanted company as he walks along the platform.

'An air raid last night,' the man says. 'A small one by all accounts but it damaged the rail tracks. We have been lucky lately. I was hoping they had forgotten us.'

Theo grunts but doesn't speak. The man could be Gestapo – though that, Theo has already decided, is unlikely.

The ground they walk on changes from gravel to concrete. Theo notes the stranger's shoes have steel tips at the heel as well as the toe. They make a distinctive double click as first the heel, and then the toe, touch the ground.

Both men walk slowly, the stranger with his briefcase and Theo with his kitbag, shouldered high. Theo, unwilling to start a conversation, continues to respond to the man's questions with grunts. The man lives in Berlin, he says. It has been badly damaged by bombs.

'Though not as badly as our northern cities,' he says. 'So how is Bremen? I hear it suffered badly last summer.'

Theo swallows. Even between close friends such talk is unknown.

After more than four years of war Party paranoia has reached a peak. Not only do suspected dissenters now vanish, so do their families, their friends and their distant relations. Theo, on his boat, is occasionally outspoken but he trusts all his crew – or he did until now. What else does this man know? Has one of the new men been talking? It could be William, a former Hitlerjugend boy... not that Theo holds membership of the Hitler Youth against anyone these days. The kids don't have a choice, they reach the age of fourteen and their parents put their name on the role – and if they do not do that then they suffer the consequences, they lose their jobs and their homes.

Yes, Bremen is all but destroyed. But why ask about Bremen? That Theo is a submariner is obvious to those that know uniforms, but he could just as easily have come from any one of the northern ports.

As they near the station concourse the man stops, turns to Theo and frowns. 'I understand the U-boat construction yards at Bremen have taken a beating.'

The man is expecting an answer. If it is a test, it is a crude one. Theo mumbles a response barely loud enough for the stranger to hear:

'It is not right to ask such questions.'

'I apologise, Kapitänleutnant, how insensitive of me, how indiscreet, you will forgive me.' He resumes his walk and his questions. 'You travel to Berlin? I only ask because you will find nowhere to stay. People will assume last night's bombing is the start of a campaign, and because of that you will find yourself sleeping in a shelter with many hundreds of others. Some of them can be quite unsavoury.'

Theo shakes his head. He wants to laugh. To him, crammed in a shelter with bombs raining down is normal. He is a U-boat man. Unsavoury is part of his life.

It is time to break from the stranger. Deciding to test his suspicions that the man does indeed have a peculiar interest in him he lengthens his pace. Changing direction he joins the most distant checkpoint queue.

The woman and boy from his compartment, labouring under the weight of their case, stand in front of him in the queue. The woman presents her papers to a ticket inspector who takes them, glances at them, hands them back and waves the woman and boy through. Theo, his papers ready, hands them over. The woman checks them and hands them back. As Theo is folding them ready to slip them back into his canvas wallet, the woman snatches them back and holds them high.

CHAPTER SIX

A GOOD HOUR HAD PASSED since Mitchell told Spargo they were about to leave for Inverness. The man had become sidetracked, inevitable in the circumstances, Spargo supposed. He regretted not being more forceful with Mitchell at the start because if he had brought his own car he would be well on his way home by now. When Mitchell wasn't in the cottage he was in the incident van. And whenever he walked between them he called out to Spargo:

'Be with you in a minute or two...'

Words that were starting to grate.

Spargo stood near the schoolhouse in the rain, inspecting the flora growing in the stone wall. When he tired of that he ventured further afield. A stroll down the road, a walk to the beach, perhaps – though not a beach in the proper sense because there was very little sand, just patches of pebbles and a mile-long stretch of boulders and collapsed cliffs.

The walk was not a success. When he reached the turning circle at the end of the road and the police turned him back. He walked back up the road, past his mother's cottage and Mitchell's parked car. He followed the stone wall bordering the grounds of the mine house, stopping when he reached the twin stone pillars that once held the entrance gates to the grounds. One pillar was still standing, the other had fallen. It was now a tumble of stone blocking the drive.

The stone wall continued well beyond the limits of the mine house grounds. Further along the road stood a similar pair of stone pillars at the entrance to what had once been the mine's plant yard, the store for the mine's surplus machinery and its stockpile of ore. The yard was empty now, one of the valley's flat fields of green.

Spargo stared at the mine house. The three acres of grounds had once seemed huge to him. At least half of it had been cultivated, and like other gardens in Kilcreg it had grown vegetables rather than flowers. When Spargo was eight he had planted seeds in a patch of ground near the front door of the mine house, marigolds, he remembered, flowers that beamed like small suns. He glanced left and right in the hope he would see their descendants. There was no trace of them. Wrong time of year anyway.

The house stood well back, almost at the foot of the hillside. Spargo made his way to it, picking his way through a wilderness of tall tufted grass. In more southerly climes this would now be a jungle of brambles, bracken, and self-seeded trees. Such growth didn't happen here. Here the winter winds reduced even the most hardened, determined gardeners to tears, slicing through everything, freezing the sap, beating down all but the toughest of the land's native firs.

Spargo and his mother stayed on in the building long after Samuel Spargo died - rattled around in it, his mother had said. She knew it was only be a matter of time before her boy left home, and when that happened she would move somewhere smaller. And John would leave Kilcreg, she had no doubts about that. The youngsters all did.

Morag was still living in the mine house when winter winds felled the chimney stack. She wrote to him, saying how it had come through the roof in the night, tearing through beams and rafters and ending up in the hall. Mercifully she was unharmed, but the damage done to the house was so severe the building was declared unsafe. Spargo was in Zambia and couldn't return.

Spargo's efforts to get his mother to leave Kilcreg failed miserably. Her good memories of the place outnumbered the bad, she said in her letters, and Kilcreg was where all her friends were. By good fortune the first cottage on the road into Kilcreg – the one opposite the school – came up for sale. By the time Spargo got leave to return to Kilcreg, his mother had bought the place and moved in.

The mine house was a sorry sight now. Old floorboards had been nailed across what was once the front door. On them, scrawled in black paint, were the words DANGEROUS STRUCTURE, KEEP OUT. The four large front windows had been blinded by sheets of thick plywood nailed firmly in place.

Turning from the house Spargo looked towards Kilcreg, to the cottage where his mother had died – at the hands of a madman, or what? Remembering, guiltily, that he hadn't called Jez he took out his mobile. Remembering, too, that Kilcreg was no place to use mobile phones he headed for the mist-clad hillside.

Many years ago Spargo had clambered all over these hills. At his fittest he had managed to scale the valley side in less than ten minutes. Now, if he could even manage to get to the top, it would take him thirty minutes at least. By the time he reached the seagull-winged tree near the top of the slope a sharp breeze had sprung up and was shifting the mist. It reminded him of that saying of his father's – Cornish, he supposed – that if you don't like the weather, just wait a while…

The signal bars on Spargo's mobile jumped suddenly, nothing one second to full-strength the next. He tapped a key. Brought up Jez's number. Down in the valley the headlights of a parked car flashed on and off. It was Mitchell, ready to leave.

⚜

At times like this Jez wished she had a car of her own. She blamed her home town of Edinburgh with its convenient buses – that and the fact she had attended a school and then a university within walking distance of home. She had inherited her father's love of rocks, and to his great pleasure she'd graduated in geology with First Class Honours. Now she lectured full-time. Same city. Same university. Same walking distance.

She was born in Zambia. Her parents had met there, she knew the story well. He worked at a mine called Roan Antelope and her mother was the daughter of a diplomat. Her first school was on the mine township, her second in Edinburgh (expatriate rules were that when you got older you were sent home to boarding school). It was a future that had, at the time, scared her. But it didn't happen. Days before she was due to fly to Edinburgh, on her own, she overheard a parental row she didn't understand. Days later her father resigned from his job. Within a few weeks she, her father and her mother, were living in Edinburgh.

The phone call from her father came just after midday. He was at Kilcreg, he told her. He had accompanied a policeman there, a detective called Mitchell. She listened without interrupting and then, when he finished, she started her questions. Despite her insistence he refused to explain why he was there and why the police were involved. He sounded distressed.

Rather than argue with her father at a time like this, as soon as the call was over she cancelled her seminar with final year geology, jumped on her motorbike, and rode home.

Her bike was small and intended for town. She had never taken it out of the city, so riding it to Inverness didn't even cross her mind. She could take boyfriend Joby's car, she was on his insurance and had driven it a few times. But that wasn't really an option. There was no way she would tackle the A9 in a soft-top kit car she had driven only on Sunday mornings in half-empty car parks. Flying from Edinburgh Airport to Inverness was a non-starter. Even if she could get a seat it would be a short-notice, full-cost flight she could ill-afford. That left the train, cheaper but tedious, a nineteenth-century solution to a twenty-first century travel problem. A one hundred and twenty mile journey taking over three hours. Or five, if you caught the slow train.

The bike journey from the university's King's Buildings on the south side of the city brought Jez to Edinburgh's Meadows and Bruntsfield Links, a kilometre of close-mown parkland and fine old trees. Jez took roads around it and arrived, eventually, at the lane behind the ground floor apartment she owned.

Jez had sole access to the high walled garden behind her house. A few years ago, intending to grow her own vegetables, she dug up the grass, spent money on gardening tools and a shed to keep them in. What she hadn't realised was that at some stage in their history the flats had been renovated, and what looked like good soil was a veneer of earth above deep builders' rubble. Not one for giving up she salvaged a small piece of ground in which she planted seeds. One weekend when she was away, someone shouldered open the gate to the lane behind the garden, prised the padlock off the shed door and stole her tools. All of them. Now the much more heavily padlocked tool shed was a home for her newly purchased motorbike.

Back in her flat she tried, unsuccessfully, to call her father. Frustrated, she stuffed a few necessities into an overnight bag, tapped the number of a taxi firm into her phone and then, deciding she should try her father again, she cancelled the call.

'It's Jez,' she said when he answered. 'Where are you?'

'Hi, love. On my way to Inverness.'

'I'm coming up. I'm catching the train. I'll let you know when I get there and you can pick me up from the station.'

'Jez… no… don't… I'm not staying. I'm coming home.'

'Why were you at Kilcreg? Why were you with the police?'

'I still am. I can't talk now, I'll tell you later. Must go.'

She kept talking but he had gone. She took the phone from her ear and stared at it, as if it were to blame.

She had been pacing her sitting room, her phone clamped to her ear. Though she hadn't taken much notice of what was going on outside she was fairly sure the young man now walking away from the house had been copying down the names on the doorbells.

❧

Morag's funeral was a small affair attended by Spargo, Jez, and a handful of Kilcreg residents who Spargo recognised but didn't really remember. Detective Sergeant Mitchell made a brief appearance, keeping his distance before slipping silently away before the end.

Spargo saw and heard little of the short service. Childhood memories blocked reality, throwing him back to the mine house and its garden, the sound of his mother's voice calling him, a warning to wash his hands and face and scrub the mud from his knees before his father came home. She had loved him, protected him, and after his father died she'd brought him up single-handed. And what had he done in return? He had wallpapered and painted her house. Fixed leaks in her roof. Hadn't been there when she needed him most.

Again he recalled how he'd tried to persuade her to leave Kilcreg. Many times, four or five at least. He lifted his head and stared at the coffin. Lying to himself about such things made no sense. Twice, he corrected. Twice since she moved to her cottage. Once when the bus service ceased and again when the doctor retired. She'd told him that having no bus and no doctor made no difference. She was never ill and she never went anywhere.

He hadn't persisted. He'd had his own reasons. He was living in Edinburgh at the time and was thinking of moving house. The last thing he and Theresa needed was the added complication of buying a house with a granny-flat.

More guilt.

Jez tugged at his sleeve, bringing him back. People were moving, shuffling between rows of chairs, staring at the ground, waiting for him to go first. If he caught their eye they forced weak smiles. Someone slapped his back and said she had gone to a better place – which wouldn't be difficult – and someone in a surreal but determined whisper said they would get the bastards that did it.

Get them? He didn't think so.

'You're not sleeping, Dad,' Jez said later, seated in the black Daimler limo that took them away. 'Are you having your dreams again?'

Shrugging off the question he shook his head. In the days since his mother's murder his imaginings were as disturbing as ever and it was not a subject he wanted to discuss, not with Jez. He didn't know how much her mother had told her about his problem and he was not about to expand on it.

'Surprised your mother didn't come,' he muttered. It wasn't true. He wasn't surprised at all. She was organising a trade mission to the Far East and had phoned Jez from Bangkok to express her condolences. 'Kilcreg always was a bit rural for her,' he added.

'You know that's not fair. She loved it.'

'She didn't like the rain. Or the countryside. She didn't like Scotland much either. Sorry Love. Not another word, I promise.'

Unlike his own marriage his mother's had been a happy one, she'd been content with her lot. He corrected himself: his own marriage had been a happy one in its early years. Perhaps he could have been more tolerant, perhaps he should not have spent half his life abroad on consulting jobs. He certainly shouldn't have brought his work worries home with him. Then, of course, there were his imaginings.

Over the years he had sought other explanations for his visions. After Campbell in Zambia blew holes in his theory he had latched on to mines. Mines were responsible. When he was nine years old his father took him underground at Kilcreg. By mining standards the shaft they descended wasn't deep. To the young Spargo, who at the time had never even seen a lift, the journey in the cage to the mine's lowest level was a descent into hell. Excitement at the prospect of going where his father went each day on his tour of inspection soon changed to fear – fear he dare not exhibit as he followed his father along narrow workings, ankle deep in syrupy mud.

Unlike the Zambian mines, the Kilcreg shaft and its underground drives were unlit. Father and son carried cap lamps, young Spargo's fixed to a coal miner's helmet several sizes too big for him. The weight of the lamp, combined with the heavy rubber cable linking it to the battery on the leather belt around his waist caused the helmet to slip and twist, a motion he could correct only by gripping the helmet with one hand as he walked.

Claustrophobic passages led to underground voids. Stopes, his father told him – voids left behind when the ore had been mined. Each one he saw was large enough to house two or three double-deck buses. In the largest of these his father switched off their lamps and they stood side by side in blackness and silence. Silence punctuated only by sounds of their breathing and a regular drip-drip-drip from somewhere far off.

Spargo, scared, had opened his eyes wide and waited, expecting them to become accustomed to the dark like at night in his bedroom. But there was nothing. It was, he thought at the time, like having no eyes.

It was inconceivable to Spargo that such huge voids lurked beneath the ground he walked on and played on. Were they under the houses in Kilcreg? Under the Mine House and the school? It was also inconceivable that he – young Spargo – could ever find himself in a situation worse than this. His trousers were soaked. His wellies were filled with wet mud. The battery belt was so big and heavy that his free hand, the hand not holding his cap, struggled to keep it in place.

But worse was to come.

When they returned to the shaft his father realised they couldn't use the cage to ascend to the surface. The ore skip – the huge steel tub hanging beneath the cage – was being used to raise ore to the surface. These skip operations, his father told him, could not be interrupted.

Running up one side of the shaft, adjacent to the vertical rails that guided the cage and the ore skip, were small wooden platforms, one above the other and quite far apart. The timbers supporting each platform were jammed against the rock walls and held there by wooden wedges. Long wooden ladders linked one platform to the next. There were no handrails, not on the platforms or ladders. Nothing to stop a man – or a boy – slipping and falling into darkness and certain death.

Young Spargo cried when he was told to start climbing. His father told him that if he didn't climb out then the alternative was to wait for three hours for the cage to become free. So with aching arms and legs he struggled up ladders from ledge to ledge. Every few minutes, when the ore skip roared past like a piston, he wrapped his arms around the ladder in case the wind accompanying the passing monster tore him away from it.

His search for explanations for his imaginings didn't stop there. If they weren't rooted in his first trip underground, then they came from the stories. Not all the miners at Kilcreg were Scots. Some, like his father, came from Cornwall and they told tales of disasters. Disasters like the one at Levant.

Back in the days before cages, miners descended Levant Mine's shaft on a man-engine. Its very name had invoked fear in young Spargo. The man-engine, the old miners explained, was a long wooden rod that ran the full depth of the shaft. At the surface it was attached to a rocking beam driven by steam. It rose and fell, raising the rod up and down. Fixed in the shaft were small wooden platforms like those he had come up in the manway. Smaller platforms were fixed to the rod, and each one could carry a man. When the rod rose and fell the men stepped off and on, from the moving platform to the fixed one and then back again. This allowed them to travel up or down, as they wished.

Several times in his life Spargo had tried to imagine one shift of men and boys going underground at the same time as another shift came up. He never quite got his mind around it. Never quite worked out the logistics.

One hundred years ago the pin holding the moving rod to the rocking beam at Levant snapped. Two shifts of miners plunged to their deaths. 'Broken arms,' the Kilcreg miners told him, as if they had been there themselves. 'Broken legs, broken necks and broken bodies. Men and boys, some as young as yourself, piled up in black water at the bottom of the shaft, dead and drowned'. And if that wasn't enough for the young Spargo there was another mine, Wheal Oates where the ocean broke through to the subsea workings. Unsurprisingly, everyone died there, too.

To Spargo, these are the reasons for his visions, the nights when the white ghosts walk, the men, the women and the children who drift past in silence, white ghosts that turn to him, stare at him with unseeing eyes. Then he wakes. He always wakes. If he doesn't wake, he knows he will sleep for ever. These are the things he has kept from his mother. Kept from everyone.

Ghosts, he told his mother and the doctor. Dead miners, he told Theresa years later during long, sleepless nights – which, seeing as how he was working underground in Zambia at the time, was not the wisest choice of explanations. He dismissed her concerns by explaining Roan Antelope wasn't in the least like Kilcreg: Kilcreg was dark and claustrophobic, while the Zambian workings he mapped and measured each day were illuminated by bright mercury floodlamps. The mines were, he attempted to explain to her, far better lit than most underground car parks.

She told him to seek help. When he refused she booked an appointment with a specialist – a shrink, Spargo said. That she had done such a thing led to rows. Rows and sleepless nights meant tiredness and tension. Tiredness and tension meant more rows and more sleepless nights. Theresa was now living with a top civil servant in Brussels. And very happily, so Jez had once tactlessly told him.

It wasn't just Theresa who'd quizzed him. Jez had done it too. He had dismissed her concerns, blaming it all on that first trip underground.

For a while she accepted his explanation. Then, a couple of years ago and out of the blue, she challenged him about it. Told him his timing was muddled.

'Gran once told me you were having those dreams long before your trip underground with your father.'

So they wouldn't have to return to Edinburgh immediately after the funeral, Spargo had booked them both into a local hotel. One his way there, to prove to himself that things were back to normal, he switched on his mobile phone. As the black Daimler turned onto the hotel drive his phone rang, filling the car's reverentially plush interior with a coarse, sacrilegious ring tone. Glancing guiltily at the driver's mirror he rummaged through his pockets, Jez staring in disbelief as he retrieved it and pressed buttons.

'For god's sake, Dad! Don't answer it! Switch it off!'

In the days between his mother's death and the funeral he had kept working. He had kept his business appointments, trying but failing to put what had happened to his mother to the back of his mind. Flying to London had helped. He had spent five days at a mining show in the hope of meeting potential clients. With business the way it was, he needed everything he could get.

The oily voice on his mobile brought it all back – the man in the light cotton suit who had drifted past Spargo's small display stand, a mobile held to his ear. He was one of those irritatingly ageless men, perhaps mid-thirties but probably older. Not so much elegant as dapper. More a high-class pimp than a mining man.

He was the man with no name. Visitors to the exhibition were issued with badges and the man's wasn't showing. Finally he stopped and proffered a hand and a handshake. It was unexpectedly firm and powdery dry.

'Meester Spargo,' the man had said. 'Meester John Spargo. My name is Luis Benares. You are a mining consultant.'

Spargo knew that already. It said so on his badge and on his stand. Trying to place the man's accent he had nodded and smiled. Not quite Spanish. South American, possibly. Perhaps Portuguese.

Flicking through Spargo's brochures they talked about mines. It didn't take Spargo long to realise that Benares, despite professing to represent several mining companies and contractors, knew absolutely nothing about mining.

Now, in the Daimler, Benares was on Spargo's mobile.

'Please, Mister Spargo, where are you? I am at Barajas International Arrivals. But I think you are not here.'

As the Daimler pulled up at the front of the hotel Spargo kept the phone to his ear. He flicked back his cuff so he could read the date on his watch.

'Mr Benares, I am so sorry, I am in Scotland. Something came up.' He swivelled in his seat and met Jez's stare. 'A death in the family,' he added. 'A close relative. My mother, actually.'

'My condolences, Mr Spargo. I am sure we can reschedule your visit. Please telephone me at a time more convenient to yourself.'

'I met him at the mining show,' Spargo explained to Jez over dinner. 'He says he represents a man who could use my services. I was supposed to fly to Madrid today.'

He took out his wallet, selected a business card and passed it to Jez. 'BarConSA,' she said, studying it. 'Odd name.'

'It's probably Bar Consulting SA. Or Bar Contracting.'

'There's no address.'

'There's a Telex number.'

'Who the hell uses Telex these days?' she mumbled as she turned the card over. 'There's nothing. No phone number.'

'He said BarConSa will pay all expenses for my visit, plus two days of my time at top rate. I have nothing to lose. When I made the arrangements my diary was free. I thought the funeral would be weeks away.'

'So your Mr Benares isn't a happy bunny.'

'He was okay about it. He wants to reschedule.'

She grunted. 'You should go. It'll help take your mind off things.'

'I can't, can I? There's the house to clear. There's all the legal stuff.'

'There's no rush. The cottage isn't going anywhere. If you want help then I can stay for a day or two. Or I can ask Joby.'

'Thanks,' he said. 'I can handle it. I'll stay up here a couple of days to get things rolling.' It was one of those things. However much he tried, he just couldn't ask favours of someone called Joby who, he assumed, occasionally slept with his daughter. He knew he was being unreasonable but he just couldn't help it. 'I don't want him here,' he added, regretting the words as he said them. 'There's no need, I mean. As you said, there's no hurry.'

'I don't know what you've got against him. Don't tell me in a few weeks that I didn't offer to help.'

Spargo had ordered seafood. When it came he picked at it with his fork. Stabbed at the cod and prawn pieces. He had ordered Chablis, a Premier Cru, pushing the boat out in memory of his mother. He wanted to make it a celebration of her life… or something. The waitress had filled his glass. So far it remained untouched.

'Here's to Gran,' he said, smiling at Jez and raising his glass. As it touched his lips he felt tears come and he left the room quickly, out through reception and into the cold, not stopping until he reached the seclusion of the firs beyond the bright lights of the car park. There he doubled up, and wept.

Next morning he checked out and drove Jez to the station. The sky was cloudless and the late autumn sun lit her hair from behind, filtering through it and tinting it amber. It looked so like her mother's. It reminded Spargo of bright days, never dark ones. He waited until the train pulled out. Waved as it snaked away.

To help clear his mother's house Spargo hired a man with a van. When he arrived at Kilcreg the van was already there, parked in his mother's short drive, backed up near the front door.

During the day the driver, Stuart Main, amazed Spargo by performing Godzilla-like feats such as lifting the fridge into his van single-handed. Though Spargo did his best to do his share of the work it wasn't long before he realised he was hindering rather than helping, so instead of doing the big stuff he carried small items to the van, made tea, and wished he'd had the presence of mind to bring a packed lunch like Stuart Main had done.

By mid-afternoon everything, with the exception of several items of furniture to be collected later by auctioneer's men, was stowed securely in the back of Main's van.

Both men stood at the garden gate, no longer strangers.

'I heard you lived here once,' Main said. 'Heard you're the son of the manager of the old mine. You're a mining engineer yourself, I'm told.'

'Who said?'

'Word gets around. You know what it's like, Mr Spargo, everyone into everyone else's business. So where was the mine?'

Spargo didn't want questions. He had done in one day what he thought would take two. Now he wanted to get away.

'I never lived in this house,' he said. 'I lived there.' He pointed up the road to the mine house, swinging his arm in a sweeping gesture to encompass the whole hillside behind it. 'The mine was up on the moor.'

Main stayed looking at the mine house. 'I've been here before,' he said. 'Came when I was a boy. I thought the mine was in the valley. I remember a compound full of rusty junk.'

'That was the plant yard. They stored the heavy stuff there, broken underground locomotives, spare rail and old pumps. The mine was reached up a track.' Spargo stretched out an arm, pointing beyond the old yard. 'There, the gash in the hillside, overgrown now. It's fifteen years at least since I went up there. There's nothing up on the moor now, just a building or two. They dismantled everything and filled in the shaft.'

'Didn't realise there was a shaft.'

'It was sunk in the late nineteen-thirties. Before that, the main entrance to the mine was in the sea cliffs. My father said they collapsed into the bay... the cliffs, I mean. There are boulders there the size of buses.' He swivelled on his heel, looked down the street towards the sea and did the pointing thing. Main looked. From where they stood they could see only houses.

'Time I was leaving, Mr Spargo.'

Spargo dipped a hand into his back pocket, took out a mix of banknotes and counted them out. He added a few more to the price they'd agreed.

'Generous of you. Very generous...'

Main's van pulled away in a haze of blue smoke. Spargo watched it pass by the long wall of the old plant yard and commence its climb up the hill. Heard gears change as the hill steepened. At very top of the hill its brake lights flashed as it took the sharp bend.

Spargo blinked. He was tired, though thanks to Main's efforts, nowhere near as tired has he might have been. Twice during the day the man had commented that he had cleared many houses belong to elderly people and this was one of the easiest – nothing in the garage except a few gardening tools and nothing at all in the attic. Spargo told Main what he'd told Mitchell – that his mother, like his father, didn't keep what she didn't need. It was a fine dictum. One he should apply to himself.

He turned and looked back at the cottage. Its now curtain-less windows looked back at him, hollow and ghostly. With luck the place wouldn't be on the market for long before somebody bought it. He would rather give the place away than have it crumble away like the school.

Everything his mother had owned was now crossing the high moor on a single lane road, her books and her bedding, curtains and cutlery, pot-plants and pictures. It would be sold and the proceeds given to charity. The few things that had been dear to Spargo long ago were safe in the boot of his car.

Sea mist drifted in, as did fine drizzle. Spargo flexed his arms in mock-exercise as if fooling himself he was fit. Earlier he had watched fifty-something Main heave a garden roller up a ramp and into his van using his Sumo-wrestler's build to propel the thing upwards. The roller had belonged to Spargo's father and was so difficult to push that Spargo had never used it. Who uses garden rollers these days, anyway?

Gravel crunched beneath his feet as he walked to the side door. In the kitchen again he reached up, flipped a switch in the box above the door and checked the electricity was really off by trying a light switch. It was part of a ritual, one his father had performed in the mine house on the few occasions they all went on holiday. Water off, electricity off, windows secure and doors locked. Once done, Spargo stepped outside, turned the key in the lock and then stood for a while, ticking things off his mental list. He had finished. There was nothing more to do.

What seemed so wrong to Spargo was to leave Kilcreg without speaking to Rosie. She still hadn't returned. He could come back to see her, he supposed, but in his heart he knew it wouldn't happen. The gate to the drive, always open, now thudded closed on a part of his life. Not on a part of his childhood – that had happened years ago when he left home – but on something more recent, more evil.

At the top of the hill he pulled into a passing bay, got out and looked down the valley, first at the cottage and then at mine house. Had the weather been better he might have walked back down the hill to the plant yard, perhaps even attempted to walk up the miners' track to the mine. Or perhaps not.

❧

Midge Rollo slid into the driving seat of his small black Fiat and pulled away from the pumps. The belated payment for services – services so far only partly rendered – had arrived in the post, a padded envelope containing used banknotes. With cash in his pocket he had taxed his car and filled up its tank. The Fiat was well known to the police, who for reasons best known to themselves pulled him over fairly regularly. Tax and insurance wouldn't stop it happening. But why give them the satisfaction of finding something wrong?

Mr Luis had left Edinburgh the same day he'd arrived. Refusing Midge's offer of a bus ride to the airport he had taken a taxi. He had also refused the pistol, with a curt comment that he had not asked for it and didn't want it. Last night, in his Gran's kitchen, Midge had stripped the gun down, cleaned the parts and reassembled them. Dead-easy. He'd been doing it with replicas for years.

Mr Luis's departure meant Midge had changed from minder to watcher. His new task, Mr Luis told him, was to familiarise himself with the Spargo woman's movements, with her work, and with her friends.

For a couple of days he'd hung around in the road outside her house but had felt too conspicuous – what with the kiddie's playground so close and the young mothers and grannies who eyed him suspiciously. He now knew the times Jessica Spargo left for work – on a motorbike she kept in a shed – but because he'd no vehicle he didn't know where she went. She came home at odd hours. Sometimes she was picked up in a grey Volvo driven by a man old enough to be her father. At the end of each day, as instructed by Mr Luis, Midge wrote out neatly the things he had learned and then sent them, in an envelope, to a London address.

Having the Fiat back on the road didn't make things much easier. He had pictured himself parking up the road from the flat with the car heater on and a tape playing, but residents' parking zones conspired against him. He ended up parking two streets away and walking, as before.

Today, like every other day, he found a space and parked neatly. He stepped out of the car and inspected his parking, checking his wheels were tucked close to the kerb. Always conscious of what had happened to Robbie he found the nearest ticket machine and fed it with coins. Back at his car he stuck the ticket in his windscreen. Unstuck it again and adjusted it. Got it square.

As Midge was walking across the entrance to the lane behind the houses, a motorbike came out fast and missed him by inches. The bike wobbled, the engine stalled. The rider lifted the helmet visor, looked at Midge, and mumbled apologies. Midge stared at her. Went on staring while Jessica Spargo restarted her bike and continued out onto the road.

CHAPTER SEVEN

THE TICKET INSPECTOR who snatched Theo's papers says nothing. She glances over Theo's shoulder and gives an almost imperceptible nod to someone behind him, someone in the queue. Theo turns. The stranger from the train is there, he flashes Theo a smile.

'Kapitänleutnant,' he says. 'Take your papers and walk on. I wish to speak with you.' The ticket inspector is holding Theo's papers high, keeping them from him. At a nod from the stranger she hands them back. Theo takes a few steps past the checkpoint and stops. The stranger speaks again. 'Forgive my inquisitiveness. Do you know Berlin?'

'I do not.'

'And you are hoping to continue your journey beyond the city?'

'I am. How do you know these things?'

'Unless you are a fool you will not be travelling east, so I assume you hope to go south. That will not be easy for you.'

'I have a permit to travel.'

'Such a permit allows you to travel, it does not provide you with the means. Is that not so? Trains for passengers are rare, Kapitän.'

'I understand that.'

He takes care with his words. Even the most innocent responses hold dangers. All responses would beg the same question: *So who told you that, Kapitänleutnant?*

'As you may have guessed, I know this railway station. Despite what I told your fellow passengers you will find no transport to take you further tonight.'

'That does not trouble me.'

'I am sure it does not. Please listen to what I have to say. I can help you – not to travel south, for that is your own concern – but tomorrow I shall travel to Berlin, I have transport. I have a place in Potsdam where I will stay tonight. I can find a bed for you.'

'That is considerate of you. But I shall make my own arrangements.'

'Kapitänleutnant, I must now telephone for a car. When I telephone I can also ask that you be given a meal and a bed for the night. It is up to you.'

Passengers from the train, seeing there are no buses or taxis, mill around in the concourse. Experienced travellers, accepting that they are stranded, are taking over the waiting rooms and staking claims to sheltered alcoves. The stranger speaks again.

'Tell me? First thing tomorrow I will leave for Berlin. You can accompany me there if you wish, or you can make your own way.'

Theo looks the stranger in the eye and nods. There can be no harm in it. The sooner he gets to Berlin, the sooner he travels south to his son.

The saloon that arrives for them is driven by a girl in Luftwaffe uniform who alights from the car and salutes stiffly, her arm held straight and high, a salute accompanied by an inevitable and overly-enthusiastic *Heil Hitler*. The salute is for the stranger and not for him. Confirmation the man holds higher rank than he does.

The girl attempts to take the stranger's bag but he tugs it back. Surprised and embarrassed she apologises and turns her attention to Theo, seeking his consent with a quick, enquiring glance before taking his kitbag. The brief smile he gives her is not returned. By the time she is back from the car's boot the stranger is already in the car. She holds the door open for Theo, and salutes him. Clicks her heels. So much wasted energy.

Potsdam is dark and deserted. Their car creeps forwards, guided only by a pool of yellow light from its blackout-masked headlights. Other than that there are no lights at all, no streetlights, no lights in buildings and no other vehicles.

Apart from the girl's salutation no words have been spoken. It is a strange world in which people dare not talk freely. What talk there is speaks of war, of hollow victories, of food production figures and praise for the leadership. Theo, when on his boat, talks with trusted colleagues about failures, about those who call themselves leaders, about the paranoia of the Führer and the prancings of Göring. Even Dönitz, their Grand Admiral, seems to toe the party line. And what about last summer's attempt on Hitler's life? Surely that means his own generals doubt him? Rumours abound that Feldmarschall Rommel was involved in the plot and now he is dead, his car conveniently strafed by an enemy plane. Germany, Theo muses, remains a fantasy land, a Thousand Year Reich doomed to die.

'We will arrive very soon, Herr Kapitän. I would not submit you to yet more long distance travel.'

Theo's smile is not seen. Long distance for him is the German Ocean, the Norwegian Sea and the Denmark Strait to the North Atlantic. His journeys take weeks, not days.

Fat raindrops attack the car's roof. Wipers come on and move lazily. Smear the screen. The driver changes gear and the car slows to walking pace. With such rain and poor lights it is a miracle she can see anything.

Unexpectedly the car turns sharply and stops. Theo, whose view through the car's windscreen resembles the slow-moving frames of a cinematograph film sees, ahead of him, a white barrier like those at the entrance to dockyards. From the darkness comes a running man holding an oil lamp. Car windows are lowered and papers presented, checked and handed back; the barrier rises, hinged at one end. The car moves on.

Dim headlights pick out concrete roads and cropped grass. On Theo's left, looming from the darkness, is a many-windowed building. The stranger speaks, the driver nods. The car changes direction and drifts, silently but for the hiss of its tyres on wet concrete, towards the main doorway of the building. It stops, with just a touch on the brakes, at the foot of a flight of stone steps.

Though the driver moves quickly she is beaten to the stranger's door by a uniformed Luftwaffe officer who runs down the steps from the building's main door. Out of compassion or pity Theo waits for the girl to open his door, and as he clambers out she salutes him, her arm held high. He returns a naval salute with his hand flat, his fingers to the peak of his cap. Refusing his help she struggles with his kitbag, heaving it from the car's boot, on to her shoulder and up the stone steps.

The stranger and the Luftwaffe officer have gone on ahead. They are already through the double doors of the building and standing just inside, talking loudly, laughing and joking.

Theo shelters from the rain under the flat stone canopy of the entrance and watches the car turn. Sees twin pools of yellow light sweep across more neatly trimmed grass. A great lawn. Probably a sports field. He can smell it, sweet and newly mown, a smell he has not known for years.

The double doors swing open. The stranger comes up behind him, places a hand on his shoulder and turns him.

'Major Shomburg, this is Kapitänleutnant Theodor Volker. I have promised him a bed for the night, so please arrange it for me. Tomorrow morning he will accompany me to Berlin.'

That Theo was introduced by name didn't surprise him. He had presented his papers at the station and again at the checkpoint. Clearly, the man has keen eyes. Theo senses this is not the place for a naval salute, and for Shomburg he extends his arm smartly. Shomburg is not wearing a cap so the salute is not returned. Instead he nods and clicks heels.

'Will the Kapitänleutnant be joining you for dinner, Herr Generalmajor?'

Theo bites his lip. The stranger's high rank shocks him. He knows naval ranks but finds those of the other services confusing. He is fairly sure a generalmajor is four ranks above him at least. In naval terms, a Vice-Admiral.

The stranger, the Generalmajor, swivels on his heel and scans Theo from head to toe. He takes in – perhaps for the first time in decent lighting – Theo's well-worn jacket, his grubby-topped cap, his heavy serge trousers and his seaboots of soft dull leather, boots more suited to a fisherman than a Kriegsmarine officer. And his beard. A beard trimmed, not quite to perfection, by his bosun.

'I think not, Shomburg. Show our friend to the officer's mess. Find someone to accompany him, someone of similar rank to himself.'

'Of course, Herr Generalmajor.'

Again the Generalmajor regards Theo. 'Kapitänleutnant, tomorrow you will be at this very spot at seven o'clock precisely.' There is the trace of a smile. 'That is, of course, zero seven hundred hours. Not nineteen hundred hours.'

Theo spends the evening with youngsters, though not by choice. He is accompanied not by an officer of his own rank, but a non-commissioned orderly who guides him through corridors to the Junior Mess. The notice boards on the walls confirm his suspicions. He has been brought to a Luftwaffe training school.

In the mess he is introduced to young airmen, fresh-faced and fresh-laundered in what look to him like naval midshipmen's blue waistcoats. The white twill trousers they wear have knife-sharp creases. He does not want this; what he wants most of all is a bath and a bed. What he gets instead is idolization and beer. And more beer. He is U-boat commander, a hero.

'You have seen much action of course, Kapitänleutnant? We do not expect details, but can you tell us a little?'

Theo humours them, telling them what they want to hear, exaggerating the strength and the skills of his crew. He recalls how, at the end of his last mission, his gunners brought down two aircraft. What he fails to tell them is his boat was caught by surprise on the surface and one of the aircraft they brought down was one of their own – and cannon fire from the enemy aircraft tore the heads off his gunners and punctured his boat's ballast tanks.

He wants to tell them about merchant seamen from Allied cargo ships choking on oil, screaming for help from the U-boat crew that condemned them to death. To tell such truths would be unwelcome, defeatist – even treasonable – talk. He tells them instead of the thrill of the chase, of torpedo runs in the dark, the crowds on the quay when they leave on a mission. Of the bouquets, the brass bands and the girls of the signals corps at Saint-Nazaire. Past glories, all gone.

'Is it wise to name places, Herr Kapitänleutnant?'

Theo nods pensively. 'It is of no importance. Saint-Nazaire and our southern ports are now in enemy hands, you surely know that.'

'We will drive the scum into the sea, Herr Kapitänleutnant. It is our destiny.'

Their belief in the Führer is absolute. Their indoctrination is total, the result of exposure since birth to icons and emblems, symbols of magic and mystery. Most of all they believe in a faultless, omnipotent Germany. For the first time in years he is close to tears. In a few weeks so many of these youngsters will surely die.

Far too much beer. Time to go before he spoils it for them.

'It is time for me to sleep, my friends. I have had a long day.'

They lift their glasses to him. He leaves them to their beer, and for what little is left of the night he sleeps badly, his waking hours spent listening for the drone of bombers, the thud of distant bombs and a call to the shelters – a call that doesn't come. Tonight Potsdam is safe.

Wishing he had risen in time to eat breakfast, Theo arrives at the double doors at five minutes to seven. Today there is no smell of mown grass, just the smell of a damp morning and a thin, all-pervading smell of burnt timber.

'I trust you slept well, Kapitänleutnant Volker?'

The question is more of an order than a question and it demands a positive answer. 'Thank you, Herr Generalmajor, I slept well.'

Theo expected the generalmajor to be in uniform but he is dressed as before. He also expects to be picked up by a staff car, perhaps the one with the girl. What arrives, dead on time, is a canvas-topped lorry. Its arrival does not surprise the Generalmajor.

'In these days of hardship it is not always possible to travel in the style normally accorded to one's rank, Kapitänleutnant. I shall ride with the driver. I am sure there is room for you in the back.'

Theo peers over the tailgate and seeing the truck is empty he heaves up his kitbag and scrambles in after it. He thumps on the driver's cab, a signal that he is on board, the sits on the tailgate, gripping a steel hoop that supports the truck's canvas top. He sees, beyond the mown grass, rows of ancient tanks and armoured cars. Further along, holed up in bays between trees, are Königstigers – Tiger Tanks – the Reich's finest. He wonders why they are here, rather than in the south or east, where they are needed most.

The service road they are on opens out to a wide concrete apron. On the far side of it is a concrete roofed bomb shelter with wide open doors. The truck pulls up beside them and the Generalmajor climbs down. He calls to an airman:

'Where is Oberinspektor Krawczac? Find him. Bring him to me.'

With steel tips clicking the Generalmajor crosses the concrete and enters the shelter's wide doors, returning minutes later with a man carrying a clipboard. Airmen in overalls, pulling handcarts loaded with wooden crates, follow the two men out onto the concrete.

Theo jumps down. He watches the Generalmajor take the clipboard, squint at it, take glasses from his pocket and put them on. As each crate is loaded onto the truck the man – Krawczac, Theo assumes – calls out the number stencilled on the crates. The Generalmajor nods. Makes marks on his clipboard.

The loading is efficient and fast. When they resume their journey Theo is no longer alone. He shares what little space remains in the truck with an elderly, uniformed guard. Theo feels in his coat pocket for his pipe and tobacco. The guard watches him silently. Real tobacco is a rarity – and this naval man has two tins of it.

'Not explosives?' Theo asks, tapping a crate with his fingers. 'Am I permitted to smoke?'

The guard shrugs. He is carrying a well-worn, ancient rifle that he jams into a gap between crates, takes off his helmet and goes through his pockets. He finds, and then unrolls, a thin leather tobacco pouch. Knowing he has no tobacco, only papers for roll-ups, he watches Theo tug good-quality black twist from a half-full tin, transfer it in small pinches to his pipe and then pack it down with his thumb.

Theo passes the tin to the man, who feigns surprise and then nods acceptance. He balances the tin on his knee and picks at its contents sparingly. He rolls the strands of tobacco between his palms and transfers it to the paper.

'Luftwaffe?' Theo asks. 'These days there are so many uniforms.'

The guard nods. Theo offers his lighter to the man, flicking the flint wheel as he holds it out. The lighter's flame is orange and smoky and its wick glows red at its edges. The fuel is impure, supplied to him by his boat's chief engineer – distilled from the boat's diesel fuel, Theo suspects.

The guard has his roll-up between his lips. When Theo touches the end with the flame a length of the paper flares up and Theo wonders what it is made from. These days little is what it seems: They make rubber from coal, and coffee from roast acorns.

Theo taps the crate he is sitting on. 'Vital spares?' he asks. 'Equipment for our glorious air force?'

The man snorts, shrugs, and draws hard on his cigarette. A third of it vanishes in a bright orange glow. He coughs, gently.

'Treasures of the Reich,' he says, winking. 'Recovered from those that oughtn't to have had them.'

Theo doesn't look like an officer. His leather jacket has no badges of rank and the thin braid of yellow around the peak of his cap is oil-stained and grubby. And he is in the back of the truck, not up front with the high-ranker.

'You a U-boat man?'

Theo nods. The man takes one last pull on his cigarette before crushing the fragments that remain under his boot, grinding them around until they are unrecognisable.

'Wouldn't catch me doing your job. Wouldn't get me in one of those tin coffins.'

'You get used to it.'

'Not me.'

Theo takes short puffs on his pipe. He is no longer used to it and it isn't long before he bangs out its contents on the heel of his boot. He is about to crush the embers when the man shoves the boot aside, jams himself down between the crates and starts sorting through the ash with his fingers, picking out strands of tobacco. He transfers his finds to his fold-over wallet.

'You going right through?' he asks.

'Through?'

'Right through. To Schönebeck.'

'To Berlin. I've got shore leave. Got a son down south. Going to see him.'

'South? You mean Steglitz? Templehof?'

'Near Ingolstadt. It's north of Munich.'

'Shit! Not a chance. You'll not get there.'

'Is the enemy that close?'

'If I knew where those bastards were I wouldn't tell you, would I?

What I do know is there's no trains. Not for the likes of you and me.'

They have reached Berlin. They pass through shattered streets, like those in Potsdam. Whole streets have vanished; women and children labour with barrows and baskets piled high with bricks; human chains of workers trail back into side streets, an army of ants passing tiles, bricks and timber from hand to hand. In the main streets are hills built from rubble, some of brick and stone, others of window frames, roof timbers and floorboards.

Time was when the enemy dropped its bombs on railway yards, docks and factories. Now it drops them on houses, hospitals and shops. To Theo, this scale of damage is not new. He has seen the devastation in the ports. But houses, hospitals and schools?

'Do you know Berlin?' he asks the man. 'Do you know what station I need for Munich?'

'Anhalter. That's if the bastards didn't get it last night.'

'Where are we going now?'

'Air Ministry, Wilhelmstrasse. Anhalter's one block away. You can walk there.'

Ridges of rubble have realigned streets. Traffic is delayed and diverted by clearance work. The smell of smoke is overpowering and occasionally it can be seen, dense columns of black curling skywards. They rise so high their tops are cut off by the wind, thinned out and carried away.

The guard is a tour guide of devastation:

'Brother in law's in that lot,' he says, pointing to a fire truck. 'Says they can't cope. Last year the Führer took fire units from Hamburg and Bremen, said we need them here.' Aware of his careless words he glances at Theo. The submariner seems unmoved. 'A wise move,' the man adds, in an attempt to redeem himself. 'This is our capital city.'

Theo massages his forehead with his fingertips. These are things he does not know. Hamburg, gutted by fire, fifty-thousand dead in one week. And the Führer moved the city's fire trucks to Berlin?

They are passing the Tiergarten, woodland in the heart of Berlin. Though Theo hasn't seen the place before, he has heard of it. If there is one place in the city that shows how bad things have become, this is it; what was once parkland is studded with bomb craters, fallen trees and shattered stumps. He gazes awestruck at the flak tower – a sixty-metre-high concrete cube bristling with anti-aircraft guns that dominates the skyline. It is surely the tallest man made structure he has ever seen.

'Grandson's in the flak crew there,' the guard says. 'Does a good job, gives the bastards something to think about. He's a good kid. Fifteen years old next month.'

Theo nods. They fight this war with children. He gets youngsters on his boat but they are not that young, thank god. The war will soon end. Perhaps another year, perhaps another month. They will lose, he knows that too. So what then, foreign rule? Years of oppression? Will there be resistance, partisans fighting the victors, like in France?

'Wilhelmstrasse,' The guard says, loudly. 'The heart of our Reich. Reich Chancellery coming up now!'

It is a peculiar, retrospective commentary. From the back of the truck they see only what they have passed, it is a half-look at everything. The guard reels off names of more buildings as the truck trundles on. Strangely, compared with others parts of the city, these buildings have suffered little.

'Air Ministry,' he says. 'This is it. You ever seen a building like it?'

They pass a wall of pale stone with five storeys of windows. It is the largest office building Theo has seen – though not as large as some underground voids in the Harz mines. In Theo's mind no building can beat those for grandeur.

The road they turn into is narrow, much less grand than Wilhelmstrasse. Halfway along it is the main entrance to the Ministry with its high railings and tall stone gateposts surmounted by bronze eagles, each twice the height of a man. Ironically the birds have closed wings; to Theo they look more like the American eagle than the more common spread-eagle of the Reich.

Staff cars litter the courtyard; armed guards in Luftwaffe uniform stand at the gates. Nervousness is a rare feeling for Theo and it comes to him now. The building was built to impress and it succeeds. He pulls himself together. Any second now the truck will stop and he will be on his way, off to Anhalter Station and the trains to his boy. He will jump down, sling his kitbag over his shoulder, walk to the truck's cab and thank the Generalmajor for his kindness. He will salute smartly. And, sea boots willing, give a heel-click. He speaks to the guard:

'I need directions. Which way is Anhalter?'

The guard shrugs. 'Looks to me like most roads are impassable. Best you walk back to Wilhelmstrasse and ask somebody.'

The truck doesn't stop at the main entrance. It drives the whole length of the building and turns down a lane.

'Schutzstaffel and Staatspolitzei,' the guard says, nodding at the high walled building across the street. 'Headquarters, of course. Another of my grandsons is there. Privileged position. Good safe job.'

'SS?'

'No, Staatspolitzei. Still a boy. Recruited straight into the Gestapo from the Hitlerjugend. What do you think of that, eh?'

The Air Ministry is even bigger than Theo realised. Behind it, on each end of it, are massive extensions, huge wings with hundreds of windows. One of the extensions has taken a direct hit by bombs. Apart from that, the place looks undamaged.

The truck turns again and stops at twin gates. Theo stands up, holds on to the canvas and leans around to get a better view. His jacket is tugged from behind.

'Sit down, man! Put your cap on!'

Two sentries look in, first at Theo and then at the guard. Unusually, they don't demand papers and the truck moves on, into the ministry grounds. There are more staff cars here, not parked randomly like those at the front but lined up neatly as if for inspection, their chrome trim and chrome radiators gleaming in the sun. How, Theo wonders, can there be time for polishing paintwork in a world of such hell?

Uniformed drivers – women, elderly men and one youngster – stand smoking, huddled in a circle like peak-capped penguins. As the truck approaches they turn away. One catches sight of the officer in the cab and throws up a salute. Cigarettes vanish in well-practised moves.

The truck grinds in low gear past boarded up windows. Much of the ground floor is protected from bomb-blasts by high walls of sandbags. These, and concrete blast walls, protect the rear entrances to the building. The truck stops at one of these and the Generalmajor appears at the tailgate, surprising the guard, who jumps up and salutes. He is ignored.

'Kapitänleutnant, we have arrived at the Air Ministry. Climb down, please, bring your bag and come with me. Your papers will be checked. Please have them ready.'

The guard's eyes widen, the U-boat man is an officer, he has been tricked, made to gossip idly. He tries to recall the things he has said but his mind swims with thoughts and he cannot concentrate. Theo turns to him, winks, and slips a tin of tobacco into his hand.

Theo follows the Generalmajor around a wall of sandbags, into the building and through high corridors. He thanks him for his kindness and hospitality and for his lift to Berlin. The man keeps walking, doesn't seem to have heard. His footsteps make the familiar double click, except that in here there are echoes. For a man with a limp, he walks fast.

Another corridor, then down flights of stairs. The place is a warren of passages. Theo tries again:

'I am grateful to you, Herr Generalmajor. But if I am to – '

The man half turns his head, speaking as he walks.

'Keep following me, Kapitänleutnant.'

Theo has his papers in his hand, but so far nobody has asked for them. He is sweating, partly from the effort of carrying his heavy kitbag and partly from fear – not the fear that comes before combat but fear of the unknown. He has done nothing wrong, he is a good officer who has served the Reich well. It is true he often says what he thinks, but only when amongst friends.

One side of the corridor is bare wall. The other is a labyrinth of rooms and side corridors along which uniformed staff scurry with papers, ghost-like figures beneath silver-blue lamps. Then another corridor, dank and deserted, bleak and unpainted. It ends at an open door, heavy steel like others. Not exactly a cell door, but very much like one.

The room beyond the door is small, lit by a sealed bulkhead lamp like those on board ship. Theo stands in the doorway but he doesn't go in. He places his kitbag at his feet, turns to the Generalmajor and stares at him, not something he would normally dare do. He has placed seamen in custody himself, escorted by two or three ratings. Never, in his limited experience of such matters, would an officer of this man's rank be present. Never would such a man be expected to guard a prisoner.

'I am Kapitänleutnant Theodor Volker. I am a loyal Kriegsmarine officer.'

'I know very well who you are, Kapitänleutnant. Please pick up your bag and go into the room.'

CHAPTER EIGHT

THE MISTY DRIZZLE AT KILCREG became fierce, drenching rain. Spargo, oblivious to it, had changed his mind, turned his car in the road and was now driving back down the hill. Thanks to Stuart Main's efficiency he was early, he didn't need to leave for home. Not yet, anyway.

Spargo turned off the road and stopped the Volvo in the entrance to the plant yard. Though his destination was the mine house, its front drive was blocked by stone from the gate pillars, whereas the plant yard's entrance was clear. Driving further into the yard was unsafe for his tyres; the surface of the yard was studded with nuts, bolts, washers and other small steel scrap.

It had been a private joke amongst Kilcreg miners that there was probably more tungsten in the old steel scrap machinery in the plant yard than there was in all the ore they mined. Despite his father's pronouncements about disposing of unwanted junk, in truth he couldn't throw anything away. Damaged equipment was kept in old buildings or out in the yard. To young Spargo, the mine's plant yard with its old engines and mining equipment had been an Aladdin's Cave of treasures.

It was the same at home, nothing was ever thrown out. Things no longer wanted, such as old lampshades, old suitcases and vacuum cleaners with burnt-out motors, were safely stored away. Ironically, what his father used to say about the attic was true – it really was empty. The things the Spargo family no longer used were kept in a shed on the edge of the plant yard; occasionally the young Spargo would go there with his father to look for things amongst the junk, the vases and pots, the Christmas tree lights and old books.

The question Spargo never thought to ask his father came to him as he drove up the hill: why did his father trudge all the way to the dank dirty shed when there was perfectly good storage space in the mine house attic? Why had his father said *if it's ready for the attic then it's ready for the tip?*

The comments he'd made to Mitchell came back to him – whoever murdered his mother had got the wrong house. He'd also said there was nowhere in Kilcreg worth burgling, but somebody clearly thought there was. What if their information was years out of date? What if they'd searched the wrong Spargo house?

Spargo, screwdriver and claw hammer in one hand and hand lamp in the other, set off towards the mine house, making his way there by way of the plant yard. Though the yard was cleared years ago, traces of things long gone still remained: a flat slab of concrete was all that was left of the mechanical workshops and blacksmith's shop; a rectangular depression marked the place where a tall stack of sleepers once stood; heavy steel bolts, brown with onion-layered rust, stuck up through the grass. Once, the ground was all black ash and clinker, brought from the steam boiler at the mine and rolled flat, like tarmac. That too was still there, visible occasionally through a veneer of small weeds.

Spargo stepped through a gap in the fence dividing the plant yard from the mine house grounds. The house, ahead of him now, had been constructed from dark grey stone. Its extension, built on its left-hand side, was a simple, one-up and one-down affair under a lean-to slate roof. It had been constructed in wartime out of concrete blockwork, then rendered with grey cement in an attempt to make it blend in. To the young Spargo it had always been part of the house. Now he saw it for what it was: artless, bomb shelter architecture.

Over the years the plywood sheets nailed over the windows had loosened. As Spargo neared the house the wind got behind them and they flapped with a regular, thudding beat. The planks across the front door were fixed in a criss-cross pattern by nails driven into the mortar. A case-opener – a jemmy – might have eased them out; Spargo, carrying only the small tools salvaged from his mother's garage, didn't even attempt it. And anyway, tearing wood from the front of the house wasn't an option because the house could be seen from the road.

Like the back of the cottage, the back of the mine house faced the hillside. In it were several tall windows and a back door that led into the kitchen. This doorway, like the one at the front, was heavily boarded, and the windows were covered by ply. By levering one of the plywood sheets with his screwdriver he managed to get his hands behind it. It was rotten. It tore away easily.

The kitchen window frame behind the plywood was glassless. Rather than climb up onto the windowsill Spargo leant over it and slithered snake-like into the kitchen, a task made easier by whoever had removed the large Belfast sink that once stood there.

Had the room not been bare it might have triggered emotions, but Spargo felt none. Not only had the sink gone, so had everything else. Whoever had gutted the place – he assumed it was builders – had taken the door to the walk-in larder and the door to the hall, complete with its frame. Rectangles on the walls and floor marked where cupboards and shelves had been – the mine house, though built more than a century ago, had a fitted kitchen with floor to ceiling cupboards and a built-in, wood-fired range.

The floorboards, still covered by the original brown linoleum, felt sound underfoot, they didn't bounce when he crossed to the hall doorway. Once there he switched on his lamp, playing its beam lamp on the pile of felled masonry that had once been the main chimney stack. Not only had the falling stack torn through the roof, it had smashed its way through the hall ceiling, the hall floorboards and the strong beams beneath them. Broken slates lay scattered like playing cards and, at his feet, sprouting from the ground beneath rotting floorboards, was a crop of tall weeds. High above him, wind laced with rain swirled through the gash in the roof with an eerie, hollow howl.

It took Spargo a while to realise why the hall seemed so huge. The main staircase, an elegant structure of polished mahogany, was no longer there. The balcony-style landing that gave access to the bedrooms and bathroom had gone too, as had the doors to the upstairs rooms. Now, these doorways sat high in the wall, like eye sockets in a square, hollow skull.

Spargo played the lamp on the hall ceiling. Sheets of lath and plaster, still attached to broken beams, dangled precariously above his head. Off to one side of the gash, above where the balcony had been, was a hatch that once gave access to the attic. Now that the staircase and balcony had gone, the only way to reach it would be with a three-section extending ladder, set up in the hall on the rickety floor. He didn't have one. Wouldn't dare do such a thing anyway.

He stopped looking up. In his heart he knew that searching was pointless, he was wasting his time. Had there been anything in the house to find, then whoever stripped the place bare would have found it.

Curiosity took him into the ground floor rooms. The dining room, once kept for best, was as bare as the kitchen, its fireplace and fittings torn out and taken. The sitting room too, was empty. Even the light fittings, switches and sockets had gone.

The two rooms in the extension were accessible through a door at the end of a corridor – not that the door would be there now. Spargo pointed the lamp in that direction and saw he was right. The door had gone.

He hesitated before entering the room and he wasn't sure why. The floor was sound, under the lino it was solid concrete, he knew that. It was just that he had never liked that part of the house, it was different and felt claustrophobic, even to him as a boy.

The room stank of rot and its wallpaper, black-streaked and spotted with mould, peeled at its top edge and hung down like rotting net curtains. To him, this room had three lives; in his earliest recollection of it there were beds with metal ends; later, when he was six years old, it became his father's office, transferred from the mine buildings when they needed more space. Lastly – and this was the memory that hurt most of all – the room became a store for his late father's paperwork and files, his brown oilskin waterproofs and his mining helmet. Spargo had hated it. Hated the room and its contents.

The extension had its own staircase, narrow and steep and built into one wall. Surprisingly it still had its small wooden door and he went to it, lifted its metal latch and swung the door back. Surprisingly, too, the stairs were still there. Lamp in hand he placed a foot gingerly on the wooden step, then the next and the next. The staircase led directly into the upstairs room and, when he reached it, he again did his testing thing. The floor was sound.

He hadn't expected to see a trapdoor in the room's ceiling. That the extension should have its own attic hadn't occurred to him, despite the fact the building was a lean-to and the room's ceiling was flat – which meant there was dead space overhead. He reached up. Managed to touch the trapdoor with his fingertips.

Thirty minutes later he was back in the room, standing on the stepladder he had taken from Rose Munro's garage after beating the padlock on the door with a half-brick until the hasp and staple broke away. He knew the stepladder would be there. Long ago he'd fixed brackets to the garage wall so she could hang it up.

If he couldn't go into the main attic, at least he could look into this one, stand on the steps and check with the lamp. Simple and safe. He stood on the steps, pushed up the hatch and shoved it aside. Then, climbing higher, he lifted his lamp and inspected the void. Apart from a thick layer of dust on the wooden joists there was nothing. No hidden treasure. No pots of gold.

What Spargo hadn't expected to see was a dark triangular patch, high on the house wall. It was off in one corner of the attic and he puzzled over it, angling the lamp beam to see it more clearly. It took him a while to work out that though most of the lean-to roof was lower than the main roof, the dark patch was a gap where the two overlapped. There was, after all, a way into the mine house roof.

CHAPTER NINE

THE BASEMENT ROOM in the Air Ministry building stinks of damp. It is small, little more than a cell; its ceiling and walls are concrete, painted pastel green. Halfway along the left wall is a sink and above it, screwed to the wall, is a polished sheet of steel to serve as a mirror. Beyond the sink, in the far left corner of the room, is a lavatory pan with no seat, screened from the door by a short wall of bricks – shiny pastel green, like the walls. A stackable, steel framed chair with a brown canvas seat stands by the bed; the bed itself, against the right hand wall, is a slab of concrete topped with flat wooden boards on which has been placed a thin mattress. A towel, two neatly folded grey blankets and a horsehair-stuffed pillow are stacked where a bedhead would be, had Hitler's Reich bothered with such things.

Fixed to the wall between the lavatory and the bed is an electric heater. Theo's gaze traces the route of the black steel pipe that carries its cables, along the wall behind the bed and up to switch near the door. He reaches out and flips it down. The heater hums. Whatever else he may die from in this place it won't be from cold.

The bed is the least of Theo's worries; when tired he can sleep almost anywhere. He drops down and sits on its edge, reaches down to unlace his boots and kicks them off. They fly across the room and he goes for them. Places them neatly, side by side.

A clear head and fast responses have kept him alive in this war and yet he let down his guard, he fell into a trap. It seems so clear now. The man in the carriage – Helmut Saur – moved from his compartment to make space for the Generalmajor. Or did it start before that? Was another unfortunate passenger hauled away to make space in the carriage for him, Theodor Volker? And there is another thing:

his name. He'd assumed the Generalmajor saw it on his passbook. That, he realises now, was unlikely. This morning the man produced reading glasses to check the list of crates.

The biggest puzzle of all is why a senior officer, a *very* senior officer, should have done this, it isn't as if Theo holds high rank. And why a Luftwaffe man, why not the Kriegsmarine or the police? Or, if it they believe he has committed a crime against the state – god forbid – why not the Gestapo?

He wonders if he should have protested more forcefully. But you don't protest, do you, not these days. He has seen what happens to those who do, seen a crewman kicked and beaten, dragged off by men who refused to give explanations. He recalls how polite they were when they came to the dockside, insisting he need not trouble himself such matters, that they would inform the Kriegsmarine, they would write the reports.

Theo has slept. Somewhere far off a pump is running, water is flowing. There are other noises, all muffled, all distant. Shaking off sleep he stumbles to the sink, runs water and splashes it on his face. The room has no ventilation and has become over-hot. As he switches off the heater he notices that the heavy metal door is slightly ajar. He hesitates before touching it, wondering if it has been like that since the Generalmajor left. Wonders, also, if it was left unlocked deliberately. The door opens inwards; though there is no door handle on his side of the door, that does not mean it cannot be opened; slowly and silently, using his fingertips, he eases it back.

Compared with the room Theo just left, the corridor feels cold and damp. It is well below ground and the outside wall, if indeed it is an outside wall, has no windows. Like his room it is lit dimly with bulkhead lights and he stands looking down it, attempting to identify the noises he hears. Then, walking slowly back the way he came with the Generalmajor, he passes other rooms. Their doors are open, their rooms unlit. All but one - a washroom - are packed with old files.

When he came with the Generalmajor the prison-like, steel bar gate across the end of the corridor was open, swung back against the corridor wall. Now it is locked shut and he shakes it, more from frustration than in the hope it will open. That it is locked doesn't surprise him. After going to so much trouble they would hardly let him walk free.

There are voices, far off. Sounds echo confusingly and it is only when the voices get close that Theo realises two men at least are descending steps beyond the barred gate. One is the Generalmajor, he can tell by the walk. Scared of being caught Theo runs the length of the corridor, back to his room like a misbehaving child. By the time he hears the clang of the barred gate he is sitting on the edge of his bed with the door fully closed. Then the Generalmajor is there, leaning on the door. It opens unexpectedly and he topples into the room. The man with him shakes his head and laughs loudly.

'Well, you clever old bastard, you did it! And single-handed! Didn't think you still had it in you. I owe you a drink, maybe several. Though you may have to wait some time.'

Both men keep laughing. They ignore Theo, who watches the new man, sees he wears the uniform and insignia of a Luftwaffe Major. Theo stands up. Reaches for his naval cap. Places it on his head and salutes.

Still the men ignore him. He notes that though the newcomer is three ranks below the Generalmajor they converse as if they are equals, swapping jokes at Theo's expense, commenting on the size of the room, that to a submariner it must seem like a ballroom. The newcomer runs a finger around the inside of his shirt collar and remarks on the room's heat.

'I suppose we should expect this from a bloody submariner...'

He swings the black briefcase he is carrying, hurling it across the room. It lands on the bed.

'This is Kapitänleutnant Theodor Volker,' the Generalmajor says to the man, quietly and deliberately. 'Present and correct. Though when I say correct, Walter, he is unlikely to pass any inspection of mine. Are all U-boat men as scruffy as this one?'

'I don't know any, thank god. Though I suspect they are.'

'I can leave him with you now?'

'Of course. An excellent job, my friend. Truly excellent!'

The men laugh again and the Generalmajor leaves, pulling the door closed behind him. The newcomer stares at Theo for a few seconds then turns his attention to the wall heater.

'Turn that bloody thing off!'

'It is turned off.'

'It is turned off, Herr Major!'

Whatever humour the Luftwaffe men might have shared is not to be shared with Theo. He goes to repeat the man's words but is interrupted before he can speak. The major is staring at Theo's leather jacket.

'Good god man, you should see yourself! You are a Kriegsmarine lieutenant! What is that thing you are wearing? Where are your badges of rank?'

Then, spotting Theo's boots beside the bed and realising the submariner is standing to attention in his socks, he commences a torrent of abuse about naval men in general and submariners in particular.

Theo stays at attention. Making no attempt to explain, he simply apologises. Explanations are excuses. They have no place here.

'Herr Major,' he says when the man has calmed. 'Why am I here?'

He gets no reply. Instead the man goes to the door, realises there is no handle on the inside and curses everyone, Theo and the Generalmajor, for imprisoning him in the room.

'I can open it, Herr Major.'

'Leave it. Sit down.' He wags his hand. 'Not on the chair, on the bed.'

Theo obeys. The man grabs the chair, turns it around and sits down straddling it, resting his arms on its back and his chin on his arms.

Theo senses a change. If this is an interrogation, the man has gone soft. Or perhaps this is the way they do it. Scare you. Then relax you. Then maybe they hang you or shoot you.

The man rabbit-jumps the chair forwards until he is close. Much too close. So close to Theo he has nowhere to look but straight into disturbing, bright blue eyes. He tries, and fails, to assess the man's age. His fair hair is cropped short and thinning, and there are hints of grey near the ears. But the eyes are those of a much younger man.

Theo realises he is assessing his opponent. He stops abruptly and runs a hand through his own hair. Hair thick and wiry. Brown once. Now almost white.

'Kapitänleutnant,' the man says. 'You are making me feel uncomfortable.'

'I am sorry, Herr Major. That was not my intention.'

'You are very confident, Kapitän. Perhaps overconfident.'

'I have done nothing wrong.'

'You really do not know me, do you? You do not remember me.'

'I'm sorry, Herr Major. I know no Luftwaffe men.'

The major takes a silver case from his pocket. 'Cigarette?'

'I smoke a pipe, Herr Major.'

'Not while I'm here you don't.'

'No, Herr Major.'

The man returns the silver case to his pocket, the cigarettes untouched.

'Have you swum again in the Zweigkanal, Theodor?'

Theo frowns. He has had enough. Maybe all Luftwaffe men are as strange as Göring, their leader. Is he in the company of madmen, madmen who construct meaningless sentences and use secret codes like in children's games? Have you swum again in the Zweigkanal?

Then Theo remembers. It starts with the eyes, their sharpness, their blueness. Eyes belonging not to a Luftwaffe major but to a boy he once knew.

'I have swum in the Zweigkanal, Walter,' he says slowly, his eyes again on the major's. 'But not since that day.'

CHAPTER TEN

SPARGO HAULED HIMSELF into the cathedral-like void. Watery daylight from the gash in the roof cut through ancient dust stirred up as he moved, dust that caught in his throat and nose and made him sneeze. As he expected, the main attic floor was not boarded over. The floor joists beneath his feet support the lath and plaster ceiling of the room below. Like in the smaller attic, one false step and his foot would go through it.

He was right about the daylight. Though it wasn't bright, once his eyes became accustomed to it he could see the whole attic. Apart from a large galvanized water tank sitting on timber beams at the other end of the void, the place was empty. No old suitcases, no lampshades or old paintings, no chairs.

Beneath the hole in the roof was an even bigger hole in the attic floor. Roof slates, and the occasional block of stone that hadn't made it down to the hall, lay scattered on the joists and laths. Fine, silvery streaks of rain drifted down through the gash in the roof. Lit from above, it seemed as if every raindrop had its own internal light.

Stepping carefully he approached the hole. The closer he got the less safe he felt – until finally his feelings got the better of him and he backed away. The similarities between the attic and underground workings were uncanny, the dangers were similar: dark voids and deep drops. But in mines there is one big difference – the ground doesn't bounce up and down when you walk.

Using his lamp he probed the dark corners. In an attempt to see behind the water tank he stepped sideways and lit it with his lamp. It didn't look safe. The beams it sat on sloped gently towards the hole and the whole assembly appeared, from where he stood, to be held in place by two water pipes fixed to its side.

He was sure that if he trod carefully and kept well away from the hole, he would be able to reach the tank safely. It seemed to be the only place in the roof where something could be concealed, either behind it or under it.

Getting to the tank meant skirting the hole; skirting the hole meant stepping on roof beams that sagged under his weight. He trod carefully, testing beams before putting all his weight on them. All went well until one of the beams, seemingly safe, twisted to one side as he stepped onto it. The water tank jerked, slipping off its base with an ominous hollow thud.

By the time Spargo realised what was happening the tank was sliding towards the hole, picking up speed, skidding and grinding and dragging its pipes. Sure that if he stayed where he was the tank would miss him, he froze. Then, unexpectedly, one of the pipes snagged a roof beam and swung the tank towards him like a ball on a chain. As he threw himself sideways the tank and its pipes – flailing like tentacles – sliced across the place he'd been standing. For all of five seconds it teetered on the edge of the hole and then toppled, its pipes whipping the air as they smashed at the timbers, cracking more beams as the whole mess of steel tore through the floor. Then, finally, a deep hollow boom as the tank hit the hall floor.

Spargo, safe from the tank, swam in the filth and clawed at the timbers. Under his weight the nails holding the thin wooden laths that supported the floor ripped away from the beams with a machine-gun-like chatter. Chunks of ceiling plaster broke away, fell to the hall floor and burst like small bombs. Had he not been standing astride a beam when the floor gave way he would have plunged to his death. Instead, when he lost his grip on everything, both feet went through the ceiling.

Rain fell heavily through the hole in the roof. It fell on the unconscious figure of Spargo, no longer clinging to the beam that supported him but lying face down astride it with both legs through the hall ceiling. Aroused by the rain he came round slowly, tightening his fingers around a wooden beam he could feel but not see, clinging to it the way a shipwrecked sailor might cling to a spar. The intense pain in his groin came to him gradually, a pain the like of which he hadn't experienced since his schooldays when he'd been kicked in the groin in the melees that passed as school sport. Though this was worse. Much worse.

His legs, held firm by clusters of shattered laths as sharp as sharks' teeth, had no feeling. Scared he no longer even had legs, he felt for them, found his left and then his right. Found something else too – the unmistakable, slippery feel of warm blood.

Still face down, he tried lifting a leg. When it didn't respond he tried lifting the other, managing to drag it up far enough to hook his foot over a beam. As he did so a tingling in his toes spread slowly through his body, pins and needles first and then vicious, knife-stab pains. Finally, crying with pain, he pulled the other leg free and crawled sideways, crab-like, until he was supported by several firm beams.

At first he thought the flickering light that came from the hall was a rescuer, someone who had heard the tank fall, heard his cries and come to investigate. Encouraged, he called out. Hearing nothing but falling rain, he called out again. No longer able to stand he began a long crawl back to the extension, beam by beam, easing himself along as if crawling on shards of glass. Twice during his journey the pain overpowered him. Made him vomit.

His slow and painful entrance to the hall was greeted not by rescuers with torches but by his very own hand lamp. Having survived the fall it lay on its back amongst rubble and dirt, its beam blocked now and again by breeze-blown, leafy weeds.

His trousers were bloody; slivers of lath had shredded the fabric and torn into his skin. Cuts to his calves seeped blood. One cut, deeper than the rest, had a sliver of wood sticking from it and was bleeding profusely. Scared that if he passed out again he might bleed to death, he sat on a block of masonry and removed his shirt. He was about to rip it into bandages when he remembered the first aid kit in his car.

As he bent down to retrieve his lamp its beam picked out the water tank, distorted and split by the fall. His eyes then focussed on something beyond it, a pyramid shape he hadn't seen before. Holding the beam steady he limped towards it – not a pyramid but a box-shaped package about the size of a car battery. That it was heavy was obvious, One of its corners had embedded itself in the floorboards.

Spargo stared down at it. Whatever it was, somebody had wrapped it in many layers of canvas and then bound it with wire. He attempted to crouch down to examine it more closely but the pain was too great. Reluctantly he returned to the kitchen, struggled out of the window and limped back to his car.

CHAPTER ELEVEN

Theo barely recognises Walter Wolff. The resemblance to the boy he once knew ends at the eyes. A sickle-shaped scar like the first quarter of the moon crosses his cheek from his right ear to his chin. When Wolff was young he wore his hair long and now it is cropped short. He is around Theo's height. Though he has bulked out, he is not overweight.

Theo can't avoid staring. His old friend's father held a government post in the town where they lived. When Walter was fourteen his father was promoted and the family moved to Munich.

'Have I changed so much, Kapitänleutnant, that you did not recognise me?'

Theo notes the persisting formality.

'It has been fifteen years.'

'Surely more than fifteen?'

'It only feels like more. Perhaps I didn't expect the uniform. The last I heard was that you had moved to Munich with your parents. Also that you joined the Schutzstaffel.'

'Then you were misinformed. As you rightly say, I moved to Munich. I joined the Hitlerjugend and later the Luftwaffe, not the SS. But enough of this, there will soon be time for such talk. You look tired. You have had a long journey.'

'Only from Bremen.'

'Careless talk, Kapitänleutnant!'

'I apologise. I assumed you knew everything about me.'

Wolff stands up, turns the chair and sits on it properly. He looks towards the briefcase on the bed and beckons to it, flicking his fingers.

'Pass that to me.'

Theo does as he is asked. Wolff takes from it a folder made of thin card. As if to refresh his memory he scans its pages.

'Biscay. Saint Nazaire. Then Trondheim to Bremen, your last mission. What went wrong?'

Theo swallows. Maybe Walter's presence is a coincidence after all.

'A Luftwaffe major knows these things?'

Wolff flicks pages. Keeps his eyes on the papers.

'All about you, yes, did you not just say that? I know you were a proficient chief engineer and that you are now an excellent U-boat commander. You are also a good German, despite being a little free with your tongue.'

'Again, I apologise.'

'Apologies are meaningless and pointless. I am not referring to your comments to me, I am speaking more generally. You spent last evening with recruits. I have been told you spoke very freely. Now answer my question. Your voyage. What went wrong?'

'I have made my report.'

'So I see. You were caught on the surface by a British bomber, a Wellington. Did your luck run out, would you say?'

'I do not trust to luck.'

'I do not trust to luck Herr Major!'

'I do not trust to luck Herr Major!'

'So, what went wrong?'

'It is difficult to say, Herr Major. It was after midnight. I had surfaced to recharge my batteries. The sea was rough. The seaman on watch failed to hear the plane's engines until it was upon us.'

'And this seaman, how did you deal with him?'

'It is there, in my report. Herr Major.'

'There is nothing here about disciplining this man.'

'There was nothing left of him to discipline. And very little left of my two gunners.'

'Very well. So why are you here?'

'Herr Major?'

'I mean why are you in Berlin?'

'I wish to visit my son. I told the Generalmajor.'

'Really? If you told him that, then he should have told me. He is an old friend of mine. He was injured in France and now has a less taxing job in Potsdam. He is a very talented gentleman. He has been watching you from the day you disembarked.'

Theo stays quiet. He finds that hard to believe.

'It says here you are married. Your wife and son are dead'.

'My wife is dead. My son is alive.'

Wolff frowns. Taking a pen from his pocket he strikes out words in the file and writes a correction.

'So, you have a son. How old is he? Where is he?'

'Three years old. He lives with his grandparents.'

'Very pleasant. Lucky for you. Ah, I forgot. You do not believe in luck.'

'His grandparents are old and unwell. I have used up three days of my leave already. If this is some kind of social meeting then we must get together some other time.'

Theo swallows. The words just slipped out. Wolff stares at him, his face set hard.

'So you think I have time for social visits?' The words are harsh, and hissed through Wolff's teeth. 'Do you suppose I spent the last few months having you checked and followed so I can pass the time of day with you? Do you think the Generalmajor spent the last week dragging himself around those shitholes you've been in simply to get you here so I can tell you that you look like a refugee? There is one thing you can be sure of, Kapitänleutnant Volker, you will not be visiting your son!'

Wolff stands up, paces to the open door and returns to the chair. He turns it and then straddles it again. Props his elbows on the chair's back.

'You are not a Party member. Why is that?'

'I was never much of a joiner.'

'But you joined the Kriegsmarine.'

'Why have I been brought here?'

'That is not your concern. I ask the questions. Did you volunteer for naval service?'

'As did many others.'

'You had no need to volunteer. You were offered a position on the mines in Lorraine. You accepted.'

'I did not accept. I was told mining engineers were needed in France and I said I would consider it.'

'You joined the navy because you did not want to go to France.'

'I was told they used forced labour on the mines. I am a mining engineer, not a prison warder.'

'You listened to idle talk. Lorraine would have been an easy life for you, you would merely have been advising the guards. But you refused to help the Reich.'

'I did not refuse. I considered the mines and then joined the navy. Is that why I'm here? It was no crime. Why this is of interest to the Luftwaffe? Why did you have me followed?'

Wolff smiles. 'Theodor, Theodor, so many questions! No, that is not why you are here. And you are beginning to irritate me… exactly one year ago you were disciplined for striking a superior in a bar-room brawl.'

'The man was drunk and offensive.'

'I have heard that most U-boat men on shore are fairly offensive, drunk or sober. You were at fault.'

'I was at fault for striking the man and I was disciplined. If I have done anything wrong, Herr Major, surely it is a matter for Naval High Command.'

'Forget Naval High Command. If your return to Bremen is delayed then the correct authorities will be notified.'

'If, Herr Major?'

Wolff has picked up the file and he writes as he speaks. Makes comments and corrections.

'Despite your occasional misdemeanours you appear to obey naval orders to the letter.'

'I am a good German Officer.'

'Nevertheless, the commander of a U-boat enjoys a certain freedom?'

'No more than the commander of any other vessel.'

'That is not what I have heard. However, that is not my concern.' He turns pages. Several fall from the file and Theo moves quickly, picking them up and handing them back. He glances at them for clues but learns nothing. 'Your last command...' Wolff continues. 'I am told you sailed your damaged vessel to Trondheim against all odds. I am told your weapons were out of action and you were unable to submerge.'

'My actions were no different to those of other commanders.'

'Would you say you are a survivor?'

'Aren't we all, those that remain?'

'I asked you a question. Don't answer my questions with your own questions.'

'I have survived so far. My wife has not.'

'And you hold yourself responsible for that?' Theo's mouth locks as he searches for words. 'Calm yourself, Kapitänleutnant. I did not say you were responsible, I merely asked you if you held yourself responsible.'

'I was not with her. I was not there to help her.'

'And your son?'

'I believe my son is unharmed.'

'I remember Erika from school. I am sorry she is dead. How did it happen?'

'I'm sure it says in your papers.'

'Never mind what it says in my papers. I want to hear it from you.'

'She had moved to Hamburg. She died in a bombing raid. Her parents travelled there and found Peter in an orphanage. Erika had already been buried.'

'And for this you hate the enemy?'

'I hate this war and the things it does to people.'

'But you hate the enemy.'

'I hate what they have to do and what we have to do.'

'You would be wise to keep such thoughts to yourself.'

'It is how I feel.'

'You have changed, Kapitänleutnant. You were the quiet one. What happened to the young man I once knew?'

'War changes people.'

They lock eyes. Theo holds the stare.

'So it does, Theodor, so it does. Tell me, when you were at mining school you visited England, is that not so?'

If that is what it says in your notes, Theo tells himself, then it must be right.

'No. I visited Scotland, not England. It's no secret. There were many such exchanges. Mining engineers came to us and we went to them.'

'So you have friends there?'

'A mining engineer visited our mines in the Hartz. Later I travelled to Scotland and stayed with his family, nothing more. These things were not unusual. It happened several years before this war started.'

'And do you still contact him?'

'Herr Major! Of course I do not contact him!'

'Did you contact him in the years before the war?'

'We swapped Christmas greetings. Possibly a letter or two. May I ask why you want to know these things?'

'I wish to convince myself you are as reliable and trustworthy as this report makes you out to be.'

'Am I supposed to feel flattered?'

'You are not supposed to feel anything. I warn you again, treat your superiors with respect or suffer the consequences. I shall leave you here to consider your position. When I return I want to hear that you will co-operate with me fully and without question.'

'And if I do not, Herr Major? May I continue my journey?'

'If you do not, Theodor, you will never again see your son.'

CHAPTER TWELVE

SPARGO'S HOTEL SERVED BREAKFAST but not evening meals. Had he known that before he arrived he would have stayed elsewhere. He could drive to Inverness now, he supposed, but the drive from Kilcreg had been hell and he didn't feel up to it. Whenever he put his foot on his car's clutch he'd had indescribable pain in his legs and groin.

Deciding that food was the last of his priorities he ordered a coffee from the bar, then changed his mind and carried back to his table a double whisky, three bags of crisps and some nuts.

Not only had the drive been hell, the whole day had been hell. He had attended to his injuries as best as he could. He managed, with great difficulty and even greater pain, to remove most of the large splinters of wood from his flesh and then bind the wounds tightly with bandages from his car.

The canvas wrapping around the package he found was bound with thick copper wire, twisted tight with pliers. He had tried to unwind it, and when that failed he dug down through the rotting canvas with his screwdriver. Eventually he reached what, in poor light, looked like rusty steel.

With what little strength he had left he'd trundled the package to the kitchen, heaved it up on to the windowsill and pushed it outside. Rather than attempt to take it to his car he had, reluctantly, driven his car over the rough ground to the back of the house. He'd been so convinced the package was what his mother's killer had been seeking, that when he reached Inverness he took it straight to the police. The desk officer took one look at him and called an ambulance.

Now he sat alone in the hotel bar, picking at crisps and nuts. Sipping at the whisky he remembered the no alcohol warning he'd been given at Raigmore when they dosed him with painkillers. He limped to the bar again. Came back with a coffee.

'Looks like you've lost fifty dollars and won five.' The voice was distant and had a soft Texan drawl. 'Don't much like drinking alone,' it continued. 'You mind if I come over?'

Spargo grunted. The last thing he needed was company. He swivelled in his chair and caught sight of a tall, lean man lifting a chair.

'Couldn't help noticing you were driving a Volvo,' the man said as he carried the chair towards Spargo's table. 'Great cars. Had one just like it in the Gulf.'

Spargo willed the man to go away. It didn't work. He turned again, this time seeing him properly for the first time and taking in his weather-worn features and long dark sideboards. Also the white shirt, the white designer jeans and the jewellery. Draped around the man's neck was a heavy chain – solid gold, Spargo guessed. On it hung a heavy medallion – more gold – that swung hypnotically when the man moved.

And there was still more gold, two signet rings, a watch and its expanding strap. The only metallic object he wore that wasn't gold was a heavy belt buckle of brass. There was, Spargo realised, something of Elvis about the man.

'You want a drink?'

'Thanks, no, I'm okay.'

Mock Elvis looked him up and down. 'You been in the wars? What the heck happened?'

Since his hospital visit Spargo had changed clothes. His hands were still stained with antiseptic and dressed with cotton pads. One side of his face had abrasions that had been treated and left exposed. The worst damage, to his torn thighs and calves, didn't show.

Spargo didn't comment. Tried a switched-on smile.

The man smiled back. 'You here on vacation?'

'No.'

'So it's work?'

'No.' Spargo wanted to walk away but couldn't quite bring himself to do it. 'I've just buried my mother,' he said instead.

It should have been the ultimate conversation stopper. It didn't stop Kalman.

'Hey, I'm sorry, I guess you don't want company right now.' He took a swig of beer. 'One sure thing,' he said as he wiped his mouth with the back of his hand. 'One day we all gonna die.'

Another sure thing was that despite Kalman's realisation that Spargo didn't want company, the man was making himself comfortable at Spargo's table.

Spargo wanted to add that not only was his mother dead, she had been murdered, beaten to death, and how did that fit with such glib observations?

'True,' he said, instead.

'You live around here?'

'Edinburgh.'

'Hey, went there a while back, spend time seeing the sights. Didn't expect to be having another vacation so soon but the boat's in dock, got pump problems, been waiting for a part from the 'States but turns out it's special, y'know? They got to make the darned thing from scratch.'

Spargo nodded as if he cared. Or understood. As if it were the most natural thing in the world for a man dressed like Elvis to need a new part for a pump.

'It's Bob, the man said, as if starting over. This time he extended a hand and Spargo shook it. 'Kalman's the name. Diving's the game.'

Spargo winced. 'Diving?'

He winced again as he realised he had make the mistake of asking Kalman a question. The man had baited the hook and Spargo had bitten. For the next two hours he listened to the story of Kalman's life, give or take a few years.

'Started on land-based oil rigs,' Kalman said. 'And then moved offshore, eventually became a diver. Made more money in the Gulf than I ever made back home – but what the heck, Spargo! The money I get now is good. Been with the same outfit a while. Like I said, the boat's in dock. So I'm taking time out to see this great country of yours.'

And so it went on. Until Spargo, more asleep than awake, excused himself and went to bed.

CHAPTER THIRTEEN

TO AVOID KALMAN NEXT MORNING, Spargo went without breakfast. Wanting to be alert for his drive home he hadn't taken his medication and was suffering all kinds of pains. By the time he was thirty minutes into the drive he was wishing he'd stayed an extra night. Then he remembered Kalman and changed his mind.

His drive south went smoothly. Before midday he had crossed the Firth of Forth, and less than thirty minutes later he turned into Jez's road. To save her the trouble of taking her overnight bag on the train he'd kept it in his car and now he was dropping it off, looking for somewhere to park, driving round the block for the second time. The third time round he got lucky, pulling in to a space just vacated by a small black Fiat driven by young man who could hardly see over its steering wheel.

Spargo had keys to Jez's flat but he didn't like to use them. It was his daughter's domain, not his. When he reached the top of the steps that led to her door he pressed the doorbell, heard it ring and then waited. It was a weekday, she wasn't home – which, considering the state he was in was a very a good thing. He unlocked her door, went inside, waited and listened. Carrying her bag he walked through to her kitchen and placed it where she would see it. No need for a note.

He missed family life. He and Theresa could have strung out their relationship for a few more years just for Jez's sake. He would have been willing to do it but then Theresa simply upped sticks and went. Despite that, Jez didn't appear to have suffered. If anything, she was more content and more stable than he was.

There was no way his daughter could have afforded to buy a place in such a desirable location on her lecturer's salary and he suspected, but had never asked, that most of the money had come from Theresa, perhaps in the hope that when Jez left university she wouldn't move back into the family home with her father.

Spargo's house in The Grange in south Edinburgh held more good memories than bad. It had been the family home, the house he and Theresa bought before prices went skywards. When they split up he bought his share of the house from her. His reason for keeping the place – it was excessively large for his needs and he should have downsized – was simple: his business wasn't doing well; mining in Britain had been dead for years and it seemed that the heydays of North Sea Oil would soon be over. If business got worse he would sell the house, buy a smaller place and use the capital to do something else. He had no idea what.

He arrived home to find his answering machine blinking. Only three messages. Time was when after even a short time away from home there would be fifty or sixty. He touched 'play'. Heard Benares' oily tones giving him a date and saying Spargo was booked Business Class to Madrid. He checked the date on his watch. His flight to Madrid was tomorrow.

Benares was waiting for Spargo at Barajas International Airport. Spargo's image of the man had been dulled by time and he took in the round face, the slicked-back black hair, the pale suit and the open-necked, yellow shirt.

'Mister Spargo! I am pleased to see you! Again, I am sorry if I inconvenienced you when I telephoned. I trust I did not interfere with the arrangements?'

Spargo tried to recall if any other of his potential clients had apologised for something that wasn't their fault. He smiled at the man and held out his hand. Got the firm, dry handshake.

'I am the one who should be apologising. What with everything...'

The niceties continued as they walked to retrieve Spargo's bags: how was the flight? How is the weather in Scotland? Only when they reached the carousels did Spargo realise they were being followed by a uniformed driver in a high-fronted peaked cap.

Benares, true to form, kept the conversation shallow but pleasant.

'This is your first visit to Madrid, yes?'

'I was here twenty years ago. I guess it has changed.'

'So-so. There is more traffic and therefore more pollution. I am sure it is the same with you. I have never been to Edinburgh. It is, of course, a city like so many others, overcrowded with people and motor cars.'

'It's not so bad. For a city it is small and compact. The traffic's nothing like – '

The baggage carousel started to move. Spargo stepped forwards awkwardly and pain from his stitched cuts made him wince. In his haste to pack and get to Heathrow he had forgotten his painkillers.

'Mister Spargo?' Benares queried, staring and frowning. 'You have pain? You have injured yourself?'

'It's nothing. I fell and cut myself. It gets sore sometimes.'

Benares nodded. Turned his attention to the carousel.

'Ah, you see, the baggage, it arrives!'

Spargo entered Madrid in a spotlessly clean Mercedes. By accident or design its pale fawn paintwork and leather upholstery were identical in colour to the driver's smart suit, his cap and his suede shoes.

The car turned onto the tree-lined Castellano and drove west through dense traffic. Spargo tried to recall the buildings as they passed them, finally deciding this was not a part of the city he had seen before. His last visit had been short and he'd had no time for sightseeing. All his trips abroad were like that, his clients always seemed to be on their way to somebody more important than him. Benares, at least in this respect, was a breath of fresh air.

As in London, all attempts to converse with the man about business failed miserably. At the oil show, trying to discover what the man really wanted, Spargo had asked most of the questions. He hadn't progressed far.

'My employer will explain,' Benares said back then. He said it again now, this time adding: 'I am merely his agent.'

The Mercedes turned off the main street into a road named Orense, a side road lined with a strange mix of properties. Old Spanish buildings with ornate stonework and ironwork balconies sat uncomfortably beside dark glass and steel.

In a maze of small streets the driver slowed the car, turned his wheel sharply and aimed for parked cars at the kerbside. Spargo tensed. He hadn't noticed the gap between them, nor the steep ramp beyond it. The Mercedes slipped deftly down the concrete slope, under a barrier, and into a dark basement car park.

Fluorescent tubes flickered. The place was huge and empty, theirs was the only car. Spargo's imagination worked overtime, placing him well below decks in a vast aircraft carrier. A lift big enough to accommodate twenty people took them up through the building. Spargo, standing in a back corner, wondered if it had ever carried that number.

He wasn't taken to the flight deck of his imagination but to the top floor in a seven storey building. Following Benares out of the lift he stepped into what he mistook for the reception area of a small hotel. It was freshly decorated, and brightly lit by halogen spots in the ceiling. Across the room, with its back to the wall, stood a small reception desk with two swivel chairs. Both were empty. Close to the desk were a sofa and armchair, each upholstered in yellow leather, and a glass topped table with what looked like magazines.

Spargo, his hands behind his back, took note of the layout. All lights were on. There were three offices at least, all with half open, half-glazed doors. He listened for sounds of staff working but heard nothing. He looked for nameplates. A sign on a door near the lift said SALIDA – exit – one of the few Spanish words he knew.

'Is this BarConSA's office?'

'BarConSa has many offices. But yes, Mister Spargo, Mr Bar does own the building. Now, make yourself comfortable, please sit down, I have telephone calls to make. Should you wish to refresh yourself there is a cloakroom.' He gestured to a corridor. 'It is along there.'

Spargo positioned himself in the middle of the sofa, then changing his mind and moved to one end of it. At the sound of the lift motor Benares, about to enter a nearby office, stopped and stared at the lift doors. The motor stopped. The doors didn't open. Nobody came.

What Spargo had mistaken for magazines turned out to be shipping directories, airline timetables and international phone books, stacked neatly on the glass-topped table. Like everything else in the place, the pile was free from dust. Spargo, flicking through them, observed that the directories were all twelve years old. Even dentists' waiting rooms had newer reading material than this.

Bored, Spargo listened to Benares talking on an office phone. Though he was unable to understand a single word, he was aware that every so often the man cursed, slammed down the handset, picked it up again and tapped in more numbers. With every call he became more agitated and his voice more high-pitched. Fifteen minutes passed and Benares was still at it, still phoning, still cursing and redialling.

The only thing on the reception desk was a leather-bound diary. Spargo reached for it, opened it, and flicked through its pages. Not a single word had been written. Also, it was ten years old.

Spargo, thirsty, set off down the corridor. Shoving the door marked with the outline of a man he walked to a sink and turned the tap. Concerned the water might also be at least twelve years old he let it run for a while before cupping his hands under it and taking deep gulps. He also took the opportunity to drop his trousers and examine the surgical dressings – passably clean with a slight seep of blood. He'd been given replacements. As with his painkillers, he'd left them at home. Out in the corridor again he heard Benares, still phoning.

Wondering not for the first time why he was there, Spargo looked through the glass portholes in the doors in the corridor, peering into furnished offices, all brightly lit. One door stood ajar and he pushed it open. It swung back more easily than he'd expected and hit the wall with a thud. He waited, expecting Benares to appear. When he did not, Spargo entered the room.

CHAPTER FOURTEEN

THOUGH THE BRIGHT SPANISH SUN was more than capable of illuminating the room Spargo had entered, its efforts were supplemented by an array of halogen spotlights recessed into the ceiling. The furniture, in complete contrast to the glass and yellow leather of the foyer, were, at least to Spargo's eyes, valuable antiques. A long mahogany table down the middle of the room was so precisely positioned between the long sidewalls that the distances might well have been measured. Tucked under each long side of the table were five ornate chairs. The carpet, Spargo noticed, was twice as thick as the one in reception. Its repeating design – a fleur-de-lis motif – added a classical touch to what was otherwise an inescapably boring, shoebox shaped room.

At the far end of the room a high-backed armchair stood throne-like. Its seat cushion, Spargo saw when he reached it, was four inches higher than all the others. He wiped a finger along the back of the chair and found no trace of dust. It was, he thought, a boardroom without a Chairman or board of directors. A captains' table without a captain or crew.

At the room's only window he gazed down to a courtyard, deep-walled and dark. In the midst of these office buildings is washing on a line, a child's buggy, a red ride-on car. Madrid, he remembered, is like that.

He had taken little notice of the pictures on the walls when he walked down the room. He had assumed they were photographs of chairmen long-gone, pictures similar to those he had seen on the walls of the old mining internationals in the City of London. Now, as he walked back towards the door, he realised he was wrong.

The first picture he stopped at was not a photograph of a man, it was a photograph of a painting of a man. He frowned. A black and white photo of an old painting didn't look right. What made it more ridiculous was that it was mounted in a black wooden frame, behind glass. There were more like that, a total of ten on each wall. One that particularly attracted his attention was a head and shoulders portrait of a young woman in mediaeval dress. Or a man, perhaps? He couldn't tell.

Spargo had no doubts about the gender of the subject in the picture next to it. Even allowing for the fact it should have been in colour, the woman's eyes still followed him around the room. Why would anyone bother to hang such a poor version of the original in a company boardroom? And why monochrome?

'An old and fascinating collection, Mister Spargo, do you not think?'

Spargo jumped. Benares had slipped silently into the room and was standing behind him, up close. There was no telling how long he had been there. Benares continued:

'I am told that the previous owners of this building became bankrupt. These photographs were left on the walls and Mr Bar could find no reason why they should not remain here. Now, you must forgive me for keeping you waiting. It appears that Mr Bar is indisposed. I have finally located him and I am pleased to say that this evening he will join us for dinner. Meanwhile perhaps you would like something to drink?'

Spargo stood in the foyer of his hotel staring out at the road through a wall of smoked glass. A taxi rank, a row of shops. Hordes of scurrying shoppers even at this late hour. The day had not gone well. At five this morning he had showered, shaved and dressed. He had gone without breakfast, driven to Edinburgh Airport, flown to Heathrow and then on to Madrid. He had been taken to an office resembling a landlocked Marie Celeste and wasted two hours there. He was offered a drink that never came – he would have preferred a large gin but had been offered a coffee. Benares had searched for it in the office's small kitchen. There was no coffee. Not only had Benares failed to produce Mr Bar, he had failed to find a drink of any kind.

Benares had then summoned a taxi that took them to a tapas bar a five minute walk away. The export strength G&T Spargo ordered when he arrived was closely followed by another, accompanied by small plates of snacks that did little to counter the numbing effects the alcohol was having on his brain. His saving grace was that Benares seemed oblivious to these things and, like him, sat quietly on stools at the bar until it was time to leave.

He had expected a taxi but Benares called for the Mercedes. It arrived within minutes, driven by a chauffeur who resembled a uniformed orang-utan. The car deposited Spargo at a hotel a stone's throw from the American Embassy and then it vanished, with Benares, into dense Madrid traffic.

Now, in the late evening, Spargo saw the Mercedes again, dead on time with Benares in the back, mannequin-slick in a fresh, cream-coloured suit and off-white shoes. Spargo, as always, had travelled light and had little more than he stood up in. His suit looked like crumpled linen – his own fault for not removing his jacket before dozing off in the plane. He slid into the back of the car beside Benares.

'Mister Spargo, how are you this evening? Regrettably Mr Bar is unable to dine with us tonight but we shall visit him tomorrow, it is all arranged. Now, do you know the Calle de Serrano? It is like your Bond Street in London or your George Street in Edinburgh. In Serrano there is a small but exclusive restaurant much favoured by Mr Bar, where a table has been reserved for us.'

Spargo said nothing. He felt there was nothing to say. The Mercedes swung in a tight circle, turned a corner, and almost immediately pulled in at the curb. Spargo, wondering if he was about to be dumped out on the pavement for not speaking, saw they had arrived at their destination – the restaurant favoured, but presumably not visited that often, by Mr Bar.

At Benares' approach the restaurant's plate glass door it was snatched open from the inside by a man in a black tailcoat and a scarlet cummerbund. He bowed low to Benares and addressed him by name. He peered suspiciously at Spargo, who gave a brief, forced smile.

Tailcoat guided them to an alcove screened from other diners by twin curtains. Red velvet, Spargo noted. Red like the paintwork, the carpet, the ornate tasselled lampshades and, of course, tailcoat's cummerbund. The red lampshades cast a glow across Benares. Lit his pale suit red.

The place looked expensive. Spargo hoped he'd got his facts right about Bar meeting all the expenses. BarConSa clearly had money; they owned office blocks and travelled in style in an expensive car; they had booked him into a five-star and now were taking him to dinner; and they were paying – of course they were paying…

He gave Benares an approving nod. 'Nice place!'

'As you say, Mister Spargo, nice place. Tell me, how does one become a miner? Is it in your family? Is your father a miner?'

'I am a mining engineer, Mr Benares, not a miner.'

'There is a difference?'

'I spent four years at university. I have a degree in mining engineering and I am a Chartered Engineer. I am sure BarConSA wouldn't expect anything less from a consultant.'

'And your father? Does he mine for coal?'

'My father died when I was young. He mined for tin in Cornwall. In the nineteen-thirties he moved to Scotland to manage a scheelite mine.'

'What is scheelite?'

'An ore of tungsten, the strongest metal known. It is added to steel to improve its strength and quality.' He wondered if he had got that right, there were so many new metals around these days. Not that it mattered, because Benares wouldn't know and wouldn't care. The man was already bored. He was playing with his blood-coloured cloth napkin, part-camouflaged by the table's red cloth.

Spargo relaxed. This was smalltalk, and essential preliminary for what was about to come – the discussions, the real business. But the smalltalk continued. Spargo tried, in vain, to turn the conversation to BarConSA and what they wanted from him.

In London, Spargo had discovered that Benares knew nothing about mining. Now, over the meal, he discovered that the man knew nothing about BarConSA's plans for him. Or if he did, he did not intend to divulge them.

Early the following morning Spargo packed his bags and took the lift to reception. The bill was presented to him and he looked at the total, wincing as he converted it to pounds sterling. It was enough to feel a small family for a week.

'It is for you to check and approve, Senör,' the receptionist said. 'For your signature only. It is to be charged to a private account.'

Spargo, doing his best not to look relieved, signed on the line, picked up his bags and walked to the smoked glass. The fawn Mercedes was there, at the roadside.

'No Mr Benares this morning?' Spargo asked the driver as the car moved away. The man grunted and pulled out into traffic. Spargo repeated the question. The man replied in Spanish. Instead of turning in the road towards Castellano the car kept going. Five minutes later they were heading north out of the city in heavy traffic. After passing three overhead signs saying Aeropuerto, Spargo asked more questions. Received only grunts.

Settling back into plush leather he considered last night's meal, his barely-cooked slab of beef that had occupied the entire surface of what Spargo initially thought was a serving plate. Then Benares was given one too. It came without vegetables. Or anything else.

It had been a bizarre end to a bizarre day, Benares pouring away money as if it were water. The Rioja was a select year and must have cost a small fortune – Mister Bar's favourite, Benares had said. Spargo had wondered then, as he was wondering now, if Bar actually existed.

The Mercedes crossed three lanes and positioned itself for the airport. Benares was dumping him, sending him home. Either Bar hadn't been able to make it or else he, Spargo, hadn't made the grade in some way. Was it the way he'd held his knife and fork? Was it his crumpled suit? Was it because he had failed to eat barely one third of the outrageous slab of meat?

Not that it mattered. Providing BarConSA paid up he would be out of pocket only by the cost of fuel for his drive to the airport at home – also the small fortune it would cost him to get his car out of the airport's car park. Worst of all was the wasted time. What little consulting work Spargo had still needed to be done. What with clearing the cottage and later the funeral, he was behind with his work.

'I want Internacionales,' Spargo snapped, noticing another sign. 'You are taking me to the Nacionales. I do not want an internal flight.'

True to form the driver said nothing. He stopped the car, got out, opened Spargo's door wide and went to the boot for Spargo's bag.

'You get out of car! Por favor!'

'Wrong terminal,' Spargo said. 'You take me Internacionales. Internacionales vamos.'

Vamos sounded right so he said it again, this time louder. The driver shook his head.

Spargo didn't see Benares come up behind the driver. But that was the way of the man.

'Mr Spargo, you cannot sit in the car for all of the day. I see you have your bag, that is good. You have checked out of the hotel? Yes?'

Benares wore a three-quarter length alpaca coat. It was draped over his shoulders Al Capone style. It protected yet another immaculately pressed suit.

'Today we shall fly to Almeria. It is in the south east of Spain, in Andalucia. You have heard of it, possibly?'

Spargo, numbed, swung a leg out of the car and eased himself up. He went to pick up his bag but the driver got to it first.

'Almeria,' Spargo said. 'Yes, I've heard of it.'

He wasn't sure whether Benares' unexpected presence made him feel better or worse. He had already convinced himself that in a few hours he would be home, pouring himself a well-earned whisky. He wanted to complain that he should have been warned about all this but he couldn't bring himself to do it. He believed the unwritten maxim that the client is always right. Or at least, he believed it until the client was hooked.

What made Benares' revelations more bearable was that Andalucia was rich in minerals, probably the right place to be if you owned Spanish mines. The downside was that if this was an example of the kind of organisation he could expect throughout the project – if indeed there was a project – then things didn't look good.

'We leave in forty minutes, ' Benares said, turning to Spargo who now lagged behind. 'It is necessary to hurry.'

Spargo picked up speed. Drew level with the man.

'Are you sure Mr Bar is there?' he asked.

'Of course! I have organised it! Would I lie to you, Mister Spargo?'

CHAPTER FIFTEEN

BY LATE EVENING THEO WONDERS if Walter will ever return to the basement room. Several times during late afternoon the wall light flickers, and shortly after nine o'clock the power fails completely. It returns thirty minutes later, as does the sound of footsteps. They are the first distinct sounds Theo has heard since Wolff locked the steel gate.

Though Theo hears two sets of footsteps, Wolff enters the room alone. He orders Theo to strip naked and he is obeyed without question. When it is done Walter opens the door to a short, overweight man in Luftwaffe uniform. Taking a cloth tape measure from his pocket the man advances on Theo and then stops, observing Theo's body the way a cattle buyer might appraise cows at an auction.

Nobody speaks. Theo, in the middle of the room, raises his arms in expectation of being measured. The man, clearly a tailor, shakes his head. He doesn't need measurements. Still silent the man salutes the naked Theo and leaves the room.

'It seems that you are a standard size,' Wolff says. 'Get dressed. Tomorrow, when I return, you will do the same as you have just done. That man must not see your naval uniform.'

The tailor returns the following morning holding a varnished wooden coat hanger on which is a neatly pressed Luftwaffe uniform. Draped over his arm is more clothing that he places carefully on the bed, smoothing out creases with strokes of his hand. Walter is carrying a Luftwaffe kitbag that he upends on the bed, spilling out shirts, socks and underclothes. Theo watches with interest. The fact Walter is carrying the kit rather than a low-ranking orderly implies that whatever he is doing is secret.

Theo dresses under the eye of the tailor, who tugs at the fabric and smooths out the creases. From a trouser pocket he takes a folding clothes brush, flips up the bristles and brushes Theo down. When he is finished he stands back, inspects his work one last time, then turns and salutes Walter.

'Herr Major! Tunic, one; trousers, two pairs; greatcoat, one; underwear, three sets; shoes, two pairs; belts – '

'Yes, yes, I have eyes, I can count. Give me that…!'

He beckons with impatient fingers and is given a docket to sign. When the man has gone Theo flexes first his arms and each leg. Despite not having been measured, the uniform fits perfectly. Walter stands in the corner and watches. Stroking his chin he nods his approval.

'I have no right to wear this uniform,' Theo says. 'It is a breach of regulations.'

'Keep your observations to yourself. Ask no questions and follow my instructions, you are an actor, you are playing a part. From now on you will wear this uniform. Cut that fungus from your face and you might even look like a Luftwaffe officer.'

'What are these stripes? What is this rank?'

'Are you unfamiliar with the ranks of our military?'

'I spend my time at sea. I have never had reason or time to learn the distinguishing marks of our other forces.'

'It is the rank of Hauptmann. It is an equivalent rank to your own.'

'Tell me what you want from me. I know nothing about our air force or our aircraft. What am I to say when I am questioned? How shall I answer?'

'Questioned? Why should you be questioned?'

'In conversation. If a senior officer speaks to me what do I say?'

'You spent four uneventful years behind a desk, administrating the anti-aircraft defences in a large city. Nobody will be stupid enough to ask you which city or what you did there – and if they do, you will not be stupid enough to attempt to answer them. And you are wrong when you say you know nothing. Surely as a naval commander you are able to identify aircraft? Surely you can distinguish the enemy from friends? Get your kitbag. No, not that one, your naval kitbag. Empty it out.'

Theo does as he is told. Wolff rummages through the bag's contents, shoving small items aside as if they are contaminated. Realising Theo is watching he wags his finger and points to the sink.

'That beard… it resembles a whore's yard brush. Remove it, every bit of it. I want you clean shaven. While you are shaving I shall take your naval items. I want everything, your sea boots and these binoculars. What are these?'

Wolff is reaching across the bed. Not everything tipped out of the kitbag when it was upended. Several books remain jammed inside. Wolff opens one and turns pages. Theo protests.

'They contain private writings.'

'Diaries, you mean? That is foolish.'

'They are personal.'

'Do they contain accounts of naval actions?'

'They do not. I have mentioned no names and no places.'

Wolff sits on the bed, thumbing pages while Theo shaves. Finally he gathers up the books and throws them onto a pile that has been growing in size.

'It surprises me you waste naval stationery on such trivia. The Generalmajor will see they are destroyed with the rest of your things.'

'They are of no importance, Walter. They are – '

Wolff fixes Theo with a glare. But instead of the outburst Theo expects, Wolff speaks quietly, in measured tones.

'God, you look human at last, more like the Theodor I knew. Take note that you will never again call me Walter. Never, you understand? You will refer to me always as Major Wolff, even when we are alone. Now, sit down on that chair and listen to what I have to say. From now you are Hauptmann Theodor Vogel. Repeat?'

'This is not – '

'Shut your mouth! Who are you?'

'Hauptmann Theodor Vogel. Herr Major!'

Wolff is nodding. 'Very good. And again?'

'Hauptmann Theodor Vogel. Herr Major!'

'Soon the Generalmajor will come with new documents. He will give you a carbon copy of your Luftwaffe service record. Once you have memorised it you will place it on the pile.'

Wolff stoops, searches through the pile and picks out a pen. He unscrews the top and runs the nib across the back of his hand. There is ink.

'When I have gone, Vogel, you will practice your signature. It will not be in the documents, it is for you to invent. Use one of your precious books. Get used to writing it. Perfect it.'

'This isn't possible, Herr Major! You can't simply change my life!'

'You are wrong, Vogel. I have done it. You agreed to it.'

'You gave me no choice.'

'You had a choice. You agreed to co-operate.'

'Hobson's Choice, Herr Major.'

'Hobson? What is Hobson?'

'A British saying. It is Hobson's Choice when you are given only one option.'

'You are impertinent, Hauptmann Vogel, and you are wrong. Again, I allow you to choose. Either I have your full co-operation or you leave this building in a wooden box.'

Next morning Theo leaves Berlin in the truck that brought him there, still with the crates but no longer with the guard. Instead of the Generalmajor as company he has Wolff and he sits in the front on a bench seat, sandwiched between him and the driver. Nobody speaks. There is nothing to say.

Theo passes the time by dredging up memories. Not only has his old friend Walter lost all trace of compassion, his appearance has changed almost beyond recognition. As a boy he was lean. Skinny, even. And there is the scar.

Most clearly of all Theo remembers the day he saved Walter's life, the summer's day when they rode their bikes to the marshalling yards at Braunschweig to watch engines shunting, building long trains of wagons to take ingots of copper, lead and zinc from the smelters. How old was he then, fourteen? The day was hot, he remembers. To cool down after their long ride they dumped their bikes beside the canal, stripped off their clothes and swam in the still water. Walter, always reckless, swam under the moored barges. He didn't return.

The truck heads north. Theo doesn't know Berlin but he knows his directions. In the streets men in shiny shoes and business suits step over burned timbers. Others, mostly women and children carrying baskets of rubble, labour like ants to clear the streets.

At last Wolff speaks.

'That fat-gut Churchill says he will do to Berlin what he's done to Hamburg.'

He is about to say more but his words are cut short by the driver, responding unexpectedly with obscenities aimed at the Allies. Wolff lets it pass. Such hatred is understandable. All around them are blackened tooth-sockets that were once Berlin's buildings. Those dragged from the ruins are there too, their bodies hidden under sheets of pale canvas – a direct hit on a shelter. It was what happened to Erica, they said.

With the exception of a military convoy, most of the vehicles on the roads to the north of Berlin are horse-drawn and ancient. It as if every horse and wagon in Germany has been pressed into service.

Broken down vehicles and diversions turn a three hour journey into five. The final few miles are along lanes through dense woodland whose verges have been churned up by tyres. Theo assumes he is nearing an airfield, built for the defence of Berlin. He is wrong.

The truck slows to walking pace as it approaches farm buildings. A man dressed overalls crosses in front of them and stops by the roadside to wave. Further on they reach gatehouses built of stone, each with an archway surmounted by crests. Though there is no gate the driver slows down, drifting the truck forwards with his foot on the clutch. Theo, sure the gatehouses are unmanned, is surprised when an airman with a rifle slung on his shoulder steps out, stands in the lane and signals them to stop.

The airman's cuff is embroidered with the name General Göring in fine silver thread.

When he sees the cab contains officers he ignores the driver, walks to Wolff's door, salutes him and asks for their papers. Wolff slides the window open and hands out three passbooks and permits. The guard opens them in turn and flicks through them, glancing at photos and faces. He hands back Wolff's and the driver's but concentrates hard on Theo's. Then, without speaking and still holding Theo's papers, he turns on his heel and walks back to the gatehouse.

Theo, attempting to appear disinterested, peers ahead, out of the windscreen at a forest track so straight and so long it appears to converge on a single, distant point. It is perfect perspective. It distracts him for all of three seconds.

When Theo first inspected his Luftwaffe papers he saw that they'd taken the photo from his Kriegsmarine passbook. Conveniently for them the photo was old, taken before he grew his beard. Less conveniently it showed the shoulders of his naval tunic with the stripes of the rank he had held back then – a junior lieutenant, a Leutnant zur See. Staining now masked the stripes. It was as if drink had been spilled on the photo.

Theo feels fear he felt in Berlin. Could his papers contain a deliberate error, something the airman is meant to spot? Is he here simply to be arrested, taken away and questioned as part of a dastardly plot only Walter and the Generalmajor understand? Surely, after all that has happened in the last forty eight hours, anything is possible.

A Luftwaffe officer in a forage cap appears in the archway. He is taller and slimmer than the airman and his tunic, like the airman's, bears the General Göring braid. The man, a Hauptmann like himself, struts smartly over, salutes Wolff, and frowns at Theo.

'Herr Hauptmann – with respect – your passbook and photograph… this damage is unacceptable. I must urge you to obtain a replacement as soon as it is possible to do so.'

Theo hopes his relief doesn't show. He waits for Walter to speak on his behalf but to his surprise he does not. Theo acknowledges the officer with a nod but it is not enough, his papers are not handed back.

'Herr Hauptmann, I apologise. My documents sustained damage in a bombing raid. There has not been time to – '

The heel of Wolff's shoe crushes Theo's foot. The pain is unexpected and cuts Theo short. Walter interrupts by reaching out for Theo's passbook and waggling his fingers until it is handed over. He takes it and inspects it.

'Hauptmann Vogel is my personal assistant. I was not aware of this damage and I shall see to it that the matter is resolved immediately.'

Walter does the waggling fingers thing again, this time pointing to

Theo's travel permit. The officer hands it over.

'I await your orders, Herr Major!'

It is a military expression of subservience, one Theo discourages in his boat crews. The officer takes a step back and salutes again. Walter responds by sliding the window closed and pointing to the track ahead. The driver engages gear and pulls slowly away.

Theo stands in a disused barrack hut that smells faintly of wood smoke. He watches Walter, who walks the length of the hut and shoves a closed door with his foot. Theo, inquisitive, follows him.

The room at the end of the hut is twice the size of the one in the Air Ministry basement. It is not at all cell-like and contains two beds, two chairs and a table. Fixed high on one wall is a bookshelf with books stacked in piles. Between the beds, beside the room's only window, is a small wood-burning stove. Theo, near the door, can feel its warmth. Walter goes to it, tugs up the coiled wire handle and peers inside. Theo mumbles.

'Someone knew we were coming.'

'Of course. Unless you want to freeze to death in the night you had better find logs. This thing is nearly out.'

Unsure which of the two beds Walter will choose Theo drops his kitbag on the floor. Each of the window's small panes has been painted brown, and in the centre of one of them someone has scratched the paint to leave a small square of clear glass. Theo walks to it and looks through it. Sees only dark-trunked firs.

'This will be your room while you are here, Hauptmann Vogel. You will find it cramped but comfortable. There will be more room when one of these beds is removed. I shall arrange that.'

Theo nods absently. The name and rank Walter uses sounds wrong, as was Theo's assumption they would share the room. And, in his opinion, the room is not in the least bit cramped.

Walter continues: 'You will not fraternise with the staff here. You will not use the communal facilities such as the officer's mess, nor will you venture near the house, do you understand?'

Theo grunts a response. He has ceased to worry about why he is here and his mind dwells on smaller things, such as what staff and what house Walter might be referring to, and how he will eat if he cannot use the officers' mess.

He asks Walter. The food, Walter replies, will be brought to him.

'Am I a prisoner? Can I not leave this room?'

Walter's expression seems to question Theo's sanity. He frowns. Then he laughs out loud.

'God in Heaven, Theodor! You are free to leave this building and walk on the estate. The troops here will be told you are my personal assistant and you are not to be disturbed.'

Theo stays quiet. Walter is careless for using Theo's real name. Careless, too, for using an old photograph in his new passbook.

'I saw no house.'

'There is a mansion not far from here. It is off limits to service personnel.'

'What are my duties?'

'Duties?'

'As your personal assistant.'

Walter turns his back, steps to the window and looks out through the unpainted square.

'You have no duties. I have work to do. In a few days it will be complete. Until then I suggest you keep out of the way. Do you read?'

'Read?'

'Books, Theodor!'

'Kriegsmarine seamanship manuals. I don't suppose you have any.'

Theo's attempt at humour falls flat. Walter reaches up and takes a book from the shelf.

'Mein Kampf, have you read it? It is the account of our Führer's struggle against the Jews and Marxists.'

Spargo shrugged. It was the most boring book he had ever attempted to read.

'It was required reading at school,' he says. 'Surely you remember? I prefer mining books, Agricola, perhaps? de re metallica? No, I don't suppose they have it. Tell me why you used that photo on my passbook. Why didn't you have another taken?'

'I would have thought it was obvious. You had just shaved off your beard. Your chin looked – it still looks – as rosy as a whore's ass, while the rest of your face is tanned. On a new photograph the difference would have shown. I admit I was not expecting such vigilance on the part of a mere Luftwaffe gatekeeper. Now, I have to go, I have work to do. I said you are free to leave this room, Theodor, but I suggest you do not do that until I have explained to others who you are and why you are here. Tomorrow I shall come for you.'

Walter leaves, walking the length of the outer room with long strides. As the barrack door slams behind him Theo heaves his kitbag on to one of the beds, upends it, and then wishes he hadn't. There are no drawers or cupboards. Nowhere to store his kit.

Fixed to the wall beside the door is a clock with a moonfaced dial and black hands. Theo compares its time with the time on his wristwatch. They differ by six minutes. Because he does not know which is correct he splits the difference and sets his watch accordingly.

Theo's need to check and recheck all things – every switch and instrument, every valve and dial – is a habit bordering on obsession that started in the mines. Not only do you check and recheck, you watch your back and the backs of your colleagues, those that are next to you, behind you and ahead of you, above and below you. He knows his obsession and he lives with it, it has kept him alive. Though, if this is true, how did he get himself mixed up with the Generalmajor? With Walter?

The answer is simple. He wrongly assumed the enemy was on the outside. He was not expecting an attack from within.

Opposite the door to his room is another and he goes to it, opens it and enters a washroom built for twenty men, lavatories down one side and showers and lockers down the other. Once, two long rows of sinks faced each other down the middle of the room. Now only six remain, facing one another. Only two of them have taps.

Theo walks to the shower cubicles. Their doors have been removed, as have the shower heads. Walking past the sinks he pauses, turns on a tap and is surprised the water runs clear. From somewhere above him comes the trickle of a tank refilling.

Stacked against one wall of the washroom is a log pile big enough to keep the stove in his room fuelled for weeks. To one side of it, in the ceiling, is a hole for a stove pipe and he assumes that the stove, like the sinks, the taps and the showers, have been taken to equip other buildings. The light fittings have gone too, as have those in his room. For the first time for days he smiles. In a few hours he will be in the dark – even more in the dark than he is already.

During the drive from the gatehouse to this place he took little notice of his surroundings. Now, outside for the first time, he stands still and listens. Unlike the track past the farm, this one, one the truck turned on to, is muddy and rutted. It has rained recently, and now the branches of tall firs are being shaken by a cool breeze. The only sound Theo hears is the faint hiss of raindrops, falling from branches onto long grass.

There is water nearby, he can sense it. It is something to do with the light, the extra brightness water brings to the sky. When the breeze changes direction he hears other sounds, the hum of distant engines and the occasional raised voice, even the whinny of a horse. No doubt the troops Walter mentioned are billeted in newer, better quarters that this, in huts with decent plumbing and electric light, huts without holes in the roof and which don't smell of damp.

Back in his room he selects a book from the shelf, opens it, reads a few lines and returns it. Books exercise the mind, not the body. He knows from experience that his recent lapses in concentration result from a lack of physical exercise that borders on laziness.

Ten minutes later he emerges from the hut in Luftwaffe training shorts, a vest and light shoes. He glances up and down the track. Seeing nobody, he commences a slow, steady trot.

He runs for fifteen minutes and then stops for a break, bending over, bracing his arms on his knees and breathing deeply. The air is cold; his lungs hurt; he is short of breath and his calves ache. It shocks him that he is so unfit. He hasn't run properly since his training days. Running on the spot on a U-boat's steel deck is no substitute for this.

Retracing his steps at a less intense pace he hears an engine, perhaps a motorbike. Long before it appears he veers off into sparse woodland and runs again.

The run, that becomes a hobbling walk, brings him to calm water. The air is fresh but has the odour of damp vegetation, not at all like the sea. He is sure he is at the edge of a long lake or a wide river. Its far bank is no more than a kilometre away. Its ends – if it has ends – are so far away he cannot see them.

He sits on the bank, dangling bare legs in the water like his crew do on safe, sunny days. It reminds him of two boys on the banks of a canal, side by side with their feet in brown water. Boys who are the best of friends. Boys who share bread and sausage.

That thing people say: *War changes people* – trite but true. It is not just Walter who has changed. He, Theo, has changed too, a change that started in the mines when he encountered accidents, some of them fatal. Accidents happen, his father had said. But this war is no accident. Shooting and bombing are deliberate acts.

Back on the track he reaches the barrack hut at the same time as a man riding a bicycle. The man is old, and dressed in the white trousers and gold-buttoned tunic of an officer's orderly. The bicycle he rides has a carrying frame on its front, and noticing Theo he steps from the machine and leans it against the hut wall. He salutes, then heaves a hamper-like basket out of the carrying frame and stands holding it, as if waiting for orders.

The man has difficulty carrying the basket so Theo opens the hut door for him and attempts to take the basket. The man shrugs him off, tightens his grip, and mumbling apologies he heads for Theo's room. He sets the basket down, clicks heels, executes a smart but slow about-turn and leaves.

Despite having travelled on the front of a bicycle, the meal is one of the best Theo has ever eaten. The food is hot, it is cooked properly and tastes fresh – produce, he suspects, from the farm they passed.

Next morning Theo wakes early. In the chill of the washroom he shaves himself cautiously, his new safety razor – thankfully with a new blade – skates over tender flesh. In his room he dresses self-consciously in a uniform that still feels to him more like ceremonial dress than real clothes. The cap is stiff and uncomfortable. The calf-length black leather boots make him feel like a horseman. Finally he heaves the greatcoat on to his shoulders. It is heavy and restricts movement.

As he fastens the long row of buttons up the front of the greatcoat the aged orderly brings a breakfast of bread, sausage, egg, and lukewarm coffee in a white china pot. The man apologises for interrupting him, places the tray in the room, and then departs.

Soon Walter comes. A harsh-smelling roll-up protrudes from his lips and he attempts to talk without removing it. He splutters, coughs, takes it out and replaces it, this time holding it between finger and thumb with his little finger extended like a tea-drinking Englishman. He takes down a metal mug from the bookshelf, fills it with coffee, sips it and complains it is cold. Placing the pot on the top of the stove he realises that it, too, is cold. He opens the top, looks inside, and curses. The criticism Theo expects for letting the stove go out doesn't come. Instead Walter is pensive. He walks to the window and looks out through the hole in the paint.

'What do you know about our Reichsmarschall, Theodor?'

'I know what all men know, that he commands our air forces. He holds the highest military rank in the Reich. I know he was one of the Führer's strongest supporters when he first formed the Party.'

'He still is one of Hitler's strongest supporters. What is not so well known about the Reichsmarschall is that he is a collector of art. Did you know that?'

'I know nothing more about him.'

'He is an avid collector. Fanatical, some say. He and our Führer compete for the best items. They trade, they come to agreements. As you can imagine, our Führer gets the pieces he wants. At least, those he knows about.'

'They still do this? They play with trinkets while our country is threatened?'

'They have civilian and military units to doing it for them. The spoils of war, Theodor… Hauptmann Vogel.'

Theo knows from trusted colleagues that agents of the Reich take art from churches, museums and mansions. He has heard the expression they use – purchased at gunpoint – and he has laughed at it with the rest of them. It is right, they all agreed, that the conqueror takes all.

Theo waits for more. Walter opens the window and empties the cold coffee outside.

'Why are you telling me this? There are many things it is better not to know. I have no interest in the affairs of our leaders. I am an officer in the Kriegsmarine. I hold minor rank.'

Walter stays facing the window. It is still open and he is looking outside.

'No, you are an officer in the Luftwaffe. Listen to what I have to say and keep your thoughts to yourself, your opinions are of no importance. I have been told you were present in Potsdam when the truck that brought us here was loaded with those wooden crates, is that correct?'

'It is correct. The crates contain art treasures.'

Walter falls silent. His expression hardens. Theo realises, too late, that his comment was gratuitous and stupid. Inwardly he blames tiredness.

'And you learned this from whom?' Walter asks. 'The Generalmajor?'

'Not from the Generalmajor.'

'Then from whom? You have spoken to nobody.' Walter turns and stares. 'From the guard in the truck? You were with him, of course.'

'From nobody. I made a simple guess. You are talking of treasure of the Reich and of wooden crates.'

'Very well. We travelled here with the last of the Reichsmarschall's possessions to be moved from his offices and houses in Berlin. Now everything is here.'

'Where is here? I do not know where you have brought me.'

'The armband worn by the officer at the gate, it meant nothing to you?'

'There are so many armbands.'

'If you had bothered to look at that particular one you would have seen it said General Göring.'

'I can't read embroidery.'

·'Watch your tongue.'

'I apologise, Herr Major.'

Walter's stare hardens.

'You are at Carinhall, the Reichsmarschall's shooting lodge, some might say his mansion. We are in the Schorfheide, a hunting region. You have heard of it?'

'No, Herr Major.'

Walter closes the window, glances around the room and turns up his collar. 'Come, I want to talk. We will go outside. This place is depressing.'

The morning is cold. The air outside is damp and a mist hangs in the treetops. Theo walks side by side with Walter, who despite having complained about the cold is not wearing his greatcoat but has it draped over his shoulders.

Without his beard, Theo feels the cold. With unfamiliar boots he walks like a man whose shoes are too small. The only walking he has done in these boots is on concrete floors. Here, the ground is uneven.

'I have things to say to you,' Walter says. 'I am going to confide in you. What I say must not be repeated. I am sure there is no need for me to explain to you what will happen to you – and to your son – if you are foolish enough to betray my trust.'

That Walter wishes to confide anything at all is bad news. The man is part of a plan, perhaps the instigator of it. There is no way of knowing if it is sanctioned from on high or if, as Theo suspects, he is being dragged into something dishonourable. It is well known that the state treats its detractors without mercy. The slaughter following the attempt on the Führer's life was swift and vicious – the suspects, together with their families, their relatives and friends, were rounded up, tortured and hanged.

'What is all this?' Theo asks. 'Why am I here?'

The big-engine drone of a generator, always in the background, gets louder. There are other sounds, voices carried on a bracing breeze and the ring of a hammer on metal. There is also the unmistakable pounding of distant, galloping hooves.

Theo continues: 'Tell me why we are at Reichsmarschall's house. Are you planning to assassinate him? Am I to be a scapegoat? Is that why I am here?'

The angry outburst he expects doesn't come. Walter is looking away, stifling laughter.

'God in Heaven, Theodor! If that isn't the most ridiculous thing I have ever heard! It offends me you should think me capable of such a thing.' He takes a silk handkerchief from a trouser pocket and dabs each eye in turn. 'What a thought, Theo, eh? What a thought! Take care, my friend. By rights I should have you arrested for even thinking such things.'

Theo, walking bolt upright and noticeably tense, breathes more freely. It is the first time he has seen Walter's genuine amusement since the man joked with the Generalmajor. He wants to respond to the comment but he dare not. To him, Walter has developed a split personality, one minute an officer of the Reich and the next his boyhood friend.

'Let me tell you, Theodor. I assume you aware our enemies have invaded France?'

'There are rumours. I do not subscribe to rumours.'

'So tell me what you have heard.'

'I have heard they are at our borders. They will be driven back. To say otherwise is defeatist talk.'

'Defeatist talk? It is only a matter of time before we are overrun from the east and from the south and the west. It appears our enemies are in a race to see which of their rabble bands can steal the most from our country. Because of this our treasures must be protected. The Reichsmarschall's collection must be preserved.'

'So I am here to help you to move boxes.'

'You are here because I trust you.'

'You know longer know me. There must be others you could have called upon.'

Walter turns and inspects Theo, cap to boots and then back again. His eyes fix on Theo's.

'Let me be the judge of that. You look passably smart – and bloody uncomfortable. I thought you old sea dogs could handle the cold?'

Through a plantation of slender pines Theo gets his first glimpse of Carinhall. What at first he mistakes for a large stone-built barn turns out to be a Medieval style hall with a roof of red pantiles, only one part of a rambling collection of interconnecting, impressively large buildings and surrounding courtyards. Some of the outlying buildings are linked by covered walkways, constructed from massive timbers like those used to build quays. It is the style of the place that surprises Theo, it is a scaled up hunting lodge fit for a prince.

From a door in an outbuilding come two Luftwaffe men wearing tunics bearing the Göring armband. Like the others Theo has seen they are members of the Reichsmarschall's own regiment, the equivalent of the Leibstandarte, the Führer's elite guard. As they pass Walter and Theo they salute with a drillmaster's *eyes right*.

Apart from the guards at the estate entrance, the place appears undefended. There are no gun emplacements, no blast walls. It is as if here in the forest there is no war; no bombs have fallen on Berlin and the northern ports; Erica is still alive, and Peter safe at home.

Walter is beckoning.

'Come! Why do you dawdle? I have brought you here simply to show you that everything from here on is forbidden to you. Through that passage is the Reichsmarschall's house. You will not go there.'

Walter, closely followed by Theo, enters what looks like a stable block. Theo expects to see the horses he heard earlier but the interior of the building has been gutted and refurbished with a row of small rooms. All but one of their doors are open, revealing small windowless offices with bare metal desks and wooden chairs. Screwed to each door, at eye level, is a small brass frame, all empty except for one on the closed door. Slipped into it, typed on a slip of white card, is Walter's name and rank. There is no title, nothing to say what Walter does.

Walter, key in hand, unlocks the door. The furnishings are sparse here: a metal desk, a wooden filing cabinet and three chairs.

'Sit down, Hauptmann Vogel, make yourself comfortable. Would you like coffee? Hot coffee? Real coffee? Before Theo can answer Walter is yelling down the corridor to unseen ears. From some way off, like an echo, comes a curt reply.

'Now, Hauptmann Vogel. Where was I?'

'The Reichsmarschall's collection.'

'Yes. I told you to sit down, so do it. Our Führer's personal collection of artistic works is being transported to safety. You are a mining man, possibly you have heard of Altaussee?'

'It is a salt mine in Austria. I know nothing about salt mines, they are quite different to metal mines. If that is why you want me you have chosen the wrong man.'

Walter is in an unusually good mood and he laughs. Then, as if fearing he may be overheard, he lowers his voice. 'After what I told you about our Hermann, do you really think he wants to store his collection in a mine with Adolf's pieces? The Führer considers his as treasures as belonging to the Reich. Göring considers his loot to be his own.'

'His loot?'

'The last thing Göring wants is for the Führer to know what he has. The crates you have seen… a bunker is being constructed for them in the south, near Berchtesgaden. You may have heard the Führer also has a stronghold there. My guess is that the bunker is closer to Hitler than Göring would like, but I suspect he has no choice in the matter.'

This is dangerous talk and Theo wants no part of it. He is no longer concerned Walter may be out to trap him, he is more anxious they will be overheard – perhaps by whoever is tapping on Walter's door now.

The aged orderly who brings Theo his meals is standing in the corridor carrying a tray. He apologises to Walter for having brought only one cup and he scurries away to get another one. While he is gone the two men say nothing; when he returns with a second cup he brings a message that Walter is needed elsewhere. The man leaves and Walter curses, opens his briefcase, grabs papers and holds them out.

'Here, take these. What I have to tell you can wait. Take the papers to your room, read them and remember what you read. Then burn them in the stove.'

'They are stamped confidential.'

'It is your service history. I'm not expecting you to tell me what you think of it because I am not interested. From now on you are this man. Get used to it, Hauptmann!'

CHAPTER SIXTEEN

OSCAR BAR DID NOT LIVE IN ALMERIA. He lived to the north of the small town of Mojácar, a fifty mile journey from the airport undertaken at speed in a Mercedes that, for a second or two, Spargo thought was the car from Madrid.

Benares sat beside Spargo in the rear of the car and hummed softly. Spargo, sneaking a surreptitious glance, saw him picking at his fingernails with the point of a blade, scraping them white underneath and then flicking the bits from his lap. Spargo had assumed the knife was a penknife. A second glance showed it was a switchblade with an ornate wooden handle and a slim, curved blade. Benares, aware he was being watched, turned to Spargo with a brief smile. He folded the knife in the palm of his hand. It locked with a click.

Spargo, numbed by the bizarre string of events, realised as he gazed out of the car window that he had been there before. What was once a quiet coastal road was now a highway servicing hotels and timeshares, seafront restaurants and bars. He came here when he while at university and visited mines in the hills. Were they still there, he wondered? The whole thing about mines is you dig away everything worth digging and then close them down.

Just as Spargo convinced himself that the entire Mediterranean coast had been ruined by rambling developments, everything changed. The road narrowed. Hugging the coast it wound into coves and out onto headlands. Though the view inland was obscured by low cliffs the view out to sea was quite stunning. He compared it with Kilcreg. There, grey sea blended with grey sky. Here, waveless blue sea joined clear, cloudless sky.

The inland cliffs bored him but they wouldn't bore Jez. Spargo had never encouraged his daughter to study geology and he wondered if it was in her genes, a love of the Earth that passed from grandfather to son, and son to daughter. Far more likely she was entranced by the minerals he brought back from his trips abroad and if that was the case then it pleased him. He always assumed Jez would follow Theresa into politics and then law. It also pleased him that Theresa had not been at all impressed by their daughter's choice of career.

Jez had done well. At university she was awarded a First. Years later, as Doctor Jessica Spargo, she took a temporary lecturing job that soon became permanent. The fact that she stayed in Edinburgh was the only thing they had disagreed on, the only time he'd interfered. There were other places in the world, he told her.

But then, he had been everywhere and look where it had got him. Yesterday Madrid. Today Andalucia. A trip that was looking increasingly like a fool's errand.

The sea view was still there but the low cliffs had gone, replaced by tight narrow valleys that sliced up through the hills. Ravines, he supposed. Jez would know the correct term.

'Are we there yet?' he asked. The humour was lost on Benares. The man turned his head and looked up the hill.

'Indeed we are, Mister Spargo.'

Indicators clicked. The car turned inland. They hadn't gone far before the road they were on changed from firm tarmac to a rock-strewn track. A road better suited to a four-by-four than an executive car.

The Mercedes ascended effortlessly in a cloud of pale dust. High up, the track levelled out. Spargo guessed that at some time in its history the hillside had been quarried; rocks and rubble had been dumped over the edge, tumbling towards the sea to form a wide slope of boulders. All done long ago, Spargo told himself, noting the short stunted trees that studded the slope. He had seen such quarries before, chunks cut out of hillsides to leave ugly, flat scars, homes to tall weeds and abandoned, rusting machinery. But not this one. This site had been flattened and cleared.

Spargo saw, up ahead, a single storey villa with a red tiled roof, a house that would not have looked out of place on the Tyrol. It was an eagles' nest, he decided. An eagles' nest with a sea view to die for.

The long flat drive forming the approach to the villa had been dressed with gravel, its edges raked out in curved swathes like a Zen temple garden. The driver slowed the car to a crawl. Tried not to disturb the fine patterns.

'So!' exclaimed Benares. 'We have arrived, Mister Spargo!'

Spargo stayed quiet. It was one of the few times Benares had imparted information voluntarily. The only time it wasn't necessary.

Still on the gravel and some way from the villa the car drew to a stop. Spargo, determined to get out of the car before the driver opened it for him, stepped out into the heat of the day and took long strides towards the villa.

Not only had Bar cleared away all traces of former industry and imported hundreds of tons of gravel for the driveway, he had also imported vast quantities of topsoil to make formal gardens. A man in a wide floppy hat stood half hidden by roses, directing a trickle of water on to neatly raked soil. With the enthusiasm of a salesman Spargo made straight for him.

Not bothering with footpaths Spargo stepped over the rose beds. Realising at the last moment that the man he was heading for was not Oscar Bar but the gardener, he changed direction mid-stride and aimed this time for a larger and more smartly dressed man seated on a patio in the shade of the house. In full flight, and having changed direction, Spargo found his new route impeded a long, rectangular swimming pool.

'Spargo...' he called out as he weaved his way around numerous obstacles. 'John Spargo,' he said again when closer, this time with hand outstretched.

The man stayed motionless. Moving only his eyes he regarded Spargo silently. Only then did Spargo realise he was sitting not on one of the patio's wooden chairs but in a motorised wheelchair. The man regarded him with an expression bordering on derision. Finally deflated, Spargo lowered his hand.

'Sit down,' the man said in English. 'You are blocking my view. Who are you anyway? What did you say your name was?'

Unfazed by Bar's attitude Spargo dipped a hand into the top pocket of his jacket and scissored out a business card between two fingers. He flipped it upright, the way a magician might produce a playing card. Bar waved it away.

Spargo, embarrassed by his failed sales pitch, calmed down.

'My name is John Spargo,' he said quietly. 'I'm a mining engineer. I am here because Mr Benares believes I can help you.'

Eyes that might once have been blue looked him up and down. If this was indeed Mr Bar then he was a heavy man, big and bald and with dark, unkempt eyebrows. And old. Very old. Much older than Spargo could have imagined. Ninety, he guessed.

Spargo grasped the back of one of the wooden chairs, swivelled it round, placed it in front of Bar and sat down on it. In case Bar would think he was invading his space he jumped it back while still sitting. Bar looked off to one side as if to avoid eye contact and then raised a hand slowly, pointing first at Spargo's shoulder and then wagging his finger from side to side. 'Still you spoil my view,' he said. He moved the finger, pointing to one side towards the open French windows. 'Sit there. I suppose that now you are here you want a drink...'

Before Spargo could respond, Bar addressed Benares, still in English. Unnoticed by Spargo, the man had come up to them. Silently.

'How about you?' Bar asked him. 'You look as if you could do with one.'

Spargo tried to place Bar's accent. Spanish, certainly, but also something else, Swedish, possibly. Bar swivelled his thick neck, tilted his head back a fraction and shouted, this time in Spanish. Several seconds passed before a motherly woman came trotting from the house, out through the French windows, untying her apron and bunching it in one hand as she closed in on Bar. When she reached the patio she saw Spargo, changed direction and went for the drinks trolley.

Drinks came in tall glasses with Tapas accompaniments in small porcelain bowls, brought by the woman from deep in the house. Spargo eyed them hungrily. Hoped he would be invited to eat.

'So, Mister Spargo,' Bar said. 'What do you do?'

'I'm a mining engineer.'

'So you said. I asked you what you do, not what you are.'

'I'm a consultant. I have my own company.'

'And how big is your company?'

'If I need assistance I can call on associates.'

In reality the only associate he'd ever had was Grant Murphy, a petroleum engineer he met and worked with when he returned to Scotland from Zambia. Murphy was a man who dabbled in mining in the way Spargo dabbled in oil. In practice the two – oil and mining, as well as Spargo and Murphy – did not mix. The partnership hadn't worked well. Hadn't worked at all. Murphy, luckily for both of them, got work in Canada and seldom returned.

'So, Mister Spargo, you are a one-man band.'

Spargo let the remark lie. Benares, still close, picked up a glass, drifted away from the table and struck up a conversation with the man with the hose.

'Mr Benares hasn't yet explained your project to me,' Spargo said.

'That is because Luis knows nothing. It is not his job to explain to you my requirements.'

Bar snapped his fingers and the woman came running. Still speaking English he demanded his cigars. When the woman made no move to obey him he repeated the demand in Spanish and she hurried away. She returned to the patio carrying a humidor that she placed on the table next to Bar.

'You do not smoke, John Spargo. I trust you will not be troubled when I do.'

Bar selected a cigar, rolled it between finger and thumb, held it to his ear and listened to it. Then he put it to his nose and smelt it. Benares, unbidden, appeared from nowhere with his knife, flicked it open, took the cigar from Bar, trimmed off one end and handed it back. The woman held out a table lighter and Bar, taking short sharp puffs, rotated the tip of the cigar in its flame.

Bar settled back and blew smoke. 'I like order, John Spargo,' he said. 'I demand the highest standards from those I employ. When I first came to this country it was governed by General Franco. Governed, John Spargo, not led from behind by political weaklings. Now in Spain we have this bastard democracy, squabbling politicos and governments of compromise. Good countries need good leaders, it is the same in business and trade. What about you, John Spargo? Are you a good leader?'

Spargo sat bemused. It wasn't the first time he had encountered a client who liked hearing his own voice. The man had denied knowing anything about him. He hadn't looked at his business card and yet he was calling him John. And how did Bar know he didn't smoke? Was it a Sherlock Holmes thing? No nicotine stains on his fingers, no harshness in his voice? And are you a good leader? He didn't know if he was or not. He hadn't really thought about it.

'I think that is for others to say.'

Bar grunted. Wrong answer. 'Was your father a good leader?'

'My father?'

'Your father, Samuel Spargo. It surprises you that I know his name? Why is that? If I did not know everything about you then I would not do business with you. It is the old Spanish way.'

'My father was manager of a small scheelite mine in Scotland. But I expect you know that already.'

'And therefore a leader of men, John Spargo. Tell me, the name Samuel. Surely that is not a Scottish name?'

Spargo paused. 'There was a time when parents gave their children biblical names. Samuel was a prophet.'

'Of course, I am aware of that. Are you a religious man, John Spargo?'

Spargo groped for a neutral answer. He wanted to get up and walk away. Religious? Not particularly. Superstitious? Definitely. But then, he had reason to be.

For the remainder of the afternoon both men drank in moderation, Bar holding centre stage in a powerful monotone, relentlessly slamming in turn the government of Spain, the European Union, and the United States for its global policing.

'What right?' he asked. 'What right have they to police the world, John Spargo?' He spat the words venomously. Benares, sitting some way off, nodded repeatedly, showing his teeth in a horse-like grin.

In late afternoon the weather changed, still warm for Spargo but not, it seemed, for Bar. He called for a jacket and a rug and for a while he stayed in his wheelchair, wrapped tightly. He grumbled incessantly about the hordes of flying insects attracted to the patio lights until an hour or so later he pronounced himself tired. He powered the wheelchair backwards, turning it to face Benares.

'Have you booked John Spargo into the hotel at Mojácar? Yes?'

Benares sat bemused but said nothing.

'Apparently he has not, John Spargo. However, I have a guest suite here that is particularly well appointed. There is a refrigerator with food and drink. If, for your own reasons, you do not wish to stay here then Luis will attempt, even at this late hour, to book you into a hotel. He is a resourceful man so I am sure he will manage to do that which he should have done already.'

The chair trundled across the patio and in through the open French windows. It kept going, across what looked like a lounge and then vanished down a corridor. Spargo, drink in hand, turned to Benares.

'Is anybody ever going to tell me why I'm here?'

'As you have just seen, Mister Spargo, Mr Bar is elderly and therefore you must make allowances. He is buying your time, is he not?'

'I've spent half the day travelling and the rest of it being quizzed about my past and my politics. Most clients who pay for my time usually want to wring every second of it from me.'

Benares shrugged. He dragged his chair into the space vacated by Bar and sat down.

'Is that not what Señor Bar is doing?'

The woman reappeared. Ignoring them she cleared away glasses. When she returned from the house she started to sweep the patio with a wide, soft besom. Benares watched impatiently. Tapped his fingers. When it was clear she wasn't going to go away he stood up and beckoned to Spargo. Spargo followed him into the house and across the lounge.

Parquet floors everywhere, Spargo noted. And panelled walls, panelled ceilings, all in dark wood. Then, finally, panelled double doors Benares opened with a flourish.

'For you, Mister Spargo. I am sure, I am certain, you will find everything you need in here.'

Benares went inside. Spargo stayed in the doorway, peering into the room. The place was bright, the lights were on. It was unexpectedly large, with a high ceiling extending into the roof space. It was, he told himself, what used to be known as a bed sitting room – a bedsit – except this was modern and luxurious. Across the room was a sofa and king size bed.

'Step inside if you please, Mister Spargo.'

A vision of his late mother swam before him, the hospital corridor, the doctor, the nurse. He did as Benares asked, doing his best to pay attention to the tour guide routine. It was as if the man was selling the place to him.

'Your bathroom, Mister Spargo…'

Benares' sweeping arm encompassed the shower, the sink, the bath, the lavatory and the gleaming, gold-plated fittings. A toothbrush, toothpaste and shaving accessories, all sealed in clear plastic, had been arranged in neat lines on a bevelled-glass shelf.

'Your cooking facilities are here,' Benares added, words that shook Spargo from dreams as they paced across parquet. Another door, another room, this time a kitchen. 'You will manage the cooking for yourself, of that I am sure. There is a microwave oven it is simple to use. In this refrigerator you will find food to your liking. Señor Bar, he is tired, he will not be dining this evening.'

Benares showed his teeth and left the room.

Along one wall of the big room was the apartment's only window. Outside, moths beat against the pane in an attempt to befriend the bright lights inside. Spargo's overnight bag was already there, sitting on a shelf near the double doors. He went to it. Carried it to the bed.

A tour of the main room, solo this time, revealed a bottle of whisky, a fifteen-year old Glenmorangie, his favourite malt. Picking up the bottle he poured a small measure into the small cut glass tumbler beside it and took a sip. Then a gulp. That this brand was here had to be a coincidence. He hadn't mentioned drink to Benares, hadn't asked for whisky in the tapas bar in Madrid, nor in the restaurant, nor the hotel.

Spargo had mixed thoughts about missing out on an evening meal with Bar. He wasn't particularly hungry, but dinner with a client was a good time to talk. But Bar seemed as reluctant as Benares to explain why he was there.

He carried the empty glass to the kitchen, put it on the sink drainer and opened the refrigerator. On its shelves were six plated meals sealed in cling film. Years ago, when Jez was younger and Spargo's marriage was intact, the family took self-catering holidays. This, he told himself as he looked at the plates in the refrigerator, was a self-catering business trip. He slid one of the plates from its shelf, pulled back the film, examined it and slipped it back. He did the same with another. And then another.

Many times in his married life Theresa accused him of being a fussy eater, yet there was nothing on these plates he did not like. He stared at the food. What was glaringly obvious about all this, he realised, reaching for the whisky glass and returning to the big room for a refill, was that Bar's chastisement of Benares for not booking a hotel was a blind. No wonder the man had looked puzzled. It was obvious, glaringly so, that Bar had every intention of keeping Spargo in his house overnight.

The room had two phones, one in the kitchen and one beside the bed. Seeing them reminded him he'd promised Jez he would call her when he arrived in Madrid, but in all the confusion he'd forgotten to do it. He sat on the edge of the bed, whisky glass in hand, and reached for the phone. He expected a ringtone. Instead he heard Bar's gruff voice.

'I am working on him,' the voice said in English. 'You must be patient. I have waited many years for this and I do not intend to compromise matters. The man is no fool.'

The reply was a slow Texan drawl.

'Okay, okay, have it your way. Try asking him if modern methods might make the mines profitable. Tell him the funds for investigations can be raised fast and easy, you got that? Fast and easy, Oscar, okay? Tell him fools and their money are easily parted – he is a mining man so he will guess what you mean. And listen to me, Oscar. You take care of your end, you understand? Ditch the loose cannon before he does more damage.'

'That is not your problem.'

'Dump him, Oscar! And this Kilcreg business, you get it moving, okay? Our man is getting antsy, wants to see something for his money.

Gets the impression he's waiting for ever.'

Spargo replaced the phone handset, gently.

The snatch of conversation on what he realised was a shared line kept him awake half the night. He tried to recall the exact words. Tried to put them in context. It made little sense.

The American had mentioned Kilcreg. Perhaps Bar's venture was there and not in Spain. But if they thought they could reopen the Kilcreg mine they must be out of their minds. And ditch the loose cannon, what was that? If reopening Kilcreg was their intention, and he was the loose cannon, how could they proceed at Kilcreg if they dumped him?

Breakfast, Benares had said, would be served on the patio at eight. Spargo, showered and dressed, drifted towards the French windows and found them locked shut.

The lounge was long, the full width of the house. At one end, well away from the French windows, the walls were lined with floor to ceiling bookcases of dark brown wood. To pass the time Spargo browsed book titles, keeping his hands clasped behind him as if to prove he'd touched nothing.

Bar's non-fiction, he noticed, was indexed by subject: Antarctica and Anatomy to Velazquez and Zoology. He checked under 'M' and was surprised to see there was nothing about mining. Moving to fiction, he found most of it was in Spanish. Recognising one of the titles, he pulled out a book.

Sandwiched between tall bookcases was a doorway to a room he'd not noticed before. The room was small and contained the usual office trappings, a desk and swivel chair, a computer and printer, a photocopier and filing cabinets. Spargo moved closer. Looked in properly.

Above the cabinets there were picture hooks but no pictures. Beneath each hook a rectangular patch of paint, untouched by the sun, showed where each picture had been. The pictures themselves were there, taken down and stacked on end under the room's only window, as if the walls had been cleared for redecoration. Spargo ventured inside. Went to the frames and picked one up.

'Do you read Spanish, John Spargo?'

Bar, it seemed, moved as silently as Benares. The man and his wheelchair were so close behind Spargo he could have reached out and touched them. Had Spargo not been holding the photo frame with both hands he might well have dropped it. Instead he dropped the paperback that had been clamped under his arm. Bar repeated his question.

'Spanish?' Spargo spluttered, seeking words. 'No, unfortunately not.

Bar was looking down at the dropped paperback.

'But you have read that particular Hemingway? In English? Does his work interest you?'

'I read one of his novels, Fifth Column. That was years ago.'

'It is a play, not a novel. But yes, the Spanish Civil War, the battle for Madrid. Do you not think it an irony that in that war the Soviets supported the Spanish Royalists?'

'I'm not much of a one for politics.'

Bar grunted, backed the wheelchair out of the room, swung it around and buzzed the length of the lounge. Turning sharply he stopped by the windows.

'Come here, John Spargo. The key to these doors is over there.' He waggled a finger at a side table. 'Unlock them for me, I need air. You say you do not know about politics. But you know about mines and to me that is acceptable, it is what you are here for. You have explained to me that your father managed a mine. Scheelite, you said. An ore of tungsten, yes? Are there other, similar mines in Scotland?'

'There are none. The mine he managed was kept going because of wartime needs. Nowadays it would be unable to compete with imports from abroad.'

'Would modern methods make such a mine profitable?'

Spargo's face twitched. It was the question set by the Texan, in context now.

'Modern methods? I doubt it. I take it you mean Kilcreg? Even if the minerals are there, they are not in commercial quantities.'

'How do you know that? Has anyone carried out investigations?'

'My father told me that government geologists explored the area in the nineteen-thirties.'

'In the nineteen-thirties, John Spargo? Are you saying exploration and extraction methods have not improved since then?'

'I don't know the extent of the old study. There could well be more mineral at great depth. Of course, the deeper it is, the more it costs to mine.'

'You are an honest man, John Spargo. But before you talk yourself out of a job would it not be worth investigating the mine further?'

'That would not be possible. There is no longer any way in to the old workings. Even if there were, the levels will be flooded.'

'I was thinking more along the lines of a drilling and sampling program. Funds for the necessary investigations can be raised easily,' he continued. 'A fool and his money are easily parted. I will have no trouble finding investors. You are a mining man, John Spargo. I am sure you understand what I mean.'

More snippets from the phone conversation.

'Tell me about BarConSA,' Spargo said. 'It's not in any of my mining directories. I can't find it on the Internet.'

'I am relieved to hear it.'

'The name… is it Bar Consulting? Bar Contracting?'

'You are concerned, John Spargo?'

'I like to know who I am working for.'

'My company is small and exclusive, we do not advertise, there is no need. You need have no worries about authenticity. When you next check your bank balance you will discover you have been adequately compensated for your stay here and your time and trouble. Speak to Benares, he will give you the details.'

'I still don't know what you want from me.'

'I regret I am not yet in a position to release details. Suffice to say that as soon as financial arrangements between the various partners are in place you shall be given the information you require. I have satisfied myself you are the person to do this work, and that is the reason you are here. Now, breakfast arrives! I suggest you sit down and enjoy it.'

It was dark when Spargo's plane arrived in Edinburgh. By the time its wheels double-bumped on the runway he was convinced he'd cracked the mystery that was Oscar Bar. The man was planning a scam. There would be a project of some kind, one that would impress Bar's investors. As soon as it was underway the offices in Madrid would be teeming with hired staff. To a curious investor the business would look active and legitimate.

Before leaving the airport he phoned Jez, and on his way home he called in to see her. Omitting the muddles in Madrid he explained where he had been. He described Bar, described the villa. He didn't mention the pictures he'd seen in Bar's office. Didn't think he should.

'So what's it about?' Jez asked. 'Is there work for you?'

'I'm sure there is. Not yet sure what. They talked about Scottish mines.'

'There are hardly any left, you know that. They're mainly opencast coal.'

'They mentioned Kilcreg. They're talking about reopening it.'

'That's ridiculous! Did you tell him it's worked out?'

Spargo shrugged. 'It's nonsense, I know.'

'So how can there be work for you?'

Jez was perched on a stool at her breakfast bar. Spargo dragged out another stool, sat on it, reached for the coffee and mumbled a response. He knew this would happen. He had been expecting to be quizzed.

'My guess is they'll produce an investment portfolio based on reopening the mine,' he said without looking at her. 'To do that they'll need a report on Kilcreg's mining potential. I've seen this kind of thing before. I told them there could be ore deep down. You're a geologist, you know it could be true. Whether it's worth mining or not is debatable. My guess is that I will be asked to produce a factual report.'

'They will take your stuff out of context. They'll dupe the investors. They will leave out all your caveats and cautions. It happens all the time.'

'What they do with my report is up to them. They will raise money for exploration, maybe get drills on site and put down a few holes.'

'And when they find pinhead-sized bits of scheelite they'll hype it up – Valuable minerals found at Kilcreg – it's pseudo-science and lies, Dad! They will raise even more money, perhaps enough to sink a shaft. When they decide they have spent enough of their investor's money they will announce that they have hit unforeseen problems and pull out completely.'

'I know all that.'

'So what will they do with what remains of the investor's money?'

'I know, I know. It will have all gone on directors' fees and running costs. It maintains lifestyles and big cars, villas overlooking the Mediterranean, empty offices in Madrid ready for the next scam. Oh – there is a nice bit of raised beach to the south of Bar's place. Pity you weren't there.'

'Don't change the subject. It's a scam. You're getting involved in a scam!'

'It's perfectly legal. Investors are gamblers. Gamblers take risks.'

'But it's wrong!'

'I won't be involved. I'll be out of it long before then.'

'It's still wrong.'

'Jez… look… it's what I need right now. Things haven't been too good lately. I don't have much work.'

There wasn't much more to be said. Spargo feigned tiredness, apologised for interrupting her and left without finishing his coffee. At home he swung his Volvo onto the twin row of paving slabs in his front garden, triggering the security lamp under the eaves and flooding the front garden with light. He took his bag from the boot, placed them on his front step, and took out his house keys.

A few years ago he'd had deadlocks fitted to his front and back doors. Each needed two turns of the key and he'd become obsessive about double-locking them. He inserted the key in the lock and turned it once. He tried to turn it a second time but it wouldn't turn – the door was already unlocked. He stood on the step, frowning. Opening the door he gave a nod of understanding. There was no mystery. Jez must have called round for some reason, perhaps to check the mail. Though if she'd done that, why hadn't she said?

Carrying his bag, Spargo stepped into the hall. Entering the house in the dark involved a strict routine: drop what you are carrying, step briskly to an alcove at the other end of the hall and type the alarm code into a panel. If you didn't know where the panel was, then even if you knew the code you wouldn't be able to find it before the alarm sounded.

All windows and external doors were alarmed. Open any one of them and the panel would start its shrill bleeps. Spargo was halfway down the hall before he noticed the silence. There were no beeps. The alarm wasn't on. Jez must have been there. She had forgotten to reset the alarm. Cautiously he switched on the hall light. The alarm panel looked dead. There was no error message, no little red light.

Switching on more lights Spargo went from room to room, checking the house, first the back door and then all the windows. Everything was as it should be. By the time he returned to his bag he was calm again. There was a fault in the system, a spider in a sensor, a blown fuse, a flat battery. It had happened before.

The light on his answering machine was flashing and he went to it. Pressed the button.

'Mr Spargo, it's Mitchell. When are you planning to come here? I have been calling your mobile. Call me as soon as you can.'

A trip to Inverness right now would be useful; he was overdue for a meeting with his mother's solicitor; he had documents to sign and a house to sell.

'As I said when you phoned,' Mitchell said when he and Spargo met. 'I sent your box to the lab. It contained only books, nothing of value. Nothing of relevance to our case.'

Spargo nodded. Felt relief. He had phoned Mitchell early that morning and then driven north. He had already seen the solicitor and estate agent. Things seemed to be panning out for him. The last thing he needed right now were more complications.

'My colleagues told me you fell through the ceiling in that old place,' Mitchell said. 'Seventeen stitches, they said.'

Spargo hadn't counted them. 'A tetanus jab and painkillers,' he said. 'I didn't fall through though, not right through.'

'Then you are a lucky man. What made you go up there?'

Spargo shrugged. He didn't want to say intuition, not to a policeman.

'You probably don't remember what I told you about my father. He said he never stored things in his roof. I began to wonder if he said it just to stop me going up there.'

Mitchell raised his eyebrows. He was nodding, slowly. Seemed to want to comment but changed his mind.

'The books,' he said. 'As you might expect, they are old. They are diaries of some sort, written in German. When they came back from the lab I sent them to a translator but he wasn't much help. As far as I'm concerned they are yours, you can take them away.'

Mitchell was holding a pencil with both hands. He swivelled it until it lined up with a side desk and then pointed it down. Spargo looked there. Freed of its canvas cladding the package he'd found looked much smaller.

'That's it?'

'That's it. A devil of a thing to open, they told me. Six layers of canvas, each layer bound with wire.'

All the canvas was there, split open and surrounding the box like petals – a great grubby sunflower with a box at its centre. The top edges of the box had a golden sheen where a grinder had sliced off its top. The metal was about a centimetre thick. No wonder he'd had trouble lifting it.

'What's it made of, did they check? It looks like brass.'

'Bronze. Someone had screwed down the lid with steel screws and they'd corroded. They all broke off when the lab tried to unscrew them. As you see, they had to cut the top off.'

Spargo went to the box and crouched down. Mitchell did the same, sliding out a slab of metal that was propped against the wall. It looked like a rectangular manhole cover, still jammed in its frame. Patches of a hard rubbery substance adhered to parts of the lid and sides of the box.

'The lab threw most of that black muck in the bin,' Mitchell said as Spargo poked at it. 'They asked if I wanted them to do tests but I told them not to bother. At first they thought it was perished rubber.'

'It isn't?'

Mitchell shrugged. 'They're not sure what it is. Not important. Not to me, anyway.'

Spargo dragged out the box. Packed inside it were two piles of books, side by side. Each book was about twice the size of a paperback and bound in what looked like leather. He picked up one and touched its cover. Mitchell nodded at it.

'The lab thinks it's sealskin.'

Spargo attempted to open the book, but stopped when the binding cracked. Returning it to the box he chose another. It opened, but its pages were stuck fast in a hard, wrinkled block.

'It's wet,' he said, frowning. 'There's water in the box.'

'I didn't send the box to the translator, only the books. They came back from him wrapped in a bin bag. He told me he soaked them to separate their pages. That puzzled me because before I sent them I went through them, they weren't stuck.' He reached down, selected one and opened it. 'The translator managed to translate a couple of pages from this one,' he continued, passing the book to Spargo. 'Did either of your parents read German?'

'My father knew a little. My mother told me that before the war he had been on an exchange programme arranged by a mining association. As part of the exchange a German mining engineer visited Kilcreg. It must have been quite a shock for him. For the German, I mean.'

'In what way?'

'Kilcreg was isolated enough when I was a boy, so think what it must have been like back in the nineteen thirties. The visitor must have thought he'd been dumped in the ass end of the world. You know what I think these are? My guess is they are German mining records that might have interested my father. Strange that my father hid them. Tell me what the translator said.'

'They were written during the war, not before it. And they are definitely not mine records. And who says your father hid them? They were in the attic. Perhaps he had help putting the box up there and when he got older it was too heavy for him to bring down.'

'He could have taken the books out of the box. He could have left the empty box up there.'

'Not if he couldn't get its lid off. Most likely he left the box there because he didn't think it worth bothering with.'

'What if he didn't know about it?'

'Are you suggesting someone else put it there?'

'Think about it. My mother was attacked for a reason. They were looking for that box, I'm sure of it. Perhaps they didn't know it contained just books. Perhaps they thought there was something valuable in it.'

Mitchell grunted. 'Who do you suggest put it there? Did anyone else live in the house? Lodgers? Friends? Relatives?'

Spargo cast his mind back. There was someone. Years ago.

'A man,' he pondered. 'Two men. They stayed in the mine house extension – you saw it, that lean-to bit – I was very young, I don't really remember them. They worked on the mine. Or one of them did, I'm not sure. The other had a bicycle, he rode off on it every morning and came back late.'

'Would it have been usual for a mine manager to have had lodgers?'

'Not really thought about it. No, I don't suppose it would.'

'You said you were young. How young? Could these men have been workers billeted on your family? What about prisoners of war?'

Spargo shook his head. 'No, it must have been after war or I wouldn't remember it. By the time I was seven my father was using the extension's ground floor room as an office, which meant they had gone by then. I can't remember much, to be honest. I can't even remember my first day at school.'

'But you remember the men?'

'You asked about lodgers. Something clicked.'

Mitchell forced a smile. 'Interesting, but hardly relevant. I'm sorry, Mr Spargo, I must get on.' His eyes assumed a life of their own, his gaze darting from Spargo to the box, from the box to the small clock on his desk and then to the door. 'I will need you to sign for these,' he said, pointing.

'Did the translator say anything about value?'

'Personal interest only, apparently. They're in such poor condition he didn't think a museum would be interested in them. I'm not sure I agree. For someone with the language, willing to take the trouble...'

'After what happened to my mother I'm not sure I want to keep them. I have no wish to drag up the past. Nor do I want to give that dubious pleasure to anyone else.'

'That's up to you, Mr Spargo. What I need is a signature. Oh, and there's the translator's notes.' He held out a large brown envelope. 'I've made you a copy. There's so little there, it's hardly worth reading.'

Spargo folded the envelope and tucked it into a pocket. Mitchell left the room and returned with a form that Spargo signed.

Outside, car engine running and heater on, Spargo took from the envelope two badly-stapled pages. Propping them against the steering wheel he started to read.

The first page of the translation contained handwritten comments. The translator had received from Northern Constabulary twelve bound notebooks in poor condition. He added that the books appeared to be diaries and he'd had difficulty separating the pages. He flipped to the second stapled sheet. On it he found a short, typed translation:

'Arrived K late afternoon. Reported to Moehle. For me, new boots and new leathers. Not before time. Still no hint of promotion. Korvettenkapitän would have had a nice ring to it'

The translator had pencilled a note that the year was nineteen forty-two. Spargo stared at the pages, turning them over in anticipation of more. Had the man really done so little? Probably just enough to demonstrate to Mitchell the books had no bearing on his case.

As Spargo slipped the papers into the envelope his mobile rang. It was Stuart Main.

'Mr Spargo. Sorry to trouble you.'

'Stuart? Problems?'

'Nothing I can't deal with, Mr Spargo. Just thought you should know I'm having a wee bit of bother with a newspaper man. He's been sniffing around, asking my neighbours if I was the man who cleared the Spargo house at Kilcreg. He was here today.'

'Did you get his name?'

'I've got his business card somewhere.' Spargo heard a clatter as Main dropped his phone. 'Sorry Mr Spargo, I must have left it in the van. He calls himself a freelance investigative journalist. Seemed to think you'd always lived in the cottage and I told him he was wrong. I didn't want to tell him anything, but you know what they're like. I didn't think you'd want him printing lies.'

'Thanks for telling me. I'm in Inverness. I've been with the police. Would you like me to call them and tell them?'

'No need. I can deal with the nosey wee shite. Just thought you should know.'

As Spargo was leaving Inverness he had a second call and he pulled in and parked. The voice was loud, harsh, and instantly recognisable.

'Hey, Old Man! How the hell are you?'

The mock middle-English was a voice from the past. If Murphy had ever possessed an Irish accent it was long-gone. For as long as Spargo had known him, his former partner had spoken like a British army officer in a nineteen fifties movie. Spargo feigned pleasure.

'Hey, Murph! Where are you?'

A slip of the tongue. The where should have been how. It was a subconscious desire to hear Murphy was far away from him as it was possible to be.

'Same old place.'

'Vancouver? Still with the same mob?'

'Still the same mob. I can't talk for long, just checking you are around. I have a meeting in Oslo in a day or so. Thought I might stop off at Shannon and fly to Turnhouse. That's if you are not too busy, of course.'

'It's Edinburgh International, not Turnhouse. It's a big place now. You won't recognise it.'

'So what are you up to? How's things?'

'Not good. You remember the time I took you to Kilcreg? You met my mother.'

'How can I forget? I slept on a sofa with my feet over the end, it was a good one foot shorter than I was. Bloody uncomfortable if you don't mind me saying.'

'Last month some bastard kicked her to death.'

Brutal words. Spargo saw no reason to hold back. Murphy gasped, then silence. Then the condolences and questions.

Spargo's back garden in Edinburgh was several feet lower than the front. It gave access to a basement room he used as a store, a room deep enough for him to hang a full-length ladder on a side wall and wide enough to have a workbench, three filing cabinets and several stacks of archive boxes along the back.

On his return from Inverness he trundled his wheelbarrow to the back of his car and tumbled the bronze box into it. In the basement he spread old towels on his workbench and laid the books on it, spacing them out in the hope they would dry. He selected one and opened it, taking care not to damage its pages. The writing, in a deliberate hand in black ink, had soaked through the paper, staining adjacent pages with a tangle of words.

For those with a command of the language the words were just about readable. On the open pages was a date, Mittwoch, Januar 10 1945. No mysteries there. Mittwoch is middle of the week, Wednesday. Spargo turned more pages. Understood nothing else.

The basement doubled as a store for items Spargo occasionally bought in bulk. Shelves held flat-packed archive boxes, paper for printers and household consumables – amongst them, paper towels. He went for a pack, started to tear off sheets and stack them beside the damp diaries. Then, settling himself on a tall stool, he worked his way slowly and painstakingly through the first book, separating pages and inserting the paper towel sheets between them.

Spargo had almost exhausted the paper pile when something in a margin caught his eye. Handwritten in black ink, several times as if practising, was a signature. Each one was neater than the last, as if getting it right mattered.

Minutes later he was in the garden, phoning Jez. He got her answering machine so he tried her mobile. She answered immediately.

'Just got home from Inverness,' he said. 'I have something to show you.'

'You mean right now?'

'I can come to your place.'

'I'm not at home, I'm at King's, I'm working late. If it's really important I can call in on my way home. I can't stay long.'

If Jez was planning to see Joby, Spargo didn't feel guilty. Her boyfriend had a key to her flat and often cooked for her, a good sign, he supposed. It revealed a degree of domestication. A brownie point, then. Probably the only one.

While he waited for Jez he went to his office to check his emails. There were very few. After deleting all the predatory spam he was left with one message:

JOHN SPARGO YOU ARE OUT OF YOUR DEPTH

Amused, Spargo wondered if the sender was referring to the whole of his life or just one particular part. Murphy was a joker. Murphy did things like that. Expecting more on the page he scrolled down but there was nothing.

The mail came from an account with a meaningless name, no doubt created just to send this one message. Last year he'd had five hundred business cards printed, all with his email address. Since then he had given away most of them. The email could have come from anyone.

CHAPTER SEVENTEEN

THEO'S ALTER EGO VOGEL has had an uneventful war. His service record shows no distinctions, no bravery awards, not even a campaign medal. Walter, Theo realises as he reads, has downgraded Theo's war efforts to those of a deskbound clerk.

Walter returns at dusk. Says he was unavoidably detained.

'Have you eaten?' he asks. 'Did my staff feed you?'

'An orderly brought food. A different man. He didn't speak. Made me feel like a zoo animal.'

'That is how it should be. They do not know who you are. This place is a privileged posting and all newcomers are a sign of change, they pose a threat. Also, the Reichsmarschall is here and they are all tense. Now come, we have work to do. Put on your greatcoat.'

A car is parked under trees. Walter walks towards the driver's door and hesitates. Asks Theo if he can drive.

'Then drive me,' Walter says. 'Make yourself useful. Drive towards the house. Keep your speed down and keep your lights switched off. They are no damn good anyway.'

Theo does as Walter says. Following his directions he drives down the road that previously they had walked down.

'Not so fast, walking pace is good. There is a crossroads here hidden by trees. If there is nothing else on the road then turn left. If you see other vehicles then wait until they have gone.'

Despite the blackout, an electric lamp lights an archway. Theo's view is restricted by neat rows of bushes and to see if the road is clear he peers around them. To his right is an archway; beyond it, in a blaze of light, is an imposing entrance to what looks like a medieval manor house. Sure nothing is coming Theo turns the steering wheel to go left and lets in the clutch but he does it too quickly and the car's engine stalls. A single headlight bears down on them from out of the trees, a motorcycle travelling fast. Theo pulls the starter. After the third attempt the engine restarts. He rams the gears into reverse and jerks the car back.

'You damn fool!' Walter snaps. 'A traffic accident on the Reichsmarschall's front drive is all I need. I should have driven.'

'I'm sorry. I have never driven an Opel.'

The motorcycle passes in front of them. It is ridden by a despatch rider who switches off his engine and drifts silently under the arch and into the courtyard, stopping at the main Carinhall door.

'Go!' Walter snaps. 'Get out of here! I will give you directions.'

'I saw a stag back there,' Theo says quietly when they are under way again. 'In the courtyard. I'm sure of it.'

'What you saw was a bronze statue. Our Hermann appointed himself Hunting Master of the Reich. He even designed his own uniform.'

'They say he was out hunting when the enemy invaded France.'

'Who says? Who are *they*?'

'It is common knowledge.'

'Then common knowledge is right. He was here. Whether or not he was hunting is another matter. It is not widely known that he has a command post here. It is most probably better for him to be here than in Berlin. The Reichsmarschall is treated by many as a joke, no doubt you heard that too. Do you know he was in Baron von Richtofen's air squadron in the Kaiser's war? Do you know he took over the fighter formation when Richtofen was killed? He was shot-up badly and still suffers from those wounds and others he received later.

'I really know nothing about him.'

'Apart from what you hear in rumours.'

'Are they all untrue?'

'Quite the contrary. The Reichsmarschall is out of favour. He failed to bomb England to its knees and now he fails again at the Russian Front. He is unable to give adequate air support or to supply our troops.'

'It would be better you did not say these things.'

'Are you saying I cannot trust you, Theodor? Switch on your lights.'

'Where is the switch?'

Walter reaches forwards and the lights come on. The headlights are masked; most of the light from the car's low wattage bulbs is blocked by steel strips, and what little gets through is aimed downwards. Driving with the headlights seems worse than driving without them.

Theo concentrates on the road. When they pass the stone gatehouses and the farm he realises he is on the road they came in on. It isn't long before the despatch rider that came to the house comes up behind them and then overtakes them, travelling fast, a rear-light glow that fades quickly.

'Where are we going?' Theo asks.

'You do not need to know.'

For all Theo knows they are returning to Berlin. During the drive he entertains fantasies about making a break for it. There would be no point travelling south, it is too late for that, it would have to be Bremen and back to his boat. He thinks up a story to tell his commandant, how he was robbed of his uniform, his papers and belongings, and how the men at an airbase lent him clothes. Or should he tell the truth, tell how he was kidnapped? Chances are that with the wrong papers he wouldn't get past the dockyard guards.

Walter has been dozing. He jerks awake, squints through the windscreen and shouts.

'Turn, turn now! Ah… that was the turning. Don't try to reverse, you can't see a thing. Keep driving. In a kilometre or so you can turn around.'

Five more minutes and they are on the right road. Up ahead is a line of vehicles parked close to what looks to Theo like a high wall. It takes Theo a while to realise that what he thought was a wall is a long train of boxcars on a railway siding. Airmen are loading them, struggling with boxes. He asks Walter where he should go but he gets no response. Walter is watching through the windscreen, concentrating on men unloading a crate from the back of a lorry. One of them stumbles; the others can't hold the crate on their own and for a second or two it teeters, then it falls. As it strikes the ground Walter is out of the car and running, shouting abuse.

Theo watches. Walter is at the truck, beating one hand on the dropped crate and waving the other in the air. Leaving Walter to rant, Theo walks beside the train towards the sound of blown steam. The boxcars jerk, their buffers clank. A locomotive is up front, being coupled to the train.

When Theo finally reaches the engine he stands in the shadows and watches its crew, one with a hand-lamp, the other with an oil can. The driver is in the cab of his engine, cleaning and checking. Lit by the glow of his firebox he is tapping gauges and adjusting brass taps. Theo recalls the times he watched such things, side by side in silence with Walter, making notes in their books – the loco's number, its wheel configurations and running gear, the place, the date and the time. The number of wagons or coaches.

And its type, course.

'P38,' he mumbles. 'Four-six-zero.'

'It is a fine locomotive, is it not?'

The voice startles him, makes him jump – an action never seen by his crewmen. The hidden voice talks on. It is deep and gruff.

'Unfortunately it is grossly underpowered.'

Theo spins on his heel. He is no more than arm's length from a man concealed partly by darkness, a man unusually large and who wears a long overcoat. Theo is aware the man can't see him properly either, he is struggling to see Theo's face.

'The trains are usually pulled by one of our Kreigslok locomotives, occasionally by two of them... do I know you?'

Theo, remembering Walter's threats, hesitates. Surely, talking to the rail superintendent can do no harm?

'No, I am sure I do not know you,' the man says. 'You have recently transferred? From where?'

'My name is Vogel. I am with Major Wolff. I have – '

Theo checks himself. Telling a stranger such things is madness.

'Ah yes. Of course. You arrived yesterday. You were with the Air Ministry in Berlin, is that not correct?'

So much for Walter's secrecy. The whole world seems to know.

'It is not right to speak of these things.'

'Very well. But it is clear to me you know about locomotives. Surely to talk about such things can do no harm?'

Theo's instinct is to say nothing, but surely the man is right. Talking about a railway locomotive can do no harm.

'I watched them when I was a boy.'

He is about to say more – that the P38 is indeed underpowered – but he is interrupted by shouts from far off. Walter is calling him. 'I apologise,' Theo says, stepping away. 'I must go.'

He hurries away. The transfer of crates has finished. The troops are slamming boxcar doors and lifting the tailgates of their trucks.

'Who was that?' Walter asks. 'I saw you talking. I told you to speak to no-one.'

'I said nothing, he did the talking. It was the station superintendent. He wanted to talk about trains.'

For the next two days Walter spends very little time with Theo. He explains he is working in the great hall of Göring's mansion. On the third day he comes early for Theo, telling him Göring is no longer at Carinhall and, at last, the two of them can work together.

Before Theo enters the vast timbered space of the great hall Walter hands him a pad and a pencil. He warns him to say nothing and to plead ignorance if questioned. Four airmen approach them along a corridor, two pulling a trolley, the others supporting two large crates it is carrying. Walter stops them. He checks the markings on the side of the boxes with those on his list.

'One crate at a time, Corporal,' he says. 'How many times must I tell you?'

The man nods and salutes. As Walter walks away the men lift one of the crates and set it down in the corridor. Walter stops, turns, and struts back to them.

'Don't leave it here, Corporal. Return it to the hall. How can the Reichsmarschall's treasures be catalogued if you leave them scattered around the place? Do you not know the value of that piece? Do you actually know what you are handling here?'

Theo stands back, watching and listening. To him, the trolley could easily have held twice as many crates. If it had been him, supervising the loading of stores and munitions he would have remonstrated with the men for not carrying enough. He makes accidental eye contact with the corporal, and feeling uneasy he glances down at his pad. As a U-boat commander, Theo excels. As an actor, he fails miserably. He turns and sets off after Walter.

'What is in the crate, the one they removed?'

'I have absolutely no idea.'

The immensity of the great hall reminds Theo of the submarine pens at Saint-Nazaire in France, though there are no other similarities because the Saint-Nazaire bunkers are square-sided and constructed of concrete whereas Göring's hall is palatial. Massive timbers span the roof. From them hang circular chandeliers the size of cartwheels, studded with electric bulbs that light the room like small suns; carpets hang on the walls between high arched windows and heavy oak beams. Tapestries, Theo realises. Like in museums.

One of the walls is bare. The tapestries, ornaments, paintings and statues that once adorned them have been packed away, taken to the railway and loaded into boxcars. The solid furnishings – tables, chairs and sideboards – have been moved, stacked at one end of the hall in a pyramid of stained and polished timber. Paintings in gilt frames have been propped against a wall like a huge deck of cards. Walter sees them and hurries towards them. Theo tags along, stepping over a roll of carpet at least as long as two torpedoes. Walter starts raving.

'Good god, those incompetents! Look at this! It is just as well the Reichsmarschall is not here!'

'Heads would roll?'

Walter glares at him. Theo raises his eyebrows. They are the only ones left in the room. Who does Walter think he is impressing?

'I have a job to do, Theodor. You might well have been a hero in your own little world but all that is behind you. It is better if you to keep your thoughts to yourself.'

'Are you responsible for all this? For moving Göring's stuff?'

'While you are here you would be wise to use his title. And no, it is not my responsibility to relocate the Reichsmarschall's treasures. I am an observer.'

Theo considers this. Walter's presence here is a sham. There is something underhand going on and he, Theo, has become a key part of it. Perhaps Göring's great hall is the place to tackle him again. He looks around. They are still alone.

'What are you up to, Walter? What have you got me into?'

Walter is unsure how to respond. Theo waits for the usual outburst and threats. Though they are alone he speaks quietly.

'I cannot tell you.'

'You cannot tell me now, or cannot tell me ever? What is going to happen to me, Walter? Will someone put a bullet in my head?'

'It is not like that.'

'Then tell me what it is like. I can hardly betray you. I'm in Göring's house, I'm carrying a blank pad, I'm pretending to assist you – '

'You are assisting me.'

'– pretending to assist you in something I know nothing about.'

'Nothing you say matters. This war will soon be over. The British and Americans are close to Strasbourg and the Soviets are already in East Prussia. We must do what we can.'

'Are they really so close?'

'This Reich is finished, Theodor. It is only a matter of time. The Reichsmarschall is transporting these items to safety. I told you that.'

'So even in these times there are trains for the Reichsmarschall?'

Theo has been kept from his son by works of art. In today's Germany, sculptures and paintings take precedence over his countrymen's lives.

'The Reichsmarschall has always had trains for his own exclusive use. To my knowledge he has at least three.'

He is about to say more when a man appears at the far end of the hall. He runs halfway to Walter and calls out.

'Major Wolff, there is a telephone call…'

Walter moves quickly. Theo follows, along a corridor to a small room with two desks. A woman is typing. The man is already there, holding the phone at arm's length, his free hand covering the mouthpiece.

'It is Herr Kropp, Herr Major.'

Walter snatches the phone, puts it to one ear, changes his mind and moves it to the other. He places the pad he is carrying on the desk and reaches for a pencil.

'Robert, Good Morning! It is a pleasure to hear from you. What can I do for you?'

Theo watches as Walter's frown deepens. The more he listens the more worried he seems. He is tapping the pencil on the pad.

'The Reichsmarschall? Are you sure of that? I was told… yes, of course, I did not mean – '

The woman is no longer typing. The room is silent. Walter holds a hand to his free ear to block out noise that isn't there.

'I didn't know he was still here. I was told he was away, preparing for his birthday celebrations. Are you sure that is who he asked for? Yes, yes of course, Robert, he is here, I shall do it immediately.'

Walter slams the phone back on its rest, grabs Theo by the arm and hauls him into the corridor.

'Tell me,' he says, his words hissed through his teeth. 'The man you were speaking to last night, what did he look like?'

'It was dark, I didn't see. A big man, hair slicked back. He wore a heavy overcoat.'

'You said he was the station superintendent. Why did you think that? I have met the station superintendent. He is thin and has only one leg. Also, he also wears a uniform, as do all railway employees.'

'I didn't know that. The station superintendent at Braunschweig wore an overcoat and a felt hat.'

Walter scowls. 'Tell me exactly what you said to him.'

'He mentioned the locomotive. He asked me if I was new here. Then he said I came from Berlin. He knew that, he didn't have to ask.'

'What else?'

'Only that I used to have an interest in trains.'

'Did you mention us? Where we used to go, you and I?'

'Why would I do that?'

'Answer me! Did you say we knew one another?'

'He knew I was with you. I think I had been mumbling to myself that the railway engine was a P38. He was in the shadows, I didn't see him properly. He said those engines were underpowered, and that the trains were usually pulled by a Kreigslok.'

'What the hell is a Kreigslok?'

'Our new wartime locomotives. I thought – '

'You seem to have excelled yourself, Theodor,' Walter hisses quietly, his eyes glancing back into the room and then fixing on

Theo's. 'Your friendly Station Superintendent just happened to be our Reichsmarschall. He wants to see us.'

Walter wipes his brow with his sleeve. Though it isn't at all cold he is sweating. Theo frowns.

'You said he had left here.'

'I was wrong. You say one word out of place to him and we are dead men. You have studied your dossier, you know what to say if you are asked. You are an administrator, not a flier. Because of your mechanical skills you gained rapid promotion but your job has always been mundane. Your job is to check requisitions for military supplies. Do understand me?'

'I don't understand why you are telling me this. We have been through this before.'

Instead of taking a direct route through the house Walter takes Theo out to the courtyard. They seem to be walking in circles. Walter has lost his composure and is scurrying, beckoning with his hand and urging Theo to keep up.

Fixed to the wall above the great door to the main house is the largest pair of antlers Theo has ever seen. For an unguarded moment they bring to mind picture-book reindeers. He tells himself he has not actually been abducted to Santa Land, it just feels like it.

A man stands in the doorway, between the two bronze stags Theo saw last night. He is uniformed and slim, so definitely not Göring. As they get closer he takes a few steps forwards, nods to Walter and speaks directly to Theo.

'Herr Hauptmann, I am Robert Kropp, I am the Reichsmarschall's valet – though I'm sure the major has told you already. I am to conduct you to the Reichsmarschall, he is expecting you. Come quickly, we must not keep him waiting.'

Walter steps forwards but is blocked, unexpectedly, by Kropp's raised hand. With a flourish Kropp turns and sweeps his arm down, deftly beckoning Theo inside while blocking Walter with his shoulder. Though no words are spoken the message is clear. The Reichsmarschall wants Hauptmann Vogel.

CHAPTER EIGHTEEN

IT DIDN'T TAKE LONG for Midge Rollo to learn the Spargo woman's routine. He even followed her into King's Buildings and checked the name on her door: Dr Jessica Spargo. Also, he worked out the man with the Volvo, the old guy he sometimes saw with her, was her father.

Dr Jessica – Midge liked the name, it made what he was doing more personal – worked a fairly predictable week. Her father did not. Midge had followed him for a while. He lived in a smart bit of town called The Grange. Big detached houses and big cars.

There was another man who visited Dr Jessica fairly regularly, a boyfriend, Midge guessed, a man in his late twenties who travelled by bus – though every so often he turned up at her flat in a wee yellow car with a black folding top. It was Friday, so no doubt he would be at the flat now, waiting for Dr Jessica to return home from work.

Midge was in his car, parked outside her work, facing the way he always faced while he waited for her. Sometimes the waiting was like watching paint dry. Other times she surprised him by leaving early. She left on time today but still she surprised him – she turned left instead of her usual right.

Midge panicked. In the daily report he left on the answering machine at the number Mr Luis had given him he was always honest. If he tailed Dr Jessica and lost her he would say so. To his embarrassment he had lost her once already, and that was a misfortune – an appropriate word. To lose her twice would be carelessness, he had read that somewhere.

He started his car and pulled away from the kerb. Misjudging the U-turn he managed to jam his car across the road at the same time as an ambulance approached in a blaze of blue lights. It managed to avoid Midge by little more than a hand's width and by the time his car had turned, Jez's bike had vanished.

Spargo, separating pages in his basement, heard the buzz of Jez's bike as she bounced in off the road. Leaving the basement he trotted up the slope beside the house and met her half way. She was removing her helmet and tossing back her hair.

'I went into the old place,' he said as a greeting. 'The mine house, I mean. I found a box.'

She walked past him and didn't reply. In the light from the basement fluorescents he caught a glimpse of disapproval. It reminded him of Theresa.

'That place is a death trap,' she mumbled. 'Didn't the chimney stack collapse? Doesn't the sign say it's a dangerous structure?'

'I was careful. I knew what I was doing. I remembered something my father used to say, that if a thing was ready to go in the roof – '

'It was ready for the tip,' Jez said, hurrying him on. 'Yes Dad, I know that. I've heard that a thou – '

'So why did he have a shed full of junk on the mine?'

'I didn't know he had. Perhaps the attic was full. Perhaps all those years he had a secret stash of junk in the roof.'

'That's the puzzle. He didn't, and it got me thinking. What if he had something up there he didn't want anyone to see?'

'God, you're not going to tell me you went up there? On your own?'

'I knew what I was doing.'

More disapproval, this time a fierce stare. 'So you said. Why are you limping?'

'I'm not.'

'When you came up to meet me you were limping.'

'As I was saying, I found a box, it was wrapped in canvas and bound tight with – '

'Never mind that. What you have done to your leg?'

'It's nothing. That isn't why I asked you here. I want you to look at these.'

He turned in the doorway. Taking pains to walk confidently he led her to his workbench.

'Diaries,' he said. 'The police had to – '

'The police?'

The squares of paper towel Spargo had placed between the pages of the diaries now showed blue and black stains. With Jez standing beside him he turned to a marked page. She noticed the signatures in the margin before her father pointed it out: Reichsmarschall Hermann Göring, in a Germanic hand. She stared at the page, then picked up the book.

'Göring was Adolf Hitler's deputy. Are you saying these books were his?'

'Göring didn't write them. The police – Mitchell, the CID man – had some pages translated... well, part of one page. They are all in the same hand, all written by a German naval officer. There's a date in this one, nineteen-forty-five.'

'Why is it wet?.' She turned her attention to the other diaries, bulging with damp paper towels. 'Were these in the roof? Of the mine house? In a box? Tell me why the CID are involved.'

'I thought Mitchell should see it.'

She grunted. 'Did he see these signatures?'

'I don't think he bothered to look through them.'

She mumbled something. Then, so Spargo could hear, 'So why would a naval officer be practising Hermann Göring's signature? And why are they wet?'

'Apparently the translator who took it upon himself to soak them. Mitchell wasn't pleased.'

Spargo started to ease more pages apart.

'Don't!' Jez snapped. 'You'll tear them!'

'I want to show you some other pages.'

'Yes, Dad, they look interesting. I'm not sure why you were so keen to show me them now. They have been in that roof for over fifty years. Another day isn't going to make any difference.'

'Whoever murdered Gran was looking for something. When I found the package I thought I'd found what they were after.'

'So you were playing detective. Why didn't you explain your

theories to the police and let them search the house?'

'I didn't see any point in troubling them. What if there'd been nothing up there?'

'What if there was only a box of old diaries?'

He smiled, picked up Mitchell's brown envelope, tipped it up and handed the folded sheets to her. She read them, turning them over as he had done, to see if there was anything on the back.

'This is the translation? Is this all?'

'That's all.'

'Because the pages of the diaries were stuck together?'

'Mitchell didn't think they were. Not before he sent them.'

'Soaking them seems an odd thing for a professional to do. What if the ink ran?'

'As you can see, some of it has. I was thinking of throwing them out. Is it worth having them looked at? Presumably my father kept them there for a reason.'

'Looked at? Translated, you mean? It's an expensive business.' She picked up a different diary but didn't attempt to open it. 'Give me a couple of days, I'll ask around at work. No promises though. I don't really know who to ask.' She turned her attention to the box, crouching down and examining it. 'They were in this? What's it made of, gunmetal?'

'Bronze.'

She put her hand into it, ran a finger around the bottom and brought it out smeared with mud.

'There's dirt in it.'

'Perhaps the translator used dirty water.'

Jez phoned next day to say she had found someone who might be able to help.

'An historian, Marie Howard. She can read old German script. I explained everything. I told her they looked like diaries and that one page had been translated. She wants to see them before she commits herself. I warned her they were in poor condition.'

'Does she want all of them?'

'Just one for now. Can you manage three o'clock, in town?'

'Today?'

'Today. This afternoon is the only time she's free.'

'No problem. Did I tell you I was meeting Murphy this evening?'

Jez fell silent. She had no time for her father's ex-partner.

'Is he staying over?' she asked.

'With me you mean? No, he's flying on to Aberdeen. He has a three hour stopover so I'm driving out to the airport to see him.'

'And you'll have a few drinks.'

'Most probably.'

'So why drive, when there is a perfectly good airport bus?'

Spargo arranged to meet Marie Howard in a bookshop in George Street. Needing the exercise he decided to walk, misjudging the distance and arriving five minutes late. Anxiously he pushed open the shop door, strode past the aisles of books and took the stairs to the coffee shop two at a time. He scanned the tables.

'You can't miss her,' Jez had said. 'She's a career academic and she looks the part, she wears her hair in a bun. Think Morningside ladies. Think Miss Jean Brodie.'

Of the several women Spargo at the tables only one had the right hair. She was, Spargo guessed, not much older than Jez. But she wore the clothes of a storybook middle aged spinster. Spargo positioned himself in front of her table and smiled. It wasn't returned. Her cup, containing a pale liquid he assumed was herbal tea, was half empty. He apologised for his lateness. Still po-faced she held out her hand, tilting it downwards as if offering it to be kissed. It seemed too dainty to shake so he held it and gave it a squeeze. She stiffened, and sat even more upright than before. Lines on her forehead deepened.

'Marie Howard,' she said. 'Jessica told me you had something that might interest me. A diary, did she say?'

She pronounced her words precisely, as if sounding the space between each one. By arriving at the coffee shop before him she had thwarted his first line of attack – he had planned to buy the drinks. He went to sit, then hesitated and pointed to her cup.

'I'll just go and get myself one of those,' he mumbled. 'Well, maybe not one of those.'

He gave her a quick, on-and-off smile and turned his back to her, sharply and deliberately. The alternative would have been to walk backwards as if retreating from royalty. At the counter he ordered an espresso, hoping a double shot of caffeine might sharpen his wits. He carried the cup to her table – most definitely her table – and set it down carefully. Shifted it sideways so it wasn't close to hers.

The diary he'd brought with him was wrapped in a carrier bag and jammed in the pocket of his leather jacket – the jacket a present from Theresa for a birthday too far away to remember. The diary was bulky and the pocket small. Standing in the short queue at the counter he had managed to extract it and unwrap it. Now he presented it to Marie Howard, across the table top, narrowly missing his coffee.

'One of twelve,' he said. 'Jez said you might be able to understand it.'

She raised her eyebrows as if taking offence. Saying nothing she reached into a soft bag, took out designer specs and placed them low on her nose. Deciding to open the diary for her, Spargo reached over and turned it to face her. Before it was right around she took over, holding its covers between finger and thumb as if extracting it from a waste bin.

She started to read, with Spargo following every eye movement. Saw her stop at the foot of the page and then track back to the top.

'Where did you get this?'

'It's one of twelve.'

She peered at him over her glasses. 'So you said. I asked where, Mr Spargo, not how many.'

'I found them. I think they belonged to my father. They've been looked at already.' He got the cold stare again as if she had been given used goods. 'The translator soaked them,' he added. 'It's why that one's damp… why they are all damp.'

To make things easier he had removed the separating sheets of paper towel. Though the pages weren't quite dry there was little chance of them sticking. She went back to her reading.

'Who did you use?'

'Use?'

Again she looked over her glasses. 'Which translator, Mr Spargo.'

'I'm not sure. Someone in Inverness, I think. A retired teacher the police use.' Realising he had the answer to her question he unfolded the interpreter's pages. 'Lewis,' he said, reading the letterhead. 'He's not Inverness, he's here in Edinburgh.'

She returned to the diary. 'The writer, Volker, appears to be writing about his crew. They are all young men and they are keen, innocent like children, he says. I'm guessing, Mr Spargo, that what you have here are papers written by a naval man taking command of a German warship. He was expecting a promotion that didn't come. He says here: 'No sign of the promotion. Korvettenkapitän Theodor Volker would have sounded good'. I happen to know Korvettenkapitän is the equivalent of Lieutenant Commander.'

Spargo picked up the translation and re-read Lewis's words. 'That's wrong. That isn't what it says.'

Without giving him time to complete his sentence she rapped the table aggressively with her knuckles and read words loudly, in German. People around them stared.

'No,' Spargo interrupted. 'I don't mean you are wrong. What I'm saying is that Lewis's translation differs from yours. Lewis simply says Korvettenkapitän would have had a nice ring to it.'

She huffed. 'That is simply the translator's style. I said it would have sounded good. He said it would have had a nice ring to it. Same thing.'

'No, not that, I didn't mean that. Lewis doesn't mention a name. He doesn't say Theodor Volker.'

'See for yourself,' she said. 'You don't have to be able to read German to see the man's name. Look at it, Mr Spargo. If you don't trust me to get it right there really is no point in continuing.'

Jez had sent him a vampire. If Marie was willing to work for free he could handle her quirkiness. If she expected him to pay then he would find someone more amicable – not that he would have any choice in the matter because Little Miss Huffy was already taking off her glasses and getting up from the table.

'I wasn't implying you were wrong,' Spargo pleaded. 'What I meant was that the translations were different. Yours is right, of course. Look at this sheet the police gave me. Why would a translator omit Volker's name?'

She settled down again, her back straight as if strapped to a plank.

'I have no idea.'

Ignoring him she concentrated again on the diary, turning the pages as if handling gold leaf. Spargo watched as he sipped his espresso. He was concerned she would come to the same conclusion as Lewis, that the diaries weren't worth the trouble of translating.

'So where is this bit about Göring?'

So that was it. Jez had told her about the signatures. It was how she had got Marie's interest, how she had set up a meeting so soon.

He took the book from her and found the marker he'd placed near the back.

'In the margin, here, Hermann Göring. Göring was Hitler's second in command.'

'I am well aware who Hermann Göring was.'

Raised eyebrows again as she read the page. She seemed hooked.

'I can't be sure,' she said after a while, 'but it appears the writer actually met Göring. He refers to things he has written elsewhere, so this isn't the first of his journals. I need to see them all, Mr Spargo.'

She closed the book, picked up her cup, and settled back as if trying to relax.

'I thought Göring ran the Luftwaffe?' Spargo said. 'Why would a naval man visit him?'

'He didn't just visit the man. From the little I've read so far it is possible he might have worked for him. There could be a book here for someone with the time to research it. Unfortunately at the moment that is not me, Mr Spargo, I can make no promises. If you want to take your items elsewhere then by all means do so.'

It was not the response he had been expecting. But as Jez had said, there was no hurry. The books had been hidden for years.

'Lewis told the police they are worthless,' he said.

'Do you mean he said the police are worthless, Mr Spargo? Or are you referring to the journals?'

He was in school again. He wondered if he should go and sit on the naughty chair.

'The books,' he said. 'The diaries.'

'They are not true diaries. I would prefer to call them journals. And I would take issue with the suggestion that they are of no value.

In fact I disagree most strongly.'

'I almost threw them out.'

'That would not have been wise.'

'Are they really valuable?'

'In terms of their content, to an historian researching this period, most definitely. Jessica told me she saw the other volumes, though she didn't inspect them. Are they all in the same condition as this one?'

'They are. I've been separating the pages and putting absorbent paper between them. Kitchen roll.'

'Don't even think of doing that. Bring the rest to me as soon as you can, I will see they are treated responsibly.'

Marie finished her tea and brushed herself down as if drinking tea left crumbs. Spargo gave her his business card. Without giving it a glance she tucked it into her bag, took out one of her own cards, inspected it, found a pen and scratched out her phone number.

'Bring them to my room. Do not telephone me, I am extraordinarily busy. If you really must contact me do it through Jessica.'

Spargo pocketed the card. Took back the journal.

'Some of the ink has run in the others too,' he said. 'I'm surprised it didn't all wash out. I'm surprised the paper didn't disintegrate.'

'I don't find it at all surprising. I am sure you are old enough to remember Indian Ink, Mr Spargo. It was waterproof, used in the days before permanent markers. The writer appears to have used it for most of his writings. Wherever he has not used it, the ink has started to run, as you say. Also, unless I'm mistaken, the pages are made from waterproofed paper. What I find surprising is that this man Lewis soaked them without your permission.'

'Maybe he thought the ink wouldn't run.'

'Is that what you believe, Mr Spargo? Have you considered the possibility he thought it would?'

CHAPTER NINETEEN

THEO'S THIGH-LENGTH BOOTS walk on Göring's soft carpets, past his paintings, his tapestries, his statues and carvings. This part of Carinhall has not yet had the attentions of the removal men. Now he climbs a staircase, one of several.

Theo follows two steps behind Kropp and climbs steadily, his mind a turmoil of thoughts as he tries to remember what he said to the man at the sidings. Had he been tactless, or stupid? He didn't think so. Even if he had, there are others who deal with detractors and those with loose tongues. One word from the man who holds the highest military rank in the land and he, Theo Volker – Theodor Vogel – would be a dead man.

More stairs – a narrow, short flight that leads to a small door. Kropp taps on it once and then, behaving the way an English butler might behave, he holds the door open and beckons to Theo. A flourish, like before.

Whatever Theo might have expected it is not this. That the stairs have brought him to a timber-framed room in the roof is no surprise; that it is so vast and so brightly lit is quite unexpected.

The loft is unfurnished. There is no room for furniture because covering the floor is the largest toy railway Theo has ever seen. There are stations and sidings, bridges and tunnels. Engines, coaches and wagons are lined up in rows. He corrects himself. These are not toys, they are models. The layout is awesome. He stands and stares at the loops and crossings, the telegraph posts and signals. There are even electric lamps inside the carriages. Near his feet is a model gun emplacement to protect the marshalling yard and its rows of wagons.

The door closes behind him and he glances back. Kropp is in the room, motionless and expressionless. Two trains are running with a continuous soft buzz, their wheels click-clicking over joins in the track. Above these sounds Theo hears a command, sharp and loud. He sees, down on both knees in a distant corner of the room, the unmistakable mass of the Reichsmarschall.

'Vogel, come! I have dropped a small screw.'

Kropp moves quickly. Göring looks up. 'No, Vogel will find it. Leave us, Robert. I have mislaid my pipe, I think it is in my study. Find it and bring it to me.'

The valet leaves. Göring struggles to his feet, raising himself the way an elephant might raise itself, rolling and struggling. The man is immense, easily the largest person Theo has ever seen. Apart from the man's size he recognises only the dark, receding, swept back hair. It is held in place with oil and a quiff has fallen over his eyes. He sweeps it back with a fat white hand.

'Come here. Help me. The screw is brass, it is very small.' He holds a finger and thumb apart, just a fraction. Theo, aware of his awkward, still unfamiliar boots, walks forwards with care. The Reichsmarschall regards him from beneath heavy, canopied brows.

'Do you have model trains, Vogel?'

'I do not, Herr Reichsmarschall.'

His voice is shaky and uneven and he coughs as if to clear his throat. He hesitates, wondering if he should repeat his words more confidently. Instead he lies face down and squints along the flat floor, something the big man couldn't do if he tried. The screw is there. He picks it up. Places it on a podgy palm.

'Good, good! But you have seen model railways?'

'Not like this one, Herr Reichsmarschall, not one so magnificent. Nor have I seen one powered by electricity, only those powered by clockwork.'

Göring looks at him with eyes that bore through his skull. He is being sized up, analysed. It unnerves him but he holds the gaze, his eyes lowered slightly so as not to stare. It is an act that feels safer than looking away – or worse still, looking down as if he has something to hide. Again he tries to shut his mind to fact he is wearing a uniform he is not entitled to wear, displaying a rank he does not hold, and carrying false papers in a name that is not his own.

Göring's stare does not falter. His lower lip is tucked frog-like under his upper one. The man is a massive, larger than life frog, far bigger than he appears to be in the few photographs Theo has seen in newspapers.

'Railways are a passion of mine,' Göring says, his ample chins quivering. 'I have track layouts elsewhere in the house and also outside. Perhaps you have seen them?'

Theo, unable to find words, shakes his head.

'No matter. You obviously know about locomotives.'

'I did not know it was you at the railhead, Herr Reichsmarschall. If I had realised then I would not –'

Göring waves a dismissive hand. 'No matter, Vogel. Stop that engine for me. Use the controller, the one on the bench. Tell me where you learned about trains.'

'When I was a boy I used to cycle to the sidings at Braunschweig. Sometimes we went to the branch line to Sauingen.'

'I don't know it.'

Göring is wearing a sleeveless leather jacket and breeches, laced below the knee. The breeches are larger than a coal sack and made from fine suede. One of his long socks has slipped slightly. Theo is sure the man cannot reach down to pull it up.

'You said we,' Göring says. 'Did you not go on these visits on your own?'

'Always with a friend.'

'You had friends. You were a lucky child. Was Major Wolff one of these friends?'

Theo pauses. He has made a mistake, but not to answer immediately is foolish. He forces a smile, as if by his pause he is reliving fond memories. This is no time to fabricate stories. One lie will only lead to another.

'He was, Herr Reichsmarschall.'

'For how long?'

'Until we were fifteen.'

'But you kept in touch?'

'Unfortunately we did not. He moved away.'

He wanted to add that Major Wolff's father was a good Party man and that's why Walter had to move. He does not. It is gratuitous information. Just one wrong word…

'But Major Wolff is still a good friend?'

'A very good friend, Reichsmarschall.' It is a lie. There is no friendship now.

Göring walks away and busies himself with controls. Something buzzes at Theo's feet and he looks down. Points change, signals click. Even these are electric.

Kropp returns, apologises for the delay and hands his master a long curved meerschaum pipe with a bowl the size and shape of a duck's egg. Göring dismisses him again and concentrates on moving railway staff, changing their positions as if it matters.

Theo had imagined the leaders of the Reich to be wild men like Hitler, excitable and impassioned. The man before him is not a warlord, he is a tame circus bear.

'Major Wolff is a good officer,' Göring says. He sits down on the only chair in the room, a kitchen armchair so large it must surely have been made for him. He takes a tobacco pouch from a pocket and presses shreds of tobacco into the bowl of the pipe Kropp brought him. 'You said you did not keep in touch? That is regrettable. When a man has friends he should keep them.'

Theo watches. Any one of his personal collection of tobacco pipes would look lost against this one. He could do with a smoke himself but he has left his pipe in his quarters. And in any case, this is hardly the time or the place. Göring slaps his pockets, fumbling and searching. He looks towards the door as if about to call Kropp. Theo, sure he can help, dips a hand into the pocket of his own tunic, takes out his lighter and flicks the wheel. There are sparks but no flame. He tries again and again, embarrassed.

Göring laughs. 'You have a shortage of petrol, Hauptmann Vogel? It is a problem we have in these times.'

Göring resumes his fumbling until he finds his own lighter. Its flame flickers near the meerschaum bowl and is sucked down into the tobacco, which crackles. He holds out the lighter to Theo.

'Here!'

'Reichsmarschall?'

'Take it, Vogel. Your need is greater than mine.'

Theo hesitates. Embarrassed again, he takes it. It is small but heavy, undoubtedly solid silver. On one side is an embossed gold eagle.

'That is kind of you, Reichsmarschall. But I can get petrol for – '

Göring fixes him with the glare of a displeased schoolmaster. Theo nods and smiles. For effect he fondles the lighter, admiring it while Göring looks on. Not yet confident enough to put it in his pocket he keeps hold of it, as if keeping it ready for use.

'It is an exquisite piece, Reichsmarschall. I shall treasure it.'

Göring grunts. There is no way to know what he is thinking. The moment appears to be forgotten as Göring bends forwards, picks up a loco and carriage, uncouples them and holds out the loco. Theo takes it. Feels sure that if he drops it he will die.

'Designed by Richard Garbe, Vogel. Did you know that?'

'I beg your pardon, Reichsmarschall?'

'The locomotive is a reproduction of the P38 you saw. It was designed by Richard Garbe. Do you know it is now the world's most numerous passenger locomotive? Our engineering is truly unbeatable. And the Class Five… do you know about the Class Five?'

'Of course, Herr Reichsmarschall. One of our locos reached two hundred kilometres per hour on the Berlin-Hamburg run. Truly an excellent run.'

'You are incorrect. Its speed was two hundred point-four kilometres per hour.'

'It is unfortunate we were beaten by the British.'

Göring turns sharply. This time the glare is withering – frightening, even – a look that conveys disbelief. The man has a very short fuse. Perhaps he is not a tame bear.

'Reichsmarschall, it is unfortunate that we no longer hold the world speed record.'

Göring looks away and tinkers with carriages. 'Unfortunate indeed, Vogel. But the British Pacifics are fine locomotives.'

'It was hardly a fair trial.'

A stare now, inquiring rather than vicious. It is accompanied by an upturned eyebrow. 'Explain?'

'Our engine pulled a 297 tonne train on a level track. The British Mallard pulled only 240 tonnes. And it was running downhill when it reached its highest speed.'

Göring's face beams like a child's story-book moon.

'Is that true?'

Theo nods.

'Then it was no contest!' Göring looks around the room at the huge expanse of track. 'I do not yet have a model of a Class Five.' He steps across track and picks up a loco. 'This is one of my favourites, Vogel, it is made by Märklin. Take it, look at the headlights on the buffer, they have real electric bulbs. Do you know we made these for the British? We made models of their own engines and we dominated their market.' He takes the loco, returns it to the track and picks up another.

'This one is from Hornby, a British company. It is a model of an electric locomotive used on the London underground railway. It is the same gauge as my layout but unfortunately it is a different voltage and I burnt out the motor. For a few seconds it ran very fast.' He laughs, mischievously. 'Come, look at these, they are steam models, they burn spirit. Real steam, Vogel! What do you think of them?'

Theo stoops and chooses the smallest one, a black shunting engine he can hold confidently without fear of dropping it. He picks it up, supporting it with both hands the way he would hold a new born child. He wonders if Göring cleans and maintains the locomotives and rolling stock or if he has staff for such things. The loco smells of warm oil and he finds himself fighting an almost uncontrollable desire to say it reminds him of the smell of his torpedo rooms.

'It is well made,' he says. 'I have never seen such a fine piece of engineering.'

'I doubt that, Vogel. You are, after all, a Luftwaffe officer. Our aircraft are second to none.'

'Of course, Herr Reichsmarschall. But I have not had the pleasure of working with any. I am a humble administrator.'

Just one wrong word…

'Don't demean yourself. Everyone plays their part.'

For two hours they play trains like small boys. Göring, taking advantage of having a younger, more nimble helper, rearranges part of the layout. Theo stays alert throughout, ensuring the man gets his way at all times and wins at all things. The Reichsmarschall, he realises, is a dangerous, competitive man.

CHAPTER TWENTY

MARIE'S PROMPT DEPARTURE from the coffee shop suited Spargo. He would drop off the diaries – the journals – on his way to the airport to meet Murphy. On his way home he changed his mind, deciding that the sooner he took the journals to Marie, the sooner she'd get hooked on their contents.

Home again, he went straight to the basement. He eased the door key from its hiding place behind the gas meter box, unlocked the door and went inside.

The basement, as always, was in darkness, its only window blocked by dense shrubs that grew close to the house. Switching on the light was always a trial because the basement door opened inwards, and for some reason the light switch was on the hinged side of the door. It had always annoyed him that he had to step around the door in the dark. Some day, he told himself, he would get around to changing it.

The lights flickered and pinged. Got brighter, slowly.

He realised, as he returned the journal in his hand to the workbench, that he hadn't yet looked at the card Marie gave him. Looking at it now he realised she wasn't at King's Buildings as he'd thought, but in a steep, tight lane off Edinburgh's Royal Mile.

It took Spargo almost an hour to remove all the soft paper from between the leaves of the journals. The pages were passably dry but the extra thickness of paper had stretched the bindings and pulled at the spines. Soon he had them encased in bubble-wrap and packed in an old rucksack. He gasped as he heaved it onto his back.

He took a bus to the National Museum on Chambers Street, a recently completed building in toffee-tinted, raspberry-ripple stone. Driving wasn't an option; parking in Edinburgh, like in all other cities he knew, was a nightmare.

With one strap of the rucksack over his shoulder he set off towards the old university buildings. Before he reached them he turned into a cobbled lane and descended to Cowgate, a low level road flanked with tall, ancient buildings. Crossing it, he started the climb up to High Street. More cobbles – properly called stone setts – streets made for horses and carts. As he walked he checked numbers on doors. Reaching the Royal Mile without finding Marie's number he turned and retraced his steps.

The place he sought was set back in a weathered stone arch. Beside its heavy wooden door was a bell push mounted on a shiny metal speaker panel. He pressed it with his thumb and waited. Pressed it again. A tinny, possibly male voice, asked his business.

'I've got books for Marie Howard,' he said. 'My name's Spargo.'

The lock clunked and he shoved the door with his foot. It opened more easily than expected and crashed back against the wall, a move earning him a frown from the man at the reception desk. Following the man's directions Spargo ventured along corridors on floors of black boards; the building was old and the boards sloped sideways, causing him to realign himself constantly, like driving a car with a steering fault. He found the right door, tapped on it and opened it.

The building was once a private house. The room Spargo entered had been a sitting- or dining room and had two tall sash windows facing north; any views it might once have had were now blocked by the grey concrete wall of a building a few feet away. The ornate plaster mouldings on the ceiling had been painted so many times the paint was peeling away in onion-like layers.

What had once been a family home was now bleak and institutional, dark and unloved. Utilitarian furniture, none of which matched, stood around the room as if placed there by removal men and not yet rearranged. Large cardboard boxes, stacked in every spare space, were still sealed with tape. Others had been ripped open and rifled through, their contents stacked untidily beside them. Shoe-horned between the box piles were two wooden desks and at one of them sat a young woman. Early twenties, Spargo guessed. He took a couple of steps towards her. Floorboards creaked.

'My name's Spargo,' he said softly. 'I've brought books for Marie.'

'Marie's out. Don't know when she'll be back. She said put the books on her desk.'

Spargo slipped the rucksack off his shoulder. When it was halfway off he lost his grip and the bag, with its journals, hit the boards with a thud.

'They said it was temporary,' the young woman said, as if conscious of the state of the place. 'So we didn't unpack. That was twelve months ago.'

Spargo too, decided not to unpack. He dragged the rucksack across the floor, shoved it in beside Marie's desk, and asked for them to be pointed out to Marie.

Murphy's blond hair had receded since the two men last met. To Spargo, his old colleague looked even shorter than when they last met, an illusion – possibly – brought about by his increase in bulk and the quilted yellow jacket he wore. Humpty Dumpty on steroids.

'Hi, Old Man!' Humpty called out as Spargo approached. 'Shit luck about your mother. They got anyone?'

'Not yet.'

'World's full of weirdoes. How's work?'

'Plodding. Still doing a bit for Parsons. And there's always the Palumbo job.'

'That's still going?'

'For ever and ever. Not much money in it now, about one day a month. Two or three if I'm lucky.' They walked to the escalator and made for one of the airport's bars where they pulled out chairs, slumping in them casually with their legs outstretched. 'There's something else in the offing,' Spargo added. 'Could be big. Ever heard of a company called BarConSA?'

Murphy shook his head. 'Can't say I have. What is it, mining?'

'So they say.'

'Sounds Spanish? South American?'

'Based in Madrid. I've been to see them.'

'Getting yourself a serious job at last.'

Spargo hesitated. Didn't like counting his chickens. He wondered, for the first time ever, if Jez's distrust of Murphy had substance after all, and if confiding in him about jobs yet to come was wise.

'Doubt it,' he said. 'Sounds a bit like the Deep Vanguard thing, remember it? Made a big show of the drilling and then fled with the cash?'

'I remember it well. Unforeseen geological problems...'

'My very words to Jez.'

'It's what they all say. How is Jessica, still at university?'

'You could say that. She got her doctorate and then took a lecturing post. Doing quite well for herself by all accounts.'

'Didn't she do geology?'

Spargo nodded. 'She's dabbling in some forensic thing at the moment, trying to set up a new course.'

'Analysing mud from shoes.'

'Don't let her hear you say that. That's exactly what I said and she wasn't amused. She's good, Murph. You know what she's like. Once she gets her teeth into something.'

'Like father like daughter.'

'She tells me forensic geology has become quite a science.'

'It's still analysing mud from shoes.'

'She'd be the first to admit it's routine. Sounds to me like the more she does the more the police come to her. She's just done an interesting hit and run. Found three distinct soil types in the muck left in the road after the smash.'

'That's fine if you've got control samples. For it to be any use you'd need a database of soil descriptions from every square metre of Britain.'

'Not if you've got dirt from a suspect vehicle. She says you'd be surprised how much muck collects in crevices under wheel arches.'

'The first thing I'd do is find a car wash and blast all the shit from under the wings.'

'That's because you think like a criminal. They don't though, do they? They don't always think straight.'

'Does this mean she's friendly with coppers?'

'There's one in particular. Not sure she's that friendly with him – though he might be preferable to the article she's with at the moment.

Calls himself a communications executive. Not sure what that is and I don't want to ask.'

'Sounds like you're running the girl's life for her. Get your arse out of her road. Let her do her own thing.'

'You don't know her, Murph. She takes no notice of what I say. So you're off to Oslo? What time's the flight?'

Murphy looked at his watch. 'If you're worrying about not having time for a few jars, I told you, I've got three bloody hours. Aberdeen tonight, meeting first thing tomorrow. I promised a colleague back home I would look at a drilling motor at Hughes. Then I'm booked out to Oslo.'

The evening was something of a success, plenty of reminiscing and swapping news. Murphy hadn't been the right business partner for Spargo. That didn't mean he wasn't a friend. Of sorts.

Taking the bus to the airport had been a good move. Spargo had every intention of catching it back into town but when the time came to leave, the skies opened. With the back of his jacket tugged up over his head he dashed through the downpour to the line-up of taxies.

Twenty minutes later he dashed again, up the path beside his car. As he did so the security light high on the corner of his house came on, and in its light Spargo took the steps to his front door in one single leap. In the shelter of the stone canopy over the door he searched for his keys, found them, inserted one in the lock, started to turn it, and froze.

Recently he had been taking extra care to double lock the door. He knew he had turned the key clockwise twice. Then, to test it, he had unlocked and relocked it. Now it unlocked after only one turn. He had no doubt at all someone had been in the house.

Inside he repeated the checks he'd made when he returned from Spain. The rooms were untouched and the windows secure. But they would be, wouldn't they? You don't come in through a window when you have a key to the door.

He began to doubt himself. Perhaps he was wrong. Maybe his unlocking and locking had been muddled – and if that were true, then perhaps he hadn't locked the basement either, or switched off its lights.

Knowing how awkward it was to ease the basement key from behind the gas meter box in the dark, he took the spare key from a hook in the hall. With an umbrella in his hand he opened the front door. Rain beat noisily on the roof of the Volvo as he dashed to the basement.

The back garden was dimly lit, not by the basement light but the bright windows of the rooms he'd just visited. He was sure he was wasting his time. The basement light was off. The door would be locked, there was no point going further. He was becoming paranoid.

He was about to turn back when he remembered the words writ large on the wall of his Kilcreg classroom – A JOB WORTH DOING IS WORTH DOING WELL – words seen every school day for years and now etched on his brain. He kept going, down to the door.

Still certain the door was locked he grabbed its handle. Half-turning his body in readiness to go back, he gave the door a shove. The door opened unexpectedly and caught off balance he tumbled into the room. So did the door key.

Spargo, stooping, ran the flat of his hand over the floor. Though he'd heard the key chink on the floor, his sweeping hand didn't find it. Standing again he reached back for the door, but that wasn't there either. He had tumbled further into the room than he realised.

Bat-like, he listened to the reflections of his own small sounds. With a floor of plain concrete and a low ceiling the place had an echo of its own, an echo familiar to Spargo, an echo it didn't have now. It was muffled, not sharp like it should be. There was someone – or something – in the basement that should not be there.

CHAPTER TWENTY-ONE

THEO TAPS ON THE DOOR of the stable block room. It is snatched open by Walter, who stands in the doorway in a collarless shirt, his uniform trousers are pulled high on dark braces. His face is pale. He stares at Theo as if unsure what to say.

'You have been gone for four hours! 'What in god's name have you been doing?'

'Three and a half hours.'

'Don't get clever with me.'

'The Reichsmarschall has a model railway in a roof of the house. We were there.'

'You have been playing toy trains? With Göring?'

Theo smiles. 'I had no choice. He is not a man to argue with.'

'You are a bloody madman! Tell me what was said!'

'Locomotives… rail track… changes to his layout. Design of some of our locomotives. Full-size ones.'

'I want the truth, Volker. I want to know what questions he asked and what answers you gave. Did he mention me?'

'Only to say that you were a trustworthy officer.'

'Nothing else?'

'Nothing.'

'You would tell me if there was anything else?'

'Göring is not what I expected. I thought he would be more aggressive, more like our other leaders. More like our Führer.'

'He is not the man he used to be, he no longer behaves like a gangster. Did you notice the pills?'

'Pills? I thought they were sugar sweets. He had them in a tin. He swallowed one every few minutes.'

'Paracodeine. He was once addicted to morphine. I'm told his body is riddled with scars from his fighter pilot days. He swallows around one hundred of those things every day and they make him docile. He is so worried about his pallor that he uses rouge.'

'How do you dare to say these things, Walter? It is not good to talk like this.'

'And why not? We are not overheard. Surely you talk of such things with your fellow U-boat officers, those you trust? Are they so special that you trust them and not me?'

'We have been through this already. I no longer know you. How can you expect me to treat you like a friend?'

Walter nods. Considering how to respond he strokes his chin. 'Yes, we have been through all this. And you are right, the fault is mine. Over the years I have not made friends easily, it is difficult to know who to trust. But enough of this. Now you've had the dubious privilege of meeting Göring. What did you think of him?'

'It's difficult to say. I'm not used to that kind of company. I felt as if I was walking on eggs. I had to watch everything I did and said.'

'What was he wearing? Was he carrying his pistol?'

'Not that I noticed. He was wearing breeches and a hunting jacket. He was dressed as if he was about to go out to shoot deer with a bow and arrow. Or maybe people.'

'You would have noticed his pistol. It is American, a Smith and Wesson revolver, a cowboy's gun. Since the attempt to kill Hitler he's armed himself with it. He even has a Stetson, a wide-brimmed cowboy hat he wears when he's hunting. He is fond of America. You would not believe how dismayed he was when they entered the war.'

'Have you been involved with him for so long?'

'I have never met him. These are things I hear. It is my job to know such things.'

Theo nods slowly. 'So tell me, Walter. What exactly is your job?'

Hoping Walter will at last open up to him, Theo suggests they eat together in Theo's hut. To his surprise Walter readily agrees, admitting he finds eating in the officer's mess difficult.

'I was a damn fool to assume the rank of Major,' he says. 'It means I am answerable to higher ranks. In this place there are many and they ask too many questions. I should have taken the rank of Generalmajor. But I was told that if I had high rank I would draw attention to myself.'

'Who told you? And how could you give yourself a higher rank?'

Walter doesn't respond. They are walking to the hut. When they reach it Theo goes for the door but Walter stops him and turns and looks back. There is nobody, nothing but the track and tall trees.

'Don't go in.' he says. 'Keep walking. We have things to discuss. Take the path through the trees.' He points. 'No, not that way. That path there…'

'You were going to tell me about your job.'

'Keep quiet, I will do the talking. I mentioned we have a crisis in Germany – come back here, don't walk on ahead. Our leaders say it is vital the Reich should not die, and some make plans to take the fight elsewhere. They believe there are countries that will support us and provide us with a base.'

'What use is a Reich without Germany? It would be like an engine without a car.'

'For the Reich to live, our leaders must be protected. It is important that they are taken to safety.'

'You sound like Dr Göbbels. You know as well as I do it's the fanaticism of our leaders that has got us into this mess.'

'Just listen! Some of our leaders saw the end when the Americans joined the war, it was unforeseen and should not have happened. The more enlightened ones have even established businesses throughout the world, did you know that?'

'How is that possible?'

'There are around two hundred Nazi owned companies in Switzerland, two hundred in Spain and one hundred in Argentina. All are financially sound. All trade on behalf of the Reich. Not openly, of course.'

'And the German people? What will they think when they hear their leaders have abandoned them?'

Walter shrugs. 'How should I know? It is not for me to justify our leader's decisions.'

'What about the Reichsmarschall?'

'Our Hermann has no plans to get out. Whatever else they say about him, he is no coward. He believes the Allies will let him continue to live the life of a medieval baron. He believes that the Allies – particularly the English aristocracy – will treat him with respect. The Englishman Lord Halifax has stayed here, at Carinhall, as have several others.'

'They will stick Göring against a wall and shoot him, just like they'll shoot the rest of them.'

'He thinks not. He no longer makes decisions or has a say in state matters. He thinks the very worst that will happen is he will be exiled. At best he'll be allowed to stay in his castle.'

'He has a castle?'

'He has places everywhere, I told you. He has a castle between Nürnburg and Bayreuth. Maybe you have heard of it – Schloss Veldenstein – he inherited it from his Jewish godfather, would you believe!'

'And what is your part in all this?'

'I am a small cog in a big machine. You are an even smaller cog. Without all its cogs a machine cannot work properly. As an engineer you must know that.'

They have reached the lake. Though they can see across the water, a thin mist fogs the far distance. Walter stops and looks around. As if concerned the trees might hear him he tugs Theo's sleeve and leads him to the water's edge.

'The Reichsmarschall will be removed safely from Germany when the time is right, even if it has to be done by force. I was given the task of finding an experienced U-boat commander, someone I could trust. You will understand my dilemma, there are few such men left. It was purely by chance I noticed your name on a list they supplied to me.'

Theo listens and makes no response. He is no conspirator, he wants no part of it. He waits for more, but Walter seems to have finished.

'Tell me why I did not receive orders to do this from Naval High Command.'

'If we are to save our leaders – against their will in some cases – it follows that they must not know our plans.'

'This cannot be. A U-boat cannot be made ready for the Reichsmarschall without the knowledge of naval high command.'

'To prepare a vessel for this needs a shipyard, not a navy. The necessary people have been informed. A vessel has been prepared and you will take command. You should consider it an honour.'

'I consider it madness! What do you think will happen when you move in on our leaders? You'll get cut down before you get within fifty metres of them. Do you think the Führer will come quietly? Do you really think the SS guards around Himmler and Bormann will stand aside for you?'

'When the time comes that is exactly what they will do. Calm yourself, it is not your problem. By involving you I am merely obeying orders.'

'And if I refuse?'

'You cannot refuse, there is too much at stake. You were the one who pressured me into telling you these things and because of that you are now part of it. While there is still hope, our leaders must remain here to fight. Only at the very last moment will they be taken to safety – though if we leave it too late then all exits will be blocked. Timing is everything.'

'And what are these exits?'

'I am not party to such detail. My guess is that from Berchtesgaden they will go to Switzerland.'

'Berchtesgaden couldn't be further from our northern ports. If Göring goes south then you won't need me. To keep him near our ports you will have to keep him here, is that what you are planning? Is that why you are here? Am I part of a kidnap plan?'

'I have told you more than is wise. Now come, Theodor. It is time to eat.'

After their meal they return to the woodland. This time they go inland, away from the lake. In a clearing they pass the only defensive position Theo has seen – an anti-aircraft gun. It is unmanned. Walter leads the way with deliberation, stopping only when they reach the top of a flight of concrete steps leading underground. Daylight is fading as they descend them, treading with care.

The steel door at the foot of the steps was made as an exit, it has no handle. There is, however, a hole for a key, a key Walter takes from his coat and turns in the lock. Holding it he attempts to tug the door open. Words hiss between his teeth.

'Help me, damn it!'

Theo reaches around him, managing to gets his fingers around the flanged edge of the door. When the gap is wide enough both men slip through into darkness, closing the door behind them. Walter throws a switch. A row of widely spaced bulbs on one wall reveal the place is not an air raid shelter as Theo expected but a low-ceilinged, white painted store, stacked to the roof with wooden crates.

'These are Hermann's best pieces from his Berlin houses. Some were in the truck that brought us here. You accompanied priceless works of art.'

'One wooden case looks much like another to me.'

'There are times when I find your humour irritating, Theodor. I suppose it's a U-boat thing.'

'You should not call me Theodor. So if they are priceless, why was there only one guard on the truck?'

'Sometimes it is better not to advertise what you are carrying. And in any case, who in Germany is going to attack a Luftwaffe truck? Now, look at the cases. I want your advice. The cases are supposed to be waterproof. What do you think?'

'They are plywood. I'm guessing it's marine ply, plywood made with waterproof glue. It won't protect the contents.'

Walter nods. 'I suspected as much. What additional protection would they need if they were to be transported by sea?'

'If they were kept in a dry hold, probably nothing more. The risk is greatest when they are being loaded and unloaded.'

'And if they were inside metal containers with watertight seals?'

Theo goes to stroke his beard but there is nothing there. 'Ammunition boxes, you mean? Still a risk, especially on a long sea journey.'

'Who said anything about a long sea journey?'

'Argentina is one of the few countries likely to welcome our leaders. Portugal also. But Portugal is in Europe, it is too close.'

Walter nods again. 'I knew I made the right choice with you. The only thing left for you to do is to learn how to keep your mouth shut. So tell me how we can keep these crates safe.'

'Salt water is corrosive, as I am sure you know. Steel corrodes easily. Bronze is best.'

'What about copper?'

'Not as good as bronze.'

'What if they were to be coated with rubber? I have been told it can be done.'

'The schnörkels on our newest boats are encased in rubber. They are metal of course. I doubt if it is possible to coat wooden cases.'

'But metal ones? If the wooden cases were to be placed in metal boxes and then coated with rubber?'

'Overdone. If the seals on the metal boxes are good enough then you probably wouldn't need the rubber. With tests and trials you – '

'There is no time for tests and trials.'

'So is this your real job? Is this what you are here for, to arrange to ship these? Also to kidnap the Reichsmarschall? Is this why you keep looking over your shoulder.'

'The transport of these items is administered by those with no knowledge of warfare. Officially I am here to advise them on security and protection. In practice, security is the work of the infantry and I leave it to them. All I have to do is to ensure that the temporary shelters provided for Göring's treasures are always adequate.'

'Temporary shelters?'

'You have seen the condition of our railways. It can take days to reach the south. My job is to ensure that when our journey is interrupted, for example by bombing, the cargo we are carrying remains unharmed.'

'You impress me. I didn't realise you had such expertise. The enemy now has a bomb that goes right through our U-boat pens. Maybe you should have designed them.'

'Ah, this is more of your humour? No, I do not have such expertise. So far I have merely identified places of shelter along road routes such as tunnels and mines. In practice my research is pointless because we shall be transporting everything by rail. When we require shelter all we need is a railway tunnel. I happen to know the location of all the rail tunnels between Berlin and Berchtesgaden. Luckily for me, so do the train drivers.'

'So you don't have any expertise. How do you get away with it? Haven't they checked up on you?'

'They have. And everything has been found to be in order.'

'Everything falsified.'

'My childhood, my schooling, my upbringing. These things are not false.'

'But everything else? Your rank?'

Theo's eyes fix on the uniform, on the pips on Walter's epaulettes. Walter shrugs.

'My rank is unimportant.'

'But is it the right uniform?'

'People believe what they see.'

'Good god, Walter! Who are you really?'

'That is the one thing I am not prepared to tell you.'

Walter wanders around the bunker reading labels and counting boxes. Theo stands near the door and mulls over this new knowledge, wondering how he can use it to his advantage.

'What's to stop me going to the Reichsmarschall and telling him what you've told me?'

Instead of the reaction he expects, Walter continues his task.

'So what have I told you, exactly?' he says, stooping and repositioning several small crates. 'You are so naïve. Do you think you are favoured in some way? You have seen the man's toy trains and you were impressed, that is the end of it. The Reichsmarschall is capricious, he surrounds himself with admirers. Take care, my friend, I am trusted. I have worked here for several months and what I have done has been faultless. When I asked permission to bring an aide here to help me with my work my request was granted without question. I was not even asked who that person would be.'

'I wasn't serious. I merely wondered if you had considered all the risks.'

'If you went to the Reichsmarschall with such ridiculous stories then at best you would leave here in a box.' He kicks one of the crates. 'But not as a work of art.'

CHAPTER TWENTY-TWO

'SO LET'S START at the beginning, shall we, Mr Spargo? Tell me why you went to the basement.'

Detective Inspector Quinn was in his late forties and surly and lean. What his head lacked in hair his eyebrows made up for, they were wide and bushy and stuck out like fur wings. Spargo sat opposite him at a table in a bleak, ill-furnished room. On a chair in the corner sat a younger man whose name Spargo couldn't remember. A man who had brought tea.

'I told you already. To check I'd locked the door.'

'Do you always do that so late at night?'

'No. As I told you, I'd been to the airport. I had a few drinks with a friend and took a taxi home. I was worried I had left the basement door unlocked. I had been there earlier, you see. I had been there for some books.'

'So you had been drinking.'

'That's what I said.'

'And you found the door unlocked?'

'I told you that earlier.'

'Mr Spargo, you may well have told someone else but you didn't tell me. It would help if you answered my questions.'

Spargo nodded. He had been through this before, first with the uniformed men who answered his call, and then on the way to this place. He struggled to keep a clear head. It had been a long day and was promising to be an even longer night. The four beers at the airport really hadn't helped.

'Mr Spargo? Concentrate please. You found the door unlocked?'

'I did. There are two keys. I keep one wedged behind the meter box fixed to the outside wall near the basement door. I had the other key with me. I keep it in the house.'

'Why did you have the key with you if the door was unlocked?'

Spargo muttered 'Christ!' to himself. What was it with the man? Or was it himself, was he was trying hard enough? Doing well in the circumstances. Probably.

'I didn't know it was unlocked. That was why I went to it. In case I found it unlocked I took a key with me so I could lock it. I was surprised to find it unlocked.'

'I don't see why you were surprised. You took a key with you, so you must have half-expected it to be unlocked.'

'I'm not sure I see the point of your question.'

'What happened to the key you keep behind the meter box?'

'Why, isn't it there?'

'I don't know. You tell me. Why did you take a key with you if there another one so close by?'

'It was raining. It was dark.'

'You said the security light was on.'

'The security light is on the front corner of the house. It doesn't light the back garden.'

'You told me the lights from your house windows lit the back garden.'

'They do, but they don't light the basement bit. Anyway, everything was wet. It was easier for me to take the key from the house. I didn't want to grope around in the dark for the other one.'

'Why didn't you take a torch with you?'

'What?'

'A torch, Mr Spargo.'

'I didn't need one.'

To Spargo it all made sense. Why it didn't to Quinn, he had no idea. Up to then he had thought all detectives argued as logically as Mitchell, but this man seemed to ask questions regardless of their usefulness. He had another try at the tea they had brought him. It was still too hot to drink. Quinn asked more questions but Spargo didn't hear them.

The younger man spoke for the first time.

'Mr Spargo… John… we realise you have had a shock, we do understand that. But you must be aware we need answers. Tell us again. Go through your actions and take your time. You went to the airport to meet a friend, Grant Murphy. You came home by taxi. You arrived there at midnight and went into your house – '

'More like eleven-thirty.'

'– you decided to check the basement because you thought you might have left the door unlocked. You went out in the rain. You said you turned the handle – '

'The knob. It's a knob.'

'– the knob. You said it was unlocked. Was there a key in the lock?'

It was the first sensible question he'd been asked. He hesitated before answering.

'I'm not sure.' Quinn went to speak but the younger man raised a hand to stop him. Spargo continued:

'If the key had been in the lock I'd probably have felt it when I grasped the door knob. The key gets in the way when you turn the knob.'

'This is important, Mr Spargo. We are trying to establish how someone got into your basement. Either you left the door unlocked, which you admit is a possibility, or else they used the key you keep behind the meter box. How did they know it was there, is it obvious?'

'Not at all obvious,' Spargo said. 'But there's another way. They might have used the one I kept in the house, the one I took with me to the basement.'

Quinn frowned. 'How could that be?'

'I have a deadlock on the front door. You have to turn the key twice –'

Quinn interrupted. 'I know what a deadlock is.'

The younger man held up his hand again. Quinn stayed open-mouthed.

'So you have to turn the front door key twice,' the younger man said. 'Go on…'

'I'm careful when I go out. I always double-lock the front door. A few times lately – three times, I think – I have returned home and only had to turn it once. Also the alarm's not working, I spent a week in Spain and when I got back it had a fault. That was the first time I noticed the door lock thing.'

'And you didn't report it?'

'Would you have been interested if I had? I checked the house. Everything was as I'd left it.'

Quinn again: 'Are you saying someone's been in your house?'

'That's what I thought at the time. The first time it happened I assumed it was my daughter, Jez. Jessica. She has a key. But it wasn't her. I asked.'

'Dr Jessica Spargo?' the younger man said. 'She's your daughter?'

'You know her?'

'I do. Please continue. You opened the basement door and you went in. Then what?'

'Fell in, more like. As I said, it was raining. I assumed the door was locked so when it opened I fell in. Then I couldn't find the light switch.'

'But you found it.'

'After three or four tries.'

Quinn said, 'It's your basement. Are you telling me you don't know where the light switch is?'

'It's on the wrong wall, it's on the hinge side of the door. I have to open the door and then walk around it. Because I fell in I was disoriented. But even before I found the light I knew something was wrong.'

'Intuition,' Quinn said.

The raised hand again, this time accompanied by a disapproving look.

'You knew?'

'The place sounded wrong. Also, it usually smells musty, there's a bit of damp. You were there, you know what it smelled like, it wasn't nice. Then I found the light switch.'

'Then what?' Quinn asked.

The image was burnt on Spargo's mind so clearly he didn't know where to begin. The room had been trashed. His stacks of archive boxes lay like felled columns, their contents, mostly folders and papers, were spewed across the floor. He thought he saw bare feet protruding from under the scattered paper, and thinking he was simply tired from his drive he rubbed his eyes. Stepping closer he saw that not only were the feel real, they were attached to bluish, bloodless legs. Stupidly – he knew that now – he had pushed aside boxes to see what else there was. Revealed a face so swollen it seemed to have been inflated with a tyre pump.

'You know what I saw,' he said.

Quinn again: 'You disturbed the scene.'

'I had to see if the man was dead.'

It was a lie. He remembered how it was, how the torso and head were covered by fallen files. One of the fluorescent tubes was old and had taken an age to reach full brightness, flickering ghostly light as he'd pushed boxes aside. He had wanted to see who it was, rather than see if he was dead.

'You had to see if the man was dead,' Quinn repeated. 'Really?'

Spargo continued, staring at Quinn.

'If his head was on one side of the room and his body on the other, I'd have known that for sure. I did what I should do, I checked for signs of life. Obviously you have been trained to tell if a man is dead by inspecting his feet.' He saw the younger man smile. 'When I cleared the files from his face I knew he was dead. I left the room immediately.'

He was remembering now, remembering clearly. At first he'd thought the boxes had been felled in a fight. The more he thought about it the more he knew it was unlikely a man with a wire around his neck could do much to defend himself. Kicked out, then. Kicked out a lot. Felled piles of boxes.

Bodies weren't new to him. In the Zambian mines he'd seen horrific accidents. This was different, this death was deliberate. In his basement he'd managed to control his stomach but he was having trouble now.

'Are you alright?' the younger man asked.

Spargo nodded. 'It's hot in here. Do you know who he is? The victim?'

He didn't particularly want to know, didn't really care. Hoped that by asking questions it would demonstrate a willingness to help.

'We don't yet know. Are you absolutely sure you've never seen him before?'

'Not as far as I know.'

Quinn grunted. 'What kind of an answer is that?'

'He wasn't that recognisable.' Spargo glanced at his watch, and then looked at it again as if he didn't believe the time. It was six hours since he called the police. 'Did he have anything on him?' he asked. 'In his clothes, I mean.'

'You saw his clothes?'

'No. I assumed you would have found them by now.'

'You mean in your basement? Why did you think his clothes might be there?'

'I assumed they would be. I thought it was sexual.'

Quinn adjusted himself in his chair. 'Sexual, Mr Spargo?'

'Well, what was I supposed to think? I thought he'd gone there with someone. I thought that a naked man – '

'Yes, Mr Spargo,' the younger man said with no trace of amusement. 'A dead, naked man. In your basement…'

Mid-morning the police let him go and he took a taxi home. He realised, as he approached his house, that he had made a mistake and redirected the driver.

'They've taken over the house and blocked off the street,' Spargo told Jez as she opened her front door.

'Who has? What house?'

He went to her kitchen, sat down on one of her tall stools and told her the whole story. She sat speechless. Said nothing at all the whole time.

'Don't you think you should have called a lawyer?' she said finally. 'Didn't they suggest it?'

'I don't need one. They're just making enquiries. I simply told them what I did and what I found. It must have happened while I was at the airport with Murphy. When they establish the time of death they will know I had nothing to do with it. Anyway, I don't suppose my solicitor would have welcomed driving from Inverness to Edinburgh in the middle of the night.'

'I've said for years you should get someone local. Anyway, the police would have found you one.'

'I'm a witness.'

'You must be their only suspect.'

'They released me, so presumably they believe me.'

He didn't quite catch what she said. Didn't want to know.

At five o'clock Quinn called Spargo's mobile and asked where he was.

'My daughter's flat,' he said. He wanted to add that seeing as how Lothian and Borders police had taken over his house, it was the only place he could go. Sanctuary, of sorts.

'I need to see you. I've got something to show you.'

Jez was in the room with him and was gesturing, pointing to the phone. He ignored her she prised it from his hands, pressed a button and put it on speaker so she could hear.

'Show me what?' Spargo asked.

Quinn's voice rasped from the speaker. 'Photographs,' Mr Spargo. I need you here now.'

Jez shook her head and pointed at the floor. Spargo frowned at her, trying to work out the words she was mouthing. Finally he got it.

'I'm at my daughter's. It would be better for me if you came here.'

Quinn paused. 'It's not at all convenient. Oh, very well, just this time. Give me the address.'

Quinn arrived alone. He placed a slim leather folder on Jez's breakfast bar, unzipped it and took out a handful of photographs he passed to Spargo, holding them carefully so Jez couldn't see them. Spargo glanced at each one of them. Wished they were black and white and not colour.

'Look at them properly,' Quinn said. 'It's not as if you haven't seen it for real. The body's been tidied up. The face is more natural.'

Spargo concentrated on the first photo, the head and shoulders of a man around thirty years old. The wire had been removed from the neck but a purple gash remained. The face was chalky white, and back to what Spargo assumed was its normal size. He stared at it, trying to work out how they got shots at that angle with the stainless steel slab behind. Did they have a camera on the mortuary ceiling? Did they climb above the corpse on a stepladder or did they tilt it up for the camera? He tried to make out the background, whether it was the floor or the wall.

'Mr Spargo?'

'Yes… no… I've never seen him before.'

'As far as you know,' Quinn said dryly.

'Do you know who it is yet?' Jez asked.

'We're working on it.'

Jez grunted. 'So that's a no?'

'It's a no, Miss – '

'It's not Miss anybody. It's Jez Spargo. Doctor Jez Spargo.'

Spargo put the photos on the table and Jez picked them up. Held her breath as she studied each one. Then she looked at Quinn and shook her head. 'I don't know who it is either. I hope you're not thinking my father had anything to do with this.' She turned to Spargo. 'Did you tell him about Gran?'

Spargo shook his head. 'It's hardly relevant.'

'God, Dad!' She faced Quinn squarely. 'My grandmother was beaten to death last month in Kilcreg. The officer dealing with the case is Detective Sergeant Mitchell. That's Northern Constabulary.'

Quinn looked from her to Spargo and back again. 'Spargo…' he muttered, 'Morag Spargo.' I knew I'd heard that name somewhere. Why didn't you tell me?'

'As I said, I didn't think it was relevant. Do you think there's a link?'

With sagging shoulders Quinn seemed to collapse in on himself. It was as if whatever weight he carried on his shoulders had increased tenfold.

'To be honest with you Miss… Doctor… I have absolutely no idea.'

'Not a happy bunny,' Jez said when Quinn left. 'We've just destroyed any case he might have had. As I said, he had only one suspect.'

Spargo wagged a finger at the table where the photos had been. 'Did he really think I could do a thing like that?'

'He thought you knew the dead man.'

'And killed him in my own house? Not the brightest thing to have done.'

'You had an argument. You lost your cool.'

'You watch too much television. So tell me why he was naked.'

'I would have thought that was obvious. You said you thought it was sexual, you even said that to Quinn. You didn't want the police comparing fibres and DNA so you took the man's clothes and you dumped them. You dumped yours as well. Come to think of it, I haven't seen that jacket you're wearing for a while.'

He stared hard at her. 'Good god! That really is not funny. The police took the clothes I was wearing. Sometimes I worry about you.'

She smiled. 'I'm simply telling you what went through Quinn's mind.'

'And now it doesn't?'

'Even he must think the probability of you murdering your own mother and then killing this man is close to zero.'

'Stupid of me not to tell him about it before.'

'You had other things on your mind. Couldn't see the wood for the trees.'

'Couldn't even see the trees. Still can't, to be honest. I can't go home. Don't want to. I need to book into somewhere for a couple of days. What's that place near the old fire station like? Know anyone who's stayed there?'

'Don't be ridiculous! You'll stay here. That's if you can cope with the folding bed.'

The thought of staying with her hadn't entered his head. Even if it had, he wouldn't have suggested it.

'It's not fair on you,' he said. 'I'll try the hotel.'

'You'll stay here. That's on the strict understanding it really is for no more than a couple of days.'

🕮

The door to Dr Jessica's flat opened. Midge sunk low in his seat. Through the car windscreen he saw two figures silhouetted in the doorway, Dr Jessica and the back of a man Midge was sure he'd not seen there before – until he turned and descended the steps. He blanched as he recognised Quinn, the man who put brother Robbie away. He sunk lower still, managing to get most of his body jammed under the steering wheel, down near the pedals.

He stayed while a car door slammed, an engine started up and a car drove away. Then he stayed there even longer in case Quinn actually knew he was there and was trying to fool him by pretending he'd left. Slowly and painfully Midge unwound himself and looked around. Saw no sign of Quinn.

Quinn was old, he couldn't be far off retirement. At that age some of them were scared of doing something stupid, being dismissed and putting their pension at risk. They slowed down, did as little as possible or nothing at all. But not Quinn. Quinn had always behaved like a Rottweiler. And as he got older he seemed to get worse.

So why had he been to see Dr Jessica? Had she complained she was being followed, being watched? If that was why Quinn was there then surely she would have been given him the number or make of his car? If so, Quinn would have walked straight to him.

Sure the visit by Quinn was something Mr Luis needed to know about, Midge fiddled with his phone, typing text: Spargo woman's flat raided by fuzz. He read it twice and then deleted it – it wouldn't do to use the name Spargo on the phone. Nor was there any point mentioning Quinn, because Mr Luis wouldn't know who the hell he was. He retyped the message: CID *called at the flat.*

Factual. To the point. What Reader's Digest readers might call epigrammatic.

CHAPTER TWENTY-THREE

THEO TAKES OFF HIS CAP and runs a hand through his hair. Walter really is an unknown quantity, friendly chats one minute and vile threats the next. The thought crosses his mind fleetingly that Walter is fooling everyone and is an enemy agent. The idea is laughable. It is replaced immediately by the more reasonable, but equally disturbing, explanation that Walter is SS or Gestapo.

The bunker they are in has more than one room; Walter has gone, down a short corridor; lights come on and go off and after a few more minutes he returns, ushering Theo out through the steel door and closing it behind them. He slips back his cuff and checks his watch.

'Up the steps! Hurry! In seven minutes Schott will bring our meals to your hut and we must be there. The reason I survive, Theodor, is because I never give anyone a reason to question my actions.'

Next morning things move quickly. Before dawn Walter lets himself into Theo's room and shakes him awake, chastising him for not being able to hold his drink.

'You look like shit! Too much beer. I would have thought you navy men were made of sterner stuff.'

'I was dozing. I wasn't asleep.'

'You could have fooled me. For a second I thought you had died.'

Theo eases himself off the bed and attempts to stand up. Yes, he had slept heavily. As for the beer, it wasn't the quantity he'd consumed, it was his unfamiliarity with alcohol. Last night, when the orderly arrived with the food, banknotes swapped hands. Instructed by Walter what to get and where to get it, the man returned some time later with his delivery boy's basket stuffed with bottles. Those they hadn't got around to opening were lined up on a bookshelf that bowed under their weight.

'Pack your kit,' Walter says. 'We leave in two hours.'

Theo rubs his eyes. He hasn't felt like this for years and he hates himself for having had to be shaken awake – a humiliation for a man who prides himself in knowing what is going on around him at all times. On board his boat, even a crewman passing his cabin door on tiptoe can wake him.

'So soon? You said days. Weeks.'

'Smarten yourself up. Shower, shave, comb that tangled mop. I want you immaculately presented. Brush yourself down. Here…'

Like a conjurer Walter produces a stiff-bristled brush he holds it out to Theo. Changing his mind he picks Theo's cap off the hook on the door, holds it up and starts brushing its fine doeskin top. Theo takes it from him, looking around as if working out what to do with it. He stumbles to the door and hangs it up.

'You shouldn't have let me get like this.'

'Blame yourself. Go and shower. Join me in my room in thirty minutes. Come in twenty minutes instead and you can share breakfast. Here, take my brush. Use it. I want you immaculate, understand?'

Theo is late. Sprucing himself up and packing his kit took longer than he expected. Missing his breakfast wasn't a problem, his stomach couldn't have handled it anyway. On his way to Walter's room he sees Walter heading towards the bunker and they meet without a greeting. A flatbed lorry reverses past them, churning grass with its wheels; an officer wearing the Göring cuff and with clipboard in hand, stands nearby. Seeing two senior officers approaching he snaps the clipboard down to his side and salutes. Walter ignores him. Theo, surprised, returns it with an unusual sharpness.

'Look at it, Vogel! Look what the damn incompetents have sent me! I asked for two covered trucks. This one hasn't even got sides!'

It has rained in the night and the sky is still heavy. The man with the clipboard looks skywards as if to see how much more rain might fall.

'They have provided tarpaulins, Herr Major.'

Walter mumbles 'Damn fool.' Then, loudly to the officer, 'We seem to have no alternative. See that you file the necessary complaint. Now get the damn thing loaded, we must be away before ten.' As if to make the point he taps his wristwatch. 'Ten, not one minute later.' He turns to Theo. 'If you want breakfast I can still arrange it.'

Theo shakes his head. 'Not hungry. Are we driving south in that?'

'No, thank god. Only to the railway sidings at Friedrichswalde.'

'Where is that?'

Walter stares at him. 'It is the place you mistook one of our most powerful leaders for a humble stationmaster. The crates will travel on one of the humble stationmaster's trains and you and I will travel with them.' He looks Theo up and down. 'You have turned yourself out smartly. For a submari – '

'You should not say that.'

'Smartly, Herr Hauptmann, yes.'

Troops appear as if from nowhere. Ten young men, little more than schoolboys, laugh and joke, run for the truck like children at play, shout abuse at the driver as he moves the vehicle forwards. Walter cups his hands to his mouth and is about to shout when Theo, unthinking, lays a steadying hand on Walter's arm.

'Leave them,' he says. 'They're kids. They are hardly off their mother's breasts.'

He thinks of Peter. The image he has of his son is a lie, a composite of boys he remembers from kindergarten and the children of relatives. He has seen his child only once. He tries to imagine that baby now, standing up. Walking and running.

The troops, working surprisingly quickly, carry selected crates from the bunker, up the concrete steps and onto the lorry. Tarpaulins are unfolded, heaved over the cargo, and lashed down with ropes. A car stops near the lorry. Walter goes to it, speaks to the driver and then calls to Theo.

'Stop dreaming, Hauptmann! Come, get in… did you pack your bags? Did you leave them outside your hut like I said?'

At Friedrichswalde the young airmen, energetic no longer, struggle to unload the crates. Some are so heavy that by rights they should be lifted by crane. To Theo it is a repetition of the activities he saw here before but this time in daylight. Again Walter curses, yelling instructions. It is as if he cannot watch any activity without shouting orders.

'Treat those crates as if they were eggs or little babies, Oberleutnant. You will find it much easier if you reverse the truck close to the boxcar.' He beckons to two airmen. 'You two, come! Take our luggage from the car. Find the guard and he will show you our compartments. Theodor, come with me. This time there is to time to inspect locomotives or talk to stationmasters.'

Walter keeps shouting as they walk beside the train. Theo winces. Wants to ask where he can get aspirin.

The train he saw here last time was a freight train. This one has carriages and only one boxcar. Also, though the train isn't particularly long, it is pulled by two locomotives.

'Not this carriage,' Walter says. 'This one is for Göring's troops. The next is a kitchen for Radmann, Göring's cook. The others hold Göring's personal staff. You already met Kropp, his valet.'

Walter mentions Kropp without malice. He stops, turns, and takes a few steps back. 'This door, I think…'

Theo grabs handrails, hauls himself up and goes to a windowless door across the corridor.

'This one?' he asks.

'That's Christa's, Göring's nurse. Turn left. Keep walking.'

'Convenient…'

'Your cynicism is misplaced. Our Hermann is a devoted husband and father.'

'But a nurse?'

'He is also a hypochondriac.'

They walk through Göring's private salon. Theo makes comparisons between this accommodation and that on his boat, his last command. It is luxury of a kind he's not seen before.

Walter walks ahead while Theo pauses at each door, stepping inside and inspecting each compartment. Finally he comes across Walter unpacking bags.

'Your cabin is the next one along,' Walter says. 'If you think it is small, bear in mind it once accommodated Hermann's chief air aide, General Bodenchatz. In better times Göring travelled with his senior military advisors.'

The cabin next door is identical to Walter's. It is certainly not small, not in comparison to cabins Theo is used to. Not all of the train is luxurious. It has a practical side, a headquarters room with fixed tables and chairs. There are telephones, a teleprinter and a radio cabin.

'You are standing in a piece of our history,' Walter says. 'The first of the campaigns to bomb England's capital city was directed from this carriage.'

'And now?'

'The days when our air forces could mount such attacks are over. Now this is merely one of Hermann's private trains. You might be interested to know that these carriages are armoured with steel plate. It is why such a small train requires two locomotives.'

Theo, still wary he has been drawn into a plot, interrupts.

'Do you think they will try to assassinate Göring?'

'Who?'

'Those that plotted against our Führer.'

'Göring certainly thinks so. The black Daimler-Benz that passed us on our way here is Göring's. His driver tells me it is the heaviest car he has ever driven, it has an eight litre engine and ten millimetres of armour plate. Having said that, I doubt if there is anyone still alive who had even the faintest involvement in the assassination attempt.'

'Is he coming?'

'Göring, you mean? With us? Good god no! If he were travelling on this train we would not be in these cabins, we would be with that rabble of airmen.' He pulls up his sleeve and studies his watch. 'Wait here. I must check all is well with the loading. We leave here in precisely eighteen minutes.'

CHAPTER TWENTY-FOUR

SPARGO WOKE AT SEVEN and showered and shaved. As he towelled himself dry his mobile rang. Jez answered it.

'That was Mitchell,' she called up the stairs. 'Sounds urgent. Says he's got something to show you. He won't say what it is but he wants you there now.'

'Inverness? Now? Quinn said I shouldn't leave Edinburgh.'

'He has no right to say that. It's not as if you were arrested and bailed.'

'I'll call him back.'

'You can't do that, he's gone into a meeting. He said you should only call if you can't make it.'

Downstairs, Spargo tried the number and got Mitchell's voicemail. Didn't bother to leave a message.

'Just go!' Jez said, frustrated. 'And take your overnight bag because I don't want you driving back today.'

'Maybe I should move up here,' Spargo told Mitchell when they met. 'Do you know how long it's taken me? I was stuck in a jam for ninety minutes. There were road works on the Forth Road Bridge and in about ten other places. That road is a joke.'

Mitchell smiled. 'Good of you to come.'

'My daughter said it was urgent. She said there was something you wanted me to see.'

Mitchell had things on his mind. He nodded, absently. They were in his office and he was thumbing through envelopes on his desk. He picked up a bundle of them and moved to the door, gesturing to Spargo to follow him. As they walked through the building Mitchell continued the questions.

'Does the name Ian Letchie mean anything to you?'

'No, should it?'

'You used Stuart Main to help clear your mother's cottage.'

'You recommended him to me.'

'No, I gave you a list of three hauliers to choose from. But that's not important. Some time ago Mr Main called me about a journalist, did you know that?'

'I didn't know he'd called you. He phoned to say a man had been asking about me. I offered to call you but he said it was no bother, he said he could deal with him.'

They entered a room, bare except for a table and chairs. Mitchell pulled one out for Spargo and sat in another.

'What do you mean, deal with him?'

'Deal with him... deal with it... I don't remember his exact words. He said it was his problem, not mine. He was being courteous by letting me know someone was snooping, that's all. I'm hoping I haven't come all this way to answer questions you could have asked on the phone. I've had a lousy few days. I got home –'

'And found a body. Yes, Mr Spargo, I know all about that. I also know the dead man's name.'

'This Ian Ritchie?'

'Ian Letchie.'

'How did you know this?'

'DI Quinn has been circulating grisly photos. One of my colleagues recognised the victim. It must have been quite a shock for you, finding him.'

Quite an understatement. Spargo went quiet as his mind filled with pictures. He swallowed. It sounded loud in the room.

'Why didn't Quinn tell me this?'

'I'm sure he'll tell you when he's ready.'

'He thinks I did it.'

'If DI Quinn thought you did it you wouldn't be here.'

Mitchell had been glancing at his watch every few minutes. Then, as if responding to the mention of his name, Quinn blustered into the room. He ignored Spargo and nodded to Mitchell.

'Damn road works! Should have been here ages ago, by rights.'

Mitchell stood up, slid his chair back against a side wall and sat down on it. Quinn did the same, dragging a chair from the table with one hand and dumping his briefcase beside it with the other. 'You told him?' he asked.

'Just.'

Spargo couldn't imagine Stuart Main swatting a fly, never mind garrotting someone. Couldn't see why he would want to.

'It couldn't have been Stuart Main.'

'What, you think Main killed Letchie?' Mitchell asked. 'Why him?'

Spargo shrugged. 'I didn't. I don't. I assumed you might.'

'Killing a reporter who asked a few questions? And after he'd told you about it?'

Spargo shook his head and wished he hadn't spoken. 'I'm trying to see the connections,' he said.

'You and me both, Mr Spargo.'

Spargo sat at the table with his fingers outspread on its top. Realising he was fumbling he moved his hands to his lap. Quinn took a notebook from his briefcase and placed it on one knee, licked a finger and thumbed pages. Spargo swivelled his chair sideways to face them. It was a mistake. Without the table he felt exposed.

'If Letchie was asking about me then he must have been following up a story. What if he knew who killed my mother?'

Mitchell shook his head. 'No, Mr Spargo. Mr Letchie could have been killed for any number of reasons quite unconnected with your mother's murder. A year ago he was poking around in a drugs case and got himself stabbed in the arm. I knew him as a kid, he was a wee brat with a history of violence. I can't say I mourn his passing. Back in his teens a woman was killed by a stolen car we knew he was driving. We just couldn't prove it.

'After he left school we had a run of burglaries we were sure were his work. Then, inexplicably, he seemed to reform. He got a job with the local paper and, according to a friend of mine, became one of the best reporters they've ever had. More recently we had a drugs problem locally and he got to the root of it, managing to tie it to Glasgow dealers. He sold the story to a national daily. There were things in his article we didn't even know about – it's difficult to see how he got hold of the information without being involved in some way. Got himself stabbed though, didn't he, so someone didn't like what he wrote. He was on the take, I'm sure of it. He drove a new Porsche. Not many of those around here.'

'Private means?'

'Not him. Family's as poor as church mice.'

'I don't see it,' Spargo said. 'If he was killed for any of these things then why do it in my house?'

'I didn't say he was killed for any of these reasons. I'm simply saying there could be motives unconnected with your mother. I don't pretend to have experience of multiple killers but I believe they tend to stick with the same method, whatever works for them. To me, your mother was beaten by someone who just lost it.'

'Are you saying my mother's death isn't murder?'

'No, Mr Spargo, I'm not. I'm saying that perhaps your mother's killer didn't go there with the intention of killing her. Perhaps things went wrong.' He turned his head, nodded towards Quinn and turned back to Spargo. 'Inspector Quinn tells me Letchie's murder was very different and not the least bit amateur. Garrotting is not a technique I would care to use if I decided to kill someone. It implies premeditation. If the wire – the garrotte – didn't come from your basement then the murderer brought it with him. He came prepared.'

Questions from Quinn now, leaning forwards nice and friendly. 'Did Ian Letchie come to see you in Edinburgh, Mr Spargo?'

'I've never seen him before. I told you that.'

'Not quite. I seem to recall you saying you didn't think you had seen him before. I'm wondering if things have changed.'

'I'm not sure what you mean.'

'What I mean is that in Edinburgh you seemed to have no idea who the man was. Now you are aware of this man's connection with Kilcreg I'm wondering if you have changed your mind? Could it be the connection has triggered memories?'

Spargo shook his head. 'No. I'm sure I have never seen the man. Tell me why I'm here. Couldn't we have done this by phone?'

Mitchell answered. 'Bear with me, Mr Spargo. I asked you here –

both of you – because early this morning we searched Mr Letchie's house.'

He left the room and returned carrying a laptop computer that he placed on the table and hinged up the screen. Soon the screen was full of thumbnail photographs. He clicked on the first one. It was a photo of the back of Spargo's mother's cottage, taken from high on the hillside.

Mitchell brought up the next, then the next, displaying pictures of the cottage, the valley and the hillsides. Some photos, all taken from high vantage points, showed Kilcreg's main street as it usually was, and others showed it littered with police vehicles. Another was a mist-shrouded zoom of Mitchell and Spargo, standing in the back garden of the cottage in the rain, Spargo with his face to the sky.

'Didn't see him, did you, Mr Spargo?'

Spargo shook his head. 'It's taken from the small fir tree on the hillside.'

Mitchell scrolled through more thumbnails and clicked on one. Spargo jumped in his seat.

'My house!'

'No surprise there,' Quinn said, leaning forwards and studying it. 'The man was a reporter. He takes pictures for his work.'

'All digital,' Mitchell said. 'We have his camera and an impressive array of telephoto lenses.'

Spargo sat quietly. Something he had seen earlier puzzled him but he wasn't sure why.

'Go back, go to Kilcreg. I want to see the pictures that don't show any police vehicles.'

He waited. Mitchell brought one up on the screen. Spargo tried to take over and Mitchell moved to stop him. Changed his mind.

'Don't screw the thing up or they'll have my head. By rights this should have gone to the lab.'

'Was there any time Kilcreg looked like that?' Spargo asked, nodding at the screen. 'When there were no police vehicles at all?'

Mitchell hesitated. 'We were there for three days and nights. These must have been taken later in the week.'

'That's not right. What's the date on this file?'

'The pictures don't have dates on them.'

'No, I mean what's the image date, the date on the file?'

'The dates don't help, they are all the same, all well after the murder. It's probably the date Letchie downloaded them from his camera.'

Spargo brought up an image that showed the back of the cottage.

'How do I make this bigger?'

Mitchell zoomed the image. Spargo squinted at the screen.

'The kitchen window's ajar,' he said.

Quinn moved closer. 'Looks closed to me.'

Spargo pointed. 'Look at the other windows. They are all the same except this one, the kitchen window. The reflection is different. That could only happen if the glass was at an angle and was reflecting something else. It means the window is open, just slightly.'

'So?'

'There are no police vehicles in any of this group of photos. Would your colleagues leave a window open when you weren't there?' At any time after the murder?'

'Not a chance. We left the place secure… and there is no incident tape anywhere, we had some strung along the back fence. It is probably still there.'

'Your point being?' Quinn asked.

'His point being,' Mitchell said, 'that Letchie was there before the murder, taking photographs. No way of knowing if it was the day before, or weeks before.'

Quinn left the room to make phone calls. Mitchell sent out for sandwiches and took Spargo back to his office, collecting coffee en route.

'There was more room where we were,' Mitchell said. 'But the room's booked for the afternoon.' He grasped the back of a chair and spun it around. 'Sit down, Mr Spargo.'

Spargo looked at his watch and wondered where the day had gone. Mitchell sat cradling a coffee mug.

'What if you are right,' he asked. 'What if some of those pictures were taken before your mother's murder?'

'You're the detective.'

'That doesn't mean I've got the answers. I didn't live there, you did.

You knew your mother, I didn't. The obvious conclusion to draw is that Letchie was checking the place out before the murder, but for what?'

'Taking pictures for somebody?'

Mitchell fell quiet. Placed a hand over his mouth, thinking.

'Such as who?'

'Such as the person who killed my mother.'

Mitchell jerked himself upright.

'Bloody obvious I suppose. But it's the most constructive thing I've heard so far.'

'Why?'

'It doesn't give us a motive for your mother's murder but it gives us one for Letchie's. Reporters sniff around, they wheedle their way into things. Sometimes I envy them. Unlike us they get away with it, they have excuses when challenged, they say they're doing a piece on development, on land use, on local schools, who lives here, who lives there. They can always find somebody willing to talk.'

'So why kill someone so useful?'

Mitchell sat silently, rotating his wedding ring six turns one way, six the other. 'Kill Mr Letchie, you mean? Outlived his usefulness? Started to get in the way? Wanted more money? Threatened to write something? Could be any number of reasons. Got out of his depth, that's for sure.'

Spargo flashed a frown. Mitchell's all-seeing eyes didn't miss it.

'Something bothering you?'

'It can wait.'

'Tell me.'

'It's nothing. A while ago someone sent me an email.'

'And?'

'Out of my depth, it said. At first I thought it was spam.'

'Who was it from?'

'I don't know. I sent a curt reply but it bounced. Whoever it was closed the sending address.'

'When was this?'

'When I got home. The day I collected the journals from you.'

When Quinn appeared in the doorway Mitchell went quiet.

'So you are calling them journals?'

It was a deliberate change of subject and Spargo played along, didn't return to the subject of emails. Feeling he should offer Quinn a chair, Spargo went to stand up. Quinn waved him back down. He crossed the room, cleared files from the corner of a side table and sat on it, his legs swinging.

'Journals, yes,' Spargo said. 'I took them to a researcher my daughter knows. The woman is a lecturer. Or something. It's what she called them. She's already found fault with the translation your man did.'

'Lewis? He only did half a page. Are you telling me it's wrong? I haven't had a bill from him yet. Perhaps I should refuse to pay.'

Quinn came to life. 'Lewis? Translator? Elderly man?'

'I've never met him,' Mitchell said. 'We use him once in a blue moon. Apparently he used to teach up here. When he retired and moved to Edinburgh we continued to use him. Elderly, yes. Must be.'

'If you're expecting a bill from the man then forget it. We have been looking into a hit-and-run. Victim's name was Lewis. Buried recently in Piershill.'

Daylight had gone. The rain that started as a few large drops on the windows of Mitchell's office now howled up the Moray Firth in long drenching sheets, hitting the seaward side of the building with a sound like thrown sand. Quinn cursed. Said he had to drive back to Edinburgh today because he had court in the morning.

'We've finished with your house,' he told Spargo before he left. 'Best you don't go back today though. Not sure who's got the keys.'

Back in his car Spargo called the motor lodge where he stayed last time and booked a room. Then he called Jez and told her his news. Said the dead man in his basement might have been reconnoitring his mother's place for someone else.

'So bizarre…!'

'And there's something else. DI Quinn was here, he drove up. He said the translator, Lewis, was killed in a hit-and-run in Edinburgh.'

Jez stayed quiet for so long Spargo asked if she was still there.

'Dad… I don't like the sound of this. Stay out of it. Please stop poking around.'

Remembering the motor lodge didn't serve evening meals Spargo drove into town, stopped near the railway station and bought a pizza. By the time he had checked in it had gone cold.

That night he dreamed not of the ghosts of dead miners but of Mitchell and Quinn on the hillside at Kilcreg, competing in an egg-rolling contest with Letchie's laptop as the prize. It beat his imaginings hands-down. Wished he could have more like that.

The motor lodge provided self-service breakfasts. Men and women in suits and crisp shirts sat at small tables with open newspapers in one hand and forks of food in the other. Still hungry from yesterday Spargo took a plate from a pile and assembled some do-it-yourself food. Poured himself coffee and carried it to a table.

'Hey, Spargo! You mind if I join you?'

Spargo stifled a groan. There was no mistaking the voice. He swivelled around, gave an insincere smile and said, without enthusiasm,

'Mr Kalman…'

The Elvis trimmings had gone. There were no trinkets, no jewellery, no heavy belt buckle. What remained was workmanlike – a spotless white tee and a pale, washed-denim jacket.

'So how're you doin', Spargo?'

Kalman transferred the contents of his breakfast tray onto what little space remained at Spargo's table. When everything was arranged as he wanted it he pulled out a chair and sat down.

'So why're you here this time, Spargo?'

To give himself time to think, Spargo cleared his throat and mumbled something about work. Kalman laughed.

'So it's mining business, Spargo? They got mines up here? Okay, you don't want to say. I respect your need to protect your contacts. You need have no worries there, I'm strictly an underwater man. Underwater, okay. Underground, no way!'

Spargo winced. Being with the man was bad enough without corny rhymes.

'Are you still on holiday?' Spargo asked, wondering if he should have used the word vacation. 'Not back on the rig?'

'Hey, Spargo, I haven't been on rigs for years. I'm Leading Diver on the Posi-Three. Didn't I say that? Thought I told you she was moored in the harbour?'

Spargo nodded. 'Yes, sorry. Bilge pump failure.'

'Turned out to be more than that. We got parts flown from Philadelphia, you believe that? Philadelphia! Now she's fixed. Due out tomorrow.'

Spargo took a bite of cold toast. He was about to ask Kalman where he and the boat were going when he remembered what happened last time he asked questions.

'We had to leave a load of gear on the bottom out there,' Kalman said. 'Recovering it should not be a problem, weather permitting. If we don't recover it this week I reckon it's gone for good. Not the safest job I've done, Spargo, that's for sure.'

Before Spargo realised it, the words were out.

'Job? What job?'

Kalman had his fork halfway to his mouth. He stopped and returned it to his plate. 'You haven't heard? I thought this whole darned country would know, way it's been spread around.' He stood up, gesturing to Spargo to stay seated. 'Stay there, Spargo. Just you stay there.'

Kalman scraped his chair back and headed for the lifts. Five minutes later he was back with a white plastic carrier bag tucked under his arm. He sat down. Placed the bag under the table.

'Can't tell you what we've been doing, Spargo, not officially,' Kalman said, reaching down. His hand returned holding a newspaper he unfolded and thrust at Spargo. His finger stabbed at an article at the foot of the page.

'We are supposed to keep this thing under wraps, Spargo,' he said. 'Then some jerk goes and prints this.'

Spargo's gaze fell on the journalist's name. He swallowed, uncomfortably.

DIVERS LOCATE SUB
by our Special Correspondent Ian Letchie

Divers recently located the wreck of a submarine in deep water near Fladen Ground off the north east coast of Scotland. A spokesman for Posidonian Enterprises, the diving company undertaking the work on behalf of a US-based trust, revealed the wreck is a German U-boat believed to have struck a mine in the Second World War. Diving the wreck has been dogged by inclement weather. The dive boat, Posidonian Explorer III, is now moored in Inverness Harbour with mechanical problems. Teams are expected to resume their work next week.

'Damn near cost me my job,' Kalman said. 'How the heck was I to know the creep was a newspaper man?'

Spargo sat quietly, trying to fit pieces into place in his mind while Kalman continued to rant.

'Ian Letchie, the reporter who wrote this, has been murdered.' Spargo said quietly and as nonchalantly as possible.

It was meant as a shocker to shut Kalman up. It hadn't worked when he told him about his mother's murder and it didn't work now. Kalman stayed cool.

'Can't say that surprises me, Spargo. Guy that pokes his nose into other people's business like that sooner or later is going to get whacked. Can't be that good at his job either, because he got it wrong. The sub didn't hit a mine, that's for sure. Also the guy couldn't even get the location right.'

'Where is Fladen? Sounds Dutch.'

'Fladen Ground. That's five hours out from here. They're fishing grounds, Spargo, one hundred metres of water. Is that deep, or what?'

Spargo tried to imagine such a depth. He had been deeper in mines, much deeper, but the thought of diving in any depth of water unnerved him. A cubic metre of water weighs a tonne. At a hundred metres depth that's one hundred tonnes of pressure on every square meter.

Kalman picked up his coffee, drank it down and went for more. Brought one back for Spargo.

'Were you the ones that found it?' Spargo asked.

'The sub? Hell no, someone else did that years ago. Posidonian are contract divers. We carry diving gear, not all that exploration shit.'

'So who's paying you? Why are they doing this? Are they planning to raise it?'

Kalman frowned, tilting his head as if he didn't understand the question. 'Why would they want to raise it?'

'Put it on show? Get some of their money back?'

Kalman laughed loud. Heads in the restaurant turned.

'Heck, these guys don't need money, Spargo! Raising her wouldn't work anyways, she's rusted to hell. The old tub would break its back if anyone were fool enough to try.'

'So why bother to explore?'

'There are some folks out there with more money than you ever dreamed of, who knows why they do these things? Call it philanthropic or whatever but these guys have spent two million dollars so far. That's on the dive, not the not exploration stuff.'

'Two million?'

As if it were no big deal, Kalman shrugged. He had brought sachets of ketchup back with the coffees and he tore them open, decorating what little was left of his meal with their contents.

'They gave us two tasks,' Kalman said, wiping his fingers on a paper serviette. He held up his hand and splayed out his fingers. Gripping his index finger as if about to teach Spargo how to count he said 'Number one, we were to positively identify the boat. The guys that found it used a ROV, that's a Remotely Operating Vehicle, a submersible with cameras. Their video showed no identifiable markings or numbers. What it did show was the sub had no deck gun, and that seemed to mean something to the money guys.'

'Is that what you're using, an ROV?'

'Hell no, we're technical divers, we breathe tri-mix – that's oxygen, nitrogen and helium – I guess you know it, it's the stuff that gives the Donald Duck voices. Oxygen on its own is poisonous below sixty metres, did you know that, Spargo? Between you and me we're well below the safe limit, but who the hell's to know.'

'Did you manage to get into the sub?'

'You bet. The bow compartment was easy, there was a darned great hole in the hull. Inside we had big problems. The watertight door from the bow was rusted shut, so from the outside I cut a hole in the hull. You can only stay at that depth for twenty-five minutes before the gas gets into your blood, Spargo. Been there right through summer and that's a fact. On my last dive I got into the engine room. Guess what I found there, Spargo?'

He looked at Spargo expectantly. Spargo just shrugged. Kalman jabbed his hand into a pocket and took out what looked like a small strip of brown plastic. He held it out. Spargo took it.

'Bakelite, Spargo, the stuff they used to make light switches, you remember?' Is this history, or what?'

Spargo looked at the strip. It was nameplate with fixing holes at each end. Two words in German had been engraved on it by machine but they meant nothing to him. Beneath them, in much smaller print, was the code U-1500. Spargo, unimpressed, handed it back.

'I told the trust guys I'd found this label and one of them flew over specially to see it. I showed it to him and he just stood there shaking his head. Said he had finally found the right sub. Said he'd found it, Spargo. Not me and my guys.'

'You said two jobs. You said identifying the sub was the first of them.'

Kalman held up his hand again. This time he clenched his second finger. 'Second thing, okay. We were to do a stem to stern search of the sub. They said look for something big. I've got something big, I told them, I have a German submarine. Inside it, they said, something big the sub was carrying. You think you've seen rust, Spargo? When the sub went down the acid from its batteries leaked out, helped the saltwater do its job of corroding every damn thing. Felt sorry for the folks that were in her when she went down. You know what gas is given off when battery acid mixes with seawater?'

'Chlorine,' Spargo said.

'Chlorine gas,' Kalman said as if Spargo hadn't spoken. 'Poor devils.'

'What makes you think they didn't get out?'

'Whole crew went down, I reckon. Hole in the bow looks like it was made from the inside, the hull's split wide open. How do you reckon that could have happened?'

Spargo shook his head and waited for the answer. Realising there wouldn't be one he volunteered his own. 'One of its torpedoes exploded.'

'Now that's the odd thing, Spargo. She had no torpedoes. No torpedo tubes either.' Spargo tried to comment but Kalman talked over him. 'There wasn't one inch of space in those boats they didn't use, Spargo. They bolted stuff to the roof and walls and when it rusts it all comes down. You disturb it, you get crushed by a ton of rusted steel. Can't say it's a job I want to do again. Never. Not ever.'

Spargo tried to imagine it. Tried to compare it with old mines. He had been into abandoned workings and seen collapses, rotting timbers with great globs of mould. It had intrigued him. Scared him.

'It's not all rust,' Kalman continued. 'They used bronze or gunmetal for some of the fittings and that don't corrode. You know what other metal don't corrode, Spargo?'

Spargo knew what was coming. Gold doesn't corrode. People kill for gold.

'And that's pewter.' Kalman reached down to the carrier bag, looked around the room to see he wasn't being watched and brought up a dish made of dull, silvery metal. Instinctively Spargo took it. The dish was bigger than a dinner plate and had a deep, broad rim. Though its underside was heavily pitted the plate had been cleaned with care. By Kalman, Spargo supposed.

'There's more where that came from,' Kalman said. 'A lot more.'

'Are you saying the sub was carrying cargo?'

He had heard of pewter being recovered from ancient wooden wrecks in the Mediterranean, but not from German U-boats in the North Sea. Old pewter goods were valuable, but nowhere near as valuable as gold. Even if the boat had been stuffed full of pewter, its value wouldn't cover Kalman's diving costs.

'Not a cargo,' Kalman said. 'A forty-eight piece dinner service. What do you think of that, a goddamn dinner service!'

Spargo shook his head. Managed to smile.

'So the crew ate off pewter?'

'No way. They ate off china plates, same as you and me. It's still there. Broken crockery everywhere. You're darned right though, pewter's not what these trust guys are after. Now don't you ask me what it is they are after, because I do not know the answer to that question, it is none of my business. I'm getting paid for identifying the sub and telling them what's inside it.'

'What else did you find?'

'We found jack shit, nothing. Whole game's been about nothing. Not only did the old tub have no deck gun, no torpedoes, it had no anti-aircraft gun on the bridge. What the hell use is a sub with no tubes? Hell, Spargo, that was what they were made for!'

'Did the trust think it was carrying gold? Is that what you think?'

'No, Spargo, that is not what I think. I did gold last year though, not for these guys but for a load of Greeks. Dived the Mediterranean Sea for an Italian corvette sunk in the nineteen-forties, supposed to have carried gold bullion but we found nothing, not so much as one ounce of the damn stuff after four month's work. Somebody had already got to it.'

'Either that or they were sold a pig in a poke.'

'A what?'

'Someone paid good money for false information.'

'You mean it was all bullshit? Yes, I guess so.'

Kalman took the pewter plate from Spargo and set it down on the table. He pointed to marks of the rim.

'See that? See those two shields? They are on every piece.'

He shoved breakfast crockery aside and slid the plate back to Spargo. Though the rim of the plate had been engraved, the markings were spoiled by fine pitting. The shields Kalman referred to sat side by side, tilted towards each other so they touched at the top.

'Who do you suppose owned it?' Kalman asked.

Spargo shook his head. Didn't know. Didn't want to know.

'I said they weren't looking for gold, Spargo,' Kalman continued. 'But there is gold.' He put the plate back in the carrier bag and rummaged around for more, like a lucky dip. 'What do you make of this?'

He passed something under the table. Spargo took it, held it furtively and looked down at it. It was heavy for its size, and though it was damaged by corrosion it was clear to him he was holding what was once a cigarette lighter. It was the kind fuelled by petrol – a long-gone wick ignited by a flint and striker wheel. All that was left was its body, now a black shell. Despite what Kalman said it was not gold.

Gold does not tarnish or corrode. This was tarnished.

'Found it near the engines in what had once been a grease-pot. I guess it had fallen into it. Turn it over, Spargo. Take a look.'

Spargo turned it. Saw a small gold eagle inlaid in its side. Not the brutal, angular Nazi eagle but one much more pleasant, the tips of its wings swept back as if caught by the wind. The blackened body of the lighter was silver, it had to be. Nobody would fix such an exquisite gold object to any other metal, except possibly platinum. But it wasn't platinum; unlike silver, platinum doesn't discolour.

Spargo hefted it in his hand. Held history. Wondered who in a naval ship might have owned such a thing.

'It's beautiful,' he said, stroking the gold with his fingertips.

He wasn't much of a one for trinkets but this one was special. For a second or two he knew how Jez felt when she was young, the years he'd jokingly called her crystal phase, the years when she believed crystals had magical powers. She had spent time gazing at them, stroking them.

He tried to analyse his feelings. He remembered the times he was underground in Zambia, the rare times when miners broke open chunks of rock and revealed vughs – voids lined with perfectly formed crystals. Not gold, but chalcopyrite, the stuff they mined every day in amorphous masses of brass-coloured rock. All that rock, so much dross concealing such beautiful things.

Spargo held out the lighter to Kalman. Kalman waved it away.

'Hey, looks like you fell in love with the thing. You keep it, Spargo.'

'I don't want it.'

Spargo turned the lighter over in his hands and fondled it, stroking the gold eagle with the tip of his thumb, feeling the contours of its sharp-pointed wings. He placed it on the table and flicked it gently with his finger. It slid across and jammed under Kalman's plate.

'What's up, Spargo? Scared you'll get gunned down by the revenue men?' He said it loudly and gave a short laugh. He reached down again and pulled something else from his bag.

This time the object thrust at Spargo was a pewter beer stein. Its hinged lid was missing. Like the plate, parts of the stein were pitted by corrosion. Spargo commented that it had no engraved shields and tried handing it back. Kalman wouldn't take it. Told Spargo to look inside it. Spargo looked. The bottom of the stein was made of glass. An attempt had been made to clean it but it was permanently stained. To show willing he held it up and looked at the ceiling light through it.'

'What do you make of it, Spargo?'

Spargo made nothing of anything. The glass was too dark. He chose a brighter ceiling light and saw the glass was engraved with the Third Reich eagle, its wings spread, its head turned to one side and a swastika gripped in its claws. Around the circumference of the glass disc were marks that at first glance Spargo thought were small scratches. He rotated the stein and realised they were not scratches, but letters:

Kapitänleutnant Theodor Volker

Hands shaking, Spargo put down the stein. Kalman regarded him anxiously, doing his head tilt thing.

'You okay? You look sick.'

'I'm fine.' For good measure he added another lie, 'Went for a run this morning. Not used to it.'

'Get yourself fit, Spargo. Get out and exercise.'

Spargo smiled. 'It's time I left. I've got a long drive.' He started to rise from his chair but Kalman waved him down.

'I need a favour, Spargo. You travel, you know the hassle of going through customs. Pewter's not that valuable but by the time I've paid duty, well, heck!'

Spargo tensed. Sure he didn't want to hear what was coming next he again rose to leave.

'I really must – '

'Spargo, hear me out, okay? I need to sell the stuff here, in Scotland. It's easy to carry dollars or your British pounds.'

'What exactly are you asking?'

Anything even remotely illegal would be out of the question, he was in more than enough trouble already. Kalman's hand returned to the bag and emerged, not with more pewter as Spargo feared, but with a folded sheet of paper torn from a pad. He flattened it out on the table to reveal a list of addresses, one in London, others in Newcastle, Glasgow and Leith. None of them was complete. In each case either a name, postcode or house number was missing. All phone numbers had been scratched through with a ball pen.

'Don't get me wrong, Spargo, I wouldn't ask anything unlawful. The stuff is from international waters. I found it. It's mine.'

'Your clients might think otherwise.'

'Things are okay with them. I told them I'd found a pewter dinner service and they told me exactly what I could do with it – they are not polite guys, Spargo.' He looked down at the paper. 'Friend of mine gave me this list. It's people who deal with stuff like this.'

'It's called receiving.'

'Hell, Spargo! No it is not. It belongs to our clients and they do not want this stuff. I have called these telephone numbers. That one...' he said, pointing, 'is a bakery in some place called Calne. Where the hell is Calne? That near here?'

'Down south. Wiltshire, I think.'

'Wilt-Shire. Okay. This one here, Glasgow, I was planning to visit. Can't now, not with the Posi-Three ready to sail.'

Spargo's gaze travelled rapidly down the list.

'That last one's not right,' he said. 'It should be road, not street. There's no such place as Easter Street in Edinburgh.'

Kalman became animated. He waved the list in the air.

'Hey, Spargo! You live in Edinburgh, that right? Well now, Spargo...'

CHAPTER
TWENTY-FIVE

GÖRING'S TRAIN LEAVES Friedrichswalde on time and heads south. Theo, travelling away from the Reichsmarschall, knows his greatest fear is unfounded. Whatever it is Walter is doing it is not a plot to kill or abduct the man. Leaving his cabin he finds Walter slouched in an armchair in Göring's salon, smoking a cigarette, his feet up on a table. Theo moves to the window, chooses a seat and then changes his mind. Moves to a spot where he cannot be seen from outside.

'We are travelling south,' he says. 'Are we returning to Berlin?'

'We go around it.'

'What if the tracks have been bombed?'

'If they have been bombed, they will be repaired.'

'Just for us?'

'I have no idea.'

'And then?'

Walter sighs. 'Don't you ever stop? Perhaps I made a mistake after all. Why can't you simply take orders like everyone else?'

'I want to know where we are going. Are we going to Berchtesgaden?'

'I told you, the shelter there is not yet complete. Part of our cargo will go to Schloss Veldenstein – the castle - the others will go to Munich.'

'You said the treasures would not be moved there until things got bad.'

'How much worse do you think they can get?'

Soon they are moved from the salon, politely and respectfully, by an old man in a rail supervisor's black trousers with a side-stripe of red. His cap is so covered with braid it would have better suited an admiral. He accompanies them to the command carriage where they sit down in upholstered, leather chairs.

A film of ice is growing on the outside of the windows, a pattern of crystals that creeps slowly upwards. Walter tells the man to turn up the heating, also to find a steward to bring coffee.

Footsteps bring the steward, also the Luftwaffe lieutenant who supervised loading. The steward pours coffee while the officer speaks quietly to Walter. When both men leave, Theo resumes his questions.

'You said things are bad. How bad? Is my son in danger?'

Walter laughs. 'From the British and Americans? I doubt it. You should fear the Soviets. They are animals, they will flood across Germany and drive out these cocksure western troops. They will not stop at Germany, they will soon rule Europe. The British will regret the day they did not join our struggle.'

'If that is all true, why are we bothering to move these treasures?'

The train stops unexpectedly with a clatter of buffers. The coffee in Theo's cup slops down his jacket. As he flicks it with his fingers to remove it he hears doors slamming and men running. Moving to the window he sees troops with rifles and rapid-fire guns. They are everywhere, out on the rail tracks and up on the roof.

Then, suddenly, all is quiet. Walter looks at his watch. 'Twenty-three seconds. Impressive, but not good enough.'

'What is happening? All this to protect a few pictures.'

'No, all this to protect our Hermann. It makes no difference whether he is on the train or not. Is it not better than having the men sitting on their arses, playing card games?

'That was a drill?'

'That was a drill.'

'You could have warned me.'

'I wanted to see your face.'

'Is it permitted to smoke in here?'

'Do you mean are you permitted to smoke? Of course. It is a railway carriage, not a submarine.'

One of the locomotives gives a short toot. It is echoed by the other loco's whistle and the troops move again, the sound of boots on the carriage roof and the staccato slam of doors. Soon the train is moving again, slowly.

THE MAN WHO PLAYED TRAINS

'Do they do that every time we stop?'

'It is not usual for us to stop. Our train has priority over all others.' He nods at the window. 'You see?'

A train has stopped in a siding to let them pass. Its carriages are packed with troops, its flatbed trucks piled with vehicles. There are trucks, troop carriers, ambulances and armoured cars.

'We get priority? Over military trains?'

'You have so much to learn, Theodor.'

Theo returns to his compartment, opens the top of his kitbag, shoves his arm down inside through tightly rolled clothes and fishes for the canvas wallet with his pipes and tobacco.

Ignoring his own lighter he searches for the one Göring gave him. He finds it, and holding it upright he tests it by pressing down on the thumb-catch. The wick cover lifts and the wick ignites. He lets it burn, attracted to the brightness of the small, clean white flame. Good lighter fuel is available, it seems. But only to some.

Staring at the flame he ponders on the futility of war. In the long term, even the victors are losers. He ponders too on the mining man he knew, Sam Spargo, wondering if he too has swapped his overalls for a military uniform and, if that is so, would they be obliged to shoot each other dead if they ever met? And what has he, Theodor Volker, done with his life? You can stencil icons of sunken ships on your conning tower but you can't stencil the dead. There is not enough room.

He fumbles with his tobacco pouch and opens it, nips a wedge of tobacco between finger and thumb, packs his pipe, flicks the lighter again and sucks the flame down to the tobacco. Returning to the command carriage he sits close to Walter, who has upended his briefcase and tipped its contents onto a table. Theatrically he sniffs the air.

'Your tobacco smells like dried pig shit.'

'It's not such a bad smoke.'

'You can get some decent stuff later.'

'From where? You said the train won't be stopping.'

'It won't be.'

Questioning Walter about such things isn't worth the effort so he sits back and draws on his pipe. Tries too hard to relax. Realising the pipe has gone out he prods the tobacco with a pencil. Gives up and puts the pipe down.

Walter speaks but doesn't look up. 'Dried pig shit doesn't burn well.'

'No.'

'None of this is new, you do realise that?'

'What isn't new?'

'Transporting paintings. Göring has been doing it for years. He has been sending them to Switzerland through diplomatic channels. He has a network of dealers and agents, not just throughout Greater Germany but also Spain, Italy and Switzerland.'

'You told me that. Are these the companies you were telling me about?'

'These companies are different, they are owned by the SS. Göring is not part of that, he has agents, not companies.'

'You said he was a collector. Why should he want to sell things?'

'He sells stuff he's not supposed to have. The art Adolf calls degenerate.'

'I thought that had all been destroyed.'

'You thought wrong. Elsewhere in the world these are tradable assets. Göring uses them to obtain more desirable pieces.'

Theo examines his fingernails. He can't remember a time when they looked so clean, his mother would have been proud of him. His father would have accused him of not working for a living.

'Are we carrying stuff to be sold? Are we using a train and troops to profit the Reichsmarschall? Does the Führer know he does this?'

'The paintings that go to Munich will probably end up in Zurich. That's Switzerland, in case you don't know where things are on land.'

'I know where Switzerland is.'

Walter reaches out, takes a cigarette from a silver box on a side table and puts it between his lips. 'Give me a light.'

Theo, without thinking, takes Göring's lighter and flicks up a flame. Walter snatches the lighter from him.

'Where did you get this?'

'From the Reichsmarschall. I offered him a light but my own

lighter had no petrol. He gave me his.'

Walter nods, seems satisfied. He inspects the lighter, lights his cigarette with it and hands it back.

'Our Hermann likes to give presents, though not usually to officers as junior as you. You must have made an impression on him. It's a valuable piece, take care of it. As I was saying, the paintings for Munich will be sent to Zurich by diplomatic bag. They end up – via our embassy – with a character called Mendl who transfers them to the vaults of the Schweizer Bank. Göring is trying to get everything transferred from there to Spain. It is not proving easy.'

'How do you know these things?'

'I have told you. It is my job to know.'

'Are we are going to Munich as well as to Schloss Veldenstein? You and me, I mean.'

'That's what I said.'

'My son is near Munich. Can I visit him?'

'You cannot.'

'For god's sake Walter! I will be so close! Is there no way?'

Walter stares but doesn't comment. He draws on his cigarette and looks down at his papers.

'Where is he, exactly? What do you mean by a few kilometres?'

'Ingolstadt.'

The train has picked up speed, the carriage is rocking. Walter walks to the end of the carriage, touching fixed objects with his fingertips to steady himself the way a drunken man might do. He stops, stands with his legs astride, and pulls out a drawer in a wide metal map chest. He slams it shut, opens another and then another. Eventually he finds what he is seeking and drags out a large map. Theo goes to him and helps spread it out.

'Show me,' Walter says, his finger on Munich. 'Where is this place, this Ingolstadt?'

Theo shoves Walter's hand away and studies the map. There is Munich, there is the autobahn.

'Here,' he says, with his finger on the paper. 'The farm is to the east of Ingolstadt. There is a village. It is near the Donau River.'

Walter says nothing. A small circle has been drawn on the map in purple pencil, one hundred and fifty kilometres to the north of Theo's finger. Much further south is another circle, not far from what was once the border between Germany and Austria.

Theo points to the northernmost circle. 'Is this Schloss Veldenstein?'

Walter nods. 'It is. The other is Berchtesgaden.'

He uses a bell push to call a steward from the kitchens. When the man arrives Walter orders more coffee.

'This time bring the good stuff, do you understand me? Do not bring that swill you serve to those uniformed peasants.'

When they are alone again Walter speaks in a near-whisper. Theo strains to hear.

'We will stop at Neuhaus,' he says. 'It is near Schloss Veldenstein. At Neuhaus the crates will be offloaded onto three trucks. You will accompany the truck that goes to the Schloss and I will travel to Munich with the other two. It is no coincidence you hold the rank of Hauptmann, Theodor. All offloading and transfers of crates must be witnessed by a trusted officer of at least that rank. The reason I cannot take you to see your son because I need you to witness the handover at the Schloss.'

'Can't someone else do it? Can't you drop me off at the farm and collect me later?'

'That is not possible. The only way that could happen is if you were to sign the handover documents in advance. I cannot believe a man like you would be prepared to do such a thing.'

Theo frowns. 'I don't understand. I thought we were travelling together to Munich and the Schloss.'

'I've changed my mind. There will be two separate convoys, therefore two separate cargo manifests. When you hand over the contents of your truck you will obtain a signature on yours.'

'I am not five years old, I understand all that. What I don't understand is your suggestion that I can sign the manifest without witnessing the transfer. Is that what you are suggesting? You are responsible for the treasures. You – '

'Stop calling them treasures, you sound like a pirate. The cargo we carry consists only of paintings.'

'Why did you suggest it?'

Walter shrugs. 'Suggest what?'

'That I sign the manifest in advance?'

'I simply said that the only way it was possible for you to visit your son was if you signed the manifest in advance. That is a fact, not a suggestion.'

'I don't understand why you mentioned it.'

'Despite what you believe I am still your friend. I have been thinking about your son. After all, a signature is a mere formality, a trivial thing in these times of war. I say again, if you wish to see your son you simply have to check what is loaded onto your truck and then sign the manifest. You will watch the truck depart for the Schloss. What can possibly go wrong? This is the Reich, not Mexico. The truck is unlikely to be attacked by masked bandits.'

'And what happens when the truck arrives there? Whoever unloads it will see I am not there. They will know the signed manifest is a fake.'

'They will never see the manifest. It will not go with the truck. I will place both your manifest and mine in an envelope that will be returned to Carinhall.'

'Why are you doing this? You said I had no chance of seeing my boy. Now you seem to be encouraging it.'

'To be honest with you I hadn't realised we would be travelling so close to him.'

Theo grapples with the implications of what they are saying. He shakes his head, in confusion rather than refusal. Walter watches him closely. Then he picks up the map, folds it up and hands it to Theo.

'Here, take it. Fold it small and tuck it inside your jacket. Now, go to your room and sleep. If you want pills for your head then look in Christa's room. You are no use to me half asleep and hung-over.'

'Tell me again. If I sign, you will take me to the farm? You will let me stay there for at least one night?'

CHAPTER TWENTY-SIX

QUINN WAS WRONG when he said the police had finished at Spargo's house. When Spargo arrived home a white van with Crimestoppers on its side was standing at the kerb, blocking his drive. Unusually, there was plenty parking space in the road so perhaps his neighbours didn't want to get too close in case finding bodies in basements was contagious. His front door was ajar and he gave it a push. Saw Quinn and a man in blue overalls standing in the hall.

'Thought you might have stayed here last night,' Quinn said as a greeting. 'Seeing as I told you we'd finished.'

'You told me you weren't sure about the key.'

'Later I realised you wouldn't need it. I remembered your daughter has one.'

'I stayed over, in Inverness. Didn't fancy driving down last night in that rain.'

Quinn gave him a raised-eyebrows, all-right-for-some look.

'As I said, we've finished. I came back to look at something one of our people found yesterday. You said your alarm wouldn't work. Want to know why? Come outside.'

The man in overalls led the way. The ladder from Spargo's basement was propped against the side wall of the house. At the top of it, within easy reach, the cover of his burglar alarm box hung like a pendulum on a short length of flex, rubbing the wall as it swung in the breeze. Quinn looked up at it.

'It wasn't like that,' he said. 'We unscrewed and checked it out.'

Spargo stayed looking up.

'It failed around the same time I found my front door wasn't double locked, I think I told you. I pressed buttons to reset it but it didn't respond. There's a back-up battery, that white thing. Even if the mains supply is cut off the alarm should still work. It's got an anti-tamper switch. If you remove the front cover the alarm sounds.'

'Except we've got the cover off and it's quiet.'

'So I see.'

'It's quiet because someone sliced through the front of the box with a fine blade – an angle grinder, my techie friend here thinks. The blade went through the case and severed the leads to the horn and the battery. It's a slick bit of work by someone who knew what they were doing. The only indication they'd done it is a narrow slit in the cover. One of our constables noticed it.'

'Observant of him.'

'Her, not him. Thing is, angle grinders make noise. We've spoken to your neighbours. Mr Cutler across the road remembers seeing a van here and a ladder against the wall. He can't remember when it was.'

'He didn't think to report it?'

'He thought the man looked official. Thought he was maintaining it for you.'

Chesterton again, Spargo thought. Do a thing blatantly enough, carry the tools of the trade, wear the right kit…

'Do you think it has anything to do with Letchie's body?'

'That was my first thought. But your basement isn't on the alarm system, so why bother to disable it?'

'Who's to say they knew that?'

Quinn gave slow nods. 'What I don't understand is why they disabled it so long ago. I find it hard to believe it was done as part of a plan to murder Letchie. What if you'd had it fixed?'

Spargo shrugged. 'So I was right, somebody did break into my house. They did it while I was in Spain, they disabled the alarm and got in with a house key. I kept one in the basement.'

'I know. We found it taped under the sink. Who else knew about it?'

'Only my daughter. Though she's had her own key for years. She's probably forgotten it is there.'

'What about your ex-wife?'

'Theresa. She lives in Brussels.'

'Was she aware you kept a key in the basement?'

'No, definitely not. You can't possibly suspect her of anything.'

'Would there be any reason for her to return to the house without you knowing?'

'What, park a van outside and go up a ladder dressed in overalls? Cut through the alarm with an angle grinder? She is a very resourceful woman so I suppose anything's possible.'

Quinn didn't respond. He didn't have to. The withering look he gave Spargo said it all.

'I'm sorry,' Spargo said. 'My wife would have no reason to return here, covertly or otherwise. Our split was painful but reasonably amicable. And she doesn't go round murdering journalists.'

Quinn didn't stay. When he and his colleague drove away Spargo checked all the rooms. That the police had searched everywhere was clear. An attempt had been made to replace the contents of cupboards and drawers neatly. To Spargo it looked as if his house had been tidied by an enthusiastic four-year-old.

The garden was the same, no stone unturned. Things he hadn't bothered with for years – a pile of concrete blocks, a water butt and the remains of a compost heap had been, respectively, moved, drained, and dug over.

The man in overalls had replaced the alarm box cover and had returned the ladder to the basement, leaving the door unlocked. Spargo stood there for a while, holding the edge of the door, before stepping inside and flicking the switch.

The files that were spewed across the floor had been gathered up and packed into boxes. An attempt had been made to stack them but it had been done so badly they were already collapsing under their own weight.

He was there to lay ghosts. To simply pretend it hadn't happened wouldn't work for him, he had tried that so many times. Whatever the truth of the old miners' tales this was real, Letchie's death wasn't fiction, Spargo had seen the body. Now, standing near the doorway, his mind saw more, saw the killer standing behind Letchie with the wire in his hands. Saw him looping it over his victim's head and tugging it tight.

And naked? It made sense to strip the victim and destroy his clothes. That made it worse. Had Letchie been stripped before the deed or after? Spargo shivered at the thought of Letchie being forced to undress, knowing what was to be his fate. Whatever Letchie had done, he didn't deserve that.

Spargo would change the place around, he decided, he would paint the walls yellow, install brighter lights and put the switch on the correct side of the door. Locking the door behind him he went back to the house. Without Quinn around the place felt normal – cosy even – and he was thankful for that, relieved the murder hadn't taken place in the house itself. He liked the place. Didn't want to sell it. Didn't want to think about how difficult that would be after what had happened.

He was behind with his work. Upstairs in his office he tried to settle, opening a report he'd been working on, managing to get to the bottom of the page before realising he hadn't absorbed a single word he'd read. Finally he gave up and went downstairs.

The bus Spargo caught took him close to Valvona and Crolla's in Elm Row. He crossed Leith Walk and entered the delicatessen through its tiny shop front. Beyond the chill cabinets the place opened up like Dr Who's Tardis. A few steps led up from the wine racks to a cook-shop and café.

When Jez was young, long before he and Theresa split up and on the rare occasions he was home, he shopped here for special ingredients, conjuring up exotic dishes that took half a day to prepare and cook. Evidence of his efforts still remained in his kitchen, the gourmet cook books and stainless steel implements, hidden away in drawers and cupboards like his herbs and spices, all well past their use-by dates. Perhaps one day he would cook like that again.

V&C did great bacon rolls; when the one he ordered arrived at his table he took his time eating it, sitting back and observing other diners. Not wanting to pay by credit card he went through his pockets for cash, searching through a hamster's nest of receipts, old tickets and wrappers. He found, in with the coins and crumpled banknotes, something that should not have been there.

Before he'd left Kalman he had been offered the tankard.

'A gift,' Kalman said. 'Take the trouble to look at this place in Leith for me and it's yours.' Spargo refused it, saying he couldn't look at the place because the police were interested in him for matters he couldn't reveal – and dabbling in suspect pewter might not be the best thing for him to be doing right now.

'I know you'll do what you can, Spargo,' Kalman said. 'You look like a guy I can trust. You got one of my cards?'

Out of politeness Spargo had taken the business card Kalman proffered. As they stood up to leave Kalman had taken Spargo's jacket off the back of his chair and held it out for him. Clearly, he had slipped the shell of the lighter into his jacket pocket – the lighter Spargo now clasped in his hand.

Bacon roll half eaten he sneaked a glance at the lighter. The gold eagle motif was no longer set in a black shell. The coins in his pocket had jostled against it, polishing the lighter case to reveal mottled, pitted silver.

If the lighter was a bribe he would have none of it, he would dump it in a bin. Out in the street again he had second thoughts. He couldn't just throw the thing away, not something made from silver and gold. Give it back to Kalman? He could do that, he supposed. He could post it. He had the man's details.

From Elm Row he took back streets to Easter Road. He had Kalman's paper and he took it out and looked for numbers on doors. Sure the place he sought would be an antique shop he stood on a corner and took it all in, the dry cleaners, the newsagents and charity shops. Nowhere sold antiques. Seeing nothing he wanted, he set off down the road.

The address he sought was not a shop but a faded, red painted door between a jewellers and a chemist. He looked up at the building. Saw three floors of flats. The name on his paper was Montgomery but there was no such name on the doorbells. On impulse he pressed one and heard it ring deep inside. When nobody came he felt relief. He hadn't intended to do this, he had come out of curiosity. But if he was ever unfortunate enough to bump into Kalman again he could say with all honesty he had visited the address without success.

Then he heard footsteps, slow and plodding. Someone old who found walking difficult.

The door was opened by a woman who gave an accusative, confrontational glare. Not old, but in her thirties and carrying a small child. She stood holding the edge of the door as if ready to close it fast – a clear message that her struggle to the door had better be worth the effort. Spargo hesitated before speaking.

'I'm looking for someone called Montgomery.'

'Then you've come to the wrong place.'

'But he lives here? Normally?'

'No thing as normal with the big shite. Been gone a year. What's he done? You police?'

'I'm not police. I was told I would find him here.'

'You a friend?'

'I've never met him.'

'You're lucky. If you see him you have my permission to give him a good kicking. He owes you money?'

'No.'

'He owes me money. Owes me twenty pound.'

Spargo bit his lip. Paying her something would at least ease his conscience. He pulled out a tenner and handed it over.

'Monty has a wee shop.'

She kept her hand out so he added another and wondered how long this could go on. He tried to interpret the look she gave him. Decided he would rather not know.

'Shop is called Pixie. Halfway up Cockburn Street.'

That was enough. He knew the street; its bottom end joined Waverley Bridge near Waverley station. Its shiny stone setts snake steeply up to High Street, part of Edinburgh's Royal Mile, with shops geared to tourists: gift shops and bars, and occult shops whose windows display polished pebbles, crystals, necklaces and brass Buddhas.

It took Spargo twenty minutes to walk there from Easter Road. He set off upwards, scanning the shop names for Pixie. It was halfway up, the woman had said. Though she hadn't said which side and he hadn't thought to ask.

At the top end of the street he crossed to the other side and worked his way down, imagining, like he'd done in Easter Road, a shop window with brass table lamps and coal scuttles, carriage lamps and picture frames. Maybe a flat iron or two and a few cracked vases. And pewter plates of course, propped up against the wall at the side of the display.

Halfway down the hill he gave up looking. He entered a dress shop and asked about Pixie. The young assistant led him back to the door and pointed across the street.

'Pixie,' she said. 'The yellow one. They changed its name last year.'

'Do you know the owner?'

She shook her head. 'Big man in his thirties. There's a few of them around here like him. Shaved heads. Leather waistcoats. Tattoos and stuff.'

The yellow shop was shoe-horned between its neighbours. Its door, off to one side, was set back behind a high step. Spargo crossed the road and stood looking into its window at a display resembling a bric-a-brac stall at a market. Mythical creatures were arranged on one side – fairies of various sizes and shapes arranged behind a handwritten piece of card folded tent-like that proclaimed them faeries. As if the alternative spelling validated it all.

Spargo stepped up and pushed the door. An old-style brass bell jangled on a coiled spring and he found himself swatting in-your-face creatures hanging from the ceiling on long strings and springs. Another jangle as the door closed. More little people were stacked up beside him and fearing they would topple if he brushed against them, he stepped back. Set more suspended things swinging.

The shop was unexpectedly deep and uncomfortably dark; display cabinets sat in an uneven row along both walls and Spargo took his time browsing, peering into cabinets as if showing real interest, inspecting clusters of crystals, bracelets and jewellery set with unnatural stones he knew were dyed quartz. Arranged on shelves above the cabinets were books on the occult, paganism and runic writings. Deeper in the shop lay more sinister artefacts, glass castings labelled as crystal skulls, and crossed bones in cast brass. Alone in a glass case sat what could well have been a human skull, shrunken and jawless with a top set of well-blackened teeth. A notice proclaimed it wasn't for sale.

Then deep red hair at the back of the shop, Dracula eye shadow and piercings that to Spargo looked painful. He guessed their owner was a girl and he wondered what age she really was under her trimmings. Could be fourteen. Probably ten years older.

'I'm looking for Montgomery,' he mumbled. 'I was told I would find him at Pixie.'

'Pixie's dead. This is Creatures.' She had been chewing gum. It was now behind her ear. When she realised he wasn't a customer she put it back in her mouth. 'You the polis?'

'I'm not police.' He nodded towards the skull in the case. 'You allowed to have that?'

'What?'

'A real head. A shrunken head.'

'Don't see it's any of your business. You an anthropologist, then?'

'I just want Montgomery. I was given his name by someone who has something for sale.'

She narrowed her eyes. 'What's your name?'

'Spargo.'

'Where you from?'

'Here. Edinburgh.'

'What's this man selling?'

'Old pewter.'

'Then you had best take it to an antique shop.'

'I want Montgomery.'

'I don't know any Montgomery.'

Spargo turned away and looked in more cabinets. Perhaps in the hope he would buy something the girl flicked a switch that brought to life a string of coloured Christmas tree lights that hung in loops on the wall. They flashed on and off, illuminating at three second intervals the contents of the cases beneath them. Remembering what was in them was, for the three second dark intervals, like Kim's Game.

In pride of place in the centre of a display case sat a bright red armband. A black swastika sat on a white circular patch. Arranged around it were military medals and buttons, a German army officer's cap badge and a small silver dagger. Small white price tags, the kind jewellers use, had been tied to each piece and placed face down. Spargo looked down at it all. He had got it all wrong. He had assumed Montgomery dealt in antiques, not wartime memorabilia.

'Who are you selling these things for?'

'They're mine.'

'They're Montgomery's. If they were yours they wouldn't be price-tagged. None of the things in the other cabinets have these tags.'

'What the fuck are you, Inspector bloody Rebus?'

Spargo straightened up and turned to face her. He took the lighter from his pocket and displayed it on his upturned palm. The gold and the newly polished silver glistened in the flashing lights. She stood and looked. Didn't touch.

'What is it?'

'It was once a lighter. I believe it's German, nineteen-thirties or forties. The eagle is gold. It's mounted on silver.'

'It's no use to me. I can't deal in unmarked gold.'

'What about Montgomery? Perhaps he's not so fussy. What's he going to say when he learns he's missed a trinket like this?'

She didn't respond. He didn't persist.

'Sorry to have troubled you,' he said.

He walked out. He was no longer bothered. He had done more for Kalman than he had meant to. Outside in the street he kept one hand in his pocket and realised, after a while, that he was stroking the gold eagle with the tip of his thumb. Realised, too, that it seemed to relax him.

Kalman's comment about him not being fit irritated him and he decided to walk home. It was all very well for Kalman, he was younger, he was fitter because he had a job that demanded it. Spargo, latterly anyway, spent most of his time at a desk. But that, he thought as he strode uphill – a thing he found incredibly tiring – was a temporary state of affairs because as soon as the BarConSA job kicked off he would be checking on drill rigs on the hills of Kilcreg. He would walk to them; he would soon be fit.

With new-found enthusiasm and completely unaware he was being followed, he crossed the Royal Mile. Ten minutes more and he was approaching the old university buildings and the University Bookshop, James Thin. He needed a decent map of Kilcreg and James Thin was the place. If they didn't have the right one in stock then he could order one.

He changed direction, went from one set of pedestrian lights to another. A man close behind him did the same, resulting in a strange dance movement that brought them face-to-face. Spargo apologised. The man, a stocky, leather-clad biker, gave a grunt.

Spargo, assuming the man had been drinking, stepped aside. The man blocked him. The crossing lights changed to green and Spargo, determined to cross and equally determined not to tangle with a drunken gorilla in motorcycle leathers, swivelled sharply and crossed the road. The gorilla followed. He reached the front door of the bookshop at the same time as Spargo.

'You got something to sell.'

A statement, not a question. Spargo looked at the sleeveless, weatherworn leather waistcoat and faded black tee-shirt. He could just about make out the word HARLEY printed across the shirt in what had once been multicolour – but clearly not permanent – inks. Shiny silver chains looped down across a Desperate Dan chest and linked, at their lower end, to a leather belt secured with a skull-and-crossbones buckle.

The biker's bare arms, smothered in tattoos and twice as thick as Spargo's, bore no resemblance to any he had seen on a human. Predictably the knuckles bore the words LOVE and HATE, tattoos so old the fingers had outgrown the artwork and left the ink thin, the letters distorted and wide. Though the man was adorned with a lot more metal than Kalman had been wearing when Spargo first met him, the biker's was less valuable. More suited to a pirate than a middle-aged rocker.

Spargo looked him in the eye.

'I'm not selling anything. You could have discovered that yourself if you'd shown yourself in the shop. Where were you, down the end behind the curtains? Are you Montgomery?'

'Who's asking?'

The man took out a brass cigarette case and extracted from it a thin, poorly-made roll-up. Placing one end of it between his lips he ignited the other with a disposable lighter. The protruding shreds of tobacco, along with half the cigarette, flared up and vanished with a crisp, crackling hiss.

'If you are Montgomery then say so. I'm nothing to do with the police. I know a man with pewter plates to sell. I'm doing him a favour.'

Some bloody favour. Maybe he should invoice Kalman for his time and trouble. The biker grunted again. He put a hand deep into one of his many pockets and Spargo, expecting a weapon, took a smart step back. The biker pulled out a scrap of paper and thrust it out.

'Nine o'clock tonight. Be there, Pal.'

CHAPTER
TWENTY-SEVEN

GÖRING'S TRAIN RUNS THROUGH THE NIGHT, stopping only for the locos to take on water and coal. Theo, surrounded by noise, sleeps well. Twelve hours after setting his head down on the bed's feather pillow he is woken by the steward, bringing breakfast.

The journey has taken less time than Theo anticipated. It is daylight when the train pulls into the rail yards at Neuhaus. It moves slowly, its wheels grinding and squealing as they negotiate tight curves on old rusting rails. Several vehicles with military markings are lined up nearby and three covered trucks, massive and multi-wheeled, stand ready with their tailgates down. When the train stops, two of the trucks snake backwards, lining themselves up with the train's boxcar doors.

Uniformed airmen are everywhere. All wear the Göring cuff and all are armed, some with automatic rifles and others with machine pistols. Loud thuds from further down the train tell Theo those doing the unloading are dropping loading ramps. Wasting no time.

Walter, Theo discovers when he arrives at the command carriage, has gone. No doubt he is outside somewhere, shouting and supervising. Theo finds him in the boxcar, doing his thing with his clipboard. Using a pencil as a pointer he waves it like a baton at this crate and that. When the two trucks are full, another back up. Walter hands Theo the clipboard and holds out a pen.

'Sign it!'

Theo shakes his head. 'I can't. Not until I've counted the crates.'

'Don't be ridiculous! The more time we waste messing about here the less chance there is of you seeing your boy.'

Theo, convinced he is doing a deal with the devil, takes the pen and signs. Walter takes the signed paper, folds it, and slips it into a long brown envelope. Then he frowns, inverts the envelope and taps the sheet out again. He unfolds it, checks it, and returns it to the envelope. He sighs.

'Good. All in order. Just for a second I thought you might have signed it Volker.'

An elderly officer, out of breath, arrives at the boxcar. Stopping in front of Walter he salutes. The man is cold, he has the collar of his greatcoat pulled high and his breath drifts like thin mist. Finally he finds breath to speak.

'My consignment for the Sch...' he seems to run out of air and he takes a deep breath. 'My consignment for the Schloss, Herr Major, it is complete.' He swivels on his heels to face Theo. 'Herr Hauptmann, I understand you are to accompany me in the escort vehicles.'

Walter interrupts him. 'The Hauptmann has a more important task to undertake for the Reichsmarschall. Your responsibility is to take your cargo to the Schloss. Documentation is all in order, it will be returned to the Reichsmarschall's secretary, Miss Limburger. Is that clear?'

The two trucks destined for Munich head south on a swathe of white concrete. Theo, in the lead truck with Walter, navigates using the map from the command carriage. They make good time on the autobahn, and when they turn onto local roads Theo folds the map. Tells the driver he knows the way from here.

The back roads are narrow and busy; horse-drawn wagons delay them and Walter, frustrated, slides open his window to curse them. He urges their driver to keep up his speed, to run the wagons off the road if need be.

The lane Theo takes them down was made for farm carts. It is the same width as the trucks and tree branches scrape their sides. It is also steep, tortuous and narrow and the deep muddy ruts in its surface are hard-frozen. Despite their immense size the truck's tyres struggle to grip. Theo apologises. Last time he was here it was not like this.

The lane flattens out and ends in a farmyard. Theo knows that beneath the lake of frozen mud and ice-filled hollows is a cobbled yard, but there is no sign of it now. Even trucks with ten wheels have trouble manoeuvring and they grind their way slowly. The ground beneath their tyres crunches and cracks under their weight.

The roofs of the buildings around the yard are clad with corrugated sheets, rusted through and in dire need of repair. Beyond them, like an isolated island in an icy swamp, stands the farmhouse, its roof similarly clad but less rusted. The front door of the farmhouse faces them, it is set back beneath a canopy that was once a full porch. Theo wonders what happened to its wooden sides.

'Can you drive closer? Right to the door?'

The driver grunts, then remembers who he is with. He mutters apologies and swings the wheel hard. The truck lurches, slithers sideways, and finally stops. Theo, in the middle of the truck's bench seat, reaches across Walter to open the door. He clambers past him and jumps down onto ice. The driver watches.

'With respect, Herr Hauptmann. Take care you do not fall.'

Theo, embarrassed, wants to explain to them that the last time he was there the farm was full of life, that it was the place where his wife Erika was born, that the first time he came here, in summer, he and Erica ran together through fields and rounded up cows, brought them for milking to a cowshed strewn with fresh straw. Back then there were pigs in the sties – pigs Erika named after people she knew, her teachers at school and her relatives.

But now there is nothing. Not one living thing.

Some of the ruts are soft shells. As Theo walks on them they collapse and spurt mud on his clothes. By the time he has taken his kitbag from the back of the truck the mud has coated his high boots. Walter slides back the window and looks out. His nose is turned up for good reason.

'God! What is that stench?'

'They farmed pigs. The last time I was here they had thirty.'

'You are certain this is the place? It looks deserted.'

'It was not always like this.'

'It seems to me it has been like this for a while. Do you want me to wait?'

Unusual generosity from Walter.

'No, they are here. I have seen someone.'

It is a lie. The place looks and feels dead.

'Rather you than me. I will return tomorrow at midday. You will be ready.'

'Tomorrow. Midday. Yes.'

The truck is reversing to where the second one is waiting. Still embarrassed Theo waves and shouts his thanks, his voice drowned by the truck engine's growl.

Theo stands at the door of the farmhouse with his kitbag beside him. As always the front door is unlocked and he flicks up its wooden latch and gives it a shove. The door opens into the parlour, a small, low-ceilinged room that was once comfortably furnished. Now, apart from two leather armchairs, it is bare. He wonders if Walter was right. Perhaps he should have asked him to wait.

He calls out as he steps inside. Treads mud on the grubby stone floor.

'Artur! Barbara!'

He puts down his bag but leaves his greatcoat on. It is as cold inside as it is outside, there is no fire in the grate – the fire that burns summer and winter – and no cooking pot hanging over it on the black iron hook. No kettle on the flat hob beside it.

The door to the back room is open. Except for the wooden drainer beside the stone sink, that room is bare too. On it are a loaf of bread and a small wedge of cheese. Both are thick with mould.

Returning to the door to scrape mud from his boots Theo calls out again. This time he hears a sound like the lifting of a door latch. It seems to have come from upstairs. And there is something else, the sound of footsteps. A patter, like a cat on a roof.

He pulls off his boots and moves quietly to the stairs, ascending the narrow passage in near darkness to the small upstairs rooms. Entering Artur and Barbara's bedroom he remembers how it was last time, the chair in the corner, the table with its oil lamp, water jug and washing bowl. Now the table is gone and the lamp, jug and bowl stand on the floor on a multi-colour rug – a rug made years ago by Erika from strips of rag she knotted through sackcloth. There are no free-standing beds. As in many rural houses, they are concealed behind panelled walls, like nests.

The small double doors to the bed stand open. Bundled on top of the hay-filled mattress is a large, square quilt. Theo recognises its embroidered patterns. What now feels like a lifetime ago he helped Erika and Barbara shred old woollens and stuff them inside it.

From where he is standing he can smell damp, stable-like odours. This is not how things should be. Barbara changes the hay in the mattress weekly and airs the beds daily, draping quilts and mattresses over windowsills in fine weather or airing them in the barn when it rains.

He checks the only other bedroom, the one where he and Erika slept for a week after they married. The bed doors are closed. Like the other room this once had an oil lamp, a washstand and an Erika rug. All are gone, including the curtains.

The room's one window, at the back of the house, overlooks fields. In case Artur and Barbara are working there Theo goes to it, wipes it clean with his sleeve, and looks out. What he sees shocks him. The fields are overgrown. Wheat – if what he sees is wheat – lies rotting and weed-ridden, flattened by frost.

The floor creaks as he steps back. A sound from behind the closed bed-doors startles him and he goes to them, opens the doors looks in. Something moves. He steps away. He knows about cornered rats, how they launch themselves at you, all teeth and bared claws. But it is not a rat concealed there, he knows that too.

A bulge in the quilt darts from one end to the other. Theo glimpses a nose and an ear and he grabs at the quilt. The child – it has to be a child – dodges away. Theo tries again, loses his balance and falls forwards.

Then, unexpectedly, he sees his boy, cross-legged at one end of the alcove, tight-lipped and staring.

'Peter,' Theo says, quietly. 'Where is your grandmother? Peter, listen to me, where is Artur? Where have they gone?'

CHAPTER
TWENTY-EIGHT

THE EDINBURGH BACKSTREET was not the sort of place you ventured into at night when alone – or perhaps at any time. There were no people and, unusually for Edinburgh, no parked cars. Spargo wondered why that might be.

On one side of the road a wire mesh fence on high concrete posts protected the back of dark warehouses. On the other side, a railway line ran high on a stone viaduct, the arches beneath it blocked off by wooden walls. Some of the walls had doors; the sign on one of them, an electricity substation, proclaimed Danger of Death.

Spargo drove slowly, his eyes straining for details. Halfway down the street he pulled into the kerb under the road's only working streetlight. He pressed a button. Heard the satisfying clunks of his door locks.

On the seat beside him was the biker's scrappy map. He picked it up and looked again at the clumsy annotation, the words *green door* and the child's treasure map arrow. Then he looked across the road at the boarded-up archways. In the orange glow from the street light all the woodwork looked brown. Against his better judgement he switched off his engine, stepped out of the car and pressed the remote. Heard the clunks.

A lone car came from behind, driving slowly with its lights on full beam. In the pure white light the wooden walls took on their true colours, some red, some blue and some black. The one directly across the road from Spargo became green, as did the door in its centre.

It wasn't the right place, it couldn't be. The door had no handle or keyhole. Weeds grew from the gap at its base, it hadn't been opened for years. His imagination conjured up the possibility the biker wanted him here, wanted him out of the way while he broke into his house and killed someone else. He pictured Letchie's swollen face and pop-out eyes. Enough was enough. He reached into his pocket for the remote.

The car that had come into the street stopped some way off. Spargo lost interest in it when its driver got out and walked back up the street. He wrongly assumed the man had kept walking away, but further up the road he had crossed to the arches. Now, Spargo realised, he was coming back down, walking slowly towards him. When Spargo stopped, the man stopped. When Spargo stepped sideways, so did the man.

Spargo was about to run to his car – having worked out that unless the figure was an Olympic sprinter he would reach it well before him – when the thud of drawn bolts made him hesitate. The green door beside him was being dragged back the inside with short, juddering tugs. Forgetting the distant figure Spargo turned sharply towards it. Saw, in dim light from inside the doorway, the biker's unmistakable bulk.

The body in Spargo's basement was big news. From the media frenzy Midge knew it had happened in Spargo's road but not Spargo's house, only discovering the latter fact a lot later when he drove there and saw police everywhere. He returned later and saw Quinn again, and a man up a ladder. He considered texting Mr Luis again but remembered he hadn't actually done it last time. In any case, he was supposed to be watching Dr Jessica, not her father.

The next time Midge returned to the road the police were gone and there was Spargo, backing his Volvo onto the road. Midge kept his distance, and when the Volvo straightened up he followed it, hanging well back. At the end of the road Spargo turned towards the city. After a mile or he turned right at the Commonwealth Pool, towards Arthur's Seat and Salisbury Crags. Midge, still some way off, was caught by red traffic lights.

At a roundabout in Holyrood Park Midge took a chance and

turned left, managing to catch up with the Volvo as it passed the tented structure of Dynamic Earth. Surprisingly, Spargo kept going. Didn't turn off towards the old town. Another half mile or so and he turned down a back street.

Midge, locally born and bred, knew every alley and lane. From the mess Spargo made of the last bit of the journey, it was clear he did not. When the Volvo finally stopped in a backstreet under the only working lamppost, Midge stopped his car and sat and watched. At first he thought Spargo might be after a woman, but if that was true he was in the wrong place. And besides, from what Midge was learning about the man, picking up women on the street was not his style.

He slumped low in his seat, grateful to whoever had smashed all but one of the street lights. Spargo was out of his car now and seemed to be dithering, inspecting the boarded up arches. Midge locked his car and walked back up the road – with luck Spargo would think he was leaving. He was sure Spargo would soon return to the Volvo. Couldn't believe anyone in their right mind would leave a car in a place like that without someone with a shotgun guarding its wheels.

Midge knew the road. One of the arches, he wasn't sure which, was the back way into wild-man Mongo's place. He stepped into the road to get a better view, and as he did so he heard the scrape of a door. Ribbons of light from a doorway lit the huge bulk of Mongo. Midge pressed himself hard against the viaduct wall, he'd had dealings with Mongo, he couldn't risk being seen. Mongo worked for the Roslin man – and the penalty for sniffing around the Roslin man would be a good kicking. Or something much worse.

※

The biker grunted. Spargo froze. He grunted again, perhaps recognition, perhaps welcome. He didn't beckon or speak, he just stood statue-like as Spargo, his thoughts on spiders, flies and parlours, stepped inside.

The biker's parlour looked and felt like a railway tunnel and was marginally brighter than out on the street. On one wall a single light bulb in a broken glass fitting provided a pool of dim light in which Spargo saw ladders, a cement mixer and buckets, a collection of old tools and a wheelbarrow. The buckets had rusted and the mixer looked ancient.

The ground beneath his feet was dry and dusty. What must once have been soil was now impregnated with discarded builders' refuse, screws and nails, brackets and hinges – debris trodden underfoot by generations of builders' boots. The biker jammed the door back in its frame. Secured it with two long bolts.

The arch was high and wide. It housed, beyond the builders' junk, what looked to Spargo like an old army hut that fitted into the arch perfectly. All he could see of it was the end facing him – two boarded-up windows and a closed wooden door. The biker grunted again and nodded towards it. When Spargo didn't move a tattooed arm propelled him forwards.

Four steps made from stacked concrete blocks led up to the door. Spargo, with the biker close behind him and invading his space, stepped up and turned the doorknob. He expected more squalor, more darkness and cold. Instead he got brilliant light, a gust of warm, moist air and the unmistakable smell of a bottled gas heater. A row of bright lights hung from the roof beams, each with a cone-shaped translucent shade. If military authenticity was intended then the effect was spoiled by the fluorescent, economy bulbs.

Spargo's first impression of the room was influenced by church halls jumble sales he'd attended with his mother, the indoor equivalent of today's car boot sales but presided over by middle-aged, matronly women. A long run of trestle tables, placed end-to end, hugged the left wall, with flags spread on them in the manner of tablecloths. Arranged on them was an assortment of military bric-a-brac: badges and medals, buckles and belts, holsters, torches, goggles and gas-masks.

The right hand side of the hut had no tables. Its floor space was taken up by much larger items – bundled camouflage netting, field telephones and shell cases, radio sets and signal lamps. Jammed tightly behind them, against the wall, a line of tailors' dummies displayed military uniforms in olive drab or black and blue and grey, their shiny plastic faces half-hidden beneath forage caps, steel helmets, or lost completely behind sinister balaclavas.

Hanging on the wall at the end of the room and arranged like a museum display, were rifles, swords, pistols and bayonets. A tripod-mounted machine gun had been set up beside a partly open door as if guarding it. A sign hanging from its muzzle proclaimed it was not for sale. Montgomery did not simply collect, he also sold. Most of the items had the same small white price tags Spargo had seen in the shop.

It did not surprise Spargo there was no pewter; it wouldn't look right amongst combat stuff. Lost for words he tried to take everything in. The biker, to one side of him, turned to him and grinned. Showed surprisingly intact white teeth. He took out his cigarettes and lit a roll-up. Like the earlier one, it burst into flame.

'Been collecting since I was a boy.'

Spargo now knew how Alice felt when she fell down the rabbit hole. It became clear to him he was expected to wander around the displays, and doing his best to treat the place as a museum he did just that. Occasionally he picked things up, inspected them and replaced them exactly as he found them.

It was during his second circuit of the room that he realised the kit on display had been arranged according to the flags it sat on. He inspected small groupings of personal items, penknives and watches, cigarette cases and lighters – lighters all made from steel or brass, not at all like the one he had. But there wouldn't be any, he realised. Not here.

'There nothing German,' he said. 'There's no Third Reich flag. There's nothing Nazi.'

Since disposing of his roll-up the biker had kept close. Keeping an eye on his stock.

'Is that what you want? Nazi?'

'I didn't come to buy. I assumed you were interested in the pewter.'

'You showed Oberon a lighter.'

Oberon. That figured. 'I showed it to get her interested. It's not for sale.'

Somewhere beyond the machine gun a floorboard creaked. Spargo turned his head and saw the door at the end open slowly. An echoing voice came from a darkened room beyond it.

'John Spargo...'

Spargo, caught off his guard, simply stared. He hadn't mentioned his name to Montgomery. Or Oberon. The door opened fully and the owner of the voice stepped into the light.

'Are you expecting to be given any more pieces like that, John?'

The accent wasn't Scots, it was Estuarine English, an Essex boy speaking sharply and quickly as if words cost him money. Its owner, short and wiry and probably in his forties, stepped through the doorway and into the light. Spargo took in the man's angular features, his high cheekbones, his high forehead and prominent cleft chin. His fair hair was long and swept back. His tweed jacket – the kind worn by a local squire on a foxhunt – hung open, as did the top two buttons of his shirt. Gold rimmed glasses set it all off, as if placed on his face as a fashion accessory.

'Pieces like what?

'Did you bring the lighter with you?'

'The lighter is not mine to sell.' It felt like a lie. Since giving the woman money he had been trying to convince himself it was now his.

'Then why did you come here, John?'

'Not sure. Curiosity?'

'Killed the cat, surely.' Seeing Spargo's expression he added 'Joke. Well, John, did you bring it? Come on, let's see the bloody thing. Nobody here is going to take it from you.'

Without a second thought Spargo took out the lighter and handed it over. He began to wonder if he had a genetic defect that got him mixed up in these things.

If the man kept the lighter, too bad, he had lost nothing. Better, perhaps, if it was out of the way.

'Nice piece,' the man said. 'Shame about the damage. Saltwater corrosion is a real bugger. Lucky for you it's silver and not brass, because brass would be long gone. But of course, you know that. Nice eagle John. Has to be gold, condition it's in. My name's Day, by the way, Nick Day. That's Day, as in 24-hour things. That's another joke, John.'

No handshakes. No proffered hands.

'It's not for sale.'

'So you keep saying.'

'I'm doing someone a favour. He had Mr Montgomery's address.'

'Montgomery is not his surname.' He turned the lighter over in his hand. 'This someone. Are you saying he sold you this?'

'What can you tell me about it?'

'It's a small chunk of gold on corroded silver.'

'So it's worthless?'

Day shrugged. 'Did I say that, John? But the lighter's not what I'm interested in, is it, you said that yourself. You asked Oberon about pewter. That would be Bob Kalman's pewter, am I right? Is he the someone we are talking about?'

'How do you know about Kalman? Who told you my name?'

'I keep an eye on the market and an ear to the ground. If something new comes up then I want to be there, know what I mean, John?'

Day perched himself on the end of a flag-draped table. The toe of his hand-made brogues didn't quite touch the floor so he pointed one down until he made contact with it. Kept it there, as if earthing himself.

'Before Ian died he told me about you. Like he told me about Bob Kalman.'

A bead of sweat ran down Spargo's spine. For a second it distracted him and he wondered if his fear showed.

'Ian?' he asked. 'Ian Letchie?'

'Ian, yes. I've known him for years. Pity about what happened. Couldn't have been very nice for you, finding him like that.'

Spargo swallowed hard. He considered making a break for the door but Montgomery's bulk seemed to occupy the whole of the bottom half of the hut. Then there was the door in the archway. Without The biker's help he'd need a tractor to drag it open.

'You and I need to talk, John, we need to take a short drive. My friend's little scout hut here is very pleasant but his heater gives off fumes, they catch in my throat.'

Spargo followed Day out of another door, into a dark lane on the other side of the railway arch. At first he was relieved Montgomery hadn't come. Then he wondered if Day was the kind of person who didn't want witnesses.

Day stopped, paused, and reached into his pocket. Hazard lights flashed close by, car doors clicked and headlights blazed. A big car, a saloon with personalised plates. Probably a Lexus. Spargo stopped too.

'Give me a good reason why I should go with you.'

'That's easy, John. The way I see it, you want to know about your lighter and I want to know about Bob Kalman's pewter. It's up to you. I'm offering information for information. If I'm wrong then keep walking. If not, then get in.'

In the city Day drove sedately and kept to the limit. Once on the Edinburgh by-pass he opened up, managing to touch 80. Spargo pulled his seat belt tighter.

'You said a short ride. This isn't a short ride.'

'Anxious are we, John? Say the word and I'll pull over. Bloody long way for you to walk home, but that's your problem.'

'Do you know who killed my mother? Did you have anything to do with it?'

Day sputtered and turned to face Spargo. 'I might be a lot of things, John, but I don't make a habit of killing people's mothers. Look at me, John. Do I look like the kind of man who goes around killing old ladies?'

Spargo kept his eyes on the road. Didn't want to say what he thought. 'But you know about it. You've heard about it.'

'I hear a lot of things. Your mother's death was all over the papers. Tell me what you know about Ian Letchie.'

'What about him? Did you have anything to do with his death?'

'Do me a favour, get this crap out of your head. I don't go around killing people. Ian came to see me the day he died – and I'd rather that bit of information didn't go any further. Just because he came to me doesn't mean I know anything about what happened afterwards. Strangled, wasn't he? Not sure I could do that to a man. If I had to kill someone it would be a bullet at long distance. Less personal, know what I mean?'

Spargo responded with an unseen grimace. Day continued:

'Ian Letchie didn't come to Edinburgh just to see me, John, he had another appointment. Don't ask me who with because I didn't ask, I assumed it was newspaper work. As I said, I've known him for years. I'm not saying he worked for me exactly but we had an understanding, a gentleman's agreement. If he found the right stuff I would find the right buyer.'

'Some people would call that receiving.'

'You're a great one for tact and diplomacy.'

'So Letchie came to you about Kalman, am I right? He told you about the submarine and the pewter.'

'No John, that's what troubles me. He should have come to me but he didn't. I learnt about the U-boat from his newspaper article. Back in summer he did a piece on a Californian firm diving a wreck. I phoned him and he said he didn't know much about it because they were playing things close to their chest. To encourage him to keep me informed up-front I gave him a bundle of notes – one thousand notes actually, John. Wish I hadn't bothered. Might as well have set fire to them. I learnt more from his press articles than from him.'

'Kalman says they are heading out to recover their equipment.'

'I'm not that fussed, John. Old warships are not my line, they're rust-buckets, there is nothing in them worth having. I was more pissed about Ian leaving me out of the loop than I was about the money.'

'What about gold? Could the boat have been carrying gold? Kalman says no, but why spend that much on exploring it?'

'What I've learned is that an American consortium funded the dive with big money. And when I say big I mean big, so big I didn't dare muscle-in on it. Who wants a knife in the ribs anyway, know what I mean John?'

'Kalman told me his job was to identify the sub,' Spargo said. 'He says he did that. He proved it was the one they were looking for. They told him to search it and he found a pewter dinner service. He told the funding guys about it but they weren't interested. Did Letchie tell you all that?'

'Not until the day he died. He opened up. Gave me the impression something had changed. You know what I think, John? I think he had some kind of deal going, and maybe it wasn't turning out as he'd hoped. Do you have any idea what that deal might have been?'

'Me? Why should I?'

'You've got the lighter. What else have you got?'

'Nothing.'

'That isn't what Ian told me. I'd hate to think you are telling me porkies, John.'

'I don't have any pewter. Kalman offered me a tankard. I refused it.'

'I don't mean pewter. Ian said Kalman gave you some books.'

Spargo stiffened. Hoped Day hadn't noticed.

'If that is what Letchie told you then he got it wrong. Kalman gave me the lighter. He said nothing about books.'

'Ian said they were from the U-boat.'

'That's ridiculous. You should have known he was lying. Books couldn't have survived down there. What are these books? Did he say anything about them?'

'He said they were diaries. He said others were looking for them so I guessed they had to be important.'

'What others? Who?'

'If he knew, he didn't say. Okay, Ian didn't actually say Kalman gave you the books. He said you had the books.'

'I don't have any books.'

'If that's true then I've been misled, I'd assumed it was the reason Ian was in your basement, to search for these books, these diaries. How is it you know Kalman, anyway?'

Spargo explained about the motor lodge and how Kalman had pestered him.

'He mentioned Letchie. He said he got him talking – though with Kalman the problem isn't getting him to talk, it's getting him to stop. He said Letchie's article almost cost him his job.'

'Shouldn't have been so free with his information, should he, John? Tell me about the pewter. Did Kalman tell you exactly what he found?'

'A dinner service, forty-eight pieces. The plate I saw has twin shields engraved on its rim. He said all the pieces have the same mark.'

'Really? And the lighter? Where did that come from?'

'He said something about the engine room.'

'So how come you've got it?'

'He offered it to me and I refused. This morning I found it in my pocket.'

'Right little Oliver Twist, you are. Is the lighter all you've got, or are you playing with me? Are you a middleman? Has Kalman offered you a percentage if you sell the pewter? You've got that lighter, what else have you got, the whole bloody dinner service?'

'I've got nothing. All I want to do is find out why my mother was killed.'

'And who killed her.'

'That's secondary. The police can do that.'

'Not sure I'd feel like that John. Whatever I just said to you about shooting, if someone did that to my mother I'd string the bastards up with my own hands.'

Day slowed the car. Spargo hadn't taken much notice of where they were going but he guessed they were on the outskirts of Roslin, somewhere above the wooded slopes of the Esk valley. Day braked harder, swinging the car onto a narrow track flanked by leafless trees. Spargo gripped his seat as Day, rather than bounce through the many potholes, attempted to fly over them.

The track ended at steel gates set in a high fence. Day slowed again but made no attempt to stop. At the very last moment the gates rolled aside and the car passed between them with inches to spare.

'Had you going there, didn't I, John?'

Security lights blazed. Dead-centre of a sea of red gravel stood a detached mock-Georgian mansion. There were no lawns or flowerbeds. In place of trees there were lights on tall poles like a floodlit stadium. Nick Day's own high-security wing. With a metallic thud the gates rolled shut behind them.

'My pad,' Day said. 'Bit remote but that's how I like it. Have to take precautions. Can't get insurance for what I keep here.'

Chippings scattered as Day swung the car in a loop and pulled up beside twin stone-coloured, glass fibre pillars supporting an equally unconvincing portico. Spargo expected the wide front door it sheltered to open unaided, but Day already had the door key out. Automation only went so far, apparently.

As on the outside, the inside of the house was ablaze with light. Day called out a greeting that was returned from deep in the house like an echo, but as a woman's voice. With keys still in his hand Day advanced on a door in the hall, unlocked it and opened it. Reached in and switched on a light.

The room had once been a garage. Its large double doors had been replaced by a brick wall which, like the other walls in the room, was lined with steel shelves piled with boxes. On the concrete floor stood large plywood tea chests lined up in rows.

'Don't like keeping stock here, John,' Day said. 'Don't have a choice though. Used to keep it in town. Place kept getting done over so I gave it to Montgomery to store his toys. Can't trust anyone these days.'

Day busied through cardboard boxes, taking off lids and checking their contents. Halfway along one shelf he stopped. Took down what looked like a cardboard shoebox and carried it to a desk.

'So, John. What do you think of this little number?'

Day was unwrapping layers of tissue. When he had finished he handed over a small dagger, its ivory handle set with deep red cut stones.

'Rubies,' Day offered. 'Genuine Third Reich, nineteen-thirties. Don't know any more about it than that.'

'What's it worth?'

'Who knows? Without rubies it could fetch a hundred dollars or so. This one, with rubies, maybe one thousand? If I could prove it once belonged to Adolf Hitler then its value would rise tenfold. Unfortunately I can't. Probably because it didn't.'

'Who did it belong to?'

Day spread his hands. 'Wish I knew, John. But you are missing my point. The history is what counts. Provenance is everything.'

Day reclaimed the dagger, re-wrapped it and returned it to its box. Selecting one of the tea chests he lifted the thin plywood top and rummaged inside, throwing balls of crumpled newspaper on the floor all around him. Then, selecting what looked like one of the larger of the balls, he tore off the paper and handed Spargo a small pewter bowl. On its rim was the same heraldic mark as on Kalman's piece. Day watched him intently.

'That's it!' Spargo said. 'That's the same!'

'What is the same as what?'

'This engraving, it's the same as the one on Kalman's plate, the touching shields, a fist clutching a ring.'

Day nodded. 'The coat of arms of German Reichsmarschall Hermann Göring and his second wife Emmy. This bowl was a wedding gift in nineteen-thirty-three. It's part of a set. I have eight items.'

'Are they valuable?'

'There you go again, John. We're talking history and you bring up the unsavoury subject of money. But seeing you asked, we're talking between fifty to one-hundred thousand dollars.'

'Even though they're pitted?'

'Collectors don't buy them so they can eat off them. The fact they're slightly damaged can increase their value.'

'This one can't be from the boat.'

'It isn't. Do you know your history, John? The Third Reich was growing. Göring was a key figure, he enjoyed patronage and was treated like a prince or a duke. Who knows how many dinner services he was given?'

'Why would a German U-boat be carrying a pewter dinner service?'

Day shrugged. 'Search me, John. Your guess is as good as mine. What else did you learn from friend Kalman?'

'Only that the boat had no armaments. Why should that be?'

'You're asking me, John? I thought that was what they built the things for, blowing our ships to buggery. Anything else?'

Several things, Spargo told himself, though he had no intention of revealing them to Day. He certainly wasn't admitting he'd ever seen the journals.

'Kalman said the sub had a hole in the bow that had been made from the inside,' Spargo said.

'So they blew themselves up. They scuttled the ship.'

'That's what I thought. But it's not the kind of thing you do in the middle of the North Sea.'

'Can't say I'm into the finer points of marine etiquette.'

'He also told me the dive cost three million. Not sure if he meant pounds or dollars.'

Day whistled. 'Three million? Are you sure?'

'It's what he said. And that didn't include the cost of finding the thing.'

Day paused. Took the bowl back and started to wrap it.

'I know about the finding bit. It was one of the few things Ian told me when I gave him the thousand. It was found during a survey for an oil pipeline back in the early eighties and marked on an oil company map as a wreck, though it didn't say what kind. It was in deep water well away from their pipe, so it didn't present them with a problem. Anything else you know?'

'I asked Kalman if the sub could have been carrying gold. He was adamant it was not.'

'How's your history, John? Did I ask you that already?'

'At school we did kings, queens and battles. Can't say it helped me much.'

'Sounds like you and me had the same history teacher. Kings and queens and the Cromwell guy. Forget all that, John, think more recent stuff. You must have seen documentaries about the Nazis. At the end of the war when things started to get hot for them they planned to leave by the back door. Hitler's henchmen, I mean.'

Spargo knew that. There were planned escape routes. If Hermann Göring had one then it hadn't worked. He was captured, stood trial, and then poisoned himself.

'Are you seriously trying to tell me Göring was planning to be on that U-boat?'

Day sighed. 'No, John. There you go again, adding two and two and making fifty. At the end of the war Göring weighed two hundred and eighty pounds. He could hardly get through doorways, let alone get into a submarine. Another small point is he thought he was innocent.'

'He was the one who set up the concentration camps.'

'In the 'thirties he imprisoned dissidents in camps. It's a myth that he set up the death camps. By the time that happened he'd fallen out of favour with Hitler.'

'But he approved of them.'

'Didn't they all? At Nuremberg Göring insisted he was innocent of any war crimes, did you know that? He believed the Allies would free him. What I'm saying, John, is that there was no reason for Göring to flee. Don't think I'm defending the man, they were all evil bastards. It's more a question of degree, some were more evil bastards than others. Perhaps Göring tried to ship his best pieces out of Germany before it all hit the fan. Or if not him, then maybe someone else was doing it for him.'

Day returned to the desk, slid open a drawer, and took out a bulging ring binder. It was strapped tight with string tied in a bow and he tugged at it. The folder sprung open. The clear plastic wallets inside it were old and they clicked and cracked as Day worked his way through it.

It was an album, Spargo realised – an album of black and white photos of smart, uniformed men.

'Nazi military elite,' Day said. 'One of Montgomery's better purchases. Bought it from an old lady at a car boot sale.' He slipped fingers into one of the plastic wallets and pulled out a photograph. To see it better he switched on a desk lamp and held the photo under it. 'Hermann Göring, Head of the Luftwaffe. But you know that already.'

Until then, the few pictures Spargo had seen of Hitler's Reichsmarschall showed a grossly overweight jackbooted Nazi. Here the man was dressed in the uniform of a First War pilot. He was young and looked passably slim.

'Those medals, Day said, pointing. 'The bottom two are the Blue Max and the Knight's Cross. The one above it is the Grand Cross of the Iron Cross. Göring was its only holder.'

'What did he do, award it to himself?'

'Göring was a fighter pilot in the First War, quite a hero by all accounts. He rarely wore the original medal, he wore a copy. History tells us the original was lost when one of his houses was hit by a bomb. Shame, that.'

Spargo tilted his head questioningly. 'Shame?'

'Shame, John. Shame because there is a man in Florida who would give half a million dollars for it.'

'You're not suggesting Kalman found it?'

'John, you really are a man who jumps to conclusions. Of course not. I am simply giving you an example of how valuable these things can be. I assumed it is something that would interest you, seeing as you've got what little is left of Göring's lighter.'

Spargo tensed as Day flipped more plastic. He took out another photo and passed it to Spargo – Göring in a high-peaked Luftwaffe cap, a man so large his military greatcoat could hardly contain him. He was standing beside a military vehicle with a Meerschaum pipe in his mouth and his hands near it as if lighting it. While Spargo inspected the photo Day produced an enlargement. It showed only the pipe and Göring's hands.

'I had this enlarged. A few years ago someone offered me a pipe he said was Göring's. This is one of several pictures I have of the man smoking. None show the pipe I was offered. It could well have been Göring's, John, but who knows? Without proof it could have been anybody's. Needless to say, I didn't buy it.'

Spargo took the enlargement from Day and held it under the desk light. Göring was holding the bowl of the pipe in one hand and a lighter in the other. Though the enlargement was grainy, the lighter had a blotch on its side, possibly an inlay.

'You think that's the same? That's a gold eagle?'

'Absolutely.'

'There could have been hundreds of lighters like that.'

'I doubt that. Göring was vain. I can't imagine him using or owning anything that wasn't unique. Nobody would dare give the man tat, know what I mean? If one of Göring's dinner services was on the sub, then why not his lighter? It's not proof, but it's as good as it gets. Without this photograph your lighter's worth thirty quid. Fifty, possibly. With it, and with some kind of proof it came from a sub carrying Göring's pewter, I can put you in touch with a buyer who'll give you five hundred at least. That's pounds, John, not dollars.'

'It's not for sale.'

'I think you said that already. Just thought you might be interested.'

'Do you deal only in Göring's stuff?'

'German Third Reich exclusively. Göring happened to have a lot of trinkets, most of them belonging to other people. Don't get me wrong. Like I told you already, I don't approve of anything those bastards did, it's just that I now make a living from it. I'm not talking about selling crap to jackbooted neo-Nazis, I'm talking serious US collectors with more money than sense. I'm talking Germans who want to buy back a slice of their warts-and-all history. My clients trust me. I know about the Third Reich, I make it my business. When I step outside my field I'm more easily fooled, know what I mean? This business is plagued with fakes and forgeries but within my own territory I can spot fakes blindfold. But Göring, yes. Lucky for the likes of me he was an obsessive collector.'

'Is this why you brought me here, to show me the photos?'

'Isn't that a good enough reason? What did you think I was going to do to you, give you a kicking? Nick your lighter?'

Spargo grimaced. It was too near the truth. Day opened a drawer, took out an envelope, picked up the photographs and slipped them into a brown envelope he sealed down and held out.

'Here, take them. They're no good to me without the lighter. Let's call it payment.'

'Payment for what?'

'Information, John.'

Spargo, deciding Day's offer was too good to miss, mumbled his thanks and took the envelope from him. While attempting to find a pocket large enough to take the envelope without folding it, he realised he was being ushered out of the room and into the hall.

From the hall, Day propelled him past a jungle of pot plants and into a sitting room furnished with reproduction chairs, tables and cupboards that appeared to have been selected at random from a furniture catalogue. Spargo expected more Third Reich regalia but there was none.

Day waved him to an armchair.

'So where do we go from here, John?'

'How do you mean?'

'Come on, John! You made the first move, you went to Montgomery so presumably you have some kind of plan. As you don't have the pewter yourself, I assume you will be contacting Kalman.'

'I'll call him first thing tomorrow and say him you are interested.

He gave me a business card with his mobile number.'

'I'd rather you didn't do that. If you are not acting as middleman there is nothing in it for you, is there, John? Why not just give me his card, go home and forget all about it? I would not be a happy bunny if Kalman sold his little nest egg to someone else, know what I mean, John?'

Day's smile was over-friendly and hinted of menace. He stood up, went to a sideboard and poured out two gins. He popped the ring pulls on cans of tonic, poured a splash into one of the glasses and handed it to Spargo. .

'Back in second or two…' he said, walking away with a glass in his hand. 'Best say hello to the lady.'

CHAPTER TWENTY-NINE

CAN THREE YEAR-OLDS TALK? Theo doesn't know. He is desperate to know where Artur and Barbara are, if they have abandoned his son or if they lie dead in the fields. He tries to see if the boy looks starved but the light isn't good enough. What he can see is that he wears three or four layers of clothing which, in such bitter cold, is a good thing.

The boy is cornered. Though his gaze is intense his eyes dart around as if waiting for Theo's next move. This time it will be fight or flight, a bared-claws leap at the stranger's face or a fast dart to freedom. The boy is moving, very slowly, back into darkness, freeing himself limb by limb from the quilt.

Theo moves suddenly, surprising the boy. Instead of trying to grab him he jumps backwards with outstretched arms, grabs the twin doors and slams them shut. They have handles but no locking catch. Inspired, he takes the black leather chin strap from his cap and binds the door handles together. The boy is trapped.

Theo has no guilt, it is better this way. The boy is scared. Chances are he would have run outside and hidden, in temperatures well below freezing.

Out in the small yard at the back of the building Theo checks the small privy and then the long washhouse – the lean-to building with its stone sink and deep copper boiler; the firebox beneath the boiler has no ash, it is no longer used; the wooden washboard beside the sink is bone dry; no clothes are hung out to dry on the rails in the roof.

Nothing has happened here for days. Maybe months.

Theo trudges around to the farmyard, shouting as he goes. He checks the two barns, the cowshed, the silage store and what was once the piggery. In the cowshed he finds a bare-ribbed, half-starved black cow that turns her dark eyes towards him. So far it is the only sign of farm life. Erika's parents are good people. They would not treat an animal like this.

Nor would they abandon Peter. Not intentionally.

Far across a field a stumbling figure drags a sled. It disappears into woodland for several minutes and reappears dragging the branch of a tree, ignoring Theo's shouts. Remembering Artur is partly deaf he climbs on a fence rail and waving his arms he calls out again.

Deciding to walk to the person he swings a leg over the fence. He is halfway over when he hears the squeal of hinges and steps back down. Artur is behind him, at the farmyard gate, bent almost double and looking older than ever. He is heavy with clothes. Around his neck is a scarf made from sacking. On his hands are woollen gloves with more holes than wool. His mud-clad boots move over frozen ground with short, almost imperceptible shuffling steps.

'Theodor? Is that you?' The man is squinting, dazzled by low sunlight. 'My god, I thought I would never see you again. What is that uniform you wear, surely it is not Kriegsmarine? Have they changed things again? Why do they always change things?'

'I thought that was you in the field. Is it Barbara?'

'No, she is sick, she is not here. She is in the hospital, she has been there for weeks. No, it is months, I think. She has grown weak. You have seen Peter? He will be pleased to see you.'

'I have seen him,' Theo says. 'He is in his bed. Artur, I am so sorry about Erika. I should have stayed on the mines. It would never have happened.'

Artur looks at the ground. For a while he says nothing.

'You are not to blame. We lost our daughter. You lost your wife. Peter lost his mother. It is done.'

'Where is the help you once had? Why is the farm like this?'

'I had three workers but they took them from me.'

'Who was that I saw in the field?'

'Paul, my neighbour. He collects windfall wood. He has lost his boy. You remember Jan? He was soldier.'

'No, I didn't know him. What about the animals? I have seen one cow. Where are the pigs?'

'They are sold.' The old man wags a hand as if to bat away questions. 'Come,' he says. 'I will get Peter for you.' He takes off his boots at the door but leaves his outdoor clothes on. 'I have no wood for the fire, Theodor. I light it only when the weather is cold.'

Theo takes off his cap and runs a hand through his hair. Cold? How cold does it have to get? A few years ago this place bustled with life. A few years more and there will be nothing but ruins.

'You should have told me things were bad. I could have sent money.'

'You know it is not my way. And what good is money when there is nothing to buy? Anyway, things are not so bad.'

'They look bad to me. Is the hospital in Ingolstadt? How do you get there, do you still have the pony and trap?'

'I have sold it. I walk. It takes me all day. So many questions, Theodor! Why do you not go upstairs yourself and see your son?'

'He won't talk to me. I was worried he would bolt so I locked him in.'

That the old man disapproves is clear from his look. 'It will take time. I will go for him.'

'Why do you keep him up there?'

'I don't. He can come and go. His bed is the warmest place, it is near the chimney and so it stays warm, even when the fire has died down. When the fire is lit he comes downstairs.'

Theo shakes his head. It is not how things should be.

'It looks to me as if it hasn't been lit for some time.'

'A week or so, perhaps. I have no wood. I burned some of the furniture but I can't burn any more, it is not right, Barbara would not forgive me. When it is not so cold I take him outside and we milk the cow and collect the eggs. You see, we still have chickens. I told you, things are not so bad.'

'Where is your axe?'

'Why do you want it?'

'Just tell me where it is.'

Theo works until dusk. He could fell trees but the wood would be green and would not burn well. Instead he fells the pig pens, first the wooden roof and then the walls, chopping the wood small and stacking it in the barn. Artur comes out and protests. He is ignored.

When Theo returns to the house Artur is sitting in one of the leather armchairs with Peter on his lap, snuggling close. Together they watch while Theo lights the fire.

'He isn't a talker,' Artur says. 'He doesn't say much. You can dress yourself though, can't you, Peter?'

The boy seems content. If he still fears Theo he shows no sign of it. Though his face is grubby and pale he looks passably fit and well. Theo sits opposite them in Barbara's chair, wondering what his son would look like if he had been brought up by Erika. Healthier, no doubt. And better dressed – the boy would be wearing clothes she made for him, not ones so ill-fitting.

He knows he should not think these things. Artur and Barbara have done their best. At least the boy is with family, he is not in a home. Theo takes out his pipe and pokes the ash bowl with a pencil he took from the train, teasing out threads of tobacco and then saving them. He taps out the ash against the stone of the fireplace and repacks the shreds of tobacco.

As always, the wick on Göring's lighter lights first time. On seeing the small bright flame Peter slips down from Artur's lap, walks to Theo and holds out his hand for the lighter.

'He walks well,' Artur says. 'He comes downstairs on his own, backwards on his hands knees.'

'I would have expected him to be able to run down them by now.'

'Give the child time. The stairs are steep. It is safer for him to descend backwards. Now, I shall get food.'

'Do you have anything?'

'I have eggs and milk. I also have cabbage and potatoes, I get them from my neighbour in exchange for the wood he takes from my land.'

'I don't understand why you don't burn the wood yourself?'

'It is wet and rotten and won't burn. He stores it in his barn to dry it. Also it is too far for me to walk.' He slaps his left knee. 'I cannot walk in the woods. My leg is bad.'

The boy is still there with his hand outstretched. The lighter is not lit and to test it is cold Theo touches it to his cheek. He holds it out and the boy takes it. Examines it. Walks to a corner with it and sits down on the floor. He tries to press down the striker but his fingers are not strong enough. He is safe. It will not light.

Letting Peter play with the lighter has broken down barriers. That night Theo places a mattress on the floor near Peter's bed, and when he is sure the child is asleep he turns up the oil lamp, takes out a notebook and starts to write; here he can record things safely; at Carinhall the risk was too great.

Lying face down on the mattress Theo describes his journey from Bremen, his encounter with the Generalmajor and his meeting with Walter. He writes about Göring and the model trains. He describes the bunker, the packing cases and the journey with Walter on Göring's train. He wants to write about Peter but the flame of the lamp dims and turns red and smoky. The lamp has run out of oil.

Theo sleeps lightly, fully dressed. When he wakes in the night he listens to Peter's breathing, breaths fast and slow that keep time with the boy's dreams. Of what does he dream, Theo wonders? Of six hens and a cow? Of the stranger that scared him?

Lying in the dark he tells himself the past is gone, there is only the future. It is something he tells his crew when times are hard, drumming it into them, saying things will get better. He knows it's a lie because as days pass in this war things only get worse, more boats lost, more folk dead, more families destroyed.

He rises early and walks in the fields. When he returns to the farmhouse he finds Arthur in the kitchen with Peter. Last night he shut in both fires and now they burn fiercely. On the open fire a pot of water boils and spits – eggs again, this time boiled. Eggs and potatoes for supper and now eggs for breakfast, no smoked ham or pork like the old days. And no sausage. He misses sausage. On the boats sausage never runs out.

He finds an excuse to check the larder and is surprised to see it is not empty. There are eggs, milk, butter and cream. There is also a cabbage, and bread with green mould. Perhaps Artur trades.

'Who is winning this war, Theo?' Artur asks.

'Not us.'

'Our generals are all fools. The Führer should get rid of them.'

'He is doing that. Maybe they should get rid of the Führer. They tried.'

'So I heard. Now, the boy needs washing. The bowl is outside on the wall.'

'Can't he do it himself?'

'He is a toddler. He is two years old. What do you expect of him?'

'He is three.'

'He can barely wash his own hands, Theodor. Give him time.' The old man opens the back door and brings in a zinc bath he slides noisily across the flagstone floor.

'See to the eggs, Theodor, or they will boil hard. Give me the water pot and then cut the bread. Wash your hands before you touch the food.'

Artur pours cold water into the bath from a tall metal jug and then adds hot water from the pot. Peter looks on and seems to mouth words.

'Bath…!'

The boy's word is mumbled and unclear. It is the first word Theo has heard from him.

'He spoke. He said bath.'

'So? Shell the eggs and put the shells in the bin. Now, come on, young man! Show your papa what you can do. Clothes off!'

Theo watches his son tug off layer after layer.

'Shouldn't the bath be closer to the fire?'

Artur slides the tub across the floor, grumbling as he does it.

'You should be doing this. You are his father.'

Peter stands with his hands wrapped around his middle, his teeth chattering gently. Theo goes to him and picks him up, tests the water with his hand and sits the boy gently in the tub. He cups the warm water in his hands, raises it up and pours it over the boy's head. The boy likes it so he does it again.

Theo Volker is bathing his son. Theo Volker, who last month pulled two of his headless crewmen off the remains of the deck gun and threw them into the sea. Theodor Volker, who now wants to weep.

'Don't play with him,' Artur snaps. 'Wash him properly. Or do you think it is women's work?'

When Peter is clean and dry Theo dresses him in clean clothes, some too small, some too big. All are old. He suspects the socks and knitted jacket were once Erika's, they are pink for a girl. All three sit on the ground and eat boiled eggs, now cold. There is no coffee, only warm milk. Peter seems happy and eats heartily.

'He will eat anything,' Artur says. 'He's a good boy. Things are not so bad.'

'Where do you get the bread?'

'When the hens lay well I have spare eggs. I trade, I told you. I get oil for the lamps.'

'I have money,' Theo says. 'I can send you enough so you don't have to worry.'

'I have told you. What can I do with money? Money is good when there are things to buy. I no longer want the farm, Theodor. I want to live in Ingolstadt near Barbara but it is hopeless. In this damn war I cannot sell the farm. Nobody will buy. You must take him, Theo…'

'Take him to Ingolstadt to see his grandmother? That would be difficult for me. I have to leave soon. They are coming for me at midday.'

'So soon?'

'I have no choice.'

Artur is quiet. He sits staring at the flames in the grate. He stands, goes to the fire and drops a piece of plank on the flames.

'You must take him, Theodor. Take him away from here.'

'Take Peter? No, that is impossible!'

'On my own I can manage. With Peter things are so hard, I cannot be responsible.'

'It is hard for us all. Now you have fires. In the barn there is enough wood to last the winter and when it is used up you can gather fallen branches. Your neighbour can help you. If the wood is wet then store it, like he does. That's what you always used to do.'

'No, Theodor, that is what Barbara and I used to do, we did it together. Do you know how much fuel I need to keep that fire in?'

Theo nods. He knows very well. Despite what he said he knows the wood he cut will last two or three months, perhaps to early Spring. Then what? Cut down the cowshed and then the barn? There will be no farm left to sell. And anyway, he has been watching Artur moving around. The man could not possibly wield a felling axe.

'It is not good for the boy here,' Artur says. 'He needs company. He needs other children.'

Theo wants to nod but he dare not. Though he is shocked by the conditions he has seen much worse; when he was a child he knew boys who lived like this. Farms have mud and dirt and they stink. Farm children get muddy and dirty, they can stink like the animals.

'I can't take him. You know I can't.'

'Then you must do something. Take him to your parents.'

'I can't do that. My father has lung disease. My mother has problems of her own.'

'Perhaps there is somewhere for him in Ingolstadt?'

'Are you suggesting an orphanage, Artur? How can you say that, after all you have done for him? He is not an orphan. He has a father.'

'And you are that father, Theodor. You must take him.'

CHAPTER THIRTY

SPARGO LEFT DAY'S FORTIFIED HOUSE in a taxi summoned and paid for by Day. He was almost home when he remembered his car was still parked in the dark street with the archways. He diverted the taxi. When it arrived he foolishly paid the driver, asking him to stay while he checked his car. The moment Spargo slammed the taxi door the man pulled away from the kerb and was gone.

Luckily the Volvo was untouched and it started first time. Spargo pulled away quickly. Didn't notice the small car parked in the shadows.

Home again, Spargo did his customary check. It had become a habit to pull onto his parking space, leave the car headlights on, walk to the front door, put the key in the lock and double-turn it. He did it now. Then, car locked and safe, he went through the house, checked all the rooms but didn't bother to go out to check the basement. He did, however, kneel down and look under his bed. Didn't find any bodies.

Amongst the many thoughts that kept Spargo awake that night was the memory of a jigsaw puzzle he bought from a jumble sale when he was young. He'd struggled to complete it only to realise, after hours of trying, that the box held pieces from more than one picture. Was that what was happening now? Was he jumbling together pieces from two – or maybe more – different puzzles? Was it possible the deaths were unconnected?

A late flight into Edinburgh Airport droned overhead, diverted from its usual flight path up the Firth of Forth. As the sound of its engines faded away Spargo finally lost track of his thoughts and fell asleep.

At some stage in the night in his half-awake dozing, Spargo decided, rightly or wrongly, that the clues to all of this lay with Lewis.

The man had deliberately misinterpreted the journal page. He had soaked the journals in the hope it would make them unreadable.

There was no point talking to Quinn about Lewis. Not only did they not get on with each other, from what Quinn said it was clear the police were treating Lewis's death as a hit and run. Did Lewis have family, he wondered?

First thing next morning he went for the copy of Lewis's letter Mitchell had given him. He had made another copy for Marie and as far as he could recall he'd returned it to a tray on his desk. It was not there now. He checked the photocopier. It wasn't there either. Then he remembered the police had taken some of his things, they had listed them on an official receipt he had clamped to the fridge with a magnet. The list was still there and he checked it. There was no mention of the letter.

The more Spargo searched, the more he was convinced the letter had been stolen. It seemed so obvious now. They – whoever they were – had been in his house, they had found Lewis's papers and the letter-heading address. They went there and watched his movements – and when the time was right they ran him down.

He could get Lewis's address from Marie, he supposed, or he could call Quinn or Mitchell. Not wanting to call either of them he tried Marie's number but got voicemail. Then, realising there could be a low-tech solution to his problem, he reached for the phone book and found Lewis. Found hundreds. Knew that without an initial he hadn't a chance.

He tried Marie again and then, plucking up courage, called Mitchell. The phone rang several times before it was answered. Mitchell wasn't there. And no, they had no idea where he was or when he was coming back. But they could take a message.

Quinn had said Lewis was buried in Piershill, a large cemetery on the east side of Edinburgh. Cemeteries have chapels, they have books of remembrance. Staff there would remember a recent burial, and if not they might know the name of the undertakers. It was a long shot, but one worth trying. It wasn't as if he had much else to do.

When Spargo reached London Road he had second thoughts. The skies had darkened and rain fell so heavily the car's wipers had trouble coping. Just as he decided to turn in the road and go home he realised he had just driven past the dark stone gateposts of Piershill. A tight U-turn brought him close to them and he parked. Walked to his boot for his umbrella. It wasn't there.

Sure the trees in the cemetery would shelter him he walked in through the gates. To his left was a cottage, once a keeper's lodge but now a monumental masons' showroom. A wheelbarrow full of swept-up leaves stood abandoned nearby. At this time of year the trees wouldn't give much shelter.

There was no office, nobody to ask. Hoping to find someone who might know he set off along paths dressed with red chippings, their colour clashing uncomfortably with the grass and the dour grey of the headstones. Somewhere to his left a train rumbled through a cutting on its way to Waverley; high overhead a helicopter droned westwards, its thudding blades scything the sky. As his mother would have said, no peace for the wicked. None for the good either, not here, not with noise like that.

In contrast to the ancient graveyards in Edinburgh's Old Town, Piershill was positively bright. No prison-bar, padlocked tombs here. Burke and Hare, Spargo thought – Edinburgh's Tomb Raiders. He smiled at his joke and then, remembering where he was, adopted a suitable, sombre expression.

Wishing he had worn boots he crossed between old monuments and glanced at inscriptions. So many children, victims of child killers diphtheria, whooping cough and smallpox. So much for the so-called good old days. Better to have noise, traffic, trains and helicopters. And real medical care.

Half an hour later and soaked to his skin, Spargo still searched. He had exhausted the newer burials and was back in the old part of the cemetery, convinced Lewis was buried in a reserved plot, perhaps a family grave – or else Quinn had got it wrong and Lewis was buried elsewhere.

On his way out he noticed a sudden change in the headstones. Rows of small, neat stones gave way to massive granite slabs. Christian crosses gave way to the Star of David and inscriptions in Hebrew. Some headstones had English translations of the Hebrew and he noted the names: Jeremy Riesenbaum, Yosef Rosen, Isaac Samuels.

Lewis, Spargo told himself, would not be amongst these.

Intending to return to his car by the shortest possible route he cut across the grass, picking a path between the huge headstones. Off to his right, dwarfed by the forest of stone, stood a small black headstone. It looked quite out of place amongst the old granite blocks and because of this he walked to it. It was obviously a recent burial. Turves had been placed to form a long, heaped-up mound. Carved into the slab of black stone were gilt letters, a line of Hebrew with English beneath:

MAREK LEWANDOWSKI

'Was he a friend of yours?'

The voice startled him. A woman's, husky and deep.

'No,' Spargo said without turning. 'I didn't know him.'

The woman who shuffled up beside him was in her mid-forties. All but her face was concealed in an outsize green parka with a sodden, fur-trimmed hood. Wet, close-cropped hair peeked out and mingled with the fur.

'Polish name, Lewandowski,' she said.

Spargo thought the comment unnecessary but he nodded anyway.

'Could he have been known as Mark Lewis?'

The parka lifted and fell as she shrugged. Raindrops fell from the fur and showered down on her boots.

'Possible, I suppose. Bit of a mouthful, Lewandowski. My father's was Beckenstein. He shortened it to Beckton.'

'Do you know what the Hebrew says?'

'Something about a friend. I don't understand much.'

There were fragments of gravel on the top edge of the headstone, placed in a neat row. Spargo nodded towards them.

'What are the stones for?'

'You are not Jewish.'

'I'm not.'

'Then it's just as well you didn't bring flowers.'

Spargo frowned, not understanding. He looked around at the other gravestones. There were no flowers at all. It explained why this part of the cemetery looked so dull.

'Tradition,' she added. 'Some visitors place a stone. It shows they've been. Shows they care.'

'So Marek has had five visitors?'

'Five visits. No way of knowing how many people.'

Lanark Road seemed never ending. To make things worse Spargo got trapped behind a bus trundling west at the pace of a snail. At least the slow speed of the bus gave him time to check the house numbers. He had just passed two-hundred. Still had a long way to go.

The headstone had given him Lewis's first name. The telephone directory at home listed several possibilities and Spargo had phoned them all. Those that answered their phones knew nothing of Mark Lewis, though there was one that interested him, the man who had answered hesitantly and hung up when Spargo mention of the name. He had called again and again but the phone went unanswered. He was driving to that address now.

The houses were large and set back from the road, most of them well hidden behind hedges. The one he sought stood in half an acre of ground, most of it down to grass in dire need of a mow. It had been built as a two bedroom bungalow and extended in every direction and tacked on to one side was a massive, flat roofed conservatory looking to Spargo as if it had been assembled from old greenhouse parts. Like the lawn, it was neglected. Weathered, silver timber showed through flaking blue paint.

Spargo took the crazy-paved path to the front door. Paint had peeled from it, long strips of blue that revealed not the wood beneath it but layers of ancient, bottle green paint. Beside the door a white plastic bell push hung free on the end of its wire. Spargo held it steady with one hand and pressed the button with the other. Hearing nothing, he pressed it again. Then he reached for the tarnished brass knocker and swung it down twice in a loud, double knock.

Out of the corner of his eye he saw movement. Stepping over weeds thriving in the flowerbeds he went to it, peering in at a conservatory window in time to catch sight of a man slipping out of the room. Returning to the door he pushed open the letterbox and spoke through it.

'I'm told you knew Mr Lewis,' he lied. 'I would like to talk to you.'

The reply he got was as old and as shaky as the house.

'Go away. I don't want to talk to you.'

'Mr Lewis did some work for the police in Inverness. Detective Sergeant Mitchell.'

'You are Mitchell?'

'I'm not Mitchell.'

The man was close to the door. Bony fingers took over from Spargo's and held the letterbox open.

'I'm not expecting you to ask me in,' Spargo said. 'I have just seen Mr Lewis's grave.'

'Go away. I don't want to talk to you.'

'I want to know about him. If you're not willing to talk then tell me who is.'

'There is nobody else. Mark had no other friends.'

'Did he live here with you?'

'Why do you ask me these things? Why are you pestering me? Mark is gone, he suffered enough. Why can't you people leave him alone?'

'What people?'

'You people.'

Spargo shivered, but not with cold. He had to talk to this man. He had to get inside.

'My name is Spargo,' he said. 'My mother was murdered. It has something to do with Mr Lewis and I want to know what it is. I want to talk to you.'

Things changed suddenly. The letterbox flap banged down and two bolts slid back. The door opened just a crack and was grabbed by a chain. Spargo, scared the man would be brandishing a weapon of some kind, took a step back. The door stayed on the chain and tousled hair appeared, then an eye that looked Spargo up and down. Then two eyes, the man's head turned sideways.

Finally the door closed and reopened minus the chain. The gap revealed a man in his late eighties, a head and shoulders shorter than Spargo and with one of his hands over his mouth. His eyes were wide, staring as if confronting a ghost. Any colour he might have had in his face had drained away.

'They have killed Morag? You are John?'

'You knew her? You knew my mother?'

They stayed on their own sides of the doorway, the man in slippers with holes at the toe. The man's shoulders, lost in a sports jacket two sizes too big, drooped forwards.

'You said they,' Spargo said. 'Who are they?'

'The ones that killed Mark. The ones that ran him down.'

The man turned his back on Spargo and shuffled inside. Spargo, the door left open for him, found himself in a dark hallway with an uncarpeted, varnished floor. Three cardboard boxes, the kind supplied by removal firms, were shoved against one wall. It was more of a wide passage than a hallway and Spargo eased past them, following the man into a sitting room that resembled a stage-set for a nineteen-fifties play.

The fireplace had been boxed in with hardboard panels and painted, like the skirting, the picture rail and the window frames, in pale lilac; in place of a real fire stood a coal effect substitute whose coals glowed red but no longer flickered; above it, on a mantel shelf that could well have been made from a painted floorboard, were around fifty black and white photographs. Some were in frames. Most were at the back, propped against the chimney breast. That they had been there for years was obvious.

The man walked to the window, stopped, turned, and regarded Spargo as thoroughly as Mitchell had done when they first met. The difference was that this man, whoever he was, took his time whereas Mitchell was a man in a hurry. Low sun silhouetted him against the window and the garden's autumnal brown leaves. Realising his guest was being dazzled he tugged at a curtain and blocked out the sun.

Spargo waited for questions. They didn't come.

'You knew my mother?' Spargo asked.

'I did.'

'Did Mr Lewis live here?'

'He did.'

Spargo's head filled with so many questions he didn't know which to ask next. But he didn't have to. The man had started to talk.

'My name is Francis Rydel. Mark was my friend. When my wife died I suggested to Mark that he come and live with me. The house was too big for me. Many years ago my mother-in-law lived here, she had her own flat. That is where Mark came to live. He had his own entrance at the back of the house. So you are John?'

'I am.'

'And Morag? She is dead? Murdered, did you say? This is a terrible thing.' He was nodding, slowly. His gaze dropped from Spargo to the carpeted floor. 'I am sorry. I do not know what to say.'

'How do you know my mother? Do you know who killed her? Do you know who killed Mark? Did you see them do it?'

Far too many questions for Rydel. He pulled a chair from beneath a table in the window, turned it around awkwardly with one hand, sat down on it and gestured for Spargo to sit in one of the room's two armchairs. Spargo stayed standing.

'Mark... yes... nobody saw it. Mark was a creature of habit. Most days he walked down the road to Balerno to catch the bus into Edinburgh. You have seen the road. On this side there is no footpath and on the other there are obstructions, they have been building houses and digging up the road. Mark has been walking where there is no pavement. I did not know this. It was very dangerous.'

The nods were continuous now, slow and deliberate. When Spargo made no comment, Rydel continued to speak.

'The policeman who came here said the car did not stop. I did not believe him.'

'You don't think it was a car?'

The nodding changed to an irritated shake of the head.

'No, no, not that! I did not believe Mark. He was scared. He was always scared. I did not believe he had a reason to be scared.'

'What was he scared of?'

Rydel shrugged. 'I do not know.'

'Is that why he changed his name?'

'That is no business of yours.'

'If it bears on my mother's death then it is very much my business.'

'It is the business of the police to discover who killed your mother. It is not yours.'

Spargo let it pass. To a point the man was right and to argue with him would be counterproductive. Rydel gestured again to one of the armchairs and again Spargo ignored him. Instead he drifted to the mantelpiece, glanced at the photographs and picked up the largest.

Rydel didn't protest. The frame had been given pride of place in the centre of the spread and showed a couple in their twenties, a young man with his hair slicked back and wearing a jacket with wide lapels. Beside him, arm in arm, stood a young woman wearing a flared, pleated dress.

'That is my wife Maureen,' Rydel said. 'Gone ten years now.'

'An old photo,' Spargo said. 'Nineteen-fifties?'

'Nineteen fifty-three.'

Rydel stood up and came over, took the photograph from him and replaced it on the shelf. As he did so Spargo noticed him slide a small unframed photograph behind it, as if deliberately concealing it.

Rydel returned to his chair and Spargo, not wishing to abuse then man's hospitality, finally sat down. Glancing around him he guessed things had stayed much the same since the man's wife died. A fine layer of dust covered everything. Even the mirror on the wall above the fire had a frosted-glass look.

Rydel broke silence. 'How did Morag die?'

'I'll tell you if you tell me why Marek Lewandowski became Mark Lewis.'

Rydel didn't respond. For almost a whole minute he sat motionless.

'Mark and I are immigrants,' he said finally. 'For people like us, changing names is not an uncommon thing to do. Sometimes it is necessary in order to fit in.'

'Did you change your name?'

'I did not. I did not see the need.'

'But Mark did. You said he was scared.'

'It does not matter. He is dead now.'

'How did you know my mother?'

'Many years ago I worked with Mark. We knew Morag Spargo. I have told you why Mark changed his name. Now it is for you to tell me what happened to Morag.'

'She was beaten to death.'

More shock tactics. As Spargo spoke Rydel did the hand over mouth thing again and stared with wide eyes. He gave a quick, disbelieving shake of his head.

'You said you worked with Mark,' Spargo continued. 'Were you a teacher too?'

'I was not.'

Rydel bit his lip and again looked at the carpet. Spargo, making connections, thought of the two men who had stayed in the mine house extension, the men who taught him how to play football and how to fish from the rocks in the bay. Could this frail figure really be one of those men? Could the other have been Mark Lewis?

'Kilcreg,' Spargo said. 'You worked at the mine with my father. You lived at the mine house, in the two room extension.'

Rydel kept his gaze on the carpet.

'I was there the other week,' Spargo said. 'In the mine house. I found a package in the roof.'

Rydel looked him in the eye for no more than a second before looking down again. 'A package? What kind of package?'

'A heavy bronze box wrapped in canvas.'

Rydel shrugged. 'That is no concern of mine.'

'That's an odd thing to say, considering you just asked what kind of package it was. I took it to the police. They opened it and found wartime journals. They sent them to Mr Lewis to be translated. They came here, to this house. Actually, he did very little work on them. And what he did was wrong.'

Spargo regretted his words. They were tactless.

'I knew nothing of Mark's work. If these journals are here then you are welcome to take them.'

'They are not here. They were returned to me.'

Rydel stood up and shuffled silently to the door. He stopped, turned, beckoned Spargo to follow, and continued his stooping shuffle. Both men passed through a long kitchen and into a passage. A central heating boiler, stripped of its white metal panels, stood near the foot of a flight of stairs and Rydel stopped and leaned on it heavily, propping himself as if preparing for the climb. Spargo noticed for the first time the man's left arm hung limp and he used his right hand for everything. The man used it now to haul himself up the stairs At the top he stopped and leant on the bannister rail.

'This was all Mark's,' he said between breaths. 'Everything on this landing. He had his own rooms. He used the box room, this one...' he said as he elbowed open a door '...as an office.'

Rydel flicked a switch and stepped to one side. The room was narrow with no window. A wooden desk had been placed against the end wall and a modern swivel chair pushed against it. There was no other furniture. The remaining space was filled with stacks of paper and files. A computer and printer stood on the desk.

'That's his? That computer?'

'It is. I know nothing about such things. Now I have to dispose of it as I have to dispose of all of his things. His clothes I have thrown away. How can I tell if there are important things in here?'

'On his computer, you mean?'

'I mean everything. He worked long hours for book publishers, I do not know which ones. I do not want to go to the trouble of contacting them all. I do not understand such things.'

Spargo lifted a box file from the top of a pile. He flipped up the lid and saw a letter from Rydel to a Sunday paper, typed fifteen years ago. Checked another stack and found documents even older.

'I'm sure you can safely destroy all of this.'

'And the computer?'

'It's not that old. Why not donate it to a school? I can check it if you like. I can delete everything from the machine.'

Spargo pulled out the desk chair and sat down. Realising the computer was still on standby he pressed a key. It sprang to life.

'I see he's got a modem.'

'What is a modem?'

'His computer is connected to the phone socket. It allows him to communicate with others. Did he use it?'

'I don't know what he did. When he came to live here he had his own telephone put in.'

Spargo, more interested in the computer than in Rydel, checked Lewis's directories on the hard drive. Unlike the rest of the office, the computer files were in good order and indexed under clients' names. Spargo checked them out and found nothing of interest. He clicked on the email icon and when mail came up he scrolled through Lewis's mail. Found nothing that interested him.

'Each morning Mark started work at six o'clock and he worked very late,' Rydel said. 'Sometimes I heard him in the early hours. It was his way. His work was his life.'

'He never relaxed.'

'That is incorrect. He listened to music, he had a stereo machine. He was a considerate man and when he listened to music he wore earphones... headphones. With his money he bought compact disks. They are costly, I know that. It is so wrong for me to throw them out.'

'Why not take them to a charity shop?'

'It is not easy for me. I have been packing his things. I have put the compact disks with his stereo, they are downstairs in boxes. Like Mark, I do not have a car, I cannot drive. Do you have a car?'

Spargo, ready with an excuse, swivelled round in the chair. He tried to imagine Rydel as the man in the photo downstairs, young and fit and newly married. God knows how the man now leaning on the door frame had managed to carry all the stuff to the boxes downstairs.

'No problem,' Spargo said, smiling. 'Of course I'll take them. My daughter knows people who do charity work.'

'Before you came I was about to make tea,' Rydel said. 'Would you like a cup?'

Spargo made all the right noises. Said he was thirsty and would appreciate that very much and he didn't take sugar, only milk. As Rydel made his way slowly down the stairs Spargo swung back to the computer. He had just about decided he was wasting his time when he noticed his own name in a deleted file. Seconds later he had restored and opened an email from Lewis. Familiar words:

JOHN SPARGO YOU ARE OUT OF YOUR DEPTH

Running water and clattering cups downstairs meant Rydel was busy. Spargo switched off the computer, hurried downstairs, went to the mantelshelf and slid out the photograph Rydel had hidden. Like all the others it was black and white, a monochrome photo with cracked emulsion and dog-eared corners. A photo, Spargo told himself, that had been in someone's wallet for a very long time. With his back to the kitchen door he examined it.

In the photograph, two men in their late teens stood side by side against a backdrop of trees. Though one was taller than the other they looked so alike they might well have been twins. Both had high foreheads, long faces and high cheekbones. Their tight-buttoned jackets had no lapels. Baggy trousers drooped over heavy boots and long leather gaiters.

Again, cups clattered. Spargo moved fast. By the time Rydel came through the doorway Spargo was sitting casually in one of the armchairs. Rydel, carrying the tray in his right hand, crossed the room and slid it onto the table.

'That photograph.' Spargo said. 'The one with the two boys. Are you one of them?'

'The taller boy is Mark. I am the other one.'

There were no denials and Spargo felt guilt. Rydel hadn't flinched, hadn't even asked which photo. The man was no fool. He knew Spargo had come down to look at it.

'You look alike,' Spargo said. 'Were you brothers?'

'We were cousins. Mark was a year older than me. The picture was taken on his eighteenth birthday. It was taken in Danzig in nineteen-thirty seven. Danzig is now Gdansk.'

'Poland?'

'Poland,' Rydel said, arranging cups. 'The books you found. You said Mark translated them?'

'He did part of one.'

'You implied he didn't do it well. That surprises me.'

'The police sent him all the journals. For some reason he only translated a small bit in only one of the volumes. I'm having them looked at by someone else, a university lecturer. She said Mark's translation is wrong. He omitted a man's name.'

Rydel was holding the teapot, filling the first cup. 'And the name Mark omitted is what?'

'Theodor Volker.'

Rydel jerked. It was as if his legs had been kicked from under him. Cups rolled off the edge of the tray. Tea spurted from the spout of the ball-shaped teapot as it slid to the edge of the table, hesitated for an instant, and then fell, exploding on the floor like a steam-filled balloon. Spargo leapt up. Rydel waved him away.

'Sit down, sit down! I will see to it!'

'You knew Theodor Volker.'

'I burnt my wrist on the teapot, that is all. The name means nothing to me. Why should it?'

'Lewis knew the name. He left it out of the translation because he didn't want it seen.'

'I told you. We never discussed work.'

'Theodor Volker was the captain of a German submarine in the Second World War. Tell me I'm right.' Rydel's face paled. Fearing the man might fall Spargo stayed close. 'Lewis sent me an email message saying I was out of my depth. I've just seen it on his computer. I was being warned off. Warned off from what, Mr Rydel?'

'I know nothing of Mark's work. I do not understand these things, these emails.' He had piled everything on the tray and was lifting it with one hand. 'You must leave,' he said. 'You are no longer welcome in my house.'

'How can you turn your back on this? Three people are dead, all murdered. Don't you think you owe it to your own cousin?'

'Three people…?'

'My mother and your friend. Also a journalist who got involved, I found his body in the basement of my house. He was looking for the journals, I'm sure of it. I want to know why they were killed.'

'I do not know why.'

'Who is Mark Lewis? Why did he recognise the name Volker? Why did you recognise it?'

'I have told you about Mark. That is what you came for. You must go now.'

'You have told me nothing.'

Rydel sighed. He placed the tray on the table and collapsed back in the chair, seemingly exhausted.

'Very well. Perhaps I owe it to you. Or if not to you, then to Morag. Listen to me, because the things I say to you now I will never repeat, do you understand? I will never repeat.'

'I understand. But in a court of law?'

'I will never repeat, John Spargo! Never!'

'I'm sorry. Yes. Please continue.'

'Very well. I will start at the beginning, it is best. In nineteen-thirty-eight Mark and I left Danzig and travelled to Rostock in Germany, that is a distance of five hundred miles. You will know that in September the following year the Germans invaded my country.'

'They invaded while we stood by and did nothing.'

'I do not want your sympathy, I do not approve of those who apologise for wrongs committed by their forebears. Besides, we were unprepared. We relied on cavalry brigades on horseback while the Germans had tanks.'

'Why did you go to Rostock?'

'My father had friends there. The Germans wanted immigrant workers. I am a Jew, Mark also. But of course, you seem to have discovered that yourself.'

'But you went to Germany. Surely you knew what had been happening there?'

'We knew. Everyone knew. We also knew what our fate would be if we stayed in Poland. Our fathers were not wealthy men but they had some money. For those lucky enough there were things that could be done.'

'New papers?'

'A new identity was only part of the problem.'

Spargo frowned. Rydel locked eyes with Spargo. 'Use your imagination, John Spargo. What is the one thing that distinguishes Jewish men from Gentiles… apart, of course, from their religious beliefs? Like all Jewish boys we were circumcised. You might think that circumcision is not something that can be reversed, but there were ways.'

Spargo looked away. Didn't want to go there.

Rydel glared at him. 'Please have the courtesy to look at me while I am talking to you.'

Spargo weathered the stare. He hadn't expected this.

'I'm sorry,' he said. 'This is none of my business. I should not have asked.'

'This is your business, you have made it your business. You insist I answer your questions yet you want to be selective about what you hear. Skin grafts, John Spargo, I can assure you it was being done. We were amongst the few lucky ones – though Mark was not as lucky as me because his operation was not a complete success, it left him scarred. The surgeon falsified documents to protect him. An accident, it said on Mark's medical certificate.' Rydel looked away, his voice tailed off. 'A childhood accident.'

'I don't understand why you're telling me this.'

'Hear me out. You know of the ghettos? The camps?'

'Of course. Everyone does.'

'Then like everyone who knows but was not there, you can only imagine what I mean when I say we were lucky. Millions were not, our families were not. Six million, John Spargo! Can you even begin to imagine such a number?'

Spargo shook his head. Wasn't sure he knew what this had to do with Mark Lewis's death. Rydel continued:

'As you rightly supposed, our fathers obtained the correct papers. Nazi Germany needed recruits, good Aryan boys. Polish, Belgian, French, Dutch. Even British. Are you aware the SS formed a British division? But that is of no relevance here. What is of relevance is that Mark and I joined the German navy, the Kriegsmarine.'

'I find that surprising.'

'Do you really? Do you doubt me? Do you have the audacity to suggest I would lie to you? We did not have the word Jew written across our foreheads – though there were many who would have liked to do that. Do you honestly think it was possible for two fit young Polish boys to live in Germany and not join their armed forces? Those in Poland who were not Jews joined up in their thousands. Can you think of a better way to have survived? Can you think of any other way to have survived? '

Both men sat quietly, Rydel gazing at the back of his hand and Spargo at the floor. Lewis's email was right, he was out of his depth. He had too many questions to ask, questions whose answers he might not want to hear.

'So you came to Scotland as a prisoner of war?'

'After the war I did not return home, I had no home to return to. Poland was annexed by the Soviets, in case you have forgotten.'

'And Lewis? He came here too?'

'In the navy we trained together. We were posted to the same vessel, a minelayer. By more good luck than planning we remained together for the rest of the war. We fought for the enemy. It is a shame I cannot forget.'

'What was the last vessel you served on?'

'I have said all I am willing to say. I cannot help you further. It is time for you to go.'

Spargo rose from the armchair as if about to leave. Instead of turning away he walked to Rydel, took the lighter from his pocket and thrust it out with the gold eagle uppermost. He had no need to ask the man if he had seen it before. Rydel's eyes widened. His head shook in denial.

'This was found in the wreck of a U-boat commanded by Kapitänleutnant Theodor Volker,' Spargo said. 'Who did it belong to?' Rydel reached out as if to take it but stopped halfway, his hand frozen. 'The boat's number was U-1500. Does that mean anything to you Mr Rydel? Was U-1500 the submarine you and Mark Lewis were serving on when the war ended?'

CHAPTER THIRTY-ONE

THERE IS A MILITARY TRUCK in Artur's farmyard. The driver is having difficulties reversing, he cannot find the right gear. Artur watches through the parlour window.

'Your friends are here. This time there is only one lorry.'

Theo is washing dishes in the kitchen. He crosses to the parlour window and stands there with Artur. Disappointed Walter is early he wipes dirt from the window and peers outside. There is only one man in the cab, a man in dark uniform.

'It's a different truck,' he mutters. 'A different driver.'

The truck's engine roars. The driver gives two bursts on the horn and then one long, impatient blast.

'Your friends are impatient fools. Do they think you are deaf and blind?'

Theo puts on his tunic and leaves it unbuttoned. As he goes for his long boots the horn sounds again. He opens the front door and waves and shouts, gesturing to the driver to stop. The cab door opens. The driver leans out and shouts back.

'You have a strange way of greeting your friends, Theodor!'

It is Walter. His cap is tilted back on his head and his tunic unbuttoned. The mud in the yard is frozen rock-hard and Theo walks on it cautiously as he heads for the truck. He realises as he gets closer that Walter's cap is new. Instead of blue-grey it is a dark, ashen grey. One of the badges it bears is the same as his own, but the cap band below it is black. Mounted in the centre of the cap band is a small silver skull.

Theo stares, open mouthed. Walter stares back.

'Close your mouth. With this stink there will be flies.'

'It is too cold for flies.'

He looks up at Walter and takes in the dark uniform, the black collar and lapels. On each lapel are badges, pairs of oak leaves in silver braid. Indicative, Theo knows, of an SS officer of high rank.

'We do not have all day, Theodor. And much as I would like the pleasure of meeting your in-laws and your son and heir, I have no intention of stepping down into ankle-deep shit.'

'It's frozen,' Theo says absently. 'Walter... if they catch you wearing that uniform you will be shot.'

Walter raises an eyebrow. 'I think not. You, of course, may well be shot for wearing yours. The difference between us is that while I am entitled to wear my Schutzstaffel uniform, you are not entitled to wear that of a Luftwaffe Hauptmann.'

'I don't believe you. You cannot be SS.'

'You are wrong. I am an Oberführer. And in case you don't understand our ranks, that is a higher rank than the one I adopted for my little Luftwaffe act. There is no equivalent rank in your Kriegsmarine. However, it approximates, I believe, to vice-Admiral. Are you coming? I do not have time to spare.'

'Do I have a choice?'

'You do not. Get your things. Can you drive one of these things?'

'I can drive a car.'

'This has several more gears and is slightly heavier. Once we get on to the autobahn you will soon learn.'

'I thought we had a driver?'

'You can see there is no driver. Fetch your bags. I will give you five minutes.'

'I need more time. You said midday.'

'Things have changed. Five minutes. Get your bags.'

'I want to take my boy with me. You can see how bad this place is.'

It is Walter's turn to look stunned. He goes to speak but closes his mouth. Tries again.

'You are insane! How old is the child?'

'Three.'

'Good god! It needs a nurse, not a fool like you.'

'His grandmother is in hospital. My father-in-law can't cope with the farm and the boy.'

Walter gives himself time to think. He examines his gloved hands, first the left, then the right, first the palms and then the backs. He places both on the steering wheel and sighs.

'Theodor, I can take your boy to Ingolstadt, there will be something for him there. There are places for such children.'

'I can care for him. After we deliver our cargo we can take him to Salzgitter on our way back to Carinhall. I will find someone there to look after him, someone at the mines. They are good people. I will pay them.'

'We cannot do that. We will travel a different route. Once I have done what I have to do then we will drive to Hamburg.'

'Then take us to a railway station.'

'You have no travel permits.'

'I have a permit for myself to travel to Hamburg. I shall tell them he is my son. I shall explain everything.'

'You are forgetting. You do not have a permit, I destroyed your papers. Do you seriously think I brought you this far so you can simply walk away from me?'

'He can travel in the back of the truck. I can get quilts.'

'It is out of the question. I am carrying cargo, there is no space.'

Theo grabs a handle beside the driver's door, pulls himself up and looks past Walter. The cab is empty except for a bag on the floor. The bench seat has room for three.

'He is small. He can travel up here, with us.'

'That is not possible, you are forgetting the checkpoints. There are ways to avoid the regular ones but I cannot avoid the random ones.'

'You can pull rank. You are an SS Oberführer.'

'And you are insane.'

Walter steps down from the cab. With a sweep of his arm he shoves Theo aside. He steps gingerly on the mud, testing it with the toes of each boot before stepping down properly. Without either of them noticing, Peter comes out in the yard, runs over and stands right beside them. He has been playing near the grate and his face is smeared black. He has his fingers in his mouth and with his free hand he reaches up and grasps the hem of Walter's tunic. Walter looks down, as if at a wild animal.

'This is him? This is your son?'

Theo expects disapproval, even disgust. But Walter just stares. 'Why does he do that? Why is he barefoot in ice-cold mud? Why does he cling to a stranger, a man he does not know?'

Theo snaps at the boy, 'Go inside, Peter!'

The boy stays, sucking his black fingers and looking up at Walter.

'He looks sick.'

'He is healthy. He is well-fed.'

'He is not. Look at him, he is pale. Our faces are red with the cold but his is white. He should see a doctor. He should be in hospital.'

Then Artur is there, averting his eyes from Walter's uniform. He scoops up the boy in his arms and heads back to the house.

'Your father-in-law is an old man. Does he care for the boy without help?'

They stand watching Artur. He is stumbling, struggling to cope with the boy's weight.

'I will take him, Theodor. If I take your child to Salzgitter then we shall be even, do you agree?'

'Even?'

'I have not forgotten you once saved my life. If I take him then we will be even. Tell me, Theo. Say it!'

Theo wants to say nobody is counting, there is no debt to pay. But if Walter believes there is no debt then he will lose this chance.

'It is agreed then. We shall be even. But Hamburg, Walter, not Salzgitter. Erica had many friends there. They will care for Peter, I am sure.'

'Very well. A life for a life, Theodor.'

'What about checkpoints? You said – '

Walter shrugs. 'We will take our chances. As you said, possibly I can take care of them.'

Theo walks to the back of the truck to see what is inside it. He climbs the four rungs of a short ladder fixed to the tailgate, pulls aside the canvas curtain, looks in and is faced with a wall of stacked crates. Down one side of the truck, between the side panel and the crates is a long narrow gap containing neatly stacked fuel cans. Walter's suitcases are there – also a kitbag Theo hasn't seen before. In the last remaining space, on the floor of the truck and immediately behind the tailgate are white muslin bags containing food.

He steps down. Walter is there, watching. Theo points to stencilled markings on the crates.

'Property of the SS? To me they look like the crates we had before. What happened, weren't they delivered? Is it where we are going now? Is it why you are early? Where is the other truck? Are these the crates I signed for as having been delivered?'

'Part of our deal is that you ask no questions. Get your bags. And bring the boy, before I change my mind. Having him in the cab is out of the question. We must make space for him in the back. We must rearrange the cargo.'

Theo makes trips to the farmhouse and brings out his bags, spare quilts and spare clothes for Peter. Artur gives him a small churn of milk and a cloth bag of bread and cheese. Peter is dressed in thick clothing, topped with an outsize overcoat whose sleeves cover his hands.

Artur carries the food to the truck and Theo carries Peter, lifting him over the tailgate, and carrying him over the fuel cans to a concealed space between crates Walter is making for him. The boy does not flinch. Soon he is lost in the quilt and a mass of spare clothes.

While Theo is there the engine growls to life, gears grind and the truck starts to move, its wheels crushing ice. By the time he struggles to the tailgate and tugs the canvas canopy aside to see out, the truck has left the farmyard and is grinding its way up the lane. All Theo can see of the farm is the barn, the rusty steel roof of the farmhouse and the pillar of pale smoke rising from its chimney.

There is no point in Theo complaining about the hurried departure, what is done is done. When this war is over he will return to the farm with Peter and thank Artur properly, perhaps even help on the farm for a while. Perhaps stay there for ever.

Hours pass before Walter pulls off the road. Theo, still in the back, stretched out uncomfortably on the fuel cans with his head close to Peter's den, is rocked and buffeted as Walter takes the truck down tracks, into dense woodland. The cab door slams; Walter's boots crunch deep snow as he walks to the tailgate; daylight streams into the truck as the corner of the canvas is lifted.

Walter's capped head is framed by canvas. He is looking for something, trying to see past Theo, squinting down the dark narrow alley.

'Behind these crates you will find a naval kitbag, it has all your old kit. Change into your naval uniform and then bring me everything I gave you in Berlin.'

'My kit? You told me you had destroyed everything of mine.'

'I lied.'

'Does that mean you still have my travel permit and my rail warrant?'

'Come, move! We do not have all day!' He wags a finger at Theo's Luftwaffe boots, damaged from when he chopped wood. 'Take those off. Your socks, too. I want everything.'

Theo shakes his head, exasperation rather than refusal. He has done a deal with the devil. In exchange he has been given his son.

Walter continues: 'It is inevitable we will be stopped. When it happens you will say you are a submariner on leave. You will show them your rail warrant and tell them that because there are no trains it is now worthless. You are returning to your dockyard by any possible means and out of the goodness of my heart I stopped at the roadside to give you a lift. It is what you will say, you will not elaborate in any way. Give me your Luftwaffe papers. You will find your old naval papers in your kitbag. Now, move! Pass me one of those fuel cans!'

Theo does as Walter asks and then goes for the kitbag. In it he finds boots, standard naval issue rather than submariner's sea boots. They are brand new, as is the cap. His white roll-neck sweater is missing, as is his old leather jacket. In their place is a standard naval tunic and a greatcoat, rolled tight. Both show his true rank. Taking care not to be seen by Walter, he transfers his Kriegsmarine notebooks from the Luftwaffe kitbag to his naval one.

Soon he is a naval officer again, smarter but less comfortable than before.

Walter has walked into the trees and is burning kit. Theo consigns his papers and kitbag to the flames, and finally his tall Luftwaffe boots.

'Shame about those,' he says. 'I was beginning to like them.'

CHAPTER THIRTY-TWO

SPARGO SAT AT HIS DESK, concentrating on a sheet of white paper. On it he'd pencilled names, Rydel and Lewis, Kalman and Stuart Main. He added Letchie, and then Day and Montgomery. He drew circles around them. Drew lines to link them.

Sure Main wasn't involved in any way he rubbed out his name. Down the left hand edge of the paper he listed more words: journals, cottage, Letchie's laptop, Lewis's email. After adding several more items he started to draw lines between these, too. Then he screwed up the paper and dropped it into his bin.

He missed working with Murphy. Seeing connections between seemingly unrelated things was something Murphy excelled at. So was Jez – but if he asked her to help there would be a big price to pay, he would have to come clean with her. Trouble was, he couldn't remember what he'd told her and what he hadn't.

'His name is Francis Rydel,' he told her that evening. 'He's old, probably in his late eighties. Lewis, the translator, was his cousin. When Rydel's wife died, Lewis moved down from Inverness to stay with him.'

'You told me Lewis was killed in a hit-and-run. Are you saying you went to his house?'

'I've got stuff from there,' he said, over-cheerful. 'A stereo and boxes of CDs for that friend of yours. The one who does the charity stuff.'

Her eyes burned. 'Dad! Stop trying to divert me! I can't believe you went there! What did you hope to achieve?'

'Not as much as I did achieve. It was Lewis who sent me that message. I also – '

'What message?'

'Didn't I tell you? An email. I told Mitchell about it.'

'But you didn't tell me.'

None of the soft chairs in Jez's sitting room were particularly comfortable and he circled around, selected the best and sat down on it. Jez stayed standing while her father explained about the email.

'It was there,' he said. 'With the deleted items.'

'I think I need a stiff drink.'

'Did I tell you I met Kalman again?'

'Who the hell is Kalman?'

Jez crossed the room, opened a cupboard and poured two gins.

Spargo told her about Kalman, and pewter plates, and Montgomery and Day. And Hermann Göring's lighter. Jez poured herself another drink.

'Useful man, Day,' Spargo added. 'Likes to make out he's a shady trader. Makes his buyers think they're getting something under the counter.'

Jez listened, nursing her glass and trying hard not to scream. Over the years her father had been in all kinds of scrapes but nothing like this. She hoped, but doubted, he was telling her everything.

'Did you show Rydel the lighter?'

Spargo nodded. 'He recognised it. I thought he was going to have a seizure.'

Jez rolled her eyes. Another dead body was all her father needed. 'And did Rydel admit to having known Volker?'

'He didn't admit to it. It was obvious he did.'

'And you think they were together on the submarine. You said its number just now. What was it?'

'U-1500.'

She jotted something on a notepad.

'And this Kalman. You said that as soon as he found out the submarine was the U-1500, the whole thing was called off?'

'No. He was then to search the boat. Then he found the pewter. The consortium wasn't interested in it.'

'How much of this do the police know? What have you told them?'

'Very little.'

'Don't you think you should? Do they know about Day?'

'No. He did me a favour.'

'Rydel, then?'

'I only met him this afternoon.'

'Of course you did, how silly of me. I suppose he's done you favours too.' She tried to calm herself. 'What about Kalman?'

'What about him?'

'Have you told the police about him?'

'How can I possibly tell them? He's trying to sell pewter so he won't have to take it through customs.'

She rolled her eyes again. Her father was protecting people. It had happened before, it happened when he and Murphy fell out. At the time she was too young to understand but her mother told her years later that Murphy had smashed up a car when drunk and her father had covered things up somehow.

'And Kalman did you a favour, of course. Gran has been murdered, and you're bimbling about, keeping all this to yourself.'

'I'm not bimbling about. I just can't seem to pull it all together. I can't prove anything.'

'That is not your job. Just because you don't like Quinn doesn't mean you shouldn't tell him what you know.'

Jez waited, watching him ponder her words. She knew she had made her point and it was tactless to pursue it.

'Any sign of your Spanish contract?' she asked.

It was the first alternative topic that came to her mind. Perhaps not the best one.

'Haven't heard anything. I can't say I'm surprised though. I got the impression it would take a few weeks.'

'Tell me about him.'

'Who?'

'Oscar Bar.'

'Why?'

'Humour me. You said just now this exploration thing cost millions. Is Bar rich enough to finance it?'

'Why should it be anything to do with Bar? Kalman said exploration of the sub is paid for by a US consortium.'

'I didn't say it was Bar. Tell me what you know about him. What's his history?'

Spargo shrugged. 'I know next to nothing about him. BarConSA's not in the mining directories. Murphy hasn't heard of them.'

'I'm talking about Bar, not his firm. You said he is old.'

'Pushing ninety. Possibly more.'

'The name Oscar doesn't sound Spanish. Not sure about Bar.'

'I thought at first he was Swedish.'

'Have you looked him up on the Internet?'

'I didn't think of it.'

That surprised her. Her father was computer literate. He used the net for mining research.

'You said Swedish. Why?'

'The mixed accent. Natural Spanish flows. It's not as smooth as Italian but you know what I mean. Bar's is guttural, his words are clipped. I got the impression he had a throat problem.'

'Maybe he is German.'

'I wondered about that. It might explain the pictures.'

'What pictures?'

'In his study in Spain. Old photographs. One was of a group of men in uniform. They could have been German.'

'Wartime? And you couldn't tell if they were German? With the possible exception of Spiderman, the Third Reich probably had the most recognisable uniforms in the history of the world.'

'If you mean caps and jackboots they weren't wearing any. Anyway, I didn't get a good look. Bar came in.'

'While you were searching his study.'

'I wasn't searching. I was early for breakfast. I was standing just inside the doorway. I simply wondered why he had taken down all his pictures. The nails were still in the wall, you could see where the pictures had been.'

'What about the rest of the pictures.'

'I didn't see them. Didn't have time.'

'What did Bar say when he found you there?'

'Not a lot.'

'You said he was old and in a wheelchair. Sounds to me he's about the right age.'

'For what?'

'Don't you think it strange he wants to hire you at the very same time as this U-boat business is going on?'

'It isn't the same time. I met Benares long before all this happened.'

'I can't agree. You said the diving started early in the year. You met Benares in London months later.'

'They didn't know it was the right boat until Kalman found that name tag. That couldn't have happened until after I met Benares.'

'What do you mean, the right boat? Surely if it was empty it was the wrong boat?'

He took a swig from his glass. 'No, it was the right boat. It was the boat they had been looking for. Kalman said it was the right boat because it had no guns or torpedo tubes. He said there was space for cargo, but apart from the pewter it seemed to have been carrying nothing.'

She listened, nodding occasionally. Found herself gazing into the middle distance like her fellow academics did.

'They paid out millions of dollars...' she mumbled, '...knowing anything found in the submarine would be worthless.' Then, no longer mumbling: 'Gold doesn't corrode. Were they looking for gold?'

Her father shook his head. 'I've been through all that. Kalman was adamant it wasn't gold.'

'But still he didn't know what it was.'

'I remember him saying the whole thing had been about nothing.'

'He said?'

'This whole game's been about nothing. His exact words.'

She looked up from the floor and her gaze met his. Suddenly things seemed so clear. She sat bolt upright and looked at her father.

'If there was anything in the submarine it would be worthless,' she said. 'Are we sure of that?'

'Absolutely. Unless it was gold. And there was no gold.'

'You know what? This Kalman friend of yours wasn't hired to look for anything.'

'What do you mean? And he's not my friend.'

'Just listen to me! Oil exploration found a wreck. Someone, later on, did more work and realised it was a submarine.'

'That might have been Kalman's firm. I'm not sure.'

'That's irrelevant. Kalman was hired to check to see if it was a certain boat – a particular German U-boat. When it turned out to be the right boat – one with no armaments – he was asked to search it. He found nothing of interest.'

'That's about right.'

She looked at him sternly. 'About right…?'

'Yes, absolutely right.'

'When I search for something I start by looking in the most likely place. Only if I don't find it there do I start to look elsewhere. The sub was the most likely place to find whatever this consortium was looking for, it was their preferred option. But whatever they wanted wasn't there, which meant it was somewhere else. They will now concentrate on the other possible places.'

'I don't buy it. Nobody in their right mind would shell out millions if there was a cheaper way. They would look in the other places first. Searching a wreck on the bottom of the North Sea has to be their very last option.'

'I said preferred option, not cheapest.'

'It's not the option I would go for.'

'You can't possibly say that without knowing their alternatives.'

She could see he hadn't got it. She would have to spell it out for him. She pressed her fingertips together prayer-like and placed them over her mouth and nose. Closed her eyes and rubbed her eyelids with her fingertips.

'Searching elsewhere might have had risks,' she said.

'And exploring a wrecked sub doesn't have risks?'

'I mean other kinds of risks.'

She let him digest it.

'Kilcreg, you mean? Do you seriously expect me to believe they were looking for Volker's journals?'

She kept her hands to her face. Her voice echoed, as if speaking through a tube.

'To me it's obvious. They were sealed in a bronze box. There was a good chance they would survive.'

'Not if they were in the U-boat.'

'I agree. The journals would be ruined because the box would eventually leak. But the box would be there and Kalman would have found it. End of story. Everyone goes home. But if the box is not there, then it is somewhere else. And perhaps the journals are still readable.'

'You've made a quantum leap from the sub to Gran's cottage.'

'It's no quantum leap. The diaries were written by Volker. Volker was on that boat. Somehow the box got from the U-boat to the roof of the mine house.'

Spargo shook his head. Whether it was disagreement or denial she couldn't tell.

'So tell me how they got there,' he asked.

'I'm a geologist, not a clairvoyant.'

'If somebody thought the journals were in Kilcreg then why didn't they look there first? For the kind of money they spent searching, they could have bought every house in the place.'

'And they would have done that, would they? Bought a village? Just the thing to do when you don't want to draw attention to yourself.'

'I didn't mean that.'

'What if their preferred way was not to break the law?' she continued. 'What if for whatever reason their preferred way was to spend millions rather than to break in to Gran's house?'

He was smirking now. 'Considerate criminals.'

'Or perhaps not criminals at all. Perhaps a consortium that put up money to search for a sub for a perfectly legitimate reason. Or what it considered to be a legitimate reason.'

'A consortium that then murders your grandmother.'

'No, not necessarily. A consortium that knew – somehow – where the journals might be if they weren't in the U-boat. A consortium that after failing to find what it expected to find on the U-boat decides to hire someone to check out Gran's cottage.'

Her father went quiet. Then he murmured 'Oh Christ...!'

'I was thinking more of Ian Letchie.'

His smirk had finally gone. She was getting through to him at last.

For a few minutes they went without speaking. Jez left the room and made coffee, strong and black. For him, to keep him awake on his drive home. For her, to keep her sharp for what she planned to do when he'd gone.

'You said you had boxes for Brenda,' she said as she carried in the mugs. 'We should bring them in from your car. I'll give her a ring tomorrow and she can pick them up.'

Halfway through coffee she made the first move. She stood up, went to the hall, slipped her coat on and opened the front door. Spargo followed. When the three boxes were inside she piled them against the wall to make space.

'Which one has the stereo?'

'Not sure. But don't hold your breath. It might have batteries and valves.'

She went for scissors and scored through parcel tape. Revealed, in the first box, an expanse of shiny steel.

'I take back what I said about valves,' he said. 'It's a CD player, it looks new. What will Brenda do with it, sell it?'

'The best stuff goes for auction. It makes sure she gets the best price.'

She opened the second box. Saw silvery plastic CD cases, packed on end. She eased her hand between them. Tugged out a handful and glanced at their covers.

'Classics,' she said. 'Haydn, Debussy, Purcell.'

Spargo opened the last box and revealed more CDs. Most were boxed sets.

'More classical,' he said. 'Complete works of Chopin. There must be at least ten disks in this set. Wasn't Chopin Polish?'

'Are you suggesting Lewis listened to it because he was Polish too?'

'Don't be so sensitive. Of course not.' He picked up another set and turned it so she could see it. 'Wagner,' he said. 'After what I learned today that surprises me.'

She took it from him, turned the pack over.

'He didn't listen to it though, did he? It's still in its wrapper.' She read out the title: 'Die Walküre – The Valkyrie. It even has its price label. Why are you surprised Lewis listened to it?'

Spargo shrugged. 'Wagner was Hitler's favourite composer. He wrote all that mythical Aryan crap.'

'You can hardly blame Wagner for Hitler liking his music. Anyway, Wagner died before Hitler was even born.'

'Wagner was anti-Semitic.'

'Most of the western world was. A lot of it still is.'

Her father held up his hands in mock-surrender, a gesture that always annoyed her. Made her feel she was the aggressor.

'What is a Valkyrie anyway?' he asked.

She shrugged. 'A flying thing. Mythical Aryan crap.'

'Touché.'

'Anyway, it's not German legend. It's Norse.'

'So what will happen to them all?' he asked, waving his hand at the boxes. 'Seems a shame to break up a collection like this.'

'Who says it'll get broken up? Brenda's no fool. If she can get the best price by selling them as a collection then that's what she'll do.'

She folded down the lids. Pushed the boxes even closer together.

'Have you heard from Marie?' he asked.

'I haven't seen her. And after everything you have just told me you can't possibly use her to translate the journals. You must take them to Quinn. Tell him about Kalman. Tell him everything.'

'Can't,' he said, shaking his head. 'I haven't got the journals. I took them to Marie the same day I met her. I left them in her room.'

As soon as her father was out of the door Jez went to her laptop. She typed the name BarConSA into the search engine and got nothing. Scanning through the notes she had been making she typed in submarine, added U-1500, and then changed submarine to U-boat. Raising her eyebrows at the number of entries that came up, she scrolled down the list. Then spent time – a lot of time – checking web pages.

Returning to the aim of her original search she typed in Oscar Bar and refined it by adding keywords. By excluding genealogy, ancestors and forebears she thinned the pages down to a few dozen and worked her way through them. One was an extract from a New York insurance company's annual report, a three hundred thousand dollar claim for goods damaged in transit. Made by an Oscar Bar of Madrid.

She reached for the phone.

'Go on line,' she said when her father answered. 'I've sent you an email.'

'What, now? It's two in the morning.'

'I've sent you a list of websites. Look at them.'

'Can't it wait?'

'No it can't. You need to see them now. Take the phone with you and stay talking to me.'

She waited. Heard grumblings and mumblings.

'Got your email,' he said.

'Click on the links.'

Another long pause. Then he was reading aloud.

'Oscar Bar, insurance claim refused… what makes you think it's the same Oscar Bar? There must be hundreds with that name.'

'In Madrid?'

'Where does it say Madrid?'

'Which website are you in? Look at the one that says Anzika.'

She clicked on it herself, a list of civil claims lodged with a Californian court. She read it out:

'Bar versus Anzika Ridge Shipping and Handling, damage to works of art in transit. You got it yet?'

'Got it. They allege packing cases were dropped by a fork lift truck at Los Angeles International Airport.'

'The claim was rejected so Bar took them to court. You said there were paintings on the wall of that boardroom in Madrid.'

'Photos of paintings. But the claim is for works of art. That doesn't have to be paintings. He could have been selling the Trevi Fountain.'

'That's in Rome, not Madrid.'

'I know that.'

'What were the artists? In the boardroom, I mean.'

'Not sure. I wouldn't know a Botticelli from a Raphael. It looked like text book stuff, a mixture of artists and styles.'

'Velazquez? Reubens and his big boobed ladies? Did the breasts follow you round the room?'

'Peter Cook,' he said. 'And it was bottoms, not breasts. Odd you should bring up the Mona Lisa, it was the only picture I recognised. The photograph was black and white and grainy, not worth hanging on the wall. And the only thing that followed me round the room was Benares. I didn't know he was there.'

'And you shouldn't have been in there, that's what you said.'

'Benares wasn't fussed. He said they were left by the previous occupants.'

'Did you believe him?'

'Not really.' He was reading her email. 'I see you've been looking up U-boats. You found a website.'

'Have you got the site up? It's awesome. They list over a thousand boats, every U-boat ever made. It also lists their commanding officers. It gives the history and fate of each boat.'

'What does it say about Theodor Volker?'

'Nothing,' she said, 'there's no mention of him. Nor is there mention of any U-boat with the number U-1500.'

CHAPTER THIRTY-THREE

THE VEHICLE WALTER DRIVES is an ammunition truck with a powerful engine and it maintains a good speed. So far, Theo has resisted Walter's attempts to make him to sit in the cab and he remains in the back with Peter. His boy is sleeping, no longer in the den but squeezed into the tight alley, cradled in his father's arms.

Theo is tired but he dare not sleep. He fears the checkpoints, not so much the soldiers manning them but the ubiquitous Gestapo – the Reich's secret police – so often present in the background. He waits nervously for Walter's the prearranged warning: three taps on the back of the cab.

He wonders again about Walter. Wonders what authority he has and what documents he carries. He tells himself that now he has Peter these things no longer matter and he tries, as he has tried several times before, to invent valid explanations for having his boy. He concludes, as he concluded each time, that there are no good reasons. The boy has no permit to travel, he has no papers at all. For that alone they will be detained.

Theo wakes to loud bangs. They come again, three hard whacks on the metal wall of the cab. Theo scoops up his boy and bundles him from the alley to the den. Peter wakes up and struggles, he will have none of it. He is well used to the dark but not to being manhandled.

Walter changes down through the gears as the truck nears the checkpoint. Theo lies flat on the fuel cans, his head and shoulders in the den trying to calm his boy. The truck stops, then creeps forwards slowly. For a minute or so Theo believes they have been waved through but he is wrong. Walter is turning the truck. He is pulling in at the roadside.

Theo hears voices, Walter's and one another. He whispers to Peter to hide under the quilt but the boy shakes his head. He wants to come out.

Someone – he hopes it is Walter – is at the back of the truck. There is a rustling of rope as lashings are unfastened. A slick of light floods in as the corner of the canvas curtain is raised. Theo turns around and crawls back to the curtain. He tries, by crouching, to block any view.

His tunic is undone but his badges of rank show. A steel-helmeted soldier, still holding the curtain, salutes him.

'Herr Kapitän, I am sorry to waken you. Your papers, please.'

Then Peter is behind him, scrambling over the cans, rocking them as he moves. Curious, the soldier places a foot on the ladder. He is about to haul himself up when an officer, curious about the delay, calls out to him and comes over. Walter intercepts him. The officer salutes and Walter, casually and with his hands clasped behind him as if out for a stroll, speaks to him quietly.

'I have to confess that my Aide is not alone, Herr Leutnant. A lady friend, you understand. These U-boat men are all alike, insatiable appetites for drink and sex. Naturally, as an officer of the Schutzstaffel I find such things deeply embarrassing.'

The helmeted soldier drops the canvas and looks away sharply. One second more and he would have seen Peter. Theo grabs the boy, clamps a hand over his mouth and drags him back to the den. Theo hears laughing. Then, mercifully, the slam of the cab door and the roar of the engine.

'I must have been out of my mind,' Walter says later. 'An insatiable appetite indeed! God knows why they didn't ask me for the woman's papers. I told them she wasn't travelling anywhere and I was driving a circular route, about to take her to back. The child must be kept quiet and hidden, Theodor! My trick worked once. It will not work again.'

They have turned off the autobahn to refuel. Theo brings the cans and Walter empties them one by one into the truck's fuel tank.

'You handled it well back there. I heard them laugh.'

'It worked only because of my uniform and because there were no bastard Gestapo... unseal more cans, it will take ten at least... also, if we are stopped at a checkpoint manned by the SS then we will be in trouble.'

'I thought you people stuck together.'

'There are limits. Even if there are no Gestapo, I might be outranked, have you thought of that?' Walter hurls an empty can into the bushes. 'At least I know what is up ahead. The Leutnant knows of two more checkpoints, one this side of Dresden and another at Görlitz. He says he's heard the Soviets are on the move again and that worries me. I'm wondering if I have left this thing too late.'

'Görlitz? Isn't it on the border?'

'If you still consider Poland to be a separate country, then yes. What matters now is that he – ' Walter gestures with his arm to Peter, now out of the truck and playing with stones ' – does not wake when we pass through them.'

Theo shakes his head. 'I can't guarantee it.'

'You must find a way.'

'It is not just Peter worrying you, is it, it's the crates. What are you up to? Why do we still have them?'

'No, you are wrong, I can handle my side of this. The problem is your boy. Do not forget our deal. You have your son, I have my secrets.'

'The life of my child is in your hands. I have no option but to trust you absolutely. We need have no secrets.'

Walter leans against the truck, standing awkwardly under the weight of a fuel can, his greatcoat unbuttoned and his cap at an angle. His stance reminds Theo of the boy he once knew.

'Very well. I have told you already that one of my tasks was to find a reliable U-boat commander. I have done that. I also told you your friend Hermann will be taken to a U-boat that is being prepared.'

'You did not tell me that. Is it your job to transport the Reichsmarschall?'

'Are you trying to catch me out? I have already told you I am responsible only for the paintings.'

'You lied to me. You told me the paintings were going south for safety. Now we are taking them to the east.'

'They are safe. They are with me.'

'You know that's not what I mean.'

'They crates we carry will be taken to one of our ports. I am not yet prepared to tell you which one.'

'You have already told me it's Hamburg. Am I to take the paintings on board a boat? Also the Reichsmarschall?'

'The paintings, yes. I am not party to arrangements concerning our leaders.'

'There is hardly enough room for the crew, never mind a truckload of crates.'

'The boat has been modified. No, that is incorrect, it is a new boat, its design has been modified, one of the torpedo rooms will be used as a store. The torpedo loading hatch… if I have got that right… has been enlarged to allow crates to be loaded. We have even attempted to get your former key crewmen assigned to this boat. We understand them to be men you know and trust.'

'And the Reichsmarschall's staff at Carinhall? What will happen when they realise you have the paintings?'

'They will not. Only a select few in Germany are party to these plans. But if they do, then you, your boy, myself and many of my colleagues will not survive.

'It would be better if I didn't know that.'

'Blame yourself. You asked me, I told you. But you need have no worries. Nobody knows about your boy, and you and I are already dead, killed near Munich yesterday when our trucks were bombed by enemy aircraft. The SS unit first on the scene will have already told Carinhall the occupants of the trucks are dead and the cargo they carried is destroyed.'

Theo's face pales. 'The troops from Neuhaus? Those escorting the other trucks? You killed them all?'

Walter laughs. 'Not me, Theodor. Why should I soil my hands when there are so many of our countrymen willing to do these things for me? The deaths were unfortunate but necessary. As a combat man I would have thought you would be used to such things.'

'In action we are killed by the enemy, not by our brothers. God, Walter! What have you got me into?'

'You are naïve, Theodore. By their incompetence and stupidity our leaders have killed many thousands of the people you call our brothers. But I have told you enough. Is the fuel tank full?'

'It's the SS, isn't it? The SS is stealing the Reichsmarschall's art!'

'It is hardly his art. But no, not stealing, we are merely diverting some of it temporarily, ensuring the most valuable items stay with him rather than in a bank vault in Switzerland. Who is to say the Swiss will stay neutral? Even if they do, do you honestly believe that when this war is over the Swiss banks will be evil enough to hold on to works of art sent to them by our Reich? Give them credit!'

'What will happen if Göring does come aboard my boat? I met him, he'll recognise me. He will know I was impersonating a Luftwaffe officer.'

'Quite the contrary. He will be safe, and thanks to you he will have a selection of his most valuable paintings. You will probably get a medal. Take care with that last can, it still has some fuel. I do not wish to see our efforts destroyed in a ball of flame.'

'Will you be on the boat?'

'Of course! Do you think I would miss an opportunity to get out of this hell? Do you think I ever want to meet a Russian carrying a gun?'

'Tell me why we are heading towards Görlitz.'

'At Carinhall I asked you about the cases, whether or not they are waterproof. You suggested bronze boxes. These should have been made by now. The crates we are carrying will be sealed inside them and the bronze boxes coated with rubber like that used for motor tyres. In what you insist on referring to as Poland there are facilities to do these things. Come, we are wasting time. Get the boy into the back and then pass down one of my bags, the smallest one. I have something to make him sleep.'

They take turns driving. Walter explains he'd planned to spend the night at an SS barracks outside Dresden but now they have the child, things must change, they must sleep in the truck.

When they can drive no more they turn down a lane and conceal the truck beneath trees. All three sit in the dark in the cab and eat sausage from the muslin bags and stale bread from the farm.

The night brings snow and a deep, penetrating cold. There is a radiator of sorts in the cab, a long pipe with fins. With the engine running it stays passably warm and Peter lies on the cab floor in a bundled up quilt.

During the night Walter grumbles incessantly about the cab's smallness. Awkwardly he fumbles in his pockets, finds a cigarette, lights it and draws on it. Its feint red glow reflects in the windscreen. Other than that there is no light at all.

Walter finishes the cigarette, slides the window to one side and flicks the butt out. Theo hears him unclip the leather flap of his holster and take out his automatic pistol. He hears the click of the safety catch, then a metallic clunk as the gun is placed near the windscreen. Theo, knowing he won't sleep, pulls up the collar of his greatcoat and leans against the door. Peter, now on his lap – a concession to Walter in the hope the extra legroom will stop him grumbling – wrestles free from Theo's arms and huddles down on the floor again, close to the heater pipe. Soon his breathing changes, as does Walter's. Both are asleep.

They wake before dawn and clear snow from the truck. The trees and hedges that concealed them during the night bend under the weight of the night's snow. Lit by the truck's headlights they glow yellow-white in a smooth, sugar-iced landscape.

Daylight takes over from headlights. Walter drives, heading east into a hazy red sun. Hoping to avoid autobahn checkpoints he takes roads not built for heavy vehicles. It is a mistake; their progress is painfully slow, impeded again by horse-drawn wagons that Walter, frustrated, delights in forcing off the road.

On decent roads again they pick up speed. By the end of the day they are through Breslau and well into Poland. Walter is determined to drive through the night but the truck's masked headlights aren't up to it. Finally he gives up, finds a farm track and stops.

While the others sleep Theo ponders on the future. Over the last few days he has begun to trust Walter, he has shown consideration and a degree of compassion. It is no comfort to know there are many others involved in this plot and Walter, though of senior rank, does not control it. Most worrying of all, Theo knows it was a mistake to take Peter from the farm. He has put the boy in harm's way. What is the expression? *Out of the frying pan, into the fire?*

CHAPTER THIRTY-FOUR

IF IT HADN'T BEEN FOR the brown envelopes delivered regularly by the postman, Midge might already have dropped his surveillance. Seeing Quinn at the Spargo woman's house had shaken him – though not nearly as much as he was shaken by the news in the papers about the body in Spargo's cellar. Midge wondering if he had been set up in some way. Wondered why Mr Luis was paying him so much money to stare at a flat.

Midge used some of the money to trade in his old Fiat for a used Alfa Romeo with alloy wheels, tinted windows and a CD player. It wasn't the make of the car that attracted him but its colour, it was silver with a shimmering hint of green. Iridescent, he'd though when he first saw it. Like the sheen on butterflies' wings.

In his mind the car had two faults. The first was that the front number plate was mounted off-centre, to one side of the grill. Asymmetrical, he had said to the dealer at Sighthill, sure the man wouldn't know what the word meant. The dealer responded that cars weren't meant to be symmetrical, and if that were the case then the steering wheel and controls would be in the middle.

Midge's second gripe was that the car had a CD player. The old Fiat did not, and over the years he had amassed a collection of tapes he now couldn't use. He still had them beside him on the seat of the Alfa, so when he kept surveillance he could rummage through them. It looked as if he had stopped for a reason.

Italian, his new car. He loved it, loved the sleek styling. Loved the burble of the exhaust.

As he drove towards Princes Street something beeped. He studied the instruments and saw no warnings. He eventually realised it was his phone and he pulled in by the roadside. Didn't want to attract the attention of the police by phoning while driving.

'Is that Rollo?'

It wasn't Mr Luis. It was a voice he'd not heard for a while.

'It's Midge.'

'Where are you?'

'Working.' The dash clock said midnight. Saying he was working was sure to impress.

'Still working for Benares?'

'Still for Mr Luis.'

'Job alright? Mail arriving alright?'

'Good money. Bought a new car today.'

'I don't give a monkey's what you do with your money, Rollo. Where are you now?'

'Driving home.'

'I asked you to get something for me.'

Midge frowned at the phone. 'Get something? For Mr Luis, you mean? He didn't take it.'

'I just asked you to get it, Rollo, I didn't say who it was for. You've got it? Is it a serious piece? I don't want any tat.'

'I've still got it. I stripped it down. I haven't tried it.'

'Jesus, Rollo! Tried it? The thought of you with anything more than a water pistol scares the shit out of me. What about rounds?'

'Five. Can't get more.'

'Five is good. Listen to me. We need to meet.'

'You're here? In Edinburgh?'

'Tomorrow at eleven, Starbucks at the Gyle. You can fill me in on what's been going on.'

Midge hesitated. 'Mr Luis says I'm not to talk to anyone about what I'm doing and you said whatever he said goes. You said – '

'Who pays you, Rollo?'

'Mr Luis.'

'Wrong. I do.'

'Okay, you do. But it's his money.'

'Where the money comes from is none of your business. Just be there, Rollo. Eleven on the dot.'

The phone went dead.

Midge had bought new CDs. He didn't want to leave them on the seat with the music tapes because it would look odd, so he opened the glove compartment, took out the car's handbook to make room for them and shoved them inside. Deciding to put the handbook under the drivers' seat he reached down with it.

The handbook went under the seat remarkably easily. Didn't encounter the bag with the gun. Thinking his new car's amazing acceleration must have forced the bag right back, he got out of the car, crouched down and groped under the seat.

The handbook was there but nothing else was. The carrier bag had never been under the seat in the Alfa. It was still in the Fiat.

In daytime, motorists used the roads on the industrial estate at Sighthill as a park-and-ride car park. Tonight, apart from the shell of a dumped and torched car, Midge's Alfa was the only vehicle there, so parking in the road was out of the question. Security men in vans patrolled the industrial estate and a lone car, so close to so many car showrooms, looked wrong.

In a flash of inspiration Midge realised the best place to hide his car would be with the cars on the showroom forecourt. He turned off the road. Found his way blocked by a barrier.

His old car was where he had left it, parked in a corner well away from the others. He worked fast, wrenching off one of the wipers, bending it to make a hook and inserting it between the window glass and the rubber seal on the passenger door. He jiggled it, gave it a tug, and the lock knob popped up. Once he had the door open he crouched down, shoved his hand under the seat and groped the gritty carpet. Tense and nervous he reached further back, then relaxed as his fingers found plastic. He dragged the carrier bag out, tucked it inside his jacket, clicked the door shut and flung away the bent wiper blade.

Spargo dropped into his bed at around three that night. Though he fell asleep immediately he didn't sleep well. He'd stayed online, studying the web pages Jez had emailed, reading lists of U-boats and their commanders. Found Volk but did not find Volker. He fared no better when he brought up the tables of U-boats. None had been allocated the number U-1500. He should have known better than to doubt his daughter.

Woken by his alarm he swung out of bed and confronted himself in the mirror. Some people managed without sleep for days but he wasn't one of them, he needed his seven or eight hours. Downstairs, snatching breakfast, he phoned Benares. The man answered immediately and addressed Spargo by name. Caller ID was nothing new. But to Spargo it was as if Benares had sneaked up on him from behind, yet again.

'It is a pleasure to hear from you,' Benares continued. 'I have good news. I am pleased to tell you the finances are in place for the first phase of our work. A contract for your services was despatched to you by express courier. Included with the contract is all the documentation you will need to make an initial appraisal of the project. Are you able to start immediately, Mister Spargo?'

'What is the contract, exactly?'

'I do not know. That is Mister Bar's business. You must assume your questions will be answered by the contents of the package. If you have problems then please telephone me.'

The package arrived within the hour. Spargo tore off its wrappings to expose tight-folded maps and a stack of reports. The contract documents were inside a yellow envelope, written in English and signed by Bar in the presence of a Madrid attorney. So much for Jez's suspicions. Bar and BarConSa were real.

Spargo carried the bundle upstairs and dumped it on his desk. He took the first file and read the label on the cover.

The name of the mine wasn't Kilcreg.

The first page in the file showed a map of part of Canada's Northwest Territories. A red circle had been drawn around a place near the map's centre. Spargo attempted to pronounce its name, Cocwaiqui. Sure BarConSa had sent the wrong documents he looked at the contract again.

How had he got it so wrong? A consortium led by BarConSA was considering the purchase of a Canadian copper mine. He, Spargo, was to provide an independent review of the proposed deal. It was small beer; reading the documents and appraising the maps would take two or three days. Drafting and finalising a response would take another three. In front of him was no more than a week's work.

What shocked him even more was the payment. He was to be paid in US dollars, half up-front and half on completion. The first cheque was there, pinned to the last page of the contract, signed by a name that mean nothing to him and drawn on a Los Angeles bank. He stared at the figures in the box. Then he read the words to make sure the decimal point was in the right place. It was a ridiculously large sum for such a small amount of work.

Over the weekend Spargo spent time on the documents, familiarising himself with the Canadian mine's underground workings. Slowly he digested data, extracted production figures and forecasts, entered them into his computer and pondered over the output. For the first time in weeks his mother's murder was forgotten.

Jez phoned on Monday. It was the first break he'd had from the mine work and he was grateful for it.

'I've managed to speak to the girl who shares Marie's room,' she said. 'Apparently Marie is away.'

'And the journals?'

'She has taken them with her. She flew out to Spain last week, to some conference or other. What are you doing right now?'

'Working.'

'I've got something to show you.'

'Now?'

'Now. I think it's important.'

This time Jez came to him. He heard the buzz of her bike as she rode right up to his door. He greeted her with a 'Hi!' and she responded by brushing silently past him into the hall. She started to strip off her bike leathers, speaking as she tugged off her boots.

'On Saturday I took some of Lewis's CDs into work to show Brenda,' she said. 'One of her music student is assembling a music collection and she asked if she could borrow some of them. Because I couldn't carry the boxes I selected a few for her. Here, look at this.'

From somewhere in the mass of leather that collapsed on the floor she took a CD boxed set and held it out to him. Waggled her hand until he took it.

'Wagner's Valkyrie,' he said. 'What's wrong with it?'

'It was still sealed in its plastic, remember? It had a James Thin price label still on the plastic film.'

He took the box from her. It was a three-disc set in a plastic case that opened front and back. He opened it and held it like a book.

'Lift the inside flap. The third Valkyrie disk isn't there.'

Tough, Spargo thought. They could hardly complain about a missing disc when they hadn't even bought it. He turned the internal flap. There were three disks.

'I thought you said one is missing? It isn't missing. Someone's put it in back to front.'

'Take it out.'

He unclipped the disk and flipped it around. It had no label. Both sides were silver.

'It's not a music CD,' Jez said. 'It's a data disk. It contains a word processor file with one hundred and twenty-two pages of text. Lewis didn't have any trouble translating the journals. He translated them all. They are on the disk.'

Spargo said nothing. With the disk still in his hand he took the stairs two at a time. He returned with his laptop, placed it on the table, booted it up and slipped the CD into the drive. Nothing happened.

Jez reached out and pressed the eject tab on the side of the laptop.

'You've put the disk in upside down.'

She flipped it over. The drive whirred into life. A menu appeared on the screen.

'How much of this have you read?'

'Nothing in detail. I flipped through the summaries Lewis added to each page. At the bottom of the page, see? The journals cover Volker's entire naval career from the day he enlisted. I can see why someone with an academic interest in that period of history might find it interesting. Other than that, I'm inclined to agree with Lewis that the journals are probably worthless.'

Spargo sighed. Until that moment he'd been sure the journals held the key to both murders.

Jez watched him while he paged through the document, pausing every so often to read text.

'You don't look disappointed,' she said.

He smiled. 'I suppose I'm not. It's a bit like closure. It sort-of finishes things.'

'Volker was real enough, he was definitely the writer and he was definitely in the German navy. There were a few things in it I found particularly interesting. You once told me your father went to Germany before the war. Can you remember when?'

'Not personally. I wasn't born.'

'Be serious.'

'A German mining engineer visited Kilcreg in the mid-thirties. My father went to Germany shortly afterwards.'

'Was that possible? The war started in thirty-nine.'

'Your Gran told me foreigners travelled freely, right up to the last few months before war was declared. My father wasn't in Germany for long. He was a member of a mining institute that arranged exchanges.'

Spargo studied Jez. She was holding something back.

'What else? What is it?'

'Guess what Theodor Volker did before he joined the Kriegsmarine.'

'Surprise me.'

'He was a mining engineer.'

'Mining was a reserved occupation. Volker wouldn't have been called up.'

'He wasn't. He volunteered.'

Spargo went quiet. None of this explained the journals. They were written during the war, not before it.

'When does the journal end?

'The last one is dated February 1945. That is three months before Germany surrendered.'

'So what was Volker doing for those last three months?'

'Your guess is as good as mine. The last entry is incomplete but it's obvious he is commanding a submarine. He doesn't say where he is.'

'He wouldn't, would he? You didn't write stuff like that.'

'He did, sometimes. Sometimes he mentions places.'

'There's something I learned from Rydel, I almost got him to admit it. I'm fairly sure he and Lewis were here as prisoners of war. My guess is the U-boat and its crew, including Volker, were captured and interned. After the war some prisoners settled in Britain, which explains how Lewis and Rydel knew my mother. When I was a boy there were two young men living in the mine house.'

'At least that might explain how the journals got here.'

'Does it? If they were prisoners of war they wouldn't have been allowed to keep stuff like that. Anyway, can you imagine them carrying something that heavy?' He nodded at the laptop. 'What else have you found?'

'A lot. When I started reading I expected a war story. Instead I got emotions. It is not pleasant reading. Two months after Volker joined the navy he heard his wife was pregnant. She moved to Hamburg to be closer to him. After the child was born she was killed in a bombing raid.'

'And her child?'

Jez shook her head.

'There is a gap in the journals when he wrote nothing for weeks. After that it's all remorse and guilt. He blames himself for what happened, saying that if he hadn't joined up she wouldn't have been in Hamburg and would have still been alive.' She glanced up at Spargo. 'I'm hungry. Have you eaten?'

'There are pizzas in the freezer.'

'When are you going to start eating real food?'

'You choose something. The freezer's full of ready-cooks.'

She slid off the stool. Ignoring the freezer she went to the fridge and started to sort through it. She lifted the lid of the waste bin and dropped things in one by one. Use-by dates exceeded, Spargo told himself. It had become a ritual. Whenever she went to his fridge she threw away half of its contents.

'There's a lasagne there somewhere.'

'In the bin.'

While she continued her assault on his fridge he ran a finger over the touchpad and inspected the contents of the CD.

'There's a folder here called 3-Valk, he said. Third Valkyre disc, do you think?'

'It's the folder you are looking at. It contains the translation. The fact Lewis gave it that name means he knew where he was going to hide the CD.'

'Why hide it?'

'When you consider what happened to him I would have thought it was obvious. He knew someone would be after him.'

'For the translation? Why think that?'

'Your guess is as good as mine. I don't have all the answers.'

'Lewis was always scared,' Spargo said. 'According to Rydel.'

'Did I tell you what Marie said when I told her Lewis had soaked the journals? She implied he soaked them to make them unreadable.'

More food packs clattered into the bin. 'What else haven't you told me?' She put a pack of something into the microwave and pressed buttons.

'If he didn't want anyone to know what Volker had written,' Spargo said, 'then making the ink run makes sense. He could hardly destroy them, not if he had to return them to the police. 'What I don't understand is why he typed it up, when all he needed to do was to read it to himself.'

'He was a professional translator. It's how he worked.'

'I don't buy it.'

'So what's your explanation?'

'I don't have one.'

'Well I do. He translated it and hid it in case anything happened to him. He wanted it found. He knew what the journals were.'

'You said there is nothing important in them.'

'Perhaps I'm wrong. Perhaps there's something I've missed, something Lewis thought important that I didn't. What you said about Wagner and anti-Semitism might be more relevant than you realised. If anything happened to Lewis, then somebody going through his things – Rydel, presumably – would see the Wagner as a cuckoo in the nest. It is out of place.'

'Except he didn't.'

'Nor did we. It's too subtle by half.'

'No it's not. It worked. We found it.'

'We didn't. We missed it. If it hadn't been for that student…'

The microwave pinged. Jez opened the door, held the pack with an oven glove and scooped its contents onto plates. Then she placed the laptop where they could both see it.

'There,' she said, pointing at the screen with her fork. 'That's as far as I read in detail. A few pages further back there is a change in his writing style.' She tapped keys with her free hand. 'Look, here, after his wife dies he starts mentioning names and places. It's almost as if he no longer cares what he writes. Here, Friedrichstrasse, a street in Berlin, the first time he mentions a location.' She paged down. Using here fork again she jabbed at the words. 'Lewis's summary says the boy is safe and living with relatives in Ingolstadt. I looked the place up, it's near Munich. Volker is trying to get there by train.'

'What date?'

'September, nineteen forty-four.'

'How old is the child?'

'Not sure. I'm guessing two years, perhaps three.' She pushed her plate to one side, stood up, and went to the hall for her bike leathers. 'I have to go. I've got geology second years in an hour. Keep reading. See if you can find anything I've missed.'

She pulled on her suit and sealed herself inside it with its full-length zip. The suit had padded shoulders and elbows that made her arms look like Popeye's.

Spargo watched. Then without a word, he leaped past her, jumped at the stairs and raced up them. 'Hang on a sec, don't go. I've something to show you.'

He came down the stairs with Bar's contract file and held it out. Jez had picked up her helmet. Put it down again and took the file from him.

'Bar's contract,' Spargo said.

'But it's Canada!' she said. 'Is this the mine? How the hell do you pronounce it? It looks native Canadian.'

'Obviously a change of plan.'

'Obviously you got it all wrong.'

He grunted. Took the file back.

'At least you've got real work out of them at last,' she said. She looked at him narrow-eyed. 'It is real work? Yes? No?'

'It's real. Upstairs there's a pile of reports this big.' He held one hand high – an exaggeration. 'And a cheque this big.' He did the size thing again.

'It's about time they came up with something, you've waited long enough. So what happened to the bronze box? I've been meaning to ask. Did you take it to Marie with the journals?'

'Do you know how heavy it is?'

'Is that a no?' She looked at the wall clock. 'I've a few minutes. Can I see it?'

'It's in the basement.'

She shoved him out of the door and followed him to the back of the house. The police had slid the bronze box under the workbench and he tried, unsuccessfully, to drag it out with his foot. He bent down, grasped the top edge and tugged it to the middle of the floor. Jez pointed to a slab of metal, propped against the wall.

'Is that the lid?'

Spargo went for it and put it on his workbench. Jez crouched beside the box. He was sure he saw her put something in her pocket.

'What's that?'

'Nothing. Just wiping my hands.' She was picking at a small patch of black adhering to the bronze. 'What's this stuff?'

'Not sure. Mitchell's people thought it was rubber.'

'This box weighs a ton. A prisoner of war couldn't have carried this thing around even if he was allowed to. It's ridiculously heavy.'

Spargo shoved it back under the bench. Ridiculously heavy just about summed it up.

'What do you think it was really made for?'

'Not for books, that's for sure. Why bronze?'

'Bronze doesn't corrode in sea water.'

She gave him a tell-me-something-new look.

'Why use a box like this for a few personal diaries? Why were they so important to Volker? We've missed something, Dad.'

When Jez had gone Spargo made himself comfortable in a soft chair, putting his feet on a low table with his laptop on his lap. Three hours later he was still there, still reading. It was gut-wrenching stuff, page after page of Volker lamenting the death of his family. Then a note from Lewis, a comment at the foot of the page: *the child is not dead.*

After the second year lecture Jez was free again. Free to set up next week's lectures and the Easter trip to Arran; free to chase up her postgrads and check on their progress; free to assess the results of the First Year Civil Engineers' attempts at mineral identification, where anything black was coal and anything white was chalk. Free to work in the mineralogical lab.

She chose the latter. She had less than a thimble-full of dirt from the bronze box. Had she been taking a proper forensic sample she would have scooped it into a sterile container rather than the creased manila envelope still containing her bank statement. The sample had dried out, which would have been inexcusable for official material. But this was not a forensic examination.

She transferred the dirt she had scraped from the bottom of the box to a Petri dish, placed it under a binocular microscope and focused on a mix of sand and clay. Some of the grains had formed clumps she broke up with a glass rod. The sand was mainly quartz, but it was not beach sand. The grains were angular rather than rounded. They hadn't been ground down by the waves.

And there was something else, another mineral. She adjusted the microscope and zoomed in on one of the grains.

Spargo was still reading when the phone rang. He had his feet up like before and the laptop, appropriately, on his lap. It was Jez, calling from work.

'What?' he asked.

'What are you doing?'

'Right now? Talking to you.' She was in no mood for his humour and he got no response to it.

'When were in the basement I took a sample from the dirt in the bottom of the box.'

'I wondered what you were up to.'

'I wondered what it could be. There's not much of it to work on, about half a teaspoonful. It's about fifty-fifty clay and sand.'

'So, not much help.'

'I wouldn't say that. You should see it for yourself.'

'See clay and sand?'

'You know you sometimes say you've never seen where I work?'

'I haven't. You keep saying you'll show me around.'

'Well now's your chance. Get in your car, Dad. Call my mobile when you arrive and I'll come out.'

Both sides of Edinburgh's West Mains Road were lined with parked cars. By the time Spargo had found a space, phoned Jez and walked back to King's Buildings, she was waiting for him at the kerb. He expected her to take him to the geology block. Instead she took him between the main buildings and into what looked like a builders' yard.

'Portacabins?' he asked.

'Our new lab units. I do my forensic stuff out here, it's the only way I can keep samples secure.'

She used a keypad on the door jam, stepped into a small lobby and handed her father a white Tyvek oversuit. Suited up, they pulled on thin overshoes and entered a compact, neat lab. It reminded Spargo of one of the geology labs at his old university, only smaller and much newer. A lot of electronics Spargo didn't recognise.

'Spectrometer,' he said with a nod at a grey box.

'Photometer,' she corrected. 'Leave it. Look at this.'

On a sheet of black paper on a bench Jez had sprinkled fine sand.

'Is that what you took from the box?'

'Part of it. It was mixed with clay. I've washed it and dried it. Switch off the lights.'

He did what she said. The white lights went out. A lamp he'd not noticed before stayed on, bathing the workbench in deep blue light. The sand on the paper glowed. It was as if the light came from inside each grain.

'What are the ones that glow yellow, fluorite?'

'No, it's too hard for fluorite. Also, fluorite tends to glow white under ultraviolet light.' She reached out, switched on another blue light and switched off the first. 'The lamp was long wave UV. This one is short wave – UV-C – so don't look at the lamp. By rights we should be wearing goggles. Trouble is, they obscure the mineral's colours.'

The grains changed from bright yellow to bright blue.

'Scheelite,' she said. 'Could be apatite, but the blue isn't quite right.'

Spargo nodded. He wasn't that interested, just wished she'd get to the point. If she was trying to impress him then she was succeeding.

'Scheelite, Dad!' she repeated. 'Scheelite! They mined scheelite at Kilcreg, it was the tungsten ore.'

Spargo nodded. 'Sorry. Wasn't thinking straight. No surprise it's scheelite, is it? Not if it was at Kilcreg.'

'You don't get it, do you? If there is scheelite in the box it's likely it was opened at Kilcreg. Somebody opened it and then resealed it.'

'So the box was once in the mine?'

'Not necessarily. The scheelite could have come from a waste tip. Or perhaps the processing plant.'

'There were no waste tips. Back then the waste went into the sea. There was no processing plant either, the ore was crushed underground and shipped out for processing.'

'The important thing is that someone at the mine opened it, Dad. Someone knew what was in it.'

'Or they wanted to check what was in it.'

She switched off the ultraviolet and put the room lights on. Outside, the keypad clicked. The inner door opened just enough for a middle-aged man to get his head through.

'Sorry Jez. Didn't know you had company.'

'My father,' she said. 'Come to see how I earn my daily bread. How was Aberdeen?'

The man nodded, acknowledging Spargo. 'Cold and windy. My father's fine,' he said. Then to Spargo: 'Broke his hip. Took me three hours to drive there.'

'Wouldn't it have been quicker to fly?'

'If there was a direct flight from Edinburgh I'd take it.'

He excused himself and closed the door. Jez waited until she heard the outer door close before she spoke.

'You told me the other day Murphy flew from Edinburgh to Aberdeen.'

Spargo nodded. 'By a late flight. He was going from there to Oslo.'

'You heard what Andy just said. There are no flights from Edinburgh to Aberdeen.'

'He must be wrong.'

'Have you ever done it?'

'I've never needed to, I've always driven. Perhaps I misheard Murph. He might have said he was driving, going on to Aberdeen.'

'Don't make excuses for him, Dad! I remember exactly what you said. You told me he had three hours to kill before his flight. He wouldn't have had three spare hours if he had been driving.'

'It doesn't make a lot of sense.'

'It does if Murphy lied to you.'

'He wouldn't do that. You don't know him. You've never liked him.'

'Whether I like him or not is irrelevant. If he said he was flying from Edinburgh to Aberdeen then he lied. Murphy lied to you, Dad!'

CHAPTER THIRTY-FIVE

THE FIRST TIME THEO VISITED Artur's farm he was courting Erika. He visited at the invitation of Artur who wished to inspect the young man, the young mining graduate who would soon be his son-in-law. Theo stayed for three nights, not in the same house as his beloved Erika but at a neighbouring farm. To Theo, brought up amongst mines and miners, the land around Ingolstadt was isolated, backward, even. Now, passing through what was once Poland, he had those feelings again. Advancements of all kinds seemed to have passed this place by.

With Walter driving the truck keeps up a good speed, he seems to have the knack of driving on ice. The few people they see on the road are heavily laden. Some have handcarts and a few, the lucky ones, have horses, half-starved like their owners. Most are women, elderly men and children. Later they encounter soldiers on foot, straggling lines of fellow countrymen heading west. Occasionally there are vehicles, all of them military.

'Russian Front,' Walter grunts. 'Refugees from the bastard communists. That we are losing this war does not surprise me. Look at them, Theodor, Germany's dregs! A defeated army!'

Theo stays quiet. Walter seems to have missed the fact most of the troops are bandaged and many have missing limbs, their progress aided by makeshift crutches; others are carried on stretchers by struggling, limping men. Walter's remark is ill-founded and offensive. Walter's war, Theo guesses, has been fought from a desk.

'Tell me,' Theo asks, 'why we are heading east when the rest of the world is moving west?'

Walter pulls the truck off the road and takes maps from his

briefcase. When he has found the right one he spreads it over the steering wheel and traces with his finger the route they are taking.

'They have come from here, the north east,' he says, tapping the sheet. 'Soon we will take this road, the southerly one. With luck we will soon be free from this rabble.'

Theo's knowledge of the seas is superb; his knowledge of the land – particularly land so far from home, is poor.

'Is that where we are going, Krakov?'

'God no! I am told Krakov is overrun by the Soviets. We turn south, I told you – look – this road here.' For Theo's benefit he draws a pencil line and, for emphasis, thickens it with several strokes. 'The Soviets will not trouble us,' he says. 'They will make straight for Berlin.'

He folds the map and half-stands, twists himself round, and gestures Theo to slide over. Changing drivers without alighting into deep snow is a tight squeeze.

'I am tired,' he murmurs. 'I shall sleep. Tonight we will not stop, I will drive through the night.'

The road that leads south takes them away from the refugees, the soldiers and the traffic. By nightfall they are the only thing on the road and driving is easy – the sky has cleared to reveal a bright, helpful moon. Walter stirs from sleep and takes over. Remains behind the wheel until Theo and Peter wake at dawn.

Without retreating troops and refugees the world is silent and bleak, the villages they pass through seem lifeless. Theo tries to imagine the landscape in summer – in peacetime – its soils tilled by folk like Artur and Barbara. The world now is so far from this peace. Such imaginings do not come easily.

By afternoon Theo dozes, his boy in his arms. He is jerked awake by Walter hitting the brakes. The truck's many wheels have a mind of their own and the truck keeps moving, slides on ice, comes to an uneasy stop against a wall of deep snow. Theo's stomach tightens and takes time to settle.

Disregarding Theo, Walter starts rummaging. 'Where the hell are we, Theodor? Give me the damned map!'

Theo finds it, unfolds it and hands it to Walter who studies it and does his finger tap thing.

'Here, this is Tichau. While you were sleeping we passed through it. If I am right then there should be a railway track to our left.'

He looks left and tries to see out. The window is iced over with frozen condensation from their breath, they can neither see through it, nor will it open. The door, too, is iced shut; the outside of the truck looks as if it has been sprayed with molten glass. Once they are moving again Walter takes his eyes off the road and looks down at Peter, down by the pipes again, bundled up tight.

'How is he?'

'I gave him one of your pills. He should sleep for some time.'

Not a whole pill. One quarter was clearly enough because the boy sleeps heavily, his breathing is noisy. He doesn't move. Doesn't twitch in his dreams like he did before.

'We have to move him,' Walter says. 'If we are where I think we are then in a few more kilometres there is a checkpoint manned by regular soldiers. They will stop us. They will look in the back but they will not search, they dare not touch SS property. The boy will be safe there.'

'But the cold! He will freeze to death!'

'I doubt that. Would you rather we left him here to be found by the army?'

They stop again, refuel the truck and move Peter. The snow at the roadside is thigh-deep but with Walter's help Peter is soon safe in the den with the quilt wrapped around him. Now Theo drives. The road is straight, long and narrow and there is more traffic, not the remnants of a retreating army this time but regimented convoys with military escorts.

'Telegraph poles to our left,' Walter says. 'It's the railway. Watch out for a bridge. Then two kilometres beyond it, go over the crossroads. I am sure we will be stopped. If so, keep your mouth shut. I will talk.'

Again Theo ponders the wilderness that surrounds him. That the Reich should bother with such places makes no sense. He supposes it was the same with the British and other Europeans when they colonised the world, when they pushed into America, Australia, India and Africa. And later, when the pioneers in North America went west through the lands of the red man to further their own ends. Now his own countrymen are doing it. But so what? Such matters have never concerned him.

Walter shouts: 'Concentrate Theodor! Checkpoint…! Slow down to walking pace. Take care not to skid. The last thing we need is for you to run down the guards.'

Theo slows, stops, and follows the routine. Present papers to the guard. A quick nod when the man salutes. Then look away as if there is something more interesting to see. The guard is a tall man with his rifle slung against his back. Pointless having it there, Theo thinks. Pistols, he decides, are much more sensible for duty like this, it takes too long to unsling a rifle. When – if ever – he returns to his boat, he will have his deck guards armed with pistols, not rifles.

That his mind is wandering doesn't surprise him. Never has his life been at stake in a way that is out of his hands – a way that endangers not only himself but a child of his own. This strange little boy who, against all odds, seems to trust him.

Walter is shouting. He does it so well. It is as if all around him are deaf.

'I want the Buna plant, soldier! Here is my authorisation, take it and read it. Hurry! I do not have all day!'

The man takes the paper. For the first time he notices Walter's high rank and it surprises him so much he forgets to salute. He gives the paper no more than a glance and hands it back.

The land surrounding them is no longer rural. It is as if a giant hand has swept away trees, hedges, farms and houses. It has been militarised, there are troops everywhere. In the distance, beyond the few remaining trees, is what appears to be part construction site and part factory complex, an immense enterprise of buildings, processing plants and oil tanks. To one side of it are vast railway marshalling yards with rows of wagons and tankers. Everything is under snow and looks oddly unused.

'Monowitz,' Walter says proudly. 'Look at it Theodor, it is like an American city!'

'A city of factories, so far from Germany.'

'But in Greater Germany, Theodor!'

'You sound like Göbbels. When we lose U-boats he tells us we are winning the war of the Atlantic. When our cities are bombed to destruction he tells us the enemy has failed yet again.'

Walter shrugs. 'Do you expect our leaders to tell the truth? Do you want them to demoralise our citizens?'

Theo stays silent. Walter doesn't know his own mind. One minute he spouts propagandist rhetoric and the next he declares the Reich is done for.

They drive on. This place is indeed a city – a city of factories set out on a grid. Theo wonders where the workers live; he has seen no houses, no accommodation blocks. Walter is examining a small, hand drawn map that he orients in the direction they are driving. He starts giving directions, left here, right there, follow the perimeter to new factory buildings…

'There!' he says. 'The grey building. Drive to the double doors and wait. I will go to find Heiss.' He consults his paper again. 'Doctor Thomas Heiss.'

He opens the door to get down and then hesitates.

'No, as my aide it is better that you should go. Find Dr Heiss, he should be here somewhere. Tell him Oberführer Wolff has arrived.'

Theo clambers down and walks through the snow to the closed steel doors. The place is the size of a hangar and banging them with his fist makes an echoing boom inside but has no other effect. Nobody comes. Then Walter is beside him, briefcase in hand. Along the road men are clearing snow, watched over by two armed soldiers. All look malnourished, the workers particularly so. To Theo they look even more starved than the prisoners that work in the dockyards.

Walter disappears down the side of the building. A few minutes later one of the double doors slides back and he is standing there with Heiss – a short bald man wearing a long white coat and small, rimless glasses. Clearly he feels the cold. He is attempting to lift the collar of the white coat but it won't stay up.

Walter turns to Theo.

'Get the truck, Kapitänleutnant, turn it and reverse it. Bring it inside so we can close these damn doors and keep out the cold.'

Theo takes time to find the right gear. Reversing isn't easy, the truck is huge and the mirrors and windows are still iced. He tries several times while Walter looks on, laughing and shouting instructions. Heiss looks on with disinterest.

The building Theo reverses into is an unfinished construction shop. Along one wall is heavy machinery, waiting to be installed.

'You come at a bad time,' Heiss says. 'I was expecting you days ago. Now there are bombing raids from the west at the east, the Americans and the Soviets. Life is so difficult.'

Theo and Walter ignore the man and he wanders off, first closing the double doors and then, walking purposefully, heading towards the far end of the building. Theo drops the truck's tailgate and, with Walter helping, both men grapple with the packing cases, lowering them one by one to the concrete floor.

Theo checks Peter. The boy is still sleeping. Soon they will have to move the crates that surround him. To make things worse, Heiss is returning, waving his arms. Complaining that officers of the Reich should not be labouring.

'Oberführer,' he says, 'we have workers to do these things! You must wait, I shall handle it, I shall fetch workers.'

He is already at the doors. Before Walter can stop him he has run outside and is shouting to the soldiers, beckoning with a waving arm.

'Damn fool,' Walter mumbles. 'The last thing we need is their help but I can't refuse, it will not look good. Leave things to me. We will move the crates to the back of the truck. The workers can lift them down.'

'What about Peter? What happens when we move the last crates?'

'I'll think of something.'

Heiss returns at the head of a column of men. 'Prisoners, Oberführer!'

He calls it out proudly, as if he'd captured them himself. The column includes the soldiers who, once inside the building, separate themselves from the others and stand aside.

'We make them work for their food and their beds,' Heiss says. 'It is good for their souls. We have ten thousand here, Herr Oberführer! Ten thousand workers!'

'All prisoners of war?' Theo asks. 'French, Polish, British? Americans, perhaps?'

Two of the men are wearing items of clothing resembling British battledress. Others have a mix of ill-fitting clothes, odd boots and fingerless gloves.

'All enemies of our Reich, Kapitänleutnant. Unfortunately we do not have enough men like these, less than two hundred. Now, leave this work to them. Guards, come! I want three men in the truck. The rest of you, move these crates and stack them neatly against the wall.'

Frantically Theo turns to speak to Walter, but he is not there. He glances this way and that but it is already too late. Three prisoners are at the rear of the truck, one of them climbing the tailgate.

So this is it, Theo thinks. This is the moment of truth…

CHAPTER THIRTY-SIX

TWO DAYS AFTER SPARGO'S VISIT to Jez's lab he had a phone call from Mitchell. The detective sounded different, less friendly and more like Quinn. Wasting no time on pleasantries he came straight to the point.

'Spargo, I'm guessing you know Kilcreg as well as anyone. Is there any way to reach your mother's place without being seen? From up on the moor, I mean. If someone came down the hillside behind you mother's place, how would get up there, is there a road?'

Spargo noted the use of his surname. He was sure that until then Mitchell had always called him Mister.

'They would have been seen coming down the hillside,' he said. 'It's a ten minute scramble down a steep grassy slope. You've seen what it's like. There is no cover. You would risk being seen from the road.'

'Really? Who by? It's not exactly the Edinburgh bypass. From what I've seen of the place I doubt if more than four cars a day use the road.'

'There are more than that.'

'In summer, maybe… and I'm betting most of those are lost holidaymakers. So what is up there? On the moor, I mean. Is there any access?'

'There's the track up the hill behind the plant yard. It's overgrown.'

'I know that, you pointed it out. No point anyone parking near the plant yard, going up that track, walking a couple of miles and then walking back down the hill further along.'

'You asked.'

'So what about other access? When I took you to Kilcreg we passed a signpost at a junction, way back along the road. Where does it go?'

'Same place. The high moor. It's always been called a drovers' road but it actually leads to the old mine buildings and then to the sea cliffs. The first mine entrance was in the cliffs. Later they sunk a shaft –'

'You told me.'

'The mine used the drovers' road was used to move ore. In wartime, when the mine increased production, the ore lorries got stuck in boggy ground. That's when they cut a new track down to the plant yard. If you are thinking of Letchie, forget it. It is definitely not classic Porsche country.'

'That's no problem. We went through his financial papers. He rents a lock-up in Inverness and we opened it up. Found a Range Rover, six months old and in showroom condition.'

'He's washed it.'

'No doubt.'

'Forensics have it?'

'Not yet. They have his Porsche. When they return it to us they will take the Range Rover. I shouldn't say this, Spargo, but I'm convinced Letchie killed your mother. We have no evidence anyone else was involved.'

'Someone else has to be involved. Otherwise who murdered Letchie?'

'I mean nobody else was involved in your mother's murder.'

Spargo went quiet. He had already reached that conclusion. 'Someone wanted Letchie dead,' he said.

Bloody obvious, really. He regretted saying it.

'That's DI Quinn's business.'

'And Lewis?'

'Also DI Quinn's business. If he wants my assistance he will ask for it and I will give it to him.'

'I've got Lewis's translation. Whatever he might have told you, he actually finished it.'

Mitchell took a while to respond. When he did, his voice had changed. It was sharp. It showed clear, renewed interest.

'He did? What, all of it? He lied to me?'

'He concealed it in his music collection.'

'And you found it? How? What do you mean by music collection?'

'CDs. Compact Disks. I went to his house. He lived with his cousin, a man called Rydel. They were both Polish. Both prisoners of war here in Scotland.'

'I thought the Poles fought with the Allies?'

'Long story.' Not one he wanted to repeat to Mitchell.

'Does DI Quinn know you went to Lewis's place?'

'No.'

'You really do push your luck, Spargo. Alright, leave things to me. I will speak to Murdoch.'

'Murdoch?'

'DI Quinn.'

'Are you going to tell him I went there?'

'If I think it necessary.'

'The translation,' Spargo said. 'Lewis had hidden it in a boxed set of Wagner CDs. His main collection had composers like Chopin and Debussy.'

'A storm in a sea of calm.'

'Couldn't have put it better myself.'

'Have you read it? The translation, I mean.'

'I've been working through it. The journals were definitely written in wartime. Volker started them when he joined the German navy. He did U-boat service. Looks as if he was involved in some way with transporting looted paintings. He doesn't say it exactly, but in nineteen-forty-four he's in Berlin, then in a place called Carinhall. He met Göring there.'

'Göring was the air force one, right?'

'He was head of the Luftwaffe and Hitler's deputy. He hoarded looted works of art. He had – '

'I know that, I've heard all that.'

'Volker describes the bronze box, right down to the screws in the lid. My daughter analysed dirt she found in the bottom of the box. It has traces of scheelite, the mineral they mined at Kilcreg. To me, it means the box was opened in the mine. The screws in the lid were supposed to be bronze, not steel. It's my guess my father – or whoever opened it – lost the originals and had to use steel ones. It's why they corroded.'

'Are you saying your father knew what was in the box?'

'I'm beginning to think it.'

'And Volker was on a U-boat?'

Mitchell went quiet. Spargo started to answer, but Mitchell interrupted.

'Could this be the wreck that's been in the papers? You know it? You've read about it?'

'I bumped into an American diver who was working on it.'

'Robert Kalman, yes. We know all about him.'

Spargo swallowed. Wondered what was coming next. 'I met him only briefly,' he said.

'Strange, that. He told me you and he were good friends.'

Spargo swallowed again. 'Not true.'

'Spargo, listen to me. Am I getting this right? Are you seriously suggesting the U-boat wreck was searched in the hope of finding looted paintings?'

'It hangs together.'

'Not in my book it doesn't. Not going to be much good, are they? How long is it, sixty years? Paintings, sixty years in salt water?'

'I'm simply telling you what I know. Volker writes that he is transporting crates in a truck. Later they are loaded on to a U-boat, though by then they are sealed in bronze boxes. I'm guessing the one I found was made to carry something else, perhaps a small art treasure. Anyway, Kalman assured me he didn't find any bronze boxes.'

'Would they have survived?'

'Probably. I'm not saying they would have stayed watertight, not for that long, not at great depth. But something would remain of them. Kalman is an experienced diver, he would have found them. He would have said.'

'Oh, would he? Not according to Customs and Excise.'

Spargo went cold. 'What do you mean?'

'My friendly Customs man tells me they have been keeping an eye on Kalman from the start. His boat has been in Inverness for a while and the day he was due to leave they boarded it and searched it. They found a pewter dinner service. Also a mug with Volker's name on it.'

'Pewter? Really?' Spargo could hardly get the words out. It sounded so shaky he wished he hadn't tried.

'We've had the San Francisco police looking into the firm he works for, an outfit called Posidonian. It seems to be above-board. We've also had the Los Angeles police checking the people who put up the exploration money, it's a trust that funds world-wide exploration of historical sites. Customs now has Kalman's underwater videos, I have seen them. They show the inside of the sub from stem to stern – not somewhere I would like to go, Spargo. If there were any crates stored on board then I didn't see them. Look, Spargo, I have to go. Send me a copy of Lewis's translation.'

Spargo, tense, breathed out. Tried to sound confident.

'No problem, I'll do it now. About Letchie's Range Rover. Call Scenes of Crime in Edinburgh. Tell them you've got a vehicle you want checking for traces of soil. Tell them it's urgent.'

'And why should I do that?'

'My daughter works with them occasionally. She's a geologist and she's good. I know you said Letchie's Range Rover has been washed, but if anybody can tell you if has been on the old drovers road across the moor, she can.'

Mitchell gave a noncommittal grunt.

'What have you done with the journals?'

'They're with a university lecturer. At the time I didn't realise Lewis had already translated them.'

'Is that wise? To let him have them, I mean.'

'It's a her, Marie Howard. Considering what I know now, no it wasn't wise. I've tried to get them back but she's away. Gone to Spain and taken them with her.'

'If I were you I'd be worried. Three people have been killed.'

'Then Spain is probably the best place for her.'

'I'm not just thinking of her, Spargo. You found the box. You've had the journals in your possession and now you have the translation. You want to know what puzzles me most about all this?'

'What?'

'What puzzles me most is why you are still alive.'

Spargo made coffee, took it to his office and phoned Jez. 'Just want to put your mind at rest,' he said. 'I've just spoken to Mitchell and told him everything. I'm about to email him the translation.'

'Has he got anywhere? With Gran?'

'Letchie had a Range Rover hidden away. I've suggested he contacts SOCO here and gets you involved. If the vehicle has been to Kilcreg, you will be able to find out by comparing soils.'

'I'd rather you didn't do things like that. They have their own procedures. If they want help they'll ask for it. I was about to phone you anyway,' she continued, 'about that dirt from the box. There is clay mixed with the scheelite. Andy worked on it yesterday evening, he used XRD.'

'XRD. X-ray diffraction.'

'So you haven't forgotten everything you learned at university.'

'I can't remember what it's used for though.'

'Think of it as a mineral DNA test. Andy also used the electron microscope on it. He found microscopic fibres he thinks are fine cloth or perhaps paper.'

'Probably from the journals. I'm not sure all this work you are doing is worth the trouble. The clay you found is probably from someone's boots.'

Spargo counted the seconds of silence. Knew he had blundered.

'That's the kind of remark I'd expect from you. You're like the rest of them here, you think forensic geology is only about analysing mud from boots.'

He didn't know much about the academic world. Years ago one of his mining lecturers warned him if he ever thought of becoming a lecturer he should first buy a stab-proof vest to protect his back from his colleagues. Jez had been involved with the forensic thing from the start and it was becoming successful. Others would be jealous.

'Jez, I'm sorry, I was out of order. What you are doing is great. So what is the clay?'

'It's a rare earth clay used in brewing as a filtration medium. It's called kieselguhr.'

Spargo's grip on the phone tightened. He knew about kieselguhr. Brewing wasn't its only use. In the days when the only alternative to gunpowder was nitro-glycerine – an explosive that went off if you simply shook it – Alfred Nobel discovered that if he mixed it with kieselguhr it became safe.

'It's also used in the manufacture of blasting gelatine,' he said. 'That's gelignite and dynamite. And the fibres… sticks of mining explosives are wrapped in waxed paper. Could the fibres be from wrappers?'

'Was there an explosives store at the mine?'

He thought about it. There must have been one but he couldn't remember where. The headframe at the top of the mineshaft had been on the high moor, tucked in a hollow. Beside the headframe stood the winding house, the generator and the ablutions block. The admin building, and the counting house where his mother worked, stood some way off, well away from the noise.

In his experience any explosives store would have been a good half-mile away from all of those buildings and he couldn't recall ever seeing one. In some mines, stocks of explosives were – and still are – kept in underground lockers close to where they are needed.

'There must have been one,' he said. 'Though I can't remember where.'

'Think about the things we know,' she said. 'The box was opened somewhere at the mine. From what we now know, it was probably kept for a while in an explosives store. Someone, most likely your father, screwed down the lid and hid the box in the roof of the mine house. What we do not know is why.'

'Hid it from who, Gran? She wouldn't have gone up there. She hated heights.'

'Hid it from you.'

'That's daft. Why me?'

'Think about it. You said your father kept stuff in a shed that would have been better stored in the attic.'

'Suitcases and old lampshades. Old clothes and toys. A damp shed was not the best place for them.'

'And did he ever take you to the shed?'

'Yes, often. Whenever he wanted to sort out stuff, or move stuff. What are you getting at?'

'You still don't see it, do you? Did you ever go to the shed on your own?'

'Many times. There was interesting stuff there. Why?'

'If all the junk had been in the attic, then instead of going to the damp shed in the plant yard you would have gone to the attic.'

'He was a strict man. He'd have forbidden it.'

'And you would have obeyed him? Pull the other one, Dad! By keeping the attic empty he made sure you would never go there. He had reasons for not letting you in the roof. Seems to me the box and its contents were the reason.'

'I don't see that. And why are you so sure the box was put there by him?'

'Are you seriously suggesting someone else put it there?'

Spargo thought about it. She was probably right.

'There is something else I've discovered,' she continued. 'I took a scraping of the black stuff on the box and sent it to a friend.'

'It's rubber.'

'Yes, that's obvious. I thought there was something odd about the way it had perished so I sent a bit away. My friend thinks it could be Buna rubber.'

'What's Buna rubber? What friend?'

'A rubber technologist at London Metropolitan University. If I can trace the source of the box it will make a good case study for one of my students. I can rarely use real cases so I need everything I can get. Did you mean what you said?'

'What?'

'What you said just now, that what I'm doing is great?'

Until now he hadn't paid much attention to her forensic geology work. In his business he didn't like the way some university lecturers undercut private consultants and used college equipment on the cheap. Maybe that should also apply to her. If she wanted to do it commercially, then she should set up a proper business.

'Do you think the work's there?' he asked.

'For what?'

'Your forensic geology stuff.'

'It's definitely there. It's more a case of convincing the police that geology can help them. In the States they really believe in it. The FBI has a forensic geology division.'

'Yes, I really do think what you're doing is great. I hear you are doing something for Quinn's friend?'

'Mud from boots.'

'Seriously?'

'Seriously. Though I'm not sure about them being friends. Tom Curtis is Quinn's boss.'

'You know Quinn's boss? Really?'

'I do. As I said, mud from boots. Someone broke into a house in Dalkeith and left mud on the carpet. Some was from the garden.'

'And you think that narrows it down a bit? What do you do next, take samples from every square mile of soil in Scotland? It could take you the rest of your life.'

'I said some was from the garden. There were also fragments of calcium carbonate.'

'Calcite? That's an oddity?' He knew all the common minerals. He was proud of his ability to distinguish the main ore of copper – chalcopyrite – from its Fool's Gold cousin, iron pyrite. Not many of his mining colleagues could do that.

'I didn't say calcite, I said calcium carbonate. It has the same mineral make-up as calcite but it it's not crystalline. Also, it's attached to grains of sand.'

'Could it be cement? Concrete?'

'That's what I thought. Some of the calcium carbonate has recrystallised in concentric rim around the grains, which means it is old. It could be lime mortar rather than modern cement.'

'You've lost me.'

'I check for oddities, Dad. Things that make a sample unique.'

'So why are the police so concerned with this particular burglary? What was taken?'

'Guns. A large collection. They go back to flintlocks but they're mainly Twentieth-Century military issue automatic pistols and revolvers. The man shouldn't have had them, they weren't licensed. A lot of other stuff was stolen too, mainly military bits and bobs. Tom says the theft would probably have gone unreported, but for a neighbour who noticed a window swinging in the wind and the police sent a car round.'

Spargo thought military. Thought Mongo. Thought Day.

'How much do you like Curtis?' he asked.

'What do you mean?'

'I mean professionally.'

'He's a great guy.'

'And he gives you work?'

'Odd bits.'

'And the burglary you told me about is one of his jobs?

'It's his case. Why?'

'Call him. He may be interested in an old builders' yard I know about. I'll send you the details. It might earn you a few Brownie points.'

Spargo's enthusiasm for the translation had waned. Though he had persevered and read to the end of it, he hadn't found a convincing reason why anyone would kill for the journals. Whoever was responsible had to be interested in larger boxes, boxes so big and heavy they couldn't possibly have been hidden in the mine house roof.

Whoever had searched his mother's cottage had the right idea. They took up the floorboards. Right hiding place, wrong house.

Spargo studied his watch. He imagined turning the hour hand on for three hours, to the time it would be when he reached Kilcreg if he left right now. And, if all went well, there would still be a couple of hours of daylight left to do what he was planning to do.

From his basement he collected tools: a crowbar, a saw and a hammer. He thought it unlikely he would actually have to take up any floorboards in the mine house because he couldn't imagine his father cutting big holes in the floor. There would be a hatch somewhere that gave access to underfloor pipes and cables. Who knows what might be hidden there? Such a hatch should be easy to find, it would probably be in a cupboard.

Spargo's Volvo came out of the bend above Kilcreg and started the long downhill run. He had done the trip so many times the car seemed to know its own way. The drive didn't take much effort. Staying awake was the problem but he'd mastered that too. No music to lull him. And when that didn't work, he opened all the car windows.

In the distance, beyond the houses, a blur of grey mist met the sea at a sharp, deep blue line. Spargo caught the feint smell of wood smoke, saw it rise form the house chimneys in pillars of grey. For a second or two he thought he saw smoke from his mother's cottage chimney but it came from behind it which meant Rosie was home, back from her daughter's. There was washing, too, drooping from her back garden carousel.

How old was Rosie, back in the early 'fifties, he wondered? The same age Jez is now? He remembered how he and his friends scrumped apples from her tree and how Rosie would chase them away. The tree was still there, wizened and unproductive. In late summer its unpruned branches bore apples no bigger than marbles.

The mine house was blocked from Spargo's view by small but steep outcrops of grey rock where, long ago, the road was cut down to lessen its steepness, to iron-out bumps. As Spargo came out from behind them he glanced to his left as he always did, down to the old plant yard and mine house.

What he saw shocked him. The smoke he smelled was not from the village, it was closer than that and it billowed in great clouds from beyond the old plant yard. At first he thought the mine house was burning. Then, as the smoke drifted, he saw the bonfire – a huge pyre of floorboards and roof beams. The flames were deep red and rose awesomely high. Even with his car windows closed he could hear the roar of the wind that fed them.

The view was new to him. For the first time in his life he could see the whole hillside, unobstructed now because the mine house, his childhood home, was no longer there. It had been razed to the ground, reduced to rubble.

Trucks and vans littered what had once been the mine house garden. What remained of the grass looked rougher than ever, chewed up by vehicles and deep-rutted by truck tyres. An excavator appeared through the smoke, its own blue exhaust blasting skywards. It stopped and manoeuvred, extending a long mantis arm that grabbed at timbers, splintering them and lifting them high. Carrying them to the fire, it heaved them on to the flames in a volcano of sparks.

Jez was relieved that she had talked with her father. He was at last seeing sense, dropping the Kilcreg thing and concentrating on his work. Also, she had done what he'd suggested – phoned Curtis and told him about the builder's yard under the arches. The tip-off had, as she'd feared, triggered a barrage of questions about the source of her knowledge.

On Curtis's insistence she had phoned her father to get answers. Instead she got an answering machine at home and voicemail on his mobile. She would have another go when she got home.

Like most apartments in the City, hers had two doorbells, one on the external, communal door, and one on the door to her flat. As she was lifting the house phone to call her father, the bell on the street door rang. She peered around the living room curtains to see who was there and saw a man's back and shoulders. Whoever it was stood too close to the door to be seen properly.

A car she recognised as an Alfa was parked across the road, half on the grass and half off it. Standing on the pavement beside it was a short, square-shouldered and overweight man who turned and looked towards her flat. It was Murphy.

With Murphy outside it could only be her father at the door. She didn't bother to use the door phone to speak to him, she just pressed the button that released the lock. At least her father had remembered how she felt about Murphy and he'd had the good sense to leave him outside. She opened the door to her flat, turning her back on it as she unzipped her leathers.

'Curtis wants you to call him,' she said. 'He was asking questions I can't answer. He wants to know how you – '

If her motorcycle leathers had not been around her ankles she might have made an attempt to defend herself. Though she didn't see who jumped her he was much lighter than Murphy. He used his whole body weight to bring her down.

Over the years Spargo had seen the mine house change gradually. Wood rotted, locks failed, windows and doors swung in the wind before finally breaking from their hinges and falling free. Chimney pots fell. Then, one day many years ago, the chimney itself toppled, its massive stones tearing like cannon-fire through the roof, the ceilings, and into the hall where it punched through the floor.

What little of the romantic remained inside Spargo had hoped the house would rot down to nothing, it would crumble to dust. He hadn't expected rape. Hadn't expected to see the house picked over by men in hard hats and bright yellow jackets.

Spargo parked in the road. Stuart Main's van was nearby, filled with row upon row of grey slates, all standing on end like long decks of cards. The man himself was returning to it, pushing a builders' barrow loaded with more slates.

Spargo put on a brave face. This was closure of some kind.

He yelled out. 'Stuart, Hi! 'They've finally done it. Finally pulled the place down.'

Brave words. Tears would have come more easily.

'Didn't expect to see you back here, Mr Spargo.'

'Flying visit.'

'They got anyone for it yet? There's a rumour the Letchie thing's connected. Wasn't that down your way?'

Spargo nodded. 'I hear the police spoke to you.'

'That Mitchell, yes. Questioned me for hours. I was fool enough to admit I'd threatened Letchie.'

Spargo nodded again as if he knew all the answers. Then he turned towards the action and waved an arm. 'Who decided to do this?'

'Another collapse, they say. Water tank fell through the roof. Probably kids. Lucky they weren't killed.'

Spargo rubbed the back of his neck. Kids? There hadn't been any children in Kilcreg for twenty years.

'Kids, yes. Probably.'

'Builder from up Thurso way doing the demolition,' Main continued. 'Hired me for the day to shift slates. The granite should fetch a good price but the timber's all wormed.'

'Have you been here all day? Have they found anything?'

'Found? What kind of thing?'

'You know what these old places are like,' Spargo said, still doing the neck-rub. 'Just wondered if my parents left anything interesting.

My mother moved house while I was working overseas. I wasn't here to help.'

Main smiled. 'There wouldn't be anything, not in there. The place was gutted, even the stairs and landing had gone. Sorry, Mr Spargo, I have to get on. I need to get another load out while there's still daylight.'

'Have they torn up the floor?'

Stuart Main frowned. Nodded towards the fire. 'Floor's there, burning, Mr Spargo. Along with the roof timbers. All rotten or wormed.'

Main apologised again and climbed into his van. Spargo turned his attention to what remained of the house. At least the builders-turned-demolishers had saved him the trouble of grovelling under floorboards. Clearly, there was nothing there. No big brothers to Volker's box.

A wasted journey then, a damn-fool idea. If the boxes had needed a crane to get them on to a U-boat – which was what Volker had written – then how could they possibly have been in the mine house?

Main's van drove towards the road with wheels spinning, hurling mud in its wake. Spargo raised a hand in farewell and felt rain on his face. Fine rain. Kilcreg rain. Icy cold. Sudden and silent.

Main's van straightened up and made its way up the hill, flashing its brake lights as it rounded the bend. Déjà vu – but not quite, because this time the van's brake lights came on and stayed on as Main pulled over to let something coming the other way to pass. It was a white sports utility vehicle the size of a small whale. Definitely not a local. Cars driven by locals were at least ten years old and looked even older, their paintwork pitted with sea-salt rust. The white SUV was shiny and new.

The vehicle came down the hill cautiously and hesitantly, as if the driver had lost his way. Spargo expected it to turn around and head back but it didn't, it parked in the road behind his Volvo. Ignoring it, Spargo turned to watch men stacking stone.

What would have become of the bronze box if he hadn't found it? Would it have been overlooked, dumped on the fire with the timbers? If so, then Volker's journals, sealed in the box, would have been reduced to black tinder.

It really was closure: no more mine house, no more mystery, no point returning here ever again. He made his way to his car, stepping carefully around ruts in the mud. Glancing up for a second he saw the driver of the SUV was out of his car and standing behind it with his elbows on its roof, steadying a pair of binoculars trained on what remained of the house.

Spargo's mobile rang. By the time he'd found it the ringing had stopped. At first it showed no signal, but as he walked it came back. Went again. Came back again and the phone rang again. It was Jez.

'He told me to call you.'

'Jez, I can't hear you. The signal's poor, I'm surpr – '

'I have to call you. He said I had to. He said – ' Jez did not scare easily but there was fear in her voice. 'He said he will phone you.'

Spargo heard a voice in the background. A man interrupting her.

'Who's that with you?'

'I'm not to say. I'm not to say where I am – '

'Jez, you're not making sense. Who's that with you?'

'They're keeping me here.'

'Who is? Let me talk to them.'

'He won't… he says he'll call you later. I'm to tell you.'

'Tell me what? Are you in Edinburgh?'

'At home.'

Spargo heard a gasp, a curse and a shriek. He guessed whoever was with her had tried to snatch the phone from her.

'Jez, give it to him! Do what he says!'

'Chocky, Dad! Tim bought it last year! Chocky!'

The phone went dead. Either it had been taken from her or he'd lost the signal. He had been walking in small circles in the mud and he stopped, stared at the phone and tried to recall her exact words. In desperation he pressed keys, first her house number and then her mobile. Both failed to connect. He had to get higher and get a better signal, and the quickest way to do that was to drive up the hill. From there he could call her back. If that didn't work he'd call Quinn.

The man at the SUV was still using the binoculars, no longer watching the workmen and the house but the hillside beyond them.

Spargo, keys in hand, blipped the remote as he neared his own car. Heard the clunk of his locks. Heard, also, a familiar voice.

'Good afternoon, Mister Spargo…'

The voice was unmistakable but so out of context. Its owner came out from behind the SUV in a familiar, pale coloured, slick suit.

'Whenever I am in this country it is raining,' Benares said calmly, holding the binoculars in one hand and pointing skywards with the other. 'Why do you think that is?' He came closer, wrapping the leather neck strap around the binoculars.

Unnecessarily tightly, Spargo thought.

CHAPTER THIRTY-SEVEN

THE FIRST SOLDIER TO CLIMB the truck's tailgate is confronted by Walter. Unknown to Theo, he has climbed into the truck to count fuel cans. Hearing the climbing soldier he crawls back and calls out to Heiss.

'You will do your job and I will do mine, Herr Doctor! This vehicle is the property of the Schutzstaffel! I cannot permit your workers to touch it!'

Heiss raises his eyebrows. He opens his mouth to respond but doesn't get the chance. Walter jumps down and is face to face with him, wagging a finger an inch from his nose.

'My colleagues in Munich assured me you would have work schedules ready for my inspection. Why do I have to remind you that I have not yet seen them?'

Heiss scowls. Again he considers responding but thinks better of it. He walks briskly away, and as soon as he is out of sight Walter calls to the soldiers. They step smartly. They salute. Walter raises an arm and points.

'My aide and I will unload the crates for you and you will move them over there, away from the doors. Start with those we have unloaded.'

The soldiers nod, salute, and instruct the workers. As soon as they are alone, Theo and Walter move Peter and place him on the driving cab floor. The boy is stirring from sleep so Theo stays with him, comforting him.

Now Peter is clear, Walter sets the men to work unloading the remaining crates, sliding them to the rear of the truck, lifting them down and stacking them with the others. Heiss returns as they are finishing their tasks. He is waving papers. He starts to speak but Walter talks over him.

'Do you have the bronze boxes? Are they ready?'

'They are ready, of course. They are stored elsewhere.'

'You were instructed to send a prototype of the box to Munich for approval. Did you do that?'

Heiss shrugs. 'There was simply no time. It was constructed to your specification, as were all the others.'

'Do you have it?'

'Of course. You can inspect it in my office. But there is no point, we have already made all of the – '

'I wish to see it. Bring it to me.'

Heiss drops his jaw, a theatrical display of disbelief.

'Oberführer, I have just been... the weight... it is bronze, it is heavy. It would be easier if you came – '

'Easier for you, possibly. We are tired, Doctor, we have been driving for days whereas you appear to have done very little. You will bring it now.'

Heiss looks around him as if hoping for help. The soldiers and workers have completed their tasks and are returning to their snow clearing work. He starts after them, as if to get them. It is a route that will take him close to the cab and to Theo and Peter.

'Doctor Heiss,' Walter says quietly, pointing to the distant end of the building. 'I assume your office is that way?'

Heiss turns and shuffles away. Once he is out of sight Walter grabs the quilt from the back of the truck and takes it to Theo.

'Heiss has gone. How is the boy?'

'Not good. He's been drugged on and off for two days. I daren't give him more. Is it true what you just said?'

'About what?'

'That only SS personnel are permitted in this truck?'

Walter smiles a rare smile. 'Don't be ridiculous.'

Walter stays for a while, standing on the steps to the cab, looking in at the bundle on the floor. Peter's hair is showing around the edge of the bulked-up quilt, an overlong, coarse brown tangle. Walter steps down quietly. Closes the cab door.

Steel wheels trundle on the concrete floor. Heiss is returning, he has loaded the prototype bronze box onto a sack truck and in the hangar-like void it rattles and clatters. In the cab Peter stirs; he is trying to fight his way out of the quilt; frustrated, he cries out. Heiss, still some way off, hears the sound. He stops, cocks his head, and listens. Walter breaks the silence.

'Come, Doctor! What are you waiting for? We do not have all day. Why have you brought me a car battery?'

'Like you instructed, I have brought you the box.'

Walter stares down at a block of black rubber. He stoops. Tries to lift it up.

'God, man, it weighs a ton!'

'It is as specified. We have coated the box with rubber but have left the lid uncoated so you can inspect it. The lid is screwed down. Beneath it is a rubber seal to make it watertight. The crates you have brought will, of course, be coated completely with the rubber.'

Walter is nodding. He looks towards the truck and calls out.

'Kapitänleutnant, your attention please!'

Theo is surprised he has been called. He has no option but to leave Peter. When he gets to the two men Walter nods at the box.

'Tell me what you think of this, Kapitänleutnant. It is merely a prototype. Others have been made to the same specification, but to the correct measurements to house each of our wooden crates.'

Theo tries to shove the box with his boot but it doesn't move. He crouches down and attempts to lift it. He manages to raise one edge and then drops it.

'Bronze,' Theo says. 'Six millimetre thick plate.' He nods his approval. It seems the right thing to do.

'What about water-tightness?' Walter asks. 'The doctor says there is a rubber seal inside. Is that suitable?'

Theo is about to respond when there is a noise in the truck. Not a cry, but bumping and banging. Peter is kicking.

'You are an expert in these things,' Walter tells Theo. 'Take the box to the cab. Under the seat you will find tools. Remove the screws. Open the top and check the seal. Tell me if it is good enough.'

Theo grabs the handles of the sack truck, turns it and pushes it to the cab. He knows Walter is going through a routine to fool Heiss. Inspecting the box is pointless because the full-size ones will already have been made. But Peter is still kicking, and Heiss is attentive, distracted by sounds from what should be an empty truck.

Frustrated, Heiss makes a move towards the cab. Walter blocks him.

'You have a job to do, Herr Doctor. Tonight you will seal my crates in your bronze boxes. Pay attention to the codes on the schedule and the number on the crates. I want the each wooden crate sealed in its correct bronze box.'

Heiss is outraged. ''Am I not to unpack the crates? I consider myself a student of the arts. I was assuming I would be able to see – '

Walter draws himself up to his full height so he can stare down at the man. While shifting the crates he unbuttoned his tunic and now he is refastening it. His cap, with its deaths-head badge and SS eagle, rests on an empty oil drum nearby. He reaches for it and places it squarely on his head.

Heiss is no longer looking at the truck. No longer listening for sounds.

'You disappoint me, Doctor. Surely it is not possible for you to know what is in these crates? Could it be you have been listening to idle gossip? Could it be you have been making enquiries you have no right to make? This is a serious matter that I must report to my superiors. They will want to know how you came by this information. They will want to know who you have told about this mission. Is that what you do, Doctor, pass confidential information to those like yourselves that have no right to know it?'

'No, Herr Oberführer! I am a loyal servant of the Reich! There are things I may have heard, but I have not repeated them. Indeed, I considered reporting what – '

He raises a hand as if about to gesticulate, to emphasise a point he is about to make. Changing his mind he lowers his hand gradually as if surrendering a weapon.

'Herr Oberführer, I have told nobody. I can honestly – '

'That will be for others to decide. My concern meanwhile is the crates. In no circumstances must they be they be tampered with. If I so much as see –'

'Of course, Herr Oberführer. I shall ensure my team works on them day and night. Do you wish to supervise?'

'Shut your mouth and get on with whatever it is you have to do. I trust you have experienced staff?'

'I wouldn't say they... yes, Herr Oberführer, of course!'

'Very well. As I said, I will leave tomorrow night.'

Heiss looks at the floor. 'That is not possible, Oberführer. The full-scale plant is not yet working, we are plagued by acts of sabotage. We have only a pilot plant manufacturing the rubber.'

'So how long? Wednesday? Thursday?'

'Two weeks, Oberführer. Possibly it can be done in ten days, but with the bombing...'

Walter argues and threatens but Heiss is unyielding. There are problems, he says. He repeats his concern that the Soviets are close.

'The camps here are closing, I can no longer get workers. Even my own prisoners will soon leave.'

Theo listens from the cab. It is as he feared. As with the French mines, these factories use slave labour. For all the problems that have befallen him lately he knows that choosing the Kriegsmarine rather than the French mines was the right choice. His crewmen might occasionally behave like stubborn pigs but at least he doesn't have to whip them to make them work.

Walter is still talking.

'If I am to be here a few days I shall need a car. I want to leave the truck here, I do not want to drive it around. Who deals with these matters?'

'The Regulating Office. You can telephone from my office.'

'Do you have a car I can use?'

'We have a small van. It has no petrol.'

'That is not a problem. I have petrol.'

'There is of course the SS, Herr Oberführer. They have their own vehicles.'

Walter pauses to think. Considers that the fewer people he meets, the better.

'Forget it, I have changed my mind, I shall keep the truck, it will cope better with the snow. I need somewhere to stay. Who deals with accommodation?'

'Again, it is the Regulating Office. There is also the SS barracks, perhaps you know it? If you came on the road from Katowice you will have passed close to it.'

'Do you happen to know Hauptsturmführer Ortmann? He is a friend of mine. I believe he is here somewhere.'

'There are many SS men in the work camps, Herr Oberführer. I confess I do not recognise the name.'

Walter nods. 'Very good, Herr Doctor. Now, leave us. You have much work to do.'

At the Regulating Office Walter refuses the duty officer's offer of beds in the officers' quarters and by late afternoon Walter, Theo and Peter are settled in a furnished army hut in an otherwise deserted part of the site, the truck parked discretely away. Theo and Walter are sprawled on beds with their caps off and their tunics unbuttoned.

Peter has recovered from the sleeping pills and is playing with a pile of sawn logs, stacking them high and laughing when they fall, it is the first time Theo has heard him laugh. Rather than use logs in the stove Theo burns gas coke he found in a bin and which burns without smoke. Though the army knows where they are, there is no point advertising their presence.

Walter nods towards Peter.

'I must have been mad to bring him, Theo. So far we have been lucky.'

'So far?'

'We still have a long way to go. A couple of days here, then another long journey. Five days at least.'

'And then?'

'And then we will be in Hamburg where you will join your new boat. You will be given new orders. I cannot say more, I am not party to every decision. Once I have safely delivered you and the crates my responsibilities are over.'

Theo doesn't comment. The man has left his bed and commandeered a threadbare, high-backed armchair. He is lying stretched out on it, one boot crossed over the other.

The room is frugally furnished with six beds, a row of lockers and two tables. Several long benches have been stacked against a wall and Theo moves from the bed, takes one down, sits on it and gazes absently, half at his boy and half at the remaining beds. He has rediscovered his pipe and is fiddling with it, cleaning it out with a knife. Walter seems more relaxed than he has been for days.

'We will not be disturbed here,' he says. 'They hate us, you know.'

'Who does?'

'The regular army. They hate us, just like you do.'

'You think that?'

'I know that. I saw it in your eyes when I arrived at the farm. I am well used to it and it doesn't trouble me. We are Germany's elite. We expect resentment and envy.'

'So you think it is envy?'

'What else? The SS rules Germany, we are like a State within a State. We have our own laws, we set our own standards. Our officers and fighting men are all equal in the sight of each other. Is that not a culture to be envied?'

Theo says nothing. He has strong opinions but this is not the time to air them.

'The future of the Fatherland is in our hands,' Walter continues. 'We have our own industries, our businesses and factories. This industrial giant, this Monowitz, it is run by us, did you know that? We succeed because we will stop at nothing to get what we want. It is our right.'

'It sounds to me like a lust for power.'

'A desire, Theodor, not a lust. There is nothing wrong with power.'

Neither Walter nor Theo hear the vehicle until it stops close by. The driver has drifted there, switching off the engine when some way off. Walter is on his feet before Theo. He scoops the boy up and passes him to Theo.

'Go to the bathroom. Lock yourself in. Stay there until I come for you.'

Carrying Peter, Theo sprints to the door at the back of the hut. It connects by corridors to others, also to the ablutions block with its laundry, sinks, showers and lavatory cubicles.

Peter is quiet. Though the place where they hide is unheated, Theo sweats, his nerve close to breaking. Time passes. All is quiet. Then, from some way off, he hears the squeak of a hinge and soft footsteps. Someone is close.

'Theodor, you can come. It was nothing, a routine patrol.'

Walter is standing at a row of sinks. Idly, he turns a tap but no water runs. The pipes are frozen. Peter, released from Theo's grasp, runs to Walter but is ignored.

'Come,' Walter says. 'Before you both freeze to death.'

At eight o'clock that evening the door of the hut is kicked open with such force it slams against the wall, bounces back and is kicked open again. Three soldiers burst in and Peter, startled, yells out. A fourth man, an army officer, comes in behind them, looks around and steps outside again, returning seconds later with a man in civilian clothes. He is about Theo's age, and short and stocky with dark, close-cropped hair. To keep out the cold he has raised the high collar of his overcoat and he peers out from between the lapels. Surveys the dim room.

CHAPTER THIRTY-EIGHT

THE MINE TRACK on the high moor ran straight, a narrow green runway through waist-high dark heather. The white SUV with Benares at the wheel rose and fell over dips and bumps like a ship on an ocean. To Spargo, beside him, it was a miracle the road was still driveable. Twin groves had been gauged in the ground, first by the steel wheels of carts and later by the mine's heavy trucks. Benares kept the wheels in the grooves as if driving in tram tracks.

Spargo, gripping a hand-hold, sat quietly. Everything had happened so quickly. Benares and the binoculars. Benares and the threats.

'Mister Spargo…' he'd said. 'The mine house is no longer there and I am told it is empty, there is nothing to be found. You and I are both wrong, yes?'

Spargo, still with Jez's pleas in mind, had shaken his head. Not sure at what.

'Mister Spargo, we are here for the same things, I think. They are not in the house, we can see that now. The men would have found them, would they not?'

'Things?'

'Boxes, Mister Spargo. Boxes.'

'What have you done with my daughter?'

Benares had frowned. 'I have done nothing with your daughter. Why do you ask such a thing?'

'You have done all this, you are responsible for this. Where is Jez? What have you done with her?'

'I have done what, Mister Spargo? I am responsible for what? Please calm yourself, it is better that way. Better also that you drive your car to your mother's house and conceal it. Do not even think of driving away.'

Spargo had protested, accusing Benares of all manner of crimes. Then he did what Benares told him to do – he left his car at his mother's empty house and clambered into the SUV.

He had supposed he was being driven back to civilisation, up the hill and out of Kilcreg. They had continued for miles until Benares slowed down, spun the wheel, and swerved onto the drover's road. The old mine track.

Instead of driving cautiously Benares kept up his speed, bouncing and lurching across hard-packed, grassy ground. Spargo nervously kept up the questions – where is my daughter? What have you done with her? Benares, seemingly relaxed, said nothing.

Ten minutes down the track Spargo had another go at him. Even went through the almost comic routine, if anything happens to my daughter...

Benares turned to him and smiled. Showed his teeth.

Spargo's concern for Jez masked his own fear. He was being abducted, taken to one of the remotest spots he knew. He pictured Letchie, naked in his basement, strangled by the garrotte – a method of killing as traditional to Spain as poisoned darts were to the Amazon.

Jez's words came to him. Chocky. And Tim. He knew no-one called Tim and the only Chocky he'd heard of was the imaginary friend in John Wyndham's sci-fi classic. If there was a connection to be made between those two names then he couldn't make it. Jez had been too subtle by half.

To one side of them the overgrown track from the plant yard came out from deep heather. For a while it ran parallel to the track they were on and then, without warning, and rather like railway lines at points, the two sets of ruts joined. The SUV lurched and bounced over them, managing to stay upright somehow.

Rain came, a drizzle that seeped from thick mist. Spargo knew that way ahead of them were cliff tops and sea. Was that where Benares was taking him? Had he planned to garrotte him like Letchie and throw him into the sea?

Benares switched on the wipers and the screen cleared. Ahead of them a dark shape, that Spargo bizarrely supposed might be a sailing ship, emerged from the mist. When closer, its hull became the mine's old counting house, the two-roomed, two-storey building where his mother once worked. Its masts became the still-standing telegraph posts that once carried the mine's phone wires.

'Is Bar here?'

'Why should Mister Bar be here?'

Spargo wondered if he'd got it wrong. Wondered if all this involved only Benares, and whoever it was with Jez.

The mine buildings once sat surrounded by a hard-rolled surface of furnace ash – a sea of black clinker like in the plant yard. That surface was now deep beneath heather. The mine shaft sunk by his father's men and now filled in had been some way off. The flat concrete slabs on which other buildings stood were still there and Spargo remembered how, long ago, he had raced across them on his bike. Now they were broken, shot through with a maze of cracks sprouting tufts of long grass.

Benares slowed down and changed gear. Turning off the track he eased the front wheels on to one of the concrete slabs, drove on it and stopped. Not happy with where he had parked he shunted up and down, tucking the vehicle tight against the counting house wall. Satisfied the SUV was now hidden he turned off the engine. He gave Spargo a shove towards the door and then clambered out himself.

The back wall of the building was higher than the front. Its corrugated asbestos roof sloped only one way and gave it the look of a huge lean-to shed. The ground floor, once a store, had in later years been used as a bothy for shepherds at lambing time; its large double door had gone; the frames of the windows in the upper floor – windows that once gave a view across the moor – were boarded over.

Benares was ahead of him, waiting at the foot of an external wooden staircase leading to the upper floor. Spargo recalled how he used to think of the place as an old-style railway signal box. Outside the door at the top of the steps was a small wooden platform, surrounded by a wooden handrail. There had been a handrail on each side of the staircase but now the one on the outside had gone. Spargo remembered how scared he had been the first time he climbed the steps. Falling off it, under the handrail, had been a real fear.

THE MAN WHO PLAYED TRAINS

But not as scared then as he was now.

'Upstairs, Mister Spargo.'

'Are you bringing my daughter here?'

'The door is not locked. Go inside.'

Spargo took the stairs slowly. Stopped on the platform and looked back. 'Chocky,' he mumbled to himself. 'Chocky…'

'Open the door, Mister Spargo.'

'Chocky,' Spargo said, this time more loudly. He stopped in the doorway and turned to Benares.

'That Canadian mine stuff you sent me to work on. You said Bar was thinking of buying the mine. That was a lie.'

Jez wasn't being subtle when she'd said those two words. She must have looked up the Cocwaiqui mine and found out how to pronounce it. And TIM, he'd guessed that too. Not a name. Initials.

'Bar can't buy that Canadian mine, can he?' Spargo continued. 'There is no real work for me because it's already been sold, bought by TIM, Triscor Incorporated Materials. Why pay me to work on a worthless project? Was it just to keep me hooked? Is that it?'

Benares ignored him. He had stopped near the top of the stairs and was gazing over the heather towards the round topped dome of Stac Dubh. The man was vulnerable. He had dropped his guard. A well-placed kick and he would go over, breaking his neck or his back. Spargo felt a rush of adrenaline and took a step forwards. Then, just as quickly, the moment passed. His engineer's mind had balanced the odds of success and found them against him. Somebody had Jez. What if Benares had a prior arrangement to phone her captors? What if there was an accomplice already in the counting house?

'I know nothing of these contractual matters,' Benares said, stepping up to the platform. 'This mine business does not interest me.'

Small grimy panes glazed the top half of the door. One pane was cracked, another replaced by a square of warped hardboard. Spargo grasped the door knob, peered through the panes and saw a bed, two chairs and a table. In his mind he also saw Letchie, naked, a wire buried in his neck. It wasn't going to happen to him.

On impulse he swung his free arm back in a sudden, scythe-like sweep. It caught Benares in the chest and he toppled backwards with arms flailing. By chance he managed to grab Spargo's jacket and had just about recovered his balance when Spargo, more in panic than combat, let fly a kick that caught the man's kneecap.

Benares gasped, shrieked, released his grip and hung motionless, the heels of his shiny brogues still on the edge of the platform and his body tilted out at an angle. With his mouth open wide and arms flailing he fell backwards. Spargo, down the steps and across the concrete, leapt into the SUV and started the engine. Though Benares had manoeuvred the 4x4 well away from the track Spargo roared forwards, unaware of a two-foot drop off the concrete slab, hidden by deep heather. The vehicle darted forwards so fast the front and back wheels made it off the slab. The back of the vehicle smashed down on the concrete. The engine stalled.

If Spargo had considered Benares would survive the drop from the staircase he might have locked all five doors. He might also have looked in the mirror, because had he done so he would have seen Benares, apparently unharmed, running towards him. He only realised the man was there when the drivers' door opened and a hand grabbed the wheel.

Benares, one hand on the wheel and the other on Spargo's trouser belt, attempted to haul him out. The SUV, still with its rear end perched on the concrete slab, lurched forwards, jumped out of gear and stopped dead as if against buffers. Spargo, not strapped in, hit his head on the screen.

Spargo knew where he was but not how he got there. He also knew he was in great pain from his head, his neck and his side. From where he lay on the concrete slab he made out Benares, an out-of-focus silhouette brushing mud from its suit.

The carpet of heather covering the ground beneath the wooden staircase was thick enough to break the fall of an elephant, Spargo realised as he stumbled back up it to the counting house. The pain in his side got worse with each step and to ease it he crossed his arms as if hugged himself. One his hands touched warm, damp flesh.

He stopped climbing. Looking down at his side he saw his shirt was cut through and blood-soaked. Cautiously his fingers explored for a wound and when he found it his legs went from under him. He tried to twist round to look at Benares but the pain was too great.

'You bastard! You stabbed me!'

'You are still breathing. Give me more trouble, Mister Spargo, and I will do it again. Next time you will not get up.'

Spargo reached the landing and kicked the door, a mistake that brought more pain. It swung open into a small damp room floored with brown linoleum – a covering so ancient it had split along the joins in the floorboards. At some stage an attempt had been made to insulate the roof by lining it with kapok, held in place by cream painted plywood. It had split along the joins, releasing grey entrails of ragged, flocked cotton.

Spargo had been there many times. Long ago it seemed to him that every inch of the place was filled with desks, chairs and wooden cabinets. His mother's desk had been on the right hand side, its place taken now by a black-and-rust bedstead with a thin grubby mattress and a red sleeping bag, still partly rolled, the carrier bag beside it bearing the logo of Tiso's of Edinburgh. Closer to him and almost filling the space that remained were three plastic garden chairs, tucked in under what might well have been one of the original office tables.

Benares came in behind him and closed the door, blocking out what remained of the daylight. He walked down the room, heels tap-tapping the lino.

'You disappoint me, Mister Spargo. I thought you were an intelligent man.'

Spargo said nothing. Didn't want to do anything that brought him more pain. Then he remembered Jez. Whatever had happened to her was his fault. The least he could do – or maybe the best he could do – was keep her safe.

'Where is my daughter?' he asked. 'Why pick on her? She has done nothing to you.'

'Your daughter? What about her? You think I have done something? What makes you think this?'

'If anything at all happens to her…'

'You are hardly in a position to threaten me. Tell me how you know of this.'

'She phoned me. When I was returning to my car. When I saw you.'

Benares frowned. Didn't reply.

Spargo turned his wounded side to Benares and lifted his jacket to show the red stain. The wound wasn't that big but the blood from it was spreading.

'I need to have this seen to. I need a doctor.'

'The cut is nothing. It is a flesh wound, a mere warning. Now, Mister Spargo, I have to leave you, I have things to do. Locking you in is pointless because you will easily find a way to escape. If you are not here when I return then you will have to live with the consequences.'

'Why am I here? If it's Volker's journals you and Bar want, I don't have them. I've got a full translation, you can have that instead.'

'And I am sure it makes interesting reading. But I have no interest in these diaries.'

'Bullshit! It's why you killed my mother and Letchie.'

'You are wrong.'

'How did you know I would be at Kilcreg? How did you know where to find me?'

'I followed you from Edinburgh.'

'I don't believe you. I'd have seen you.'

'I didn't stay behind you, I am not stupid. Once you were on your way it was obvious where you were going. By coming voluntarily you saved me considerable trouble.'

'The mine house, is that your work? Did you have it demolished?'

'The house is owned by the Kilcreg Estate. I made it known I was in the market for good building stone and roof slates and I was willing to well pay over the market price. In truth I shall resell the material at a considerable loss, but that is of no consequence.'

The inscrutable smile. The white marble tombstones. Spargo grimaced.

'So I am right. You are looking for other boxes.'

'I believe I have already told you as much. But tell me how you know of these things. Is it in Volker's writings?'

'He says there were other boxes. I'm guessing that's why you had the U-boat searched. There was nothing on it, I know that too.'

'Mister Kalman has a big mouth.'

'When you realised they weren't on the U-boat you went to my mother's house to find them. You don't have brains enough to realise the box would not have been in her cottage because she hadn't always lived there. Admit you murdered her! Admit you tried to find out what she knew about the other boxes!'

'You are wrong. I did not kill your mother. I have never met her.'

'Then it was Letchie. You are as guilty as him. You arranged it. He took pictures for you, he did your reconnaissance. It's how you knew about this place.'

'Mister Letchie did take pictures. He was recommended to me as an excellent source of information. He was paid a large amount of money to discover facts.'

'About my mother. About me.'

'Not about you, I knew all about you. It concerns me that you consider me responsible for your mother's death and I am particularly anxious Mr Bar should not hold the same view. Mister Letchie became a little over-zealous. I was not informed of his penchant for violence.'

'You're a cold-blooded bastard! You dangled money on a string. It encouraged Letchie to kill her!'

Benares had moved to the door. He had his back to Spargo, staring out through grimy panes.

'I am sorry you see it that way. I have never needed to pay people to do my killing.' Spargo shivered. The wound in his side throbbed. 'Mister Letchie took it upon himself to search your mother's house while she was still there. That was incredibly stupid of him. Had he been more diligent he would have discovered your mother had not always lived in the cottage. He could have searched the other house. Your mother need not have been troubled.'

'Troubled? So you killed...' The words came from a dry throat and Spargo tried again, this time managing to get them out. 'So you killed him... Letchie... in my house.'

'Regrettably.'

'And Lewis? You murdered him too?'

Benares raised his finger and wagged it at Spargo as if chastising a child. 'Take care, Mister Spargo, do not insult me. I did not kill Lewis. As part of Letchie's journalistic investigations he talked to Kalman.

As a result of that man's indiscretions he decided to involve himself in business that was not of his concern. Mister Letchie was a loose cannon. He had to be removed.'

Spargo winced. That expression – loose cannon – words used in Bar's villa: 'ditch the loose cannon before he does more damage…'

'Mister Letchie also learnt you had discovered a box in the old house and you had taken it to the police.'

'But why kill him at my place? What was it, some kind of twisted warning?'

'That did not enter my mind. He told me about Volker's diaries. I happened to know they were of no importance and I told him so. Possibly he did not believe me. Possibly he thought they would lead him to the items we sought. Whatever the reason, he started to act independently.'

'Then you should have stopped him.'

'Oh, I did, Mister Spargo. Unfortunately I was not in time to save the translator. In your cellar Mister Letchie admitted he had visited him. Under duress Mister Lewis said he had returned the diaries to the police without attempting a translation. Later Letchie ran the man down.'

'A hit and run. And that is why you decided to dispose of Letchie?'

'I do not have to justify my actions to you. He had killed two people. We could not allow him to kill more.'

'We? You and Bar?'

'No doubt you have already learnt from Mister Kalman that the submarine investigations were funded by a consortium. Letchie was recommended to us by a member of that consortium. We believe he learnt of our needs from that same person.'

'Why are you telling me these things?'

'I see no harm in it. At some time in the future you would have learned it yourself. I would rather you were told the truth from me than lies from others.'

Spargo's shoulders sagged, relief rather than despair. If Benares was to be trusted, for Spargo there would be a future. The man was not about to add him to his victims. Jez too, hopefully.

'What else did Lewis tell Letchie?'

'I have no idea. I could not even discover from him where Mister Lewis lived.'

'I want to speak to Jez.'

Benares shrugged. 'I am late. I have to leave.'

'Let me speak to her.'

'Maybe when I return.'

'Where are you going?'

'That is no concern of yours. Stay here, Mister Spargo. I do not wish to sound melodramatic but if you are not here upon my return then I shall make a telephone call. I am sure you understand.'

Spargo lifted his jacket again. 'This is bad. I need a doctor.'

'Mister Spargo, listen to me. Despite the fact I have never done you any harm you attempted to kill me. Had it not been for that filthy undergrowth you would now be a murderer.'

With dusk came the rain, ragged, squally gusts drifting in from the sea. It beat on the counting house roof and ran down the panes in the door, transforming Spargo's view of the heather into striped Lowry paintings. It stopped as unexpectedly as it started, vanishing inland and leaving cold air. Spargo, heeding Benares' warning, stayed inside. The pain in his side was now so great he doubted he would have made it as far as Kilcreg.

In the poor light he unfastened his trousers and dropped them. He noticed a new, clean nick in his trouser belt. Its leather had protected him, it had deflected the blade. Lifting his shirt he saw the wound was a slash rather than a stab, it didn't look deep. The blood had started to congeal but his fiddling around had disturbed it and it was bleeding again.

Had the wounding really a warning? Or had Benares, in the heat of the moment and unsure he could stop the SUV, tried to kill him? Cautiously he unbuttoned one of his cuffs. With the help of a fragment of glass from a boarded window he ripped off part of a shirt sleeve, folded it into a thick pad, pressed it to the wound and then secured it in place with his belt.

In what little light there was left to see by Spargo unrolled the sleeping bag, spread it out on the bed and lay on it. Minutes later he zipped up his jacket. Finally, feeling the cold and realising he had started to shiver, he opened the bag, got right inside it and zipped it up.

Had he not been awakened by the sound of an engine he would have sworn he had not slept at all. Feeling the pain in his side but forgetting his vulnerability he eased himself out of the bag. Gasped as his shirt snagged his wound.

Car headlights lit up the heather, twin beams that bounced up and down. The engine stopped, the bright lights vanished. Torch beams wavered, came to the stairs. Could it be Mitchell? Even better, could it be Mitchell with Jez?

Voices now, definitely Spanish. Not Mitchell but Benares. As for the person with him, the gravel-deep voice was unmistakable. Bar came up the staircase slowly, breathing heavily, cursing Benares for making him climb stairs. When he reached the platform he stood wheezing, and waited a while before shoving the door. Finally he barged in, torch in hand, painting the room with its beam. It fell on Spargo. Then it moved on, as if Spargo wasn't there.

Bar was inspecting the room. Speaking in English he pronounced the place too small, too cold and too uncomfortable. Benares, still in the doorway, answered in Spanish and Bar turned the torch on him, dazzling him with the beam. As Spargo stood up Bar grabbed a plastic chair, twisted it round and slumped on to it. Its legs splayed under his weight.

'John Spargo is my guest,' he said. 'This place is not good enough. You will find heat for him. You will bring light.'

Benares held out his arms in despair. 'I cannot!' he said. 'This place is worse than a desert, there is nothing!'

'I did not choose this place, you did. Do as I say, drive until you find something. Before you do that, bring the bottle and the glasses from the car.'

'Bring them in here?'

'Of course. Do it now. Then leave us.'

Benares paused as if about to protest but thought better of it. He left hurriedly, slamming the door.

'Why are you doing this?' Spargo asked. 'Why me? Why my daughter?'

The torch beam swivelled. It stung Spargo's eyes.

'I will ask the questions.'

Benares returned, dumped a carrier bag on the floor and left without speaking. The door slammed again.

'Things are not as they should be,' Bar said when he'd gone. 'This has not proceeded the way I had planned, John Spargo…'

Bar's arm drooped gradually. As if realising he had almost dozed off he lifted the torch sharply. When he aimed its beam at Spargo, Spargo moved out of its light. The beam followed him, dazzled him.

'I want to know why I'm here,' Spargo said. 'I want to know what you've done with my daughter.'

'Do you mind if I smoke a cigar? No, of course not. Sit down, John Spargo, this place is small enough without you wandering around. What has Luis been telling you, that I am responsible for the abduction of your daughter?'

'He has not said that. I've told him everything I know. If it is Volker's journals you want, I can get them for you. You can have the full translation, it's on my computer.'

Bar rested the torch on the table and it rolled to one side. He caught it before it went off the edge and stood it on end so its beam lit the ceiling. For the first time since the man arrived, Spargo could actually see him. He appeared to be dressed as he had been in Spain, in a lightweight suit and an open-necked shirt. His only concession to the cold was a three-quarter length overcoat, draped over his shoulders like a Mafia Don.

Silently he did the cigar ritual, trimming, rolling, and listening. He reached into one of the pockets of his coat, took out a matchbox, struck a match and lit the end of the cigar slowly, rotating it as he'd done at his villa. He took a long draw on it, sat back and sighed.

'I do not want Theodor Volker's books,' he said, exhaling a stream of smoke. 'They are of no interest to me. I knew Volker, John Spargo. I know about his books, his diaries. Many years ago I instructed him to destroy them but he was a stubborn man, he kept them and took them on his boat. I did not know it at the time.'

'If they're not important then why did three people die?'

Bar removed his cigar and blew smoke. Almost inaudibly he

mumbled 'Three? You think it is only three?'

'Where are the journals now? Where is Marie Howard?'

'Miss Howard? I am paying her to translate some documents for me. She is safe in a hotel in Madrid. You are a fool, John Spargo, your meddling put her at risk.'

'You said the journals are unimportant.'

'Did I say she was translating Volker's diaries? I did not. I am simply employing her to keep her out of harm's way.'

'I don't understand.'

'There are many things you do not understand, John Spargo. You were foolish to give her the journals. I know they are of no importance, but not everyone understands that. Sit down.'

'I'll stay standing.'

Bar pointed the cigar at Spargo and jabbed it like a finger. 'Don't be so irritating. Just sit down.'

Spargo sat back on the bed. The bending hurt his wound and he winced and gasped.

Bar watched him. 'What is the matter? What have you done to yourself?'

'Benares stabbed me. I need a doctor.'

Bar held his cigar out and tapped it with a finger. A slab of ash fell from it and splashed on the lino. Changing hands he picked up the torch, aimed it at Spargo, moving the beam up and down as if looking for a wound. Spargo lifted up the hem of his jacket to show his stained shirt. By the time he had undone his belt the torch was already back on the table.

'I asked you what you had done,' Bar said. 'I did not ask to see it.'

'Benares said you have my daughter. I want to see her.'

'I am sure Luis said nothing of the kind. I do not have your daughter, I do not know where she is and I am not responsible for her disappearance. It is none of my business.'

'He said if I left this place while he was away my daughter would suffer.'

'That was most imaginative of him. He telephoned me. He said he had heard about your daughter's abduction from you.'

'That's ridiculous. You're lying.'

'I'm sorry you think that. I have never lied to you, John Spargo.'

'Everything you've said and done since I met Benares in London has been one long lie. I was led to believe you owned a mining company. You gave me the impression you wanted me to work here, at Kilcreg. I took you for a wheelchair-bound invalid but look at you now, even that's a lie. Then there's the Canadian mine, all lies...'

'You have a contract to work on mine documents, that is what I am paying you to do. I never said you would be employed to work at Kilcreg.'

'Benares told me you and a consortium were thinking of buying it. He lied.'

'To do my bidding Luis might tell the occasional untruth. As for me being an invalid, I am no longer a fit man, I have a heart condition. My consultant tells me I must not overexert myself and for that reason I use my chair whenever I can. As for the mine and the contract, they are of no relevance. They are not the issue here.'

'Then what is the issue? Why have you brought me here?'

'I did not bring you here. You came to Kilcreg of your own accord.'

'I'm a prisoner here.'

'As I said, this is not how things should be.'

'Nothing is as it should be. You run a company nobody has heard of. Then there are the empty offices in Madrid. Then there's – '

'I find your protestations irritating. You behaved exactly as I predicted. You suspected things were not as they should be and yet you did nothing. With hindsight perhaps you should not have become involved.'

'Hindsight wasn't something that was available to me when I made my decisions.'

Bar leaned forwards. Lowered his voice.

'Listen to me. Luis has many things to do, he will be gone a long time. I am going to explain to you what I have done and why I have done it.'

'Your twisted explanations don't interest me. All I want from you is my daughter.'

'I do not know where your daughter is. Nobody was supposed to be abducted. Nobody was supposed to get hurt.'

'Then you screwed up.'

Bar sat back and concentrated on his cigar, exhaling smoke into the torch beam and watching it curl as it rose. For almost one minute the silence was broken briefly by the buzz of a turboprop plane heading north to the islands. Spargo listened as it faded away. Bar waited too.

'You are aware that during the war the Nazi leaders took it upon themselves to protect works of art?'

'Protect? Don't you mean loot?'

'You have no sense of humour. You are right of course, though those responsible for the looting would have preferred the word liberated. What do you know of these things?'

'I know what most people know. I've heard that at the end of the war most of the art was recovered from a salt mine.'

'The Altaussee mine in Austria, yes. Most of the art but by no means all of it.'

Bar had changed. Away from the villa, the Mercedes and Benares, he seemed smaller somehow. He was also uncomfortable. The room was cold and damp and the plastic chair he sat on gave little support to his back. Spargo stared at him. Bar stared back.

'You are not a young man, John Spargo. But you make the young man's mistake of seeing me as I am now, not as I used to be. Many years ago I had a vision, like others I wished for an all-powerful Reich. Fortunately for me – and for the rest of humanity – that vision did not materialise.'

'I thought you were Swedish.'

'Then you thought wrong. For more years than I care to remember I have been a citizen of Spain. That country has been good to me.'

'You said you knew Theodor Volker. What were you, a U-boat man?'

'I was not in the Kriegsmarine. I was in a different service.'

'Volker mentions Carinhall, Göring's house. He says he was taken there by a Luftwaffe officer, Walter Wolff. Did you have a hand in that?'

'I am dismayed Theodor recorded matters in such detail, it was most unwise. But yes, John Spargo, I did have a hand in it. I took him there. Against his will, as a matter of fact.'

'You? You are Walter Wolff?'

'You are no lateral thinker… or possibly you have no German. When I changed my name I spelled Bar with an umlaut. It would be pronounced Bear, not Bar. Childish, you might think, changing my name from wolf to bear. Both are animals with teeth. When I was younger that appealed to me.'

'Both predators. Both killers.'

'I prefer hunters. But enough of this, we never wanted war, not with England. I should say Britain, shouldn't I, I have no wish to be politically incorrect, that wouldn't do at all, would it, not in our brave new world. You and the bloody Americans denied us our Empire, do you realise that?'

'That doesn't interest me. You and your cronies helped Göring with his looting.'

'I did nothing of the kind. I helped to liberate art plundered by others. The war was lost, the new order was crumbling. Why should my colleagues and I not benefit from our leader's successes? Should we have stood by and watched those treasures fall into the hands of our enemies?'

'So you appropriated art from Göring's collection? You and Volker?'

Bar laughed. 'Appropriated? My friend Theodor?' The laugh brought on a deep painful cough and Bar doubled up. When he regained his breath he dropped the cigar on the floor and ground it underfoot.

'Volker practised his signature in one of his journals,' Spargo said. 'Why would he do that if he wasn't taking stuff for himself?'

'His signature? Whose signature?'

'Göring's. It's written in the margin of one of his books. It says Reichsmarschall Hermann Göring.'

'The Reichsmarschall signed himself simply Göring, he never used Hermann. And in any case, you could not be more wrong. Theodor's great failing was that he was an innocent, he would never forge anything. Ask yourself, would a guilty man have been so careless? The signatures you saw can be nothing more than doodles. The man was simply playing.'

'You took stuff out of Germany. Had you left it there it could have been restored to its owners after the war.'

'Could have been? Many things could have been, John Spargo. Are you aware that only a fraction of the recovered art was returned to its owners?'

'Presumably that's because you had already slaughtered most of them in the camps.'

'You and your victorious American friends hardly acquitted themselves with honour. Along with the bastard Soviets you raped our country. You looted everything of value, so don't blame me for the wrongs of others.'

'So you escaped. Then what?'

'I re-established my connections.'

'With other ex-Nazis.'

'With like-minded ex-officers. Also several Americans and Swiss. We established legitimate companies in Portugal and Spain.'

'And in the United States. I've seen claims you made against an airport authority.'

'I am impressed, John Spargo. But that particular item was part of a legitimate trade, I own a business that buys and sells works of art. Every year I sell many hundreds of paintings.'

'And make most of your money from the illegal ones.'

'Made, John Spargo. Made.'

'No more golden eggs?'

Bar shrugged. 'You make it sound easy. The paintings you speak of were dispersed across Europe and took many years to retrieve. When we recovered them we sold them to collectors and invested the proceeds. Some of the works are now in the United States, others in the Middle East, Japan and Russia. The last painting we recovered was sold to one of your British footballers. I can only hope he hung it the correct way up.'

'The room in Madrid, the framed photos. Benares said they were left by the previous occupants.'

'He should not have left you alone, you should not have seen them. The prints you saw are copies of photographs from books and art gallery archives. Years ago one of my late partners suggested we assemble a collection of photographs of all the paintings we could personally account for in the hope we could recover them. All the photographs were in black and white. When we recovered a painting we photographed it – in colour – before we sold it. In each case it replaced the black and white one.'

'From what I remember there were only six black and whites on the wall. Does that mean you recovered – and sold – all but those?'

'That is correct.'

'And now you have run out of money.'

'I shall never run out of money.'

'One of the photos showed a woman in a brown robe. Is that one of the paintings you thought were in the U-boat?'

'The Raphael, you mean? It is not a woman, it is a portrait of a young man. The Portrait of a Young Man, in actual fact. He is pretty, is he not? But why just that one? You said yourself there were six in black and white.'

'One was the Mona Lisa. Even I know it is in the Louvre.'

'You are wrong, John Spargo. The painting in the Louvre is not the original, it is one of many contemporary copies. It is a painting Göring should not have had. The Führer could not possibly have known he had it.'

'Do you really expect me to believe that?'

'The Louvre will tell you that in August nineteen-thirty-nine the genuine Mona Lisa was taken to a place of safety. Believe me, John Spargo, the French had no such place.'

Spargo was smiling, shaking his head.

'You smile, John Spargo. If you disbelieve me then explain to me why, so many years after the war when it really should not matter, officials at the Louvre are unwilling to reveal this so-called safe place? It is because they cannot. It is because there was no such place.'

'The painting in the Louvre has been tested. The paint is right for the era.'

'Of course. It was painted at around the same time. Is that not the meaning of the word contemporary?'

'It was X-rayed. They found changes da Vinci made to it.'

'They found many peculiar alterations that were not adequately explained, as is often the case with many old masters. The great Leonardo had pupils, John Spargo, they were encouraged to copy his original. In claiming its authenticity the Louvre behaves like the church in the matter of the Turin Shroud. Many tourists visit the Louvre to see the da Vinci, do you think they would still visit the place in such numbers if they knew the principal attraction was not genuine? Believe me, John Spargo, the Louvre does not have the original.'

'And are you now going to tell me where the original is?'

'If I could do that then you and I would not be sitting in this godforsaken hole.'

Spargo sat quietly and looked at the floor. Bar's polished shoes had scuffed in the cigar ash and spread it around.

'Are you seriously asking me to believe one of the crates you are looking for contained the Mona Lisa?'

'Who said anything about crates?'

'Benares did. When we were looking at the Mine House. He said they were not there.'

'Very well. Yes, you are correct. There should be six boxes, John Spargo, only six, you must have read that in Theodor Volker's writings. And I am not am not asking you to believe anything, I have no interest in what you believe. What I am stating is fact.'

'Why put them in crates? Why not just take them out of their frames and roll them up?'

'Tell me how it is possible to roll up a wooden panel.'

'I didn't realise. I assumed they were painted on canvas.'

'You are a man who assumes many things.'

'Tell be about Letchie. You paid him to beat up my mother and search her house.'

'Don't be ridiculous. He was employed by Luis simply to look into things. He seemed well-placed to do that. Hiring him was a mistake. He was a barbarian.'

'And this was to be the big day, was it? The day you razed the mine house to the ground and discovered the boxes and their priceless contents? That is why you are here. You brought wine and glasses. You planned a celebration.'

'A small toast to my success, yes.'

Spargo was nodding. He allowed himself just a trace of a smile. 'How could you be so wrong?'

'I am not wrong. I was in Hamburg the night Theodor's submarine was loaded, I stood on the quayside and watched it sail. Now the wreck of that vessel has been investigated. No remains of the boxes were found.'

'So you reasoned they had been brought ashore and hidden in the mine house.'

'A deduction you seem to have made yourself, John Spargo. You found Volker's box with his writings in the roof of the old house, which means he, or someone from his boat, brought it ashore. It was reasonable to assume other bronze boxes came ashore also. If it is of interest to you, the box you found was a sample sent to me by the makers for my approval. I had no use for it and I gave it to Theodor Volker.'

'That doesn't fit. Kalman said the U-boat was lying at sixty metres, that's over sixty tons per square meter of pressure. No boxes could have withstood that, not for fifty years. Spending so much money makes no sense. It would have been cheaper to look on land first.'

'Spare me the technicalities. I was well aware that if the paintings were still on the boat they would be worthless. But as they are not there, they have to be somewhere else. My task was – and still is – to discover that place.'

'But you spent millions!'

'I spent nothing. My former colleagues are dead now but the consortium still exists, there are new members and they are greedy, it was their money. Personally I had no hope of recovering the paintings. Though I would have loved to see my favourite I was willing to let her go. Do you know who she is, by the way?'

'The Mona Lisa? No idea. I thought it was her name. I'm a mining engineer not an art critic.'

Wrong answer. Bar swivelled on the plastic chair and glared.

'I find it shameful you think that as an engineer you can ignore the arts. In mines have you not seen crystals, things formed by nature? Have you not marvelled at their beauty?'

Spargo nodded.

'And is it not possible for man to reproduce such beauty in his works of art?'

'He can try.'

'But he does not succeed, is that what you are saying? You are wrong. With this particular portrait, man did succeed. The portrait is that of the wife of Francesco del Giocondo di Zandi, a prominent Florentine gentleman.'

'I know that, actually. They've just discovered that.'

'Oh? I think you will find the lady's identity has never seriously been in doubt. A few years ago papers were found that merely supported what many of us knew already.'

'You were telling me why you – they – went to so much expense searching the U-boat.'

'Very well. The consortium pledged that by the end of the Millennium they would recover all the works of art it was possible to recover. They failed, but that does not mean their quest stopped. I could not convince them that even if they could locate Theodor's boat, they would find nothing of value.'

'Even if you find the paintings in good shape there's nothing you can do with them. What's a buyer going to do, put it in a cellar and gloat over it?'

'Yes, that is exactly what they will do. For the Leonardo we have three serious buyers, one of whom is so serious he personally provided most of the exploration costs. It is the desire of the moth for the star, John Spargo. That's your poet Shelley, by the way. But I am sure you will not know that.'

'So you are blaming others. You're saying they forced you to do this.'

'Forced me? Nobody forces me. In this matter I merely act as a consultant, rather like yourself. For many years I believed my friend Theodor either completed his voyage or else he was at the bottom of the Atlantic. Did I tell you he was sailing to Argentina? He should have followed a course that took him north of your Shetland Islands and into the Atlantic. I thought he had succeeded and for many years I attempted to trace him in South America. Eventually I had to accept that his submarine did not complete its journey.'

'Kalman said the consortium had been looking for it for years.'

'Not actively. We looked into reports of newly discovered wrecks. I took little notice of this one because Theodor should not have been so far off course. As it became more and more likely this wreck was Theodor's submarine I had to ask myself why he had deviated so greatly.'

'With just a few paintings and Göring's dinner service.'

Bar laughed, his gruff bark degrading into the sharp, hacking cough.

'Precisely, John Spargo. My colleagues loaded many of the Reichsmarschall's belongings on the boat, but my six were the only ones protected properly. His estate was in disarray and they were not missed. We needed to add credibility to our little venture, making naval officials believe that requisitioning the vessel was undertaken with the Reichsmarschall's authority. They had to believe it would be used to transport him to a place of safety.

'The work was carried out in secrecy. The vessel did not officially exist. Early this year I saw a video made by Kalman. Though the submarine he was exploring had no deck gun and no torpedo tubes, I was still unsure. Several submarines had been converted in this way to carry cargo and fuel.'

'The U-boat sank miles from here. What brought you to Kilcreg?'

'I think you know the answer to that. Do Theodor's writings not explain these things? Have you not made the connection yourself?'

'My father and Volker were both mining engineers.'

Bar nodded. 'As I said, you know the reason. Theodor and I spent many weeks together. He told me of the time he visited Scotland, of the Kilcreg mine and of Samuel Spargo. After seeing Robert Kalman's videotape I told the consortium what I knew about Samuel. They persuaded me to investigate things further and so Ian Letchie was hired. I believed he was working for me – for Luis – but later I discovered I was being bypassed. Letchie was cheating, John Spargo. He was sending information directly to my Consortium associates behind my back. Because I did not pursue the Kilcreg aspects of this business enthusiastically they did not trust me, they constantly checked up on me.'

'Are they holding Jez, is that what you're saying? What good can it possibly do?'

'I do not know the answer to either of your questions, but most probably you are right. They fear I have given up looking and I am guessing your daughter is to be insurance for both you and I to continue. The boxes I am looking for, John Spargo… where could they be? Might they have been taken into the mine?'

'If that's where you are thinking of looking then think again. There is no mine. The pumps, the cage, the steelwork and timber were all stripped out. Most of the workings were below the water table, so when the pumps were turned off they flooded. The old mineshaft was capped with concrete and the buildings demolished, all except the mine house and this place. Thanks to you the mine house has now gone.'

'That was Luis. He made the decision.'

'I'm sorry. I assumed he was only obeying orders.'

Bar glared. 'There are some aspects of your British humour I do not find amusing. So, John Spargo… if not the mine, then where else could they be? Tell me about your father's friends.'

'He knew everyone for miles. He was on councils and committees, he was a well-connected, popular man. Don't even suggest we start looking for his friends. If any are still alive they'll be over one hundred. That's even older than you. Possibly.'

'You have balls, John Spargo, I'll give you that. I had you down as a wimp – do we still use that expression? I should have known better, you come from good stock. Now, tell me about the other houses in Kilcreg.'

'They're small. Most have changed hands since I lived here. They have been altered, they have had central heating put in, they have been rewired and re-plumbed. If the boxes were hidden in any of them they would have been found by now. My father was an honest man. If he had been given crates he would have taken them to the authorities. If what you say is true – '

'Stop saying that. I have told you I will not lie to you.'

'– if what you say is true and you did take these paintings, perhaps that is exactly what happened. My father would have handed the crates to the authorities and they handed them quietly back to France. God knows what deals went on back then.'

Again Bar went quiet. 'No,' he said eventually. 'That did not happen.'

'You can't be sure.'

'I cannot be sure, no. But until I prove otherwise I must assume the boxes came ashore. I must assume Samuel Spargo concealed them in the same way he concealed the box with Theodor's writings. Do you not agree with me?'

CHAPTER THIRTY-NINE

A PAIR OF OIL LAMPS hang from the roof beams of the barrack hut. The man in the overcoat strides to the first of these, reaches up and turns up the wick. The room brightens slightly. He does the same to the other but its glass is blackened and emits no more light than before. Walter, still sprawled in the armchair, regards the man with interest. He sits up straight. The officer salutes him.

'Herr Oberführer, forgive the intrusion.'

The interfering man is Gestapo, of that Theo is sure. After adjusting the lamps he walks casually to the stove and holds out his gloved hands as if warm them. Half-turning he looks at Theo and Walter.

'A cosy family gathering, Oberführer. Close the door, soldier, we must keep out the cold. The boy's mother is here? Yes?'

Peter, at the log pile, lifts a log with both hands and holds it up. The man takes it, and with his free hand he opens the stove and drops the log in. Orange sparks rise high. He reaches down and holds Peter's hand.

'A fine young man,' he says, turning to Walter. 'Very trusting. The boy is yours?'

Walter is standing now and Theo watches him anxiously. Hopes for Peter's sake Walter stays calm.

Walter says 'The boy is mine.'

Theo frowns. No doubt Walter has reasons for his lie. Perhaps he believes his high rank will have influence.

'You have permits of course? A permit to move this child? You have clearance to bring him on to military property?'

'This works is under the control of the SS,' Walter says. 'I am sure you know that.'

'But this barrack hut is army property, is it not? Again I ask you: when you presented yourselves at the guardhouse, did you declare the child?'

'I did not think it necessary.'

The man walks around the room, glancing in corners and behind beds. 'Tell me why are you here, Oberführer.'

'I cannot. It is SS business, Herr...?'

'Grünbaum. Kriminalinspektor Grünbaum. And your name, Oberführer?'

'I am sure you know it already.'

'Indeed I do, Oberführer Wolff.'

Grünbaum stoops, picks up another log and holds it out to Peter. 'Here, boy, take this to your father.'

Peter takes the log. Walter takes a step forwards and holds out his hand. At first Peter heads for him but at the last moment he changes direction and runs to Theo, the log clamped to his chest with both arms. At any other time Theo would have hugged him.

Grünbaum forces a tight, thin lipped smile.

'He is young,' Walter says. 'He does not understand.'

'Oberführer, do not insult my intelligence.'

Grünbaum picks Peter up and carries him to the stove. Theo darts forward but is grabbed by the soldiers. Walter moves fast, elbows the soldiers aside, snatches Peter from Grünbaum and hands him to Theo.

'The child is my aide's son. For reasons I do not have to explain to you there are no papers for him. I possess documents that cover this situation adequately but they are not for your eyes. I demand you take me to the senior SS officer.'

The army officer walks to Walter, tips his head in a barely noticeable nod and speaks quietly, his voice a whisper.

'I apologise, Herr Oberführer. Your pistol, please!'

Walter shakes his head and stares theatrically, an overdone expression of disbelief.

'You must be out of your mind!' Instead of complying he buttons his tunic and goes for his cap. 'Are you willing to arrest a Schutzstaffel major-general on the say-so of this fool?'

Grünbaum picks up Walter's briefcase, flips its catch and looks inside.

'Leave that! You have no right!'

Walter, for all his strutting and bluster, knows he has failed. Theo, his arms gripped by two soldiers, is powerless. Out in the snow they walk side by side like prisoners, Peter up high on Theo's shoulders. The soldiers stroll behind them, their rifles held casually. Taking up the rear, riding in the back of a small open car driven by the army officer, is Grünbaum.

Back in the admin block the soldiers leave their captives with Grünbaum in a sparsely-furnished, ill-lit room. Walter and Grünbaum sit opposite each other at a grey metal desk while Peter, with Theo close by, finds a corner to sit in.

Grünbaum is well informed. He knows everything they have done at Monowitz since they arrived.

'Lying to me is pointless, Oberführer. I know why you are here.'

'If you already know everything then I see no reason to go through this charade.'

'You came here with paintings in wooden cases. You have arranged to have them sealed in metal boxes and protected by rubber. Why is that?'

Walter is nervous. To stop his hands shaking he clamps one over the other. Theo notices. Grünbaum does not.

'I am not authorised to say. Whoever passed this information to you has committed a treasonable offence. The fact you have repeated it to me makes you as guilty as him. I insist you allow me to call Munich.'

Grünbaum doesn't listen. He reaches across the desk to where the army officer placed Walter's briefcase, drags it towards him and upends it on the desk. Its contents, a mass of papers, folders and stapled documents, slither into a pile. Some papers slide off the desk and travel across the floor as if sliding on ice.

Walter tries again. 'You are making a serious mistake. Your career in the Staatspolitzei is over, you do understand? As of this moment you are finished!'

Theo watches anxiously as Peter shuffles across the floor, picks up the papers and starts putting them back on the table.

'However,' Walter continues, looking at the boy but talking to Grünbaum, 'You are a good servant of the Reich and I understand your concern in these matters. In fact, it is commendable you have acted in the way you have done and for this reason I am willing to overlook your foolishness. That is on the condition you overlook my slight transgression in the case of the child.'

It as if Grünbaum doesn't hear him. The man selects papers at random, unfolding and reading them. One takes his attention and without any comment he jumps up, opens an inner door and hurries from the room.

'This is Heiss's work!' Walter says as the door is closing. 'I'll kill that bastard!'

'Will you get the chance? What will become of us, Walter?'

Walter's confidence has taken a beating. As Grünbaum's footsteps fade away Walter opens the door wider. Sees Grünbaum enter a room at the end of a corridor.

'Theodor, I cannot say. You must tell them everything. You must say you were on leave and you were abducted by a senior Luftwaffe officer and taken to the Air Ministry in Berlin. Tell them whatever they want to know about Carinhall, omit nothing. You now understand why I refused to answer your questions. You are not part of this. I should not have involved you – tell them that too if you wish, tell them everything you know. You will not be betraying me. It is I who has betrayed you.'

Questions fill Theo's head. Walter's words come as a surprise but he suspects he will be accused of treason anyway. At Carinhall he could easily have voiced his suspicions to Kropp. Even to the Reichsmarschall himself.

'What will happen to Peter?'

Walter sits down and stares at the half-open door. It is a question he does not want to answer. When Grünbaum returns he enters the room quietly, closes the door and sits down in his chair. He places the paper he took with him flat on the desk and looks down at it, as if reading it. To Theo it looks like a list.

'There has been a mistake,' Grünbaum says quietly. 'I have been misinformed. Please forgive me and accept my apology.' He lifts his head for barely one second, catches Walter's eye and looks down again. 'I will of course overlook the presence of the child and ensure you are not troubled again. Is there is anything I can do for you? Anything you need? You would like women? I can arrange such things.'

Theo sighs inwardly. His shoulders sag, his breathing and heartbeat return to normal. Walter sits silently for what feels like an age. When he speaks he stays calm. Doesn't curse and threaten as Theo expected.

'Can you find Hauptsturmführer Ortmann for me?'

'Of course, Herr Oberführer, anything you wish. He is a friend, perhaps?'

'He was posted to one of the camps here.'

'If he is here then I will find him. In the meantime I will have my driver take you to your hut. It is a bleak place they have given you, Herr Oberführer. Can I not take you to the officer's mess? Or, if you wish, I can arrange accommodation for all of you at a hotel in Auschwitz, we have a place in the town reserved for visiting officers of high rank such as yourself. It is not far from here. I will take you there myself, you will be well received.'

'That will not be necessary. I have paperwork to attend to, the hut is ideal. Besides, it would be better for you if the boy is not seen by others.'

Grünbaum makes an awkward attempt to organise Walter's papers.

'Leave them,' Walter says. 'I will do it. Locate Hauptsturmführer Ortmann for me. Firstly, drive us to our hut.'

The temperature outside is fifteen below zero. Despite the cold, Walter looks hot and disturbed. Back in the hut he walks to a bed and empties his briefcase on to it.

'I've been a damn fool,' he says. 'That bastard could have called any one of several telephone numbers on these papers, he could even have called Carinhall. Instead he chose – thank god – to call the first number on the first paper he found. It is the number of a friend of mine in Munich, one of the very few people who are party to this business. Open the stove for me, Theodor. It is time I burned papers.'

Grünbaum returns shortly. This time he knocks on the door and waits to be invited inside.

'Herr Oberführer, forgive the intrusion, I have good news, I have found your friend Ortmann. He apologises and says he is busy – I am sure you are aware of our problems, it is said the Soviets are less than two days away. At night, when it is quiet, we can hear gunfire. All of this means the Hauptsturmführer and his colleagues have much work to do.'

'He will not see me?'

'He will, of course, but when his work is done. He asks that you visit him at the SS barracks – ' he glances at his wristwatch '– at eleven o'clock. That is two hours from now. Do you know the barracks? Can I oblige with directions?'

Walter hands Grünbaum a pencil and pad. The man sketches a map and then leaves, backing out as if in the presence of royalty. When he has gone Walter slumps on to one of the beds.

'Gunfire, Theodor? Are the Soviets really so close?'

Shortly before eleven Walter hauls himself up from his bed and buttons his tunic, tugging at its hem in an attempt to hide creases. Theo watches him fasten the top button of his shirt, tie his tie, then position his cap neatly on his head.

'There is a mirror in the washroom.'

'What the hell would I want with a mirror?'

'Your cap isn't on square. I thought you'd like to know that.'

Walter grunts. Still standing he lifts his left foot, twists it to one side and polishes the toe of his boot on the back of his trouser leg. He does the same with the other one.

'There is a hand brush beside the stove,' he says to Theo. 'Get it and brush down my uniform.'

Theo doesn't move. Walter waits, walks to the stove, picks up the brush, bangs its bristles on the floor and starts brushing himself down with it. Theo takes the brush from him and takes over the brushing.

'I never thought of you as vain.'

'Some of us have standards to uphold.'

'Some of us fight for our country. We do not have time for such pomp.'

They set off in the truck with Theo driving, Walter sits upright, mannequin-like beside him. Peter is again on the floor, rolled in the quilt and sleeping deeply. This time there is no need for Walter's pills.

Grünbaum's map proves invaluable. The site is in blackout, there are no lights and many turnings. At military checkpoints the mere mention of the name Kriminalinspektor Grünbaum gets them waved through without fuss.

'Cross the railway,' Walter says. 'Then turn right.'

Despite the blackout elsewhere the railway yards are lit brightly and there is much movement. Wagons coupling and uncoupling. Men working.

'Slow down,' Walter grumbles. 'Or you will kill us all.'

In the poor light Theo sees, ahead of him, what appears to be a tunnel. As he gets closer he realises it is an arch in a long wall. Above it, and to either side of it, are windows. It is a watchtower, of sorts.

'Do I drive through the arch?'

Walter leans forward and peers through the windscreen. 'Not unless this truck has railway wheels.' He studies the paper Grünbaum gave him. 'According to this scribble the SS barracks are off to the right. There is still some way to go. Keep driving.'

Theo was expecting more barrack huts. What they eventually come to are substantial brick buildings that remind Theo of those at Potsdam. Walter's friend is waiting at the main entrance, and as the truck approaches he comes down the wide steps. Walter jumps down and runs to him. There is laughing, swearing and back-slapping. He grabs the man's arm and hauls him to the cab. Theo has the cab door open and they both look up at him.

'Manfred my friend, my driver is the distinguished submariner Theodor Volker, he is my aide. Do not worry, he will not be trampling through your rooms in his disgusting boots. He will not be staying with us. He has other matters to attend to.'

Ortmann has been drinking. He looks Theo up and down. Realising he is an officer he decides to salute him.

'A submariner, yes, poor bastard. And I thought this place was a shit posting!'

The two men walk away. After a few steps Walter turns, calling to Theo that there is no need for him to return, that his good friend Manfred will provide transport.

'Tomorrow morning,' he shouts. 'So do not wait up for me.'

More laughter. Theo knows these reunions, knows that by morning Walter will be unable to stand up.

Seeking somewhere to turn the truck, Theo drives on. The road he is on is narrow and has been cleared of snow, it is piled high on one side of the road. When his headlights allow, he gets glimpses, over the snow piles, of snow clad, flat fields. His view in the other direction is obscured by a high mesh fence laced with snow.

Whoever cleared the road went only so far. Faced with a wall of snow across the road Theo slithers to a stop. There is nowhere to go. In a rare moment of despair he holds his head in his hands. To reverse such a long distance is impossible, his mirrors are iced up and behind him is blackness. Despite this he attempts, and fails, to turn the truck in the road. With the truck jammed at an angle he sees in its headlights something he missed before – a gap in the fence.

The gap is deliberate, torn down to allow access. Beyond the gap are the remains of long barrack huts, some with no roofs, others with broken walls. Timbers from them have been stacked for removal. Theo eased the truck through the gap. The wind has risen and snow starts to drift, it lifts from the ground, skimming along it like windblown sand. The truck's wipers have trouble coping, they judder and bend.

Still there is nowhere to turn. Now on the inside of the fence and no longer on a road, Theo keeps going. It is a low-gear grind through deep snow. Instead of finding what he hopes for – another gap in the fence – a second fence closes in on the other side of the track. The track is not made for vehicles this size and the further he drives the narrower it becomes, he is sandwiched between them. This second fence, he realises, has close-strung barbed wire on tall concrete posts. Some of the posts have unlit electric lamps with curved, vulture-neck brackets.

The truck slithers sideways. Though its headlights are masked, the blanket of unblemished snow reflects their light and Theo sees the posts clearly, sees clusters of brown ceramic pots. Electrical insulators. The fences are electrified. If the truck slides again, if it touches the wire, he and his boy will die. He grips the steering wheel more firmly than ever and drives on, slowly and nervously. Inside the second fence there are more huts. Like the others, they are deserted.

The fences have gone; though all is still white, deep snow has been cleared; to the left side of the truck is the long building Theo saw when he arrived, he is on the other side of it and in his path, some way ahead, is the rail track that runs through the arch. It is brighter here; far to his right are railway sidings, brightly lit.

As he gets close to the railway lines he brakes gently. The wheels of the truck lock and it slides forwards, coming to a stop with its front wheels on the track. He tries to back up but the wheels spin and the truck slips sideways. From the back comes a hammering sound he's not heard before, a hammering that continues even when he turns off the engine. In a frosted side mirror he can just make out the dark shape of a man – a soldier – hitting the truck's side with the butt of a rifle.

Peter, swaddled in quilt, stirs but does not wake. Now there are two soldiers banging, one on at each door. One clambers up to the cab and grabs the door handle.

'You damn fool! Open this door!'

Theo does as the man asks. The soldier sees Theo's cap, takes his hand off the door handle and snaps to attention.

'At your orders, Kapitän. I beg your pardon, I did not realise. With respect, a train is about to leave…'

With the door open Theo can see more clearly. A locomotive is hooked-up to wagons and is coming towards him out of the sidings. Thankfully it is moving slowly, hauling a train. Smoke and steam roar as wheels seek to grip.

The two soldiers stand at the front of the truck, leaning back on it in a feeble attempt to move it off the tracks. Theo restarts the engine. This time the wheels grip.

Panic over, the soldiers light cigarettes. As the train approaches they remain at the front of the truck, warming themselves on the radiator. The locomotive moves steadily, its funnel blasting sparks in a firefly cloud. The train is long and it kinks, snakelike, rattling over points. It straightens up, aligning itself with the arch. The engine is a Kreigslok; Theo allows himself a smile.

The soldiers had been justifiably angry; the train of wagons pass barely one metre in front of Theo's truck. He imagines the look on

Walter's face if his SS colleagues had to tell him his truck had been hit by a train. Such an event would normally be no laughing matter. But in these dark times there is humour in so many things.

His smile stays for a while as if locked there. It fades when he realises the open wagons contain not goods but people, people packed so tightly they cannot sit down. Floodlights on the watchtower come on, and in their light Theo sees the scene clearly. Most of the passengers – if anyone travelling in these conditions can be called a passenger – are women, though there are children, too. All have shaved heads and all wear striped clothes resembling thin smocks; some stare absently at the truck with eyes deep in their sockets. The skin on their faces is stretched thin, like canvas. Theo wants to look away but finds he cannot.

Theo has seen death, he has seen those he worked with ripped apart by gunfire and blown apart by bombs. But this? Can people look like this and still live?

His fingers tighten on the wheel. His knuckles are white, his teeth clenched. He has bitten his lip and can taste blood in his mouth. He nods to himself. There is an easy explanation. This is a refugee camp and these are its inmates, Polish peasants driven from their land by enemies of the Reich.

For the first time in his life he believes in his leaders. If this is an example of what the Soviets can do then the Führer was right to invade them. Though he blanches at the sight of the wretches in the wagons he knows that transporting them in this way is for their own good. The Soviets are close; the only way to get these people to safety before they arrive is to move them like this.

The train drifts slowly from sight, under the brick arch like a snake with its victims. As the two soldiers move away from the front of the truck one nips the burning end of his cigarette, opens the top pocket of his tunic and slips it inside. The other man waves to Theo, salutes, draws a large circle in the air with his arm and then points up ahead: start your engine and move away now…

Theo slides a window open and calls to the man. He asks the best way to the road and the man points. There is a second archway, one Theo didn't notice.

'Cross the line here, Kapitän,' the man says, pointing down. 'There is a ramp under the snow. It is why you slipped when you stopped.'

Theo thanks him, slides the window closed and then opens it again. Calls out.

'Soldier, what is this place?'

Appearing not to understand the question, the man frowns. Not only is this naval officer lost, he is also stupid. He shakes his head.

'This is Birkenau, Kapitän,' the man replies. 'It is Auschwitz number two.'

Theo, no wiser, returns the man's salute. Easing the truck forwards he crosses the track and makes for the second arch. Soon he is back on good roads.

At the sound of Theo's voice Walter looks up from his bed. He curses, holds his head and curses again. He is still in uniform, still in his shoes. One hour after dawn he arrived in the back of a military staff car and was carried to the bed by two uniformed SS men. Now he blinks constantly as he fights to get his bearings. Finally he drags his legs off the bed and sits on the edge of it, ruffling his hair, scratching his head with both hands.

'Soldiers brought breakfast from the mess,' Theo says. 'Sausage and coffee. You want some?'

Steadying himself with both hands, Walter shoves himself up off the bed. He stands, shakily. Then sits down again, heavily.

'Must get out, Theodor. Last night I learned the Soviets have taken Krakau – that's only fifty kilometres east of here. The camps here are being evacuated.' He stands again, this time managing to balance. 'Get the boy. Pack the bags. Load the truck and drive to Heiss.'

He sits down again. Falls back on the bed. Theo leaves him, goes to his own bed and stuffs clothes into bags. He lifts Peter, and with the boy under one arm and his kitbag under the other he goes out to the truck. After stowing Peter safely in the cab he starts the engine. He returns, immediately, for Walter.

The high doors of the grey building are open. Blown snow covers part of its floor and Theo drives right in. The place looks deserted, there is no sign of Heiss or the soldiers. Walter forces himself to concentrate, sobering up quickly when he sees, propped against one wall, what appear to be flat slabs of black rubber. He walks unsteadily over to them and gestures to Theo.

'Over here, come, there are crates. Back the truck over here.'

Theo obeys. Like Walter, he assumes the crates containing the paintings have been sealed in bronze boxes and dipped in, or sprayed with, black rubber. The coating is smooth and number codes have been embossed in one corner. He attempts to lift one of them but he cannot. Walter walks away, talking loudly.

'Where has the fool put the rest of them? Help me, Theodor! We have no time!'

With Walter cursing constantly they search the building, but there is no sign of the others. Walter checks the embossed codes against those on his papers.

'At least the man started in the correct order,' he mumbles. 'These are most important ones.'

Walter wants to look elsewhere, wants to search other buildings. Theo reminds him it is he who wanted to leave the place quickly. Soon they are struggling with the black slabs, resting them on the truck's tailgate, heaving them up and sliding them in. The effort is too much for Walter and he steps away, takes a deep breath, doubles over and vomits.

'My pocket…' he says. 'Top pocket...' Theo undoes the button for him, lifts the flap and takes out a tightly folded paper. 'It is a movement permit for Peter Volker, signed by Manfred's Deputy Commandant. It will suffice. Take good care of it.'

Theo takes it and unfolds it. Muttering his thanks he places it with his own papers. His boy is legal. If they are stopped he can say Peter's other papers were burnt in a bombing raid.

They drive away through fine, drifting snow that blows from between buildings, twisting serpent-like along the Monowitz roads as if racing the truck. The cab is warm. Snowflakes touch the windscreen, they melt and vanish.

'I saw a train last night in that camp you were in.'

'I wasn't in a camp. I was in the SS barracks.'

'I went further. I needed a place to turn. There were people in open rail trucks.'

'Refugees. You saw similar trucks when we came through Dresden.'

It was true. He had seen people crammed into trucks with no room for baggage. They had looked bulky in their thick clothing, some wrapped with sacking to help keep out the cold. Walter had laughed at them and said they were Poles.

'These people didn't look like those we saw at Dresden. They had thin prison clothes. They were freezing.'

Heiss had said there were work camps. Work camps were nothing unusual. There were camps in the dockyards for prisoners of war who repaired bomb damage and cleared harbour roads. Last night there were women and children. Children like Peter. All with shaven heads.

'There were electric fences.'

'Then you were lucky you didn't touch them.'

'There were SS guards. They weren't regular army. And I heard dogs.'

'Even refugees must be kept under control.'

'They looked close to death. Did the Russians do that to them? Did they starve them?'

'For god's sake! Look where you are driving! Switch on the wipers!'

'I want to know who they were. I want to know why they are here.'

'Believe me, you do not. Just drive, Theodor. When you reach checkpoints keep going. They are abandoned.'

Theo heads for the road they came in on. The few houses they pass are quiet and despite the extreme cold their front doors are open. The railway yards are strangely silent. Theo swings the wheel and puts his foot to the boards.

🚂

Some of the bodies Theo sees by the roadside have striped clothing. Most have been stripped naked, their clothes taken by others. Skeletal, huddled bodies line roadside ditches and stain the snow red. Have the Soviets been this way already? He knows how it is done: enemy scouting parties advance along highways, they shoot up everything and then double back.

Theo, forced by the snow to drive slowly, stares out at the corpses. He knows he is finding excuses. The Soviets have not come this way, they did not do these things. These people are the Reich's undesirables, the Jews and the Gypsies, the resettled peoples - peoples deported, exiled, enslaved and starved. He shakes his head.

Walter has been dozing. He wakens and attempts to focus.

'What is it? Why so slow?'

Theo points. Before he stopped counting he had seen fifty bodies. Now there are more in the distance.

'They are dead,' Walter says. 'You have seen dead men before. Drive faster. We do not have time for this dawdling.'

'They are not men. They are women and children. My god, Walter! Look at them!'

'But they are dead all the same. Dead like we will be if the Soviets catch up with us. I might only have six paintings in this truck, Theo, but I do not intend to hand them over to uniformed Russian peasants.'

He slumps back, asleep again.

Theo ponders Walter's words. In a way he is right. There is nothing to be done but to drive. He speeds up. Changes through the gears.

There are more bodies now, scattered as if dropped from the sky. In a copse of trees he sees ten... twenty... forty. He loses count. Such carnage is beyond belief and to cope with it he pretends they're not people. Is that how the guards at the camp feel about these wretches? Is that how they cope with such hell?

He shakes his head. His comparisons are odious, cowardly. These were people, human beings like himself, like Erica, like Peter. He looks down at his boy, sleeping as always. He touches his pocket to check his papers, and Peter's, are there. Feels the flat bulge.

Ahead is a convoy, moving slowly, three trucks at least. Theo reaches it and fits in behind. Walter should be navigating, but in his condition there is no chance of that. Theo takes his eyes off the road for no more than a second as he reaches for the map, and in that second the truck in front stops and Theo stamps on the brakes. Walter, slumped in the corner of the cab, falls forwards, down onto Peter who stirs, emerges from the quilt and – unseen by Theo – clambers onto the seat.

The convoy moves again, travelling at walking pace it blocks most of the road. Theo pulls out to see past it but sees only people, they are strung out along the road as far as he can see. As the convoy approaches they move to the roadside, a ripple of movement that starts at the rear and rolls forwards. Uniformed guards converge on those that fall.

The trucks pull out to pass the procession. Theo, not part of the convoy, hangs back.

To move their charges the guards use whips and batons; one draws an automatic pistol and fires two shots into a group. Four women fall and he fires again, this time at those who help. Two more fall. Theo, stunned by what he sees, realises Peter is at the window, watching. Walter, wakened by the gunfire, shoves the boy down.

'For god's sake, Walter!' Theo says. 'Those are SS men! You outrank them all, you can stop them!'

'It is none of my business.'

'Even I outrank the bastards!'

Theo is shouting now, he has his side window open but it isn't enough. He knocks the truck out of gear, pulls on the handbrake and is about to open his door when Walter hauls him back. There are more gunshots, this time from behind the truck, all evenly spaced and deliberate. Theo turns on Walter.

'You knew about this! You knew!'

'Release the handbrake. Move on. If you don't then this rabble will be all over the road again.'

'You knew!'

'Where have you been all these years?'

'You know damn well where I've been!'

'None of this is our concern. It is not our place to judge the decisions made by our leaders.'

'You are a bloody hypocrite! You rob the bastards one minute and the next you make excuses for their crimes.'

Walter, avoiding Theo's eyes, looks ahead. 'You are being beckoned. The trucks have pulled in to let you pass. Stop being so self-righteous and drive!'

An SS man waves them on. As they drive slowly past him Walter opens his window and calls to him. There is laughter. The window slides closed.

'He said don't bother to sound your horn. If you hit a few of them you will save him a job.'

The handbrake is on again. Theo flicks up the door catch and is halfway out of the cab when Walter lunges at him and locks his arm with a frighteningly strong grip. Theo hears the click of a safety catch. Walter's Mauser jabs into his neck.

'You leave now and I'll blow your head off. Do you want to end up in a ditch like these wretches? Do you think these ghouls whipping them care about human life? You will get a bullet in your head and so will your boy. If I am lucky they will spare me – but only because I outrank them. My bet is they will kill all three of us, it is easier that way. Nobody will know. Nobody will care.'

Theo, shocked, drives on. What he sees can surely be nothing to do with the war he's been fighting. Food is short for everyone, but deliberate starvation? They must want these people to die.

Memories click together. Things are making sense. He sees shaven heads and he remembers his bosun's old sea boots, remembers how his crew laughed when the soles came loose. Remembers, also, how they went quiet when they saw that the insulation that kept their feet warm was human hair.

He feels nauseous. He will remember this day for ever, the shame, the disgust and revulsion, not for the prisoners but for those that have done this thing. What he is seeing will never leave him. It will be in his dreams.

'Peter! Get down!'

The boy is at the window again, watching the procession of misery – the men, the women and children who drift past in silence, who turn to him and stare with unseeing eyes. The boy obeys his father and slips down to the floor. He snuggles down on the cab floor and is soon asleep.

CHAPTER FORTY

OSCAR BAR TALKED ON. He had a tale to tell and a captive audience – of one – to tell it to. Hardly in a position to protest, Spargo listened.

'I am cold!' Bar snapped. He picked up the torch and shone it around the room as if to find a solution. 'Where is that damned man, he has been gone for two hours!'

Bar, expecting to gloat over paintings he'd expected to find in the mine house, had jetted-in for the day. Not expecting to stay he hadn't bothered to equip himself for cold weather. Now he drew his coat around him. Doubled it over at the front.

'Perhaps you should have thought about heating before you started all this,' Spargo said. 'Benares won't find anything. Even if he drives to Thurso he'll find nowhere open.'

'That is unhelpful,' Bar said. The torch beam found a rusting hurricane lamp standing on a shelf in a corner. 'That thing…'

'I've checked it. No fuel.'

Bar looked from the lamp to the bare mattress and then to the sleeping bag. It had been flipped base-over-top by Spargo. Bar wagged a finger.

'What is that?'

'It's a sleeping bag. All mod cons. Your friend thinks of everything.'

'He thinks of nothing. That carrier bag, bring it to me.' Spargo eased himself up, went for the bag and placed it on the table. Bar shone the torch into it and took out a bottle, cursing in Spanish as he examined its label. 'A Rioja from a second rate bodega… though in this godforsaken place that should not surprise me. My hands are arthritic, John Spargo, I am cursed by old age. You will find in the bag two wine glasses and a corkscrew. Open the bottle for me and fill the glasses. I apologise in advance for the inferior quality of the wine and the fact it will be unpalatably cold.'

Spargo had no wish to drink with the man, but nor did he want to upset him. He did as he was asked, extracted two tissue-wrapped glasses from the bag and set them down. The corkscrew wasn't needed, the bottle had a screw cap. Spargo half-filled each glass and slipped one of them across the table to Bar, who nursed the glass in his hands. When he finally took a sip his grimace said everything.

The door rattled. The old counting house had never been proof against draughts and fifty years of neglect hadn't helped. Wind found its way around the door and the boarded-up windows; the loose kapok insulation swung gently in the unsteady air.

Bar said, 'You mentioned Carinhall. What do you know of that place?'

'It was Göring's hunting lodge.'

'It was where he kept his best art pieces – bought at gunpoint as you so rightly said. Towards the end of the war I was at that place. Did I tell you this? Theodor Volker was with me. I had successfully passed myself off as what you might nowadays call a logistics expert. I fixed things, I moved things around. I provided Theodor with the uniform of a Luftwaffe officer and papers to say he was my aide.'

'Volker mentions the Friedrichstrasse in Berlin, is that where you met him? Is that when he offered to help you?'

Bar put the glass to his lips. He sipped. Grimaced again.

'Theodor offered nothing. He and I went to the same school, did he write that in his precious books? My parents moved away and he and I lost contact. Many years later, when my colleagues and I were planning to relieve the Reichsmarschall of some of his art, I learned my old friend had become a submarine commander. I needed someone I could trust and I had him brought to me. I explained what I wanted but he refused to co-operate. I found it necessary to blackmail him.'

'Something you seem particularly good at.'

Bar took another sip and put the glass down.

'Do not underestimate me, John Spargo, I do not take kindly to such criticism. You cannot even imagine what life was like in those days. Theodor was married, he had a child. Early in the war his wife moved to Hamburg. Do you know all of this? Did he write these things?'

'Not all of it.'

'His wife was killed in an air raid but the child survived, it was taken by relatives to their farm in the south of Germany. I knew Theodor was attempting to visit him. I also knew he would not get there because there were no trains.'

'You said you blackmailed him.'

'At the time I did not consider it to be blackmail. We had ways of getting things done and having a hold over a person was only one of those ways. As I told you, it was nearing the end of the war, we all knew that. Göring was planning to move his treasures to Berchtesgaden near the Austrian border.'

'The Berghof. Hitler's Eagle's Nest.'

'You are not quite correct. But yes, it was near that place. The treasures were crated and I assisted with the arrangements. I offered to take Theodor to see his son on the condition he worked for me.'

'And did he do what you told him to do? Thirteen pieces of silver.'

'I think you will find it is thirty pieces… however, I told you I blackmailed him, not that I bribed him.'

'Same thing.'

'No it is not. Perhaps you will tell me what would you have done in the same circumstances?'

'Hypothetical question. Ridiculous question, actually.'

'No, again you are wrong. Theodor Volker was willing to risk everything for a chance to visit his child. A short visit is all I offered, there was no time for longer. The Allies were advancing from the south and would soon overrun us. We believed they would raze Germany to the ground and slaughter us all. That was the propaganda. We did not know if it was true or false.'

'Why are you telling me this?'

'Because your present circumstances are not dissimilar. You are convinced I have your daughter. I am wondering what lengths you might go to in exchange for her safety.'

'If you haven't got her then what's the point?'

'Given the right motivation I might be able to influence those who have taken her.'

'I've told you already that I will do anything. Who is she with? What will they do to her?'

'My belief is that members of the consortium have your daughter. I have told you they are impatient, they say I have made promises I have not kept. I have been accused of procrastinating and keeping things from them. These accusations are true. There are things they have no right to know. Things I shall never tell them.'

He took a gulp of wine and slapped the glass back on the table. It startled Spargo. Made him jump.

'I don't see how they can put pressure on you by kidnapping Jez.'

'Oh, they can, John Spargo. Believe me, they can.'

Spargo swivelled around and reached for the sleeping bag. 'You are cold,' he said. 'Do you want this?' Without waiting for an answer he dragged the bag from the bed and draped it around Bar's shoulders. Bar didn't protest.

'Tell me,' Bar said. 'Did Theodor write in his journals what we saw when we went to the farm?'

'What farm?'

'At Ingolstadt. At the boy's grandparents' farm. They had found Theodor's boy in an orphanage in Hamburg. The farm was a squalid place and it stank. The man I saw there was old, he had no money and the farm was run down. Did Theodor admit in his writings that the boy was unwell and living like a pig?' Bar turned up his nose as he spoke. 'Did Theodor write that?'

Spargo wasn't sure it mattered. Far worse things happened back then. From what he had read about the dying throes of the Third Reich, the boy was lucky to have survived.

'Pour me more of that stuff,' Bar said. 'If nothing else it serves to quench my thirst.' Spargo poured, and handed back the glass. 'I told you I knew Theodor,' Bar continued. 'What I did not tell you was I was in his debt. When I was young he saved me from drowning.'

'I'm sorry to hear that.'

Bar lowered the glass and stared at Spargo with tired eyes. 'You are a less compassionate man than your father.'

'Leave my father out of this. You know nothing about him.'

'I have done my research. I told you already I know all about you and your family. Humour an old man, listen to what I have to say. Theodor and I were railway enthusiasts. What you English call train spotters.'

'I am Scottish.'

'Whatever. In school vacations we rode our bicycles to the railway yards at Braunschweig to watch the locomotives. When the weather was warm we would stop on the way home and swim in the canal. One day I was foolish. I swam beneath a barge and became entangled in ropes.'

'And Volker rescued you.'

Bar nodded, slowly. 'Theodor rescued me, yes. A brave but foolish gesture, he should have been more aware of the dangers. But clearly, if it were not for him I should not be here now. And please, John Spargo, refrain from making another of your cynical comments.'

'But he's not here, is he? He's dead. He must have been in that submarine. You sent the man who saved your life to his death for the price of a few paintings.'

Bar became animated, waving his arms and slopping the wine. He turned his head to one side and spat at the floor.

'You dare to say such things? What right have you to judge me? Theodor was thirty years old when he died and the world was at war.' Then, more calmly, 'I did not know he would die, he was a good man, it should not have happened. I told you we were friends and we went to the same school. When I was sixteen my father was appointed to an important post and we moved away. I did not see Theodor again until the end of the war.'

Bar sat quietly, thinking back, nursing his glass.

'The trains, John Spargo, I was telling you about trains. Göring was obsessed with them, did you know that? If I had realised Theodor still retained that particular boyish interest I might not have selected him to help me. When we arrived at Carinhall I took him to the railhead. I won't bore you with details but the Reichsmarschall took a shine to him. I will admit to you it was one of the worst moments of my life. We were grey men. We did not need such attention.

'Theodor spent the next day in the attic in the Reichsmarschall's mansion, playing with what he described as surely the most impressive model railway in Germany. Mercifully for both of us their discussions did not stray beyond the merits of different locomotives and Göring's collection of tobacco pipes.' Bar stopped, looked towards Spargo and frowned. 'Have I told you these things already?'

Spargo shook his head. He was tired and cold. His wound had stopped bleeding but the pain was still there. He no longer cared what Bar was saying.

'I'm sure Volker does mention some of these things in his journals.'

If Spargo hadn't been so cold he would have dozed off. The man was waffling now.

'The tobacco pipes, John Spargo… while they played trains the Reichsmarschall wanted to smoke. Theodor produced a lighter that didn't work and so Göring produced his own. He gave it to Theodor.'

Spargo stiffened. 'What lighter?'

'You are not listening to me! Göring gave Theodor his lighter! It was made of silver and gold! It was a valuable piece!'

Subconsciously Spargo slapped his pockets. The shell of the lighter was there, mixed with loose change and receipts. Surreptitiously he moved it from one pocket to another. But not surreptitiously enough.

'What do you have there? What is that?'

'Nothing.'

'Show me!'

Spargo took out the lighter and handed it over.

'Where did you get this?'

'Kalman.'

'Was it found on the submarine?'

'In the engine room.'

Bar rotated it, inspecting it. 'What else did the man give you?'

'Only that. He slipped it into my pocket without me knowing.'

'Why did he do that?'

'He must have realised I liked it.'

Bar grunted, sat upright, and pulled the sleeping bag tightly around him. He held the lighter in the torch beam so he could see it more clearly. 'The flint wore down,' he said, absently. 'And Theodor could not get any more of them. When he arrived at the farm he gave the lighter to his boy to play with. The child kept it with him at all times. He would not part with it. The trains, John Spargo. I was telling you about the trains…'

'You told me about them already.'

'I have not told you everything. The Reichsmarschall planned to move his treasures to the south in his private trains. You will have heard, I suspect, that the last of these journeys was a disaster. The train was abandoned in a tunnel to avoid attack from your bombers.'

'No, I haven't heard that. Were you and Volker on board?'

'Fortunately not. We were on an earlier train carrying paintings in wooden crates. At Neuhaus we transferred them to waiting lorries. Theodor assisted me, it was part of our agreement. I diverted to the farm and reunited him with his son.'

'So you said.'

'For me, travelling to the farm was a mistake, I lost three vital days. Did I tell you the wooden crates were unsuitable for a sea voyage? My colleagues made arrangements for them to be sealed inside bronze boxes. To do that we had to drive into Poland.'

'When was this?'

'Nineteen forty-five. January. Making the journey was a mistake. It was a wretched winter, the worst I have ever known. My friends and I had liberated twenty-eight of Göring's best paintings. Would you believe that while in Poland all but six of these were stolen from me?'

He laughed at his words. Wine slopped on to the sleeping bag and he looked down at it. Flipped it with his free hand.

'Stolen by your so-called friends?'

'I have no idea who stole them. Besides, there were other treasures on the submarine. I was not the only one removing Göring's art. When we eventually arrived in Hamburg with our six crates, others had already been stored on Theodor Volker's boat, though ours were the only ones so well protected. My colleagues were expecting me to accompany the cases on the submarine we had ready for Theodor but I could not do that. I had then, and I still have, a morbid fear of water and confined spaces, a legacy of the incident in the canal. In my place they put on board a Schutzstaffel officer, a pig of a man called Roth.'

'Schutzstaffel. That is SS.'

'Correct. Later I learnt Roth had in his belongings an explosive device he was supposed to wind like a clock every twenty four hours. My colleagues called it insurance. It is my belief something happened on the submarine to prevent Roth from winding his little clock.'

Spargo narrowed his eyes. 'You said earlier you weren't Luftwaffe. What were you, SS like Roth?'

Bar shrugged. 'Do not pretend to be surprised. You saw the photographs in my study. I instructed my maid to take them from the walls, I did not suppose for a moment she would then leave them where they might be seen.'

'I only looked at one. If you were in it I didn't recognise you.'

Bar dismissive it with a flick of his hand. 'It no longer matters.' He finished his drink and passed the empty glass to Spargo. Spargo picked up the bottle and tipped it. It was empty.

'You mentioned Poland,' he said. 'Why Poland?'

'You haven't been listening to me. I told you we took the crates to be sealed in bronze boxes. To be doubly sure they remained watertight they were to be encased in rubber. When we arrived at Monowitz... did I tell you about the factories there? Yes? When we arrived, the Soviets were very close.'

'What happened to Volker's boy, did he ever see him again?'

Bar looked away. 'The boy was sick, I told you that. Theodor wanted to take him with us. I told him it was not part of our deal.'

Spargo stood up, stretched his legs, walked to the door and stared out. The night was black, there was nothing to see.

'I don't understand why you are telling me this. Tell me about the translator, Lewis. What was he afraid of?'

'I did not know Lewis. I know nothing about him.'

'Someone who knew him said he was scared.'

'Is that so? As I said, I did not know the man. It was unfortunate for him he encountered Ian Letchie.'

'Lewis knew what it he was translating. He must have known Volker. It's my belief he was a member of Volker's crew.'

Bar, cocooned in the sleeping bag, had slumped down. Spargo's words alerted him and he sat upright again.

'Why do you think that? Did you meet with him before he died?'

Spargo hesitated; he had said too much; at least he'd had the sense not to mention Rydel.

'I didn't meet him. Letchie got to him first.'

'You are saying this man was in the Kriegsmarine? That he served with Theodor? Who told you this?'

'It's something I've learnt.'

'You mean like you learnt your two-times-table? This man Lewis, what is his first name?'

'Mark.'

'So, Mark Lewis. That is not a name I would have expected to have found in our military.' He laughed at his words.

'He must have changed his name.'

'Of course he changed his name. And because of that you cannot possibly have discovered Mark Lewis was a member of the boat's crew simply by reading Theodor's diaries because that name would not have been there. So where did you learn about Mr Lewis, John Spargo? Who have you spoken to?'

CHAPTER FORTY-ONE

KAPITÄNLEUTNANT VOLKER'S BOAT runs astern, into black water that stinks of spilled oil. There is no brass band on the quayside like in the old days and no women to throw flowers. A lone figure watches from the shadows, his hands in his pockets and his collar pulled high. As the vessel starts to turn he holds a hand up high, not a Nazi salute but a wave. A real wave, from Walter.

The wave goes unseen. Several hours ago, when both men parted, Walter gave no hint he would stay. Once the rubber-sealed crates had been transferred from the truck to the boat, Theo had walked away from him, angered he had been lied to yet again: Walter wasn't accompanying Theo on the voyage, it was never his intention. Nor was there any sign of Göring – not that Theo ever believed there would be.

After all the lies it came as a surprise to Theo that U-1500 actually existed, it was moored ready and waiting in the U-boat pens at Hamburg. That it was one of the only vessels undamaged by bombs was little short of miraculous.

Theo, on the boat's bridge, watches and listens. He has much on his mind. His new command is one of the Reich's biggest and newest. It is certainly one of the Reich's most peculiar.

'Forward now! Don't hit the jetty. Don't scratch my shiny new paint…'

Those on the bridge smile at the irony. Most of them know Volker, know that the state of the U-boat's paintwork is the last thing on his mind. Recent bombing raids have left wrecks in the Elbe. Navigating the river at night is hazardous, even more so at dusk.

The boat stops. Eases forwards. Starts a long, slow turn.

Standing beside Theo, the Chief Engineer relays his captain's words. His voice emerges from a speaking tube far below and men in dark coveralls obey him. The boat's twin diesels hesitate and then pick up speed. The throbbing of exhausts bounces back from the concrete quay and beats on the boat's steelwork. Makes eardrums pop. For a while the boat hangs in mid-channel. Its great bulk heels to one side like a wallowing whale and then straightens up gradually, increasing speed slowly.

Wallowing whale to sleek shark.

The exhaust smoke, thick and black, thins suddenly and the Chief Engineer peers through it, down to the deck to where the forward gun should be. Only its mountings are visible' in place of a 105mm cannon there is a neat ring of bolt holes.

Volker's boat is no shark. It is a fish without teeth.

'I do not understand, Kapitän.'

The Chief's breath hits the cold and it glows, lit from below by red lights. He stares questioningly at his captain. Not only is there no forward gun, the platform behind them – the high deck behind the bridge that they call the wintergarden – is empty except for a lookout leaning on its handrail. Its deck, too, has bolt-holes: the anti-aircraft gun that should be there is gone. The vessel is naked and vulnerable.

'What don't you understand, Chief?'

'We have no weapons. I am told the bow and aft torpedo tubes have been removed. I'm told Klaus has gone. And Bruno.'

'The weapons were not removed, they were never there. This boat was never meant to have armaments.'

The Chief Engineer, Leutnant Paul Lange, arrived days ago. Theo knows him, he is a good man. Not knowing when Theo would arrive, Lang did his work for him. He inspected the vessel, ran up the engines and checked the boat's systems.

'The changes in the forward torpedo room, Kapitän... the racks have been replaced by cabins. Who for?'

'For nobody Chief, not now. Roth tells me he has billeted himself there. That doesn't trouble me, he is well out of the way.'

'And the crates, Kapitän?'

Theo touches a finger to his lips. 'Precious cargo, Chief – not another word – even steel walls have ears…'

Theo stands thoughtfully. Lange has good right to be worried. Not only does his boat have no armaments, it is also undermanned. Whoever was responsible for assigning the boat's crew foolishly omitted the gunners, the torpedo men and the weapons artificers – crewmen who, when not needed for their special skills, performed other, vital tasks. Equally worrying is that the command structure is compromised. The designated Second Leutnant – the boat's Number One, Theo's deputy captain – did not turn up. Paul Lange will now do two jobs, it is the reason he is on the bridge and not with his engines.

Theo lifts the flap of the speaking tube, stoops and speaks into it.

'Searchlight to tower…'

Lange frowns. 'The searchlight, Captain?

'The searchlight, Chief. There is debris in the Elbe. I'm told there are timbers the size of small trucks.'

He turns to his Watch Officer. His men are scanning the sky through night glasses, heavy binoculars with large lenses, which gather more light.

'Get them to look west for Mosquitos flown by mad British pilots. They hug the land to avoid the guns, they come out of nowhere. When they bring the light use it sparingly, look for river debris. If we hit anything I'll have your head…'

Above them, on the main mast, is the mesh net of the Hohentwiel, the new radar system. It is switched off. His telegraphist, fresh from college, tells him the system is flawed, it gives out a signal the enemy can detect. There are, Theo tells himself, some advantages in having young crewmen.

For more than an hour Theo stands with Lange and the Watch Officer, using the light in brief flashes, scanning the dark water for flotsam. He knows the risks he is taking; the light is powerful and aircraft approaching across the flat northlands might see it; his boat is vulnerable here because the water is too shallow to dive.

The river is wide; in peacetime the small ports on its distant banks would show lights but in blackout there is nothing, no sign of life. To the south-west the low cloud is lit from beneath by bright flashes; though they have seen no bombers they know it is Hamburg again.

There cannot be much left of the city to bomb.

'Hamburg, Chief?'

Lange turns. In the far distance a spatter of white light cuts the horizon. A chain of tracer glows orange in air thick with dust. The chief grunts, and spits. Hamburg is his town.

'They are bastards!'

Theo watches in silence. 'Bombs rather than guns, Chief. An air raid, not an invasion. That, I suppose, is something.'

Theo grips handrails, swings into the ladderway and descends to the control room. The rope soles of his boots hit the deck plates soundlessly and he makes his way forward, past his cabin and the galley, the cold store and the latrines. This is home – his only home – a claustrophobic hell with no personal space. Today it is worse; crewmen are everywhere, they have lifted floor plates and are stowing equipment, lowering crates and cans to impossible places. Provisions yet to be stored overflow from men's bunks, from the galley, the radio room and the WC.

'Think, man!' Theo snaps. 'Show them, Bosun! If you put powdered egg under the beans then we get no egg until the beans are used up. There are three sides of bacon stacked on my bunk, I want them moved. They stink.'

Many times has he seen this confusion; he has made these mistakes himself, presided over bad stowage that left cabbages festering deep beneath canned food, forgotten by cooks and impossible to move. Overseeing stowage is not his job, but with so many green crewmen the responsibility lies with the old hands.

Back in his cabin he takes a key from his pocket, unlocks the ship's safe and reads his sealed orders for the third time. Weeks ago he mentioned Argentina to Walter but Walter didn't confirm it. These papers do.

The boat has been prepared for such a great distance. Its fuel tanks contain two hundred tonnes of oil, fuel enough for eleven thousand kilometres and his boat is well able to make the trip, it is a true sea monster, an ocean-going Type Nine boat, one of the Reich's biggest.

The great distance doesn't worry him. Others have crossed the Atlantic boats like these – men like Korvettenkapitän Hardegen in

U-123. In four months their boats sunk a million tons of shipping along the East coast of the United States. Hardegen told him the ships there were lit up as if it were Christmas. Operation Drumbeat, they called it.

But that was in 'forty-one. Since then things have changed.

Theo nods to himself. He will get there and back easily – though the orders don't mention a return trip. He wonders how his crew will take that bit of news when he tells them.

Back in the control room he sees Roth... Ludwig Roth. The man is difficult to miss. Theo's crewmen wear dark cotton coveralls, while Roth wears submariner's black leather – a practical outfit when worn by his men, but on Roth's obese frame the leather is tight and it bulges. Looks fetishist. Pornographic, even. Roth is a big man. He has a beer gut, a rare thing these days.

So what is this high-booted bastard, Theo wonders, Gestapo? He guesses the man is SS, one of Walter's mob, though one spook is much like another. He gives the man a nod of acknowledgement but does not speak. Doesn't want to be seen fraternising with the enemy.

Waiting for him in his cabin is a small French cafetiere and a white china cup and saucer. The new cooks have learned fast and he wonders who told them his likes and dislikes. Rather than sit in his desk chair he drops onto his bunk. A ten-minute break, if he's lucky.

One line in Theo's orders is typed in red: DO NOT ENGAGE WITH THE ENEMY. When he first read it he smiled. He has his sidearm – his Mauser pistol – locked in a drawer in his cabin. In the boat's small armoury are rifles and sub-machine guns, to be used by his seamen in case of close combat. The only other things that could possibly resemble armaments are flare pistols in the control room but apart from these there is absolutely nothing. Do not engage with the enemy. He smiles as he reads it again.

The prospect of a quiet voyage has been shattered by Roth. Theo has fallen foul of the man already, disobeying him by opening the sealed orders in his absence. For that he had been sworn at and threatened.

The bosun taps on his door and then opens it wide.

'Kapitän... pardon... there is a padlock and chain on the door to the bow tube room, I have spoken to Herr Roth and he refuses to remove it. He says the space belongs to him.'

Without speaking Theo stands and follows the man. The forward torpedo room – the bow tube room – is entered through a watertight door with a steel wheel in its centre, a wheel that seals and unseals it. Somebody, presumably Roth, has passed a chain through the wheel and padlocked it in place.

'The chain is ours,' the bosun says. 'He must have brought the padlock with him.'

Still Theo says nothing. He returns to the control room and finds Roth there, still leaning against the conning tower ladder. Theo stops, facing him.

'There is a lock and chain on the forward torpedo room door. I understand you put it there. I demand you remove it.'

Roth lifts his chin high. There is a squeak of new leather from the coat. He is shorter than Theo but somehow the gesture is effective in making him seem tall.

'My rank is Sturmbannführer, Kapitänleutnant Volker. You will use it when you address me.'

Sturmbannführer… the man is an SS major. In the U-boat pens in Hamburg Walter had introduced Roth as the officer who would be taking his place. Surprised and annoyed, Theo had protested and then walked away, hadn't spoken to Walter again.

'I insist you remove the padlock, Sturmbannführer. If you do not then I shall cut the chain.'

'I have sealed the compartment, Kapitänleutnant. There are no torpedoes, so therefore your men do not need access. I understand that you know what we are carrying. I am here to see that the cargo stays safe.'

'You are wrong. My crewmen need access. Again, I insist you unchain the door.'

Roth stands with folded arms. Theo looks away from him and snaps out an order. The diesels fade to a dull rumble and the boat loses way. Roth is caught off guard by the change of speed and grabs at the conning tower ladder.

'What is this? Why have the engines stopped?'

Theo stands with his arms folded. 'I am unable to proceed, Sturmbannführer. Your actions prevent my Chief Engineer inspecting the hydroplane motors and the pumps in the forward torpedo room. I intend to signal my intention to return to Hamburg.' He turns and calls loudly: 'Telegraphist!'

Roth's neck and head seem to merge into one. A flush of deep purple spreads upwards from under his leathers. He is wearing a tie and starched collar and they seem to be choking him. His voice comes in a hiss.

'You cannot break wireless silence! You will not disobey me!'

There is another gun on board, Theo can see the bulge under Roth's arm. Neither man moves. Theo's voice drops to a whisper, deliberate and sharp.

'You leave me no choice, Sturmbannführer. The safety of this vessel is my responsibility. The safety of what we are carrying is yours – though you may be aware I accompanied part of the cargo though Germany and Poland long before you – '

Theo stops. He is saying things he should not say. But it is not a problem. Roth is more concerned with protocol and politics.

'Poland? Is there such a place? Do you mean Greater Germany, Kapitänleutnant?'

Theo's heart sinks. An hour into the voyage, and then this. He cannot risk conflict. To avoid further argument he mounts the ladder and climbs to the bridge. The Chief Engineer is there. The first Watch Officer has moved to the wintergarden, where he stands with a lookout. All three peer through binoculars, searching the sky.

In better days they would have left Hamburg with an escort of converted trawlers bristling with guns. Now there is no spare fuel for such vessels and those that do manage to sail are crewed by old men and boys. Theo looks east towards the first rays of sun, a pre-dawn glow through a dark smoky sky. His breath seeps up from inside his high collar like steam from a heater. He calls to Lange.

'Clear day, Chief!'

He moves closer to him and talks quietly. When he returns below, Roth is there, watching and listening, leaning against pipes with his arms folded tight. Does he intend to stand there for the whole voyage, the best part of three months?

Theo checks the time. He knows what is about to happen, knows what the Chief will do.

An alarm bell jangles. From the speaking tube comes a shriek: 'Aircraft one-ninety!' Then a shout, from above: 'Flood! Flood! Flood!'

With gloved hands sliding on the ladder's smooth sides, men drop from the tower like abseiling raiders. Conning tower hatches thump down and are clamped in place.

The men around Theo stay calm. Even the new men are well-drilled, they spin hand-wheels and check gauges. Seamen run back and forth, closing vents and valves, reporting their actions with short sharp shouts. In the engine room the diesels are shut down – but in error they stay running after the air vents have closed and they suck air from the boat. Ears pop as the pressure drops. Crewmen clamp their hands over their ears and a cook in the galley screams with pain.

Chief Engineer Lange is there and he watches the crew, the controls and the instruments. He shouts orders and men change positions, turn hand wheels, work on the valves again. From the bow comes the rumble of compressed air as it blows out the ballast tanks. The boat lurches, tilts violently. Lange shouts again:

'She's unbalanced! All non-essential hands forward!'

Theo stands beside the ladder and watches, keeping his balance by gripping its rungs. Despite having a new crew, unfamiliar with the boat, they work well together. Lange, in his double role, holds down a mike button and repeats the order. Crewmen scramble through the boat, hauling themselves up now-sloping gangways.

The Elbe is shallow here. As the stern of the boat ploughs through thick mud the crewmen stumble and reach for support. Rudders and screws plough the river's dredged channel. The boat stops dead.

Roth is caught unawares and falls awkwardly. Theo grabs him, hauls him to his feet, brushes him down, picks up his spectacles and hands them to him. As the periscope lifts from the floor he abandons the man, straddles the scope and swivels it full-circle. Though he cannot see it, he knows that a broad slick of churned mud is being spread by the current – a clear marker in the river that can be seen from the air. Had a real enemy plane been near the Elbe, its crew would have seen the mud slick, they would know there was a boat on the bottom.

Theo turns his attention to Roth. Clearly, the man is shocked.

'I need access to the whole vessel, Sturmbannführer,' he says calmly. 'These are my reasons. Firstly, the changes to our armaments mean the bow of the boat is lighter than the stern, so when we crash-dive we move crew to help balance the boat. Secondly, all our vital controls are duplicated, so if central control fails then my crewmen need immediate access to the manual systems, some of which are in the bow tube room. Thirdly, this vessel is my responsibility. Again I ask you – '

The first statement is nonsense. His crew can adjust the trim of the boat by moving water in ballast tanks but Roth does not to know that. He squeezes a fat hand into a side pocket of his leather jacket, takes out a bunch is keys, unclips one and hands it to Volker.

'Very well, Kapitänleutnant. You will give your assurance that your crewmen will enter only when I am present.'

'Sturmbannführer, I give you my word my crew will not enter except in emergencies. The door will remain closed but unlocked.' Theo looks at Roth's chin and nods at it. 'You are injured. Shall I call the medical orderly?'

Roth wipes his chin with his hand and sees blood. Ignoring the offer he swivels on his heel, ducks through a doorway and heads for his cabin. Men stand aside. Theo looks at Lange and then at the bosun.

'Chief… Bosun… the bow tube room – no access except in my presence. Tell the crew.'

When Theo first examined his boat he was shocked by the changes. Not only are there no deck guns and torpedoes, the forward torpedo room – the bow tube room – has changed beyond recognition. In place of torpedo tubes, loading carriages and torpedo racks, there is a varnished mahogany door leading to two cabins, a washroom, a shower and a WC, all timber panelled. Both cabins have telephones. On the floor of one of the rooms is a brass-fitted box containing silver cutlery and pewter dinner plates – each plate monogrammed with two tilted shields that touch at their tops.

The cabins could pass for rooms on a luxury yacht – though the ceiling heights are barely adequate and all but one of the cabins tapers towards the bow. Though a stranger might find them claustrophobic, a U-boat man would consider them spacious.

Strapped upright against one wall in the space that remains in the tube room are the six rubber-clad crates brought by Theo. Beneath them, in a space under the deck plates normally used for storing torpedoes, are more crates, works of art from god-knows-where. All are in wooden crates, unprotected by bronze boxes and rubber.

CHAPTER FORTY-TWO

IT WAS WELL AFTER MIDNIGHT when Benares returned to the counting house. He struggled up the steps bearing boxes and bags, dumped them on the floor and returned for more. Repeated the trip three more times without saying a word.

'You have found a heater,' Bar observed. 'That is good. Leave everything else. Put it over there and turn it on.'

Benares had excelled himself. He had found an industrial heater mounted on a tripod he set up in the corner of the room, rolled a large red gas bottle towards it and connected it up. Soon it was glowing brightly.

'And lights?' Bar asked. 'You have brought us lights?'

'I have not,' he said. 'That thing gives enough light. It is unwise to light up this place.'

'You told me the window in the door faces the sea. If it is true then who can possibly see us?'

Benares, ignoring him, unloaded the bags, placing sealed packs of sandwiches, bottled water and packets of nuts on the table.

'This is all I have been able to buy.'

He tore the seal from of a sandwich pack, dragged a chair to the table, sat down and bit into a sandwich. Bar spoke in Spanish and Benares replied; a heated exchange followed that included the word *hija*.

'What about her?' Spargo asked. 'What are you saying about my daughter?

Both men went quiet. Benares turned to Spargo.

'You speak Spanish?'

Spargo enjoyed the moment and then shook his head. 'I know a few words. You were talking about my daughter.'

Bar nodded. 'Luis was saying he does not know where she is. But we believe we know who has abducted her.'

'Who?'

'Giving such information to you will not help her.'

'So you are just going to sit here?'

'That depends on you.'

Bar swivelled to face Benares. 'John Spargo believes the translator Lewis was a member of Theodor Volker's crew. How can he know such a thing?' He turned his gaze to Spargo. 'Has it not crossed your mind that if this is so then Mister Lewis might have known what became of Theodor's cargo? If what you told me is true – if this Lewis is now killed – '

'You should know,' Spargo said. 'You had him killed.'

'No, John Spargo, I did not. Keep silence and listen to me. If it was not Lewis who told you these things, who was it? If you tell me where you obtained this information then I am sure it is possible to have your daughter brought to you.'

'You said you don't know where she is.'

'I do not need to know where she is. But I know how to contact her abductors.'

Benares and Bar exchanged glances, conversed in Spanish, then turned their heads to face Spargo. Benares spoke.

'Mr Letchie was recommended to me by a member of Mister Bar's consortium. I hired him to investigate the situation here at Kilcreg.'

'The situation?'

Benares shrugged. 'He is – was – a journalist. I was told he was good at his job, a regular little detective. I did not hire him to commit acts of violence.'

'But that's – '

'Let me finish. I also hired a young man to observe your daughter.'

'I know about him. Jez pointed him out to me, he's as inconspicuous as a streaker in a dayglow jacket. She wasn't worried, she was sure he fancied the young man in the flat above hers and was stalking him. Is he the one who's abducted Jez? Against your orders, I suppose.'

Bar spoke. 'Luis tells me that until recently this man, Mr Midge

Rollo, was most reliable. Regretfully it seems this is no longer the case. As I said, he was instructed to watch over your daughter.'

'Like lions watch over their prey.'

'No, Mister Spargo, Luis employed him to watch her and if necessary to protect her, is this not so, Luis? It does seem that recently he may have switched allegiances. As I repeatedly tell you, resolving these issues is simple. Just tell me how you know these things about Theodor's crewmen. Have you determined what became of Theodor's cargo?'

'I have not. I'm sure it doesn't exist.'

'Why do I not believe you? You returned to the old house. What were you going to do, search there?'

'There was nothing there. You know that.'

'Yes, we know that now.'

Bar clamped his hands on the arms of the plastic chair. He pressed down on them, eased himself up, emerged from the sleeping bag cocoon and stood unsteadily with one hand on the table. Benares slapped a half-eaten sandwich on the table and sprang up to help him – loyalty, despite recent disputes. Clearly, Bar still pulled the man's strings. Benares, manservant and henchman. Hit man.

'Very well,' Bar said, now standing. 'If you remain stubbornly uncooperative there is nothing more to say.'

Spargo stood up and stretched each leg in turn.

'What now? Where are we going?'

'You are going nowhere. You have heat, you have a bed and you have food. I shall leave you my torch. Do not breach my confidence in you by attempting to leave.'

'So where are you going?'

'I shall return home, I am tired of all this, I have done all I can do. You are keeping things from me, John Spargo. I have protected you and yet you refuse to tell me who told you about this man Lewis.'

'Protected me? You are both mad! What about Jez? How can you expect me to tell you anything when you have already murdered three people? You'll go on killing until you get what you want. And I know who is holding Jez, it's Tony Day, he's involved in all this. That's where Jez has been taken, out to the Alcatraz he calls home.'

'John Spargo, you are right when you say we will get what we want. Was Lewis married, is that it? Did he tell his wife these things? Have you spoken to her? Did she tell you about his past?'

'He wasn't married.'

'But there is someone, John Spargo.'

Spargo nodded. He knew he had a choice – give up Rydel, an elderly man nearing the end of his time, or risk sacrificing his daughter, a young woman with so much to live for.

Bar had reached the door before Spargo spoke.

'Wait... there are things I can find out. But we will do it my way.'

Brave words. Bar shuffled towards him and they stood face to face.

'Then tell me, John Spargo. What is your way?'

'I need a phone.'

Bar hesitated, deep in thought. Then he nodded to Benares, who produced Spargo's own mobile, switched it on and checked its charge and its signal. Spargo went towards the door but Bar blocked him.

'Stay inside. You have been given your telephone. Do not try to be clever.'

'I can't let you listen.'

'Then I cannot let you phone.'

Spargo moved to the gas heater and stood in its orange glow. He unlocked his phone and soon had a ringtone. He waited. Cancelled the call and tried again, silently cursing Rydel for not answering. A glance at his watch showed him it was just after two. He was being foolish. There was no way the man would answer his phone at that time of night.

Then a click. Then a voice.

'Who is there?'

Spargo had rehearsed what to say. As soon as he heard Rydel's voice he spoke forcefully. 'My daughter...' he said. 'My daughter has been kidnapped by the men who killed Mark. If you hang up on me I will send them to question you.'

Cruel words. For a while there was silence.

Then: 'Tell me what you want from me.'

Spargo asked questions, keeping them short. All were answered. As he ended the call Benares rushed forwards, grabbed for the phone but missed. Spargo, anticipating the move, dropped the phone onto the glowing red element of the heater and with a flash of yellow and spurts of black smoke it burst into flame. Phone gone, internal directory gone. Call registers with the identity of the last person called, all gone.

Benares swore. Bar laughed. Coughing and choking, all three made for the door as the room filled with smoke. Bar stepped into the ice-cold air and the others followed, Benares still coughing and cursing.

'So, John Spargo,' Bar said. 'Was your call successful? Have you learned what you wanted to learn? If so, that is good. Now I must leave you. I am tired.'

'Leave? Now?'

'It appears I am no longer in control of this situation. You want to do it your way, so whatever you do is no longer my concern. Tell me, should Luis and I return to Madrid or should we stay? And what about your daughter, do you want Luis to attempt to find her, or do you wish to do that on your own also? Tell me, John Spargo. We are letting you do it your way.'

'I have the information you need. Take me to my daughter and I will tell you what you want to know.'

'John Spargo, the air inside this pig pen is too foul to breathe and the air out here is cold. It will take Benares two or more hours to drive me to what you people call civilisation. Perhaps, when I have rested, I will make my decisions. In the meantime you can reflect on what you have just learnt from your call.'

The engine of the departing SUV faded into the night as Spargo, alone again, dragged the heater outside and stood it on the landing. Not wanting to be without heat he scraped the remains of his phone from the now extinguished burner and fired the thing up again.

Worry and pain kept him from sleep. Between four and five o'clock he dozed. At six, sleep finally overtook him.

More than once during the following morning he considered setting off for Kilcreg, and each time he decided against it. His wound hurt badly, he wouldn't get far. Also, he had made some kind of deal with

Bar to stay put. He wasn't at all sure what that deal was.

Around midday he heard an engine. He no longer hoped for the Mitchell miracle so it had to be Benares. Slow, laboured, and most unexpected footsteps on the stairs told him Bar had come too, that despite last night's pronouncements he had not flown home. The man shuffled into the room and slumped down in the chair.

'John Spargo, I trust you had a good night?'

The words came between long, laboured breaths. The man was exhausted, his eyes dark-rimmed and set deep in their sockets. His spare facial skin was pale and puffy and sagged more than usual. Benares, behind him, looked almost as bad.

'No. It was lousy,' Spargo said. 'What did you expect?'

'It was your choice. Had you cooperated you could have spent at least some of the night at home.'

'Hospital, you mean.'

Bar grunted. 'It is eight hours since I was in this place. I spent much of that time in that damned car and no more than three hours in my hotel bed. Luis has had no sleep, he spent the night telephoning. Things have changed, John Spargo. I know where your daughter is. I know she is safe.'

Spargo ran his fingers through his hair. He wanted to thank Bar but couldn't bring himself to do it. It could be a lie. Surely it wasn't in Bar's interest to say Jez had been harmed.

'Where is she?'

'I said I would endeavour to secure your daughter's safety and I have succeeded. In return you will endeavour to recover my boxes. It seems to me I am closer to fulfilling my side of the bargain than you are to yours. Did you learn anything last night when you made your call, or are you simply stalling for time?'

'I know the boxes came ashore. I know where they were taken.'

Bar raised his eyebrows. 'Why did you not tell me this last night?'

'You didn't seem interested. You told me to sleep on it. I am told the boxes were here. That doesn't mean they are still here.'

Bar leant forwards, beckoning with his hands as if encouraging more words.

'So? Where are they? Tell me!'

'Before I tell you any more I want to speak to Jez.'

He expected a refusal. Benares was standing in the doorway and Bar waved him close, speaking in Spanish. Benares frowned, produced a mobile, and held it out to Bar who waved it away. Benares poked at buttons and held the phone to his ear.

'It is Luis,' he said in English. 'Let me speak to the woman.' Then a long pause. Then, loudly, 'You will do it! Mister Bar wishes it!'

Bar reached out and took the mobile. He listened for a few seconds, held the phone an inch away from his mouth and barked into it: 'Enough! Give her the telephone now!' He listened again. Satisfied, he passed the mobile to Spargo.

'Jez?'

'Dad?'

'Are you alright?'

'I'm okay. Murphy's here. He's got a – '

The phone went dead. Spargo heard no more. He looked at the phone as if it was responsible for ending the call. Benares snatched it from him.

'Murphy?' Spargo said to Bar, 'Grant Murphy?'

Bar gave a shrug. 'I was not responsible. It was the consortium. There was nothing I could do.'

'You've abducted him too? Why? He hasn't worked with me for years. He knows nothing about any of this.'

Jez had sounded fine. Though she didn't like Murphy, at least she was with someone she knew.

'I have not abducted Grant Murphy,' Bar said. 'When I revealed to the consortium the possible connections between Theodor Volker, Kilcreg and your late mother, they sought out someone who knew you well. Against my wishes my associates took him on board.'

Spargo shook his head. 'Murph? A member of your consortium?'

'I told you, it has not been my consortium for many years. Your friend Grant Murphy agreed to provide information about you on the condition he joined our group. He provided us with the mine plans and records Luis sent to you. It was easy for him. I believe he once worked in Canada at that particular mine.'

Spargo took it in, thought about it and looked for holes in it. He found it hard to accept that Murphy, a man he had trusted implicitly – and saved from jail on at least two occasions – could do such things.

'He lied to me,' Spargo mumbled. 'He flew from Seattle to Heathrow and then to Edinburgh. He said he was flying from Edinburgh to Aberdeen and then on to Oslo.'

Benares now, frowning a question: 'And that is a lie, Mister Spargo?'

'It was a lie because no airline flies from Edinburgh to Aberdeen.'

'Do they not? Then that was most careless of him. In any case, your friend lied to you about many things. He did not fly from Seattle that week, he was with me in Madrid, we flew together to Heathrow and from there we travelled to Edinburgh on different flights. It would have been regrettable if I had been with him when you met him at the airport, would it not? In Edinburgh he introduced me to Mister Letchie and together we went to your house. To ensure we were not disturbed I arranged for your friend Mister Murphy to spend time with you at the airport.'

'You went to my house and killed Letchie? Why did you do it there, as a warning to me?'

'He had become a liability. The opportunity to resolve that problem presented itself to me in your basement, but that was not why we went there. He wanted to show me the diaries you had found. The bronze box was there, but the diaries were not.'

'And that's why you killed him? Because the journals were not there?'

Bar interrupted: 'Of course not. He has told you why. That man was a liability. It was he who killed your mother. During Luis's many telephone calls during last night he learned Ian Letchie had also killed your translator, Mr Lewis. Now, enough of this! The remaining boxes, John Spargo! A wiser man might wish to concentrate on those!'

'Very well. I know Volker came to Kilcreg. He put a crewman ashore, a man who had been injured. By your SS man Roth.'

Bar went quiet. Then: 'That is implausible.'

'You said yourself something must have happened to prevent your man winding an explosive device.'

'Ludwig Roth was not my man. And that is not what I meant. If our submarine commanders had made a habit of landing their injured men on enemy shores I am sure we would very rapidly have run out of submarines. This injured crewman, was it the translator, Mark Lewis?'

Spargo paused, wondering how to play it. Didn't want to set them onto Rydel.

'Last night I was told some sealed boxes came ashore. They were left in the bay, hidden between rocks, behind barbed wire defences.'

'And that is all, John Spargo? I hope you are not about to tell me the boxes remained there. What became of them? Where were they taken?'

'The man I spoke to last night was the injured man. He says he was unconscious when he came ashore and learned about the sealed boxes later. He said that if they were still on the beach when the cliffs collapsed they would have been buried.'

Bar was flagging. He shook his head and closed his eyes. 'Cliffs collapsed, John Spargo…? What cliffs?'

Bar dipped a hand inside his coat, fished around for a while and brought it out empty. Benares sprang to life. From one of his own pockets he took a thin aluminium cylinder, unscrewed the end and tipped out a cigar – emergency supplies for Bar. He produced his switchblade and trimmed one end neatly. The same knife, the one with his own dried blood on it plus Benares' fingernail trimmings. Spargo flinched. Bar, cigar in mouth, leaned back.

'And this is all you discovered last night, on the telephone to your friend?'

'He's not a friend.'

'If you are unable to obtain the information we need we shall obtain it ourselves. Tell me where we can find this man.'

'It won't do you any good. I told you, he was brought ashore unconscious. He learned about the sealed crates later.'

Ash from Bar's cigar fell on the floor. Benares, tired of standing, kicked a chair across the lino and sat on it. Apart from the deep hiss of the gas heater the room was quiet, no rain beat on the roof, no wind sang through the gaps around the door. Spargo, out of ideas, stared at the floor. He had a nagging doubt. Something in Rydel's words didn't ring true.

'There is something…'

Bar and Benares came to life. Both leaned forwards, both said 'Yes?'

'I'm not saying it's good news. There used to be a sea adit in the cliffs. My father told me about it. He also told me the cliffs in the bay collapsed in the nineteen thirties.'

Bar's expectant expression vanished. 'John Spargo, what is a sea adit? Explain these things to me in proper words.'

'A gently sloping drive. A tunnel. When my father took over the Kilcreg mine this tunnel in the cliffs was its only entrance. He said it was how the mine started. He said the locals found a mineral vein high in the cliffs and they mined it for ore, they followed it deep into the ground. Years later the cliffs collapsed and destroyed the entrance, but it wasn't a problem. By then my father had sunk a shaft, which they used for the main access.'

'Why should these things interest me?'

'When I was a boy miners mentioned the old adit. I remember asking my father about it and he said the cliffs collapsed before the war. When I made the phone call last night I was told your sealed crates had been left in the bay and may have been buried by the collapse.'

'And the significance of this is?'

'If the cliffs collapsed before the war, how could they have buried packing cases left by a U-boat in 1945?'

'So you are telling me your informant last night lied to you.'

'No, he had no reason to lie to me. It means my father lied to me.'

Bar was looking at the floor. For a while he said nothing.

'Are you saying the cliff collapse was deliberate? To bury the cases?'

'I think it was deliberate, but it wouldn't have been to bury the cases, not after Volker had taken the trouble to bring them ashore. I'm thinking that perhaps my father blasted down the cliffs to seal the old adit.'

Bar looked up. He did the beckoning thing with his hand.

'Keep talking, John Spargo.'

'My daughter found mineral fragments in the bronze box with Volker's journals. That could mean the box was opened in the mine.

Perhaps my father had all the sealed crates taken there. Then he sealed the entrance by collapsing the cliffs.'

'Then they are gone,' Bar said. 'You said the mine is flooded.'

'Correct.'

'I do not pretend to understand these things, but does not the level of flooding of such a place depend on the water table? We are close to the sea. Should not the water table be at sea level here, therefore a great distance below the entrance you speak of? Did you not say it was high in the cliffs?'

'The adit entrance may be dry, but it will lead down to flooded workings. It's all irrelevant anyway. You can't get into it.'

Bar was nodding.

'Because your father brought down the cliffs...'

'Even if you found a way in, brought in pumps and spent six months pumping the mine dry, you'd find nothing. The mine was a warren of passages linking new workings with old ones.'

'You give only reasons why things cannot be done, John Spargo. Millions have been spent already. If there is any chance of success with this venture then more millions will follow. I have heard of mines being reopened, cannot this be done?'

'I am telling things as they are. You accept that if the crates are in the U-boat their contents are now worthless. Conditions in the mine will be far worse. Mine water is highly corrosive. There's probably nothing left of your boxes.'

'These cliffs you speak about. Can they be reached by road?'

'The road through Kilcreg ends at the bay. It was once possible to walk along the beach at low tide but it wasn't easy. Some of the boulders are as big as buses.'

'The track outside this building appears to continue. Luis says that in the distance there is the sea. Does the track not lead to the top of these cliffs?'

'Years ago I walked it. It was overgrown with heather. It'll be far worse now.'

'But it is driveable?'

'It's hardly walkable.'

'I need closure on this, John Spargo. If what I am seeking cannot be recovered, then I need evidence that will convince the consortium that further expenditure is futile.'

'What evidence can there be? Just ask your new associate, Murphy, he pretends to know about mining. He will tell you that anything left in a flooded mine for more than fifty years will be worthless.'

'I do not know this man Murphy. I need to convince myself, John Spargo.'

'You were willing to walk away from it last night.'

'I was not. I wished to concentrate your mind, to give you time with your thoughts. Did really think I would not return? Now, come, I wish to see this collapsed cliff.'

'See it? You had trouble walking up the steps, you've got no chance of reaching the bay.'

'There is no need for you to insult me. But regrettably you are correct, so Luis will make the journey on my behalf, you will take him there.'

'You will have to drive through Kilcreg, get down to the beach and walk to the cliffs. It's impossible, there are too many boulders.'

'Driving through Kilcreg would be most unwise. The track we came here on, does it not lead to the cliff top? Can you not drive there in the vehicle outside?'

Spargo raised his arm and pointed a finger at Benares. As he did so his shirt tugged at the dried wound and he gasped.

'I'm not going anywhere alone with that madman, not after what he did to me!'

'Just do as I say,' Bar sighed as he struggled to his feet. 'I have enough problems, I do not need more from you. And take this with you,' he said, taking the torch from the table and holding it out. 'If you find this place I want to know about it. When you return you will tell me all you can.'

From what Spargo could remember about the cliffs they were more than an hour's walk from the mine buildings. That was when he was young and fit. Now, driving was the only realistic way to get there – and if the SUV got stuck then it wasn't his problem.

Not wanting to let his only means of transport out of his sight, Bar changed his mind about staying in the counting house. With Spargo up-front and Benares driving he sat in the back seat as the SUV battled its way through deep heather. The track to the cliffs barely existed, and sudden jumps and bumps were the norm. Every one of them triggering pain in Spargo's side. His wound was open again. And it was bleeding.

Bar complained constantly about Benares' driving and the lack of room in the back of the SUV. Benares, having stalled the engine for the fourth time, took his foot off the pedals and turned off the ignition.

'I have had enough of this foolishness. I can go no further. Now we must walk.'

They had stopped on a low ridge, the last of several that ran parallel to the coast. Each ridge had promised a view of the cliff top and the sea beyond. This ridge, the last ridge, delivered the view Spargo had waited for. Spargo unlatched the door but the wind held it shut. He leaned against it. The wind dropped for a second and he fell out. More pain as he hauled himself up. Bar came up beside him.

'How long will this take?'

'Twenty minutes to get there, I guess. Half an hour to look around and another half to get back. Between one and two hours, at a guess.'

Benares, already out, went to get back in.

'It is too far to walk. I will drive closer.'

Bar snapped something in Spanish and Benares froze. Bar turned to Spargo.

'To drive further would be dangerous, would you not agree? I am concerned for this vehicle. It is my only means of return.'

Spargo agreed. Benares glared at them both and then spoke.

'Very well, Mister Spargo. You will walk ahead of me. Do not do stupid things and do not walk fast. I do not have appropriate shoes for these silly games.'

Walking fast was not on the cards. Spargo, limping and in pain, wondered if he would even reach the cliff top but despite his misgivings he reached it well before Benares. He wanted to keep away from the man. That he was a liability to Bar and his cronies was never far from his mind; where better to dispose of someone than a remote cliff top?

'It's changed,' he said.

'What has changed, Mister Spargo?'

The cliffs swept towards Kilcreg in a long, concave curve. The collapse, whether natural or caused by his father, had been massive. Boulders that really were the size of buses had tumbled into the bay far below. The last time he was here, when Jez was young, they had scrambled down the cliffs, around a maze of great boulders.

'The cliffs,' Spargo said. 'There were paths down to the bay. They've gone.'

Benares had his collar up, the lapels held together with his hand. He mumbled something Spargo didn't catch. Spargo, still wanting to keep his distance from Benares, turned towards Kilcreg and started walking. Benares, trailing well behind, followed without protest. Then, in what must have looked to Benares like a suicidal leap, Spargo jumped off the cliff edge.

By the time Benares reached the same spot Spargo was zigzagging down to the bay. He had seen a way down and his soles had deep treads, they gripped well. In the few minutes it took Benares to reach the spot where Spargo had jumped – and realised it had been on to a ledge beneath the cliff top – Spargo was well ahead. Walking near Benares he'd felt vulnerable. Halfway down the cliffs, despite the sheer drop to the rocky beach below, he did not.

Benares was sitting at the top with his legs dangling over the cliff edge. Shorter than Spargo, he was unsure how to reach the ledge. Finally he slid forwards. Landed on the ledge in a shower of soil and stones.

The cliffs were the colour of rust. Here and there they were streaked bright green from traces of metallic minerals, corroded by rain and salt spray. Coarse grass and wild flowers sprouted optimistically from precarious ledges. Endangered species.

Long ago, Spargo's father had banned him from the cliffs but he had gone there anyway, scrambling sure-footed across them and exploring them, searching for minerals and crystals. He was no longer that boy. His muscles lacked tone and the steep twists and turns took their toll; every step he took jarred his bones and tugged at his wound. Nauseous, he stopped again and looked up. Benares, in his handmade brogues, was descending. He hadn't come far.

Spargo recalled their time in Madrid. There, Benares was streetwise; here, he looked scared. In the more perilous places on the cliff face he clung to the rock like a man on a seventh floor ledge.

From where Spargo stood he could see the whole bay. At one end the cliffs turned inland, out of sight and at the other he could just make out the remains of the Kilcreg jetty. Closer to him, scoured into the rubble of rocks of the beach, were the dark hollows of rock pools – or others just like them – where he had once trawled for minnows with his net. Near the waterline was a black berm of weed and a scatter of silver-brown driftwood – wood that once a week Mr McGregor, from the shop in High Street that was no longer there, had collected for his house fires. Whenever he was asked, young Spargo had helped him with the larger timbers. Helped him drag them to the shop, where he was paid for his trouble.

What was new in the bay was the flotsam of plastic, the bottles, the bright coloured fish trays and white polystyrene. Plastic that revolutionised packaging. Revolutionised filth.

When he reached the foot of the cliffs he sat on a boulder, nursing his side and observing the progress of the man in the brogues. The route they had taken was the only safe way down to the bay. The rest of the cliff looked as if it had been piled there by the hand of a giant, a perilous rockslide of packed earth and boulders. Somewhere, high up near the top and buried beneath boulders, was the original entrance to Kilcreg Mine.

When Benares finally reached the beach he went down on one knee as if about to kiss the ground. Instead, he re-tied a shoelace. Straightened up and made his way to Spargo.

'Waste of time,' Spargo said, wagging his arm like a pointer. 'My father told me the old mine entrance was in the middle of the bay. You've seen how impossible it all is. We can go back and tell Bar there's nothing here.'

Benares scowled. Muttered a response. The crash of waves swamped his words.

'Another way,' he shouted. 'There is another way up, yes? I cannot go back that way. My shoes slip, the soles are made from leather.'

'The only other way out is to walk to Kilcreg. When you get there you'll be seen, you'll have to walk past the houses. And you can't walk from Kilcreg back to your car, it'll take hours. What about Bar? He's still at the top.'

'We will take your Volvo.'

'It's not four wheel drive. It won't even reach the counting house.'

'You told Mister Bar the cliff had collapsed. That is not correct. There is a cliff at the top of that slope, I can see it.'

'Cliffs keep collapsing, it's what they do. That bit will be fresh, perhaps five or ten years old.'

'You said the old entrance is gone, Mister Spargo. But it cannot have gone, can it? A tunnel in the cliffs cannot disappear. If I make a hole through a block of cheese and I grate the end off of the cheese, the hole might be hidden by grated cheese, but it is still there.'

'We're not talking about grated cheese we're talking about massive blocks of rock.'

'But this adit you speak of, this hole. It is still there, is it not? You understand me, I think. What if the rubble has now slipped away from it? What if the entrance is open again?'

'It won't be. If my father blasted the cliff it would have destroyed a whole length of the entrance tunnel.'

'That is what you call wishful thinking, Mister Spargo. You have no proof of that. Also, I can see many places high up that look like openings in the rock.'

'They are hollows and shadows, optical illusions. That one there, look where I'm pointing, the dark bit under the white boulder, halfway up. It looks like an entrance but it isn't. It's where a boulder has fallen out. It's like a tooth socket.'

'But I can see other places. Mister Bar asked me to verify the old entrance is no longer accessible. You are going to do it for me now, Mister Spargo.'

CHAPTER FORTY-THREE

THE WIND IS ICE-COLD, straight off the Baltic Sea. Theo, on the bridge, pulls up his collar and adjusts his scarf. Those on watch must stay vigilant – leaving port these days is like Russian roulette. As well as debris there are mines dropped into the Elbe at night by enemy aircraft. Though minesweepers work constantly they cannot clear them all.

Soon they will be in deep water and able to submerge safely. Theo will do it as routine, he will test-dive his boat, taking his crew through drills to familiarise them with their new boat. Drills that under normal circumstances would have been done days ago.

He considers dropping to periscope depth to test the new schnörkel. But if he does that he will lose speed, it will take longer to reach safer, deep water. The top of the schnörkel – the bit that breathes air for the crew and the diesels – is encased in the same rubber as the six bronze boxes. He has been told this kills radar waves and cannot be seen by the enemy's radar. How do they know such things? He is sceptical of the claims, he is an engineer, not a wireless man. He makes a mental note to ask his telegraphist; perhaps one day he will learn these things for himself.

He hears the pad of soft soles on the ladder. Chief Engineer Lange emerges from the hatch with two steaming mugs.

'I'll tell you what,' he says, gesturing to the small hatch in the deck of the bridge. 'If we have to get out of here quick, we must make sure that fat bastard comes up last.'

Theo hesitates. The comment triggers a question in the back of Theo's mind but before it can form, it is gone. Trying in vain to recall it he stares out to sea, towards the bleak islands of Heligoland Bight.

'Dangerous man, Chief. Best keep him sweet.'

'The way you do, Kapitän? How will you keep him from knowing?'

'Knowing what?'

'Sleeping Beauty.'

'Oh my god…!'

Theo leaps for the hatch. In the rush to get everything done he has forgotten about his own son. Legs through the hatch, he grips the ladder's side rails with his boots and gloved hands and drops to the control room. Thankfully, Roth is not there.

'Where is the Sturmbannführer, Bosun?'

'In the bow cabins, Kapitän.'

'I'm going aft. You have not seen me. If Roth asks for me then say I am on the bridge with the Chief.'

When he reaches the engine room he shoves the steel door and steps over the sill. Though he has done this a thousand times the heat and noise from the twin four thousand horsepower diesels still strikes him like a wave, they drown all talk and block all thought. Through the din the engine room crew converse in shouts, half-hearing, half lip reading. To block out the noise they chew paper that they jam in their ears. Theo has done it himself. He has done time on engines like these.

Mechanics in coveralls jump up as he passes. He nods to them. On his boat there are no salutes. Space is tight enough without arm-waving.

He strides between the diesels, spins the locking wheel of the bulkhead door at the end of it, steps through into what should be the aft torpedo room and swings the door shut behind him. It is quieter here. Beneath the steel floor are twin shafts that drive the boat's massive propellers, propellers that hiss as they cut through the Elbe. Like the forward torpedo room, this one has no tubes, no torpedo racks or handling gear. Instead there are eight permanent bunks. Made for Göring's staff, he supposes.

There is a man in the room, a young mechanic named Lewandowski. Unlike the oil-stained, time-served men, this seaman wears spotless grey coveralls. On his left arm is a twin yellow chevron, sewn neatly – Seaman First Class – therefore brighter than most.

Lewandowski is sitting on a wooden case, reading a book. As he sees Theo he jumps up and salutes. Winces as his fingers hit overhead pipes.

'At ease, Marek. In my boat you do not salute… how is he?'

'Sleeping, Kapitän.'

'Who else knows?'

'The mechanics, Kapitän.'

'Nobody else?'

'The diesel mechanics and artificers. And the Chief Engineer, Kapitän!'

He snaps out the words. A verbal salute.

'Relax, man, you are not at training school.'

'I await your orders, Kapitän!'

The bunks have cot-like sides of metal tubing that resemble narrow ladders placed sideways. Despite the mechanical clutter of pipework and cables, vent ducts and lamps, to a seasoned U-boat man the room is spacious. Edible stalactites of sausage, ham, and string bags of vegetables hang from the pipework.

'Does what you are doing bother you?'

'It is an honour, Kapitän.'

Theo nods. 'I trust you to empty the slop bucket and keep it clean. You told me you have young brothers you helped care for.'

'Before this war, Kapitän.'

'I would like you to wash him, will you do that for me?'

'Of course, Kapitän.'

Lewandowski walks to a bunk and looks down at the sleeping boy. Then he looks at his captain. Though he says nothing Theo can see his concern. He checks the boy is breathing and hears short, shallow breaths.

'Marek? What?'

'It is time he woke, Kapitän. He sleeps too much, I fear he is not well. Should we wake him?'

The heat in the boat can be unbearable. In contrast to the bundled-up child Theo travelled with in the truck, his boy now wears one of Theo's cotton shirts, a garment so large on him it resembles a nightshirt.

'No, that would be unwise. As soon as he wakes you will tell me. Come to me yourself, wherever I am. Tell nobody, understand?'

'Of course, Kapitän.'

'I will come when I can. It is not easy for me.'

Lewandowski goes to salute but stops halfway. Theo returns his nod.

Then Theo is gone, back through the noise. He is concerned that bringing Peter on board has endangered not only his son but also his crew. Perhaps, in his desire to quieten his boy he has gone too far. He used a whole sleeping tablet, not just a fragment. Twelve hours, Walter had said. Twelve hours at least.

Back in his cabin he drops his cap on his desk and slumps on his bunk with his head in his hands. The crime he has committed will be discovered. One way or another Roth will learn about Peter and all will be lost. He sniffs the air. Remembers the side of bacon. Though it is gone its smoky, salty smell remains on his bunk and he savours it. In a few hours the only smells in the boat will be fumes from the engines and stale sweat from the crew.

As he lies there he wonders if any of it matters. Wonders what Roth can do on a boat bound for Argentina. Buenos Aires, his orders said. In them there was no mention of the Reichsmarschall, his key staff, or the cargo they carry.

Soon all their failed leaders would flee, the Führer amongst them. What made no sense to Theo was why Göring, the man commanding the Luftwaffe, would travel by U-boat when he could fly – if not to South America then to another neutral country, Switzerland or Portugal. The man had been an airman, a fighter pilot. Surely he would never elect to travel by submarine? Or maybe he wouldn't have had a choice. Hadn't Walter said the man might be taken against his will?

Something Lange said comes back to him but a split second later it is gone. Knowing he dare not rest for more than a few minutes he stares at the grey ceiling above his bunk and considers the events of the last two days. Walter had gone back on his word, deciding time was against them, that taking Peter to Theo's parents was no longer possible. Instead he'd promised that when they reached Hamburg they would seek out Erica's friends. It would be easy to locate them, he'd said; he had friends and his friends had friends; they knew everything and everyone.

It hadn't happened. On the road into Hamburg Walter took over the driving and came straight to the dockyard. They were two days late. There was no time to drop off the boy.

Lying on his bunk, Theo's thoughts come together. For the first time in weeks he wonders how Walter kept himself so well informed. At Carinhall he had access to telephones, perhaps even a friend or two. But since then, apart from the SS colleague he met, he has been isolated, out of contact with others. Clearly, he has been working to a timetable only he knew about.

Stranger still, he helped smuggle Peter into the dockyard and on to the boat. Why risk that, if Göring and his closest staff are to be there? And Roth – Walter didn't seem surprised at the man's presence. It is as if everything – apart from the confusion at Monowitz – had been planned. Theo recalls what Walter said about the SS, that they ran the Reich. They owned its factories and most of its wealth.

Lange's words about Roth – *we must make sure that fat bastard comes up last* – come back to him, as does their significance. Compared with Roth, Reichsmarschall Göring is massive, there is no way he would fit through hatches or bulkhead doors. The whole thing was a sham. There never was a plan to bring Göring on board or reunite him with his treasures.

Theo rolls sideways and sits upright. He must not sleep, not with Roth on the loose. In a tin fish there are no secrets; in time the man will become adventurous and explore the boat, pass through the engine room and enter the aft tube room. And then what?

The face he sees in his mirror has aged ten years in the last four. Days and nights without sleep have taken their toll. His eyes are deep-set. Lines on his forehead that once came only when he frowned are there always, like tram lines. He strokes his new beard, the slowly returning submariner's badge of office. Like the hair on his head it has streaks of white. This beard, he tells himself, will be a practical beard, short and neat-trimmed. Shaving takes time and uses valuable water. A beard keeps you warm on the bridge, it breaks up fierce winds. He leans forwards, touches his brow with his fingers. Even when he tries to smile the worry lines won't go,.

At training school he was immortal. He trained in the Baltic with others – mock attacks on the surface, sixty-six in all. Then attacks when submerged, sixty-six also. Is it pagan, this number? – pagan like so many things now, the crosses and runes, the magical symbols. Then there was torpedo practice, lurking beneath the surface. Not always on the ranges. Not always dummy targets.

For those that survived, life was good.

His mind is drifting. It is a sign of tiredness and he jumps up, returns to the control room, calls his navigator and sets a new course.

Word travels quickly. Most of his crew assumed Norway and there are whispers as money changes hands, mainly bets lost. The new north-west course means they head for the north Atlantic, north-west because the English Channel and the German Sea are mined heavily by both sides. Sailing to the north of the Shetlands is the only way through.

'Tell me our route, Kapitänleutnant…'

Roth has come from his suite in the bow. His tone is condescending and casual. He is now the big guest, the man in the penthouse suite.

'As ordered, Sturmbannführer,' Theo says, tracing a finger across the chart. 'We go north of the Scottish islands to avoid minefields off Orkney Isle. Here, you see? Then west to Faeroes and Iceland. From there, south into the Atlantic Sea.'

The course he has set is more dangerous than most. The waters between Iceland and Scotland have the world's longest minefield, laid by the British at the start of the war – eight hundred kilometres of mines that have claimed at least three U-boats. Once, when he thought it might matter, Theo worked out the British had laid around one hundred thousand mines.

His orders are clear: stay submerged and take the long route. Staying submerged is a departure from normal, slower but safer. In the early years the Führer decreed that to get to the Atlantic killing grounds faster, all U-boats should run on the surface. The decision was madness. They lost many boats.

When Roth sleeps again Theo will check the charts and plan a new route. By hugging the north coast of Scotland and navigating the Pentland Firth he can reach the North Atlantic in half the time, he has done it before, he knows the risks of passing though the most policed stretch of water in the world; corvettes and destroyers from the British Scapa Flow base can outrun him easily; Wellington bombers of British Coastal Command have good radar. Some have huge floodlights to seek U-boats at night. Very few of his comrades have seen these lights and lived to tell the tale.

Tobacco is Theo's only vice. When he was based in France many of his men would go to brothels, while he sat and smoked. Digging deep in his kitbag he finds his tobacco pipes and lays them out neatly – the English Briar Sam Spargo gave him, and the pipe with the rosewood stem. There is the one with the carved meerschaum bowl, a present from Erika, a pipe he touches fondly, flipping up the hinged silver lid that covers the bowl. It is a traditional, practical pipe, ideal for rough weather, though he has never taken it up-top, he has lost several that way. He puts the briar back in his bag. Between the pipe's stem and bowl is a silver band engraved with the English maker's name. Unwise to leave it around with Roth snooping.

His tobacco pouch is almost empty. Somewhere he has a tobacco tin and he hunts for it, first in his pockets and then in his bag. He finds it, opens it, and sniffs deeply at tobacco Walter gave him. It is good stuff and he tugs at it, transfers a wad of it to his tobacco pouch. He picks strands of it between finger and thumb, packing them into the rosewood pipe and jamming them down with his finger.

It is a ritual half-done. Half done because he must not light the tobacco, not here, the air is bad enough without polluting it more. And naked flames are dangerous; when the boat's batteries are charging they emit explosive gases. From his locker Theo drags out a sweater, pulls it over his head, and exits his cabin to seek out his oilskins.

He joins the Officer of the Watch and the lookouts on the bridge. The sea is calm. All are cocooned in a dense, cotton-wool fog that traps the fumes from the diesels. He comments that the air in the boat is probably fresher and he wonders, as he always wonders on days like this, whether the enemy's radar can penetrate fog like this. Always the pessimist, he assumes that it can.

'If you cannot see,' he says to those around him, 'You can listen. Get to know the sounds made by our engines. Only when you know that sound well will you hear other sounds, sounds that should not be there, sounds made by aircraft, ships and patrol boats. Be aware this fog is thin, it is cold and it lies low. Our warm diesel exhaust rises above it and colours the fog. Aircraft flying in the clear skies above it will watch for such changes.'

He flicks the wheel on his lighter, looks at it, smells the wick and tries again. The First Watch Officer takes a box from his pocket, strikes a match and holds it out. A safe thing to do only in daylight, in fog such as this.

In different conditions the smell of his tobacco smoke would be dispersed, thinned by the wind and carried away. Today it will be sucked into the air intakes and pervade the whole boat. When he returns below his crewmen, in the hope of a turn on deck, or the bridge, or the wintergarden, will attend to him like dogs wanting treats.

Theo stands there for hours, pipe in mouth, its furnace long dead. Finally, slowly and gradually, the fog lifts. For a while it remains patchy and then, in a very short time, it is blown away southwards by a strong, icy breeze. Theo watches it leave. A retreating white wall.

Later, when Theo is again below, he calls the navigator to his cabin.

'The Firth of Pentland, Kapitän?' the young man says, his voice a whisper. 'Not the charted course?'

'You know nothing of this, Rydel. You will tell no one. The men who make bets, you will not speak to them.'

'And the Sturmbannführer?'

'Has he spoken to you?'

'He asks questions. While you were on the bridge. While you were smoking your pipe.'

Dogs wanting treats.

'Tell him nothing. He has no right to ask you and you have no authority to tell him. Refer him to me.'

The man nods. Theo looks at the small brass clock on his wall. It is late afternoon.

'The fog has cleared,' he says. 'Isn't it time for a star fix?'

Rydel frowns. 'Surely it is not yet dark?'

'Another hour and it will be. It is cold but dry up there. Don't forget to take your cigarettes to the bridge.'

The man understands and he nods again. 'But the Pentland Firth, Kapitän?'

'Later, Rydel. I will call you here. When I do, bring the appropriate charts.'

Franz Rydel, like Marek Lewandowski, is one of the boat's youngest. He is straight from the training flotilla in Hamburg and knows the Pentland Firth is a difficult, dangerous route. He also know the history, knows that at the start of this war U-boat commander Günther Prien stole into Scapa Flow and torpedoed the Royal Oak. The old British battleship was expendable but the 1,300 men who died in it were not, they were sailors like him. He remembers these things. Remembers, too, what his father used to say, that those who plan wars should be placed in the front line.

In the boat the pictures are out, they are taped to bulkheads and tucked behind fittings, photographs of girlfriends and fiancés, children and wives. The men are settling in. Theo savours the moments as he walks through his vessel.

In the aft tube room again he asks Lewandowski, 'Does he still sleep?'

The young man nods. One of the bunks opposite is now occupied by a bearded man who snores loudly. Beside him, fixed to a bulkhead, is a photo of a woman with short hair. Two children beside her stare suspiciously at the camera lens. Theo nods questioningly at the bunk.

'Stoker Fischer, Kapitän.'

'He sleeps well.'

There is nothing more to say. Theo tips down the guard rail on the side of his boy's bunk and sits for a while on the edge of the mattress. As he leaves the room he inspects the steel door. It is the tube room's only access.

'I want a door-stop on the aft tube room bulkhead door, Chief,' Theo says later in his cabin. 'A spot of weld on the hinges to stop the door opening fully. Enough for a slim man to enter, but no more. Can you do that?'

Chief Engineer Lange nods. 'I shall see to it.'

'Stoker Fischer... do you know him?'

'I have sailed with him. He is a man to be trusted.'

'I was not aware your men would be sleeping in the aft tube room. I want all but Lewandowski out of there.'

'I chose to put them there. The artificers and mechanics know about Peter. Better they sleep there than with other crewmen. There will always be at least one of my men sleeping there your boy will never be alone.'

'I have dealt with that already. Lewandowski will stay with him day and night.'

'I did not know that.'

'Are you sure your men can be trusted? Every one of them?'

'With my life, Kapitän.'

'Very well. They can stay. That door hinge, Chief. See to it now.'

Except for the dive in the Elbe and two practice dives carried out in deep water, Theo has kept the boat on the surface. He has doubled the watch on the bridge in the hope they will see other vessels and planes before they themselves are seen. Now, in the fading light, through his Zeiss glasses, Theo sees land, a dull line on the horizon. Now, on the bridge, he stands beside Chief Engineer Lange.

'Scotland, Kapitän?'

Theo nods. 'I am told the Sturmbannführer has been up here.'

'He was here when I came. Fifteen minutes ago.'

'I shall try to prevent it. If he questions you, you must say you do not know where we are. Don't try to be clever, Chief. The man may look a fool but that does not mean he is one. Did he ask questions?'

'He just stood and looked. He does not like the cold.'

Theo, about to return below, swivels on his heel and stares out at to sea. To reach the Pentland Firth they will run up the coast, submerged by day and on the surface at night. Running the Firth will save two days. Submerged, though, a deep run on motors at the pace of a snail.

He grasps the hatch handrail and puts one boot on the ladder. As he does so the lookout behind him yells out: 'Aircraft, dead ahead!'

The klaxon blares. Men scramble. At other times Theo would be last off the bridge but he is at the hatch already and dropping fast.

The tanks are flooding already, pulling the boat down. A waterfall cascades down the ladder way as the last man through the hatch slams it closed.

The pulsing rasp of the alarm is silenced. All is quiet. The control wheels that affect the boat's tilt have been superseded by modern, push-button controls. The large manual wheels are now for emergencies. Instead of attending to them the hydroplane operators watch the results of their button-pushes on the same, old large dials.

'Big one,' First Watch says. 'Wellington, possibly. Flying low.'

Theo nods. It is what these planes do. Flying low means they see silhouetted conning towers and schnörkels. Even periscopes. He stands aside, pulls a towel from around his neck and wrings it out. If the plane flies too close its crew will see turbulent water. They will be back.

Men watch dials. The boat is levelling out.

'Twenty meters... twenty-five. Thirty and holding...'

The diesels have stopped. The boat is running on its motors, cruising away from the dive spot. In the clear blue Mediterranean they would be seen at great depth. But not here.

'Hold depth! Keep silence!'

There is no need for the command, it is quiet already. Crewmen sit or stand like shop dummies. A man whispers, the Bosun glares. The second hand on the bulkhead clock moves more slowly than usual, they are sure of it. It goes around once, then twice, then three times. Now eight times. If the aircraft has seen them it will now be returning. Any second now...

Roth appears from nowhere. His leather-soled shoes click on the decking.

'There is trouble, Kapitänleutnant? Why was I not told?'

Nobody answers. Nobody looks.

'Kapitän?'

'Enemy aircraft, Sturmbannführer. Please keep silence. Please leave the control room.'

'Were we seen?'

'We will know soon enough. That we saw the aircraft is all that matters. We didn't wait around to wave to the pilot.'

Men splutter, stifling laughter. Roth colours up but says nothing. For the first time he seems to sense he is outnumbered and perhaps he should join in the laughter. He cannot, and instead he attempts a weak smile. If it gets as far as his face the crew do not see it.

Theo snaps an instruction. 'Periscope depth!'

The hydroplane men play their buttons. Drive motors hum. A booming hiss of compressed air says the tanks are blown.

'Watch it, Chief!'

Lange nods. There is no need to explain. The compressed air filling the ballast tanks forces out water to lighten the boat. Too much air, too soon, and it will escape with the blown water and erupt from the sea like a wallowing whale. The hydroplane men watch the Papenburg – a tall, water-filled tube that shows fine-depth. By carefully trimming the boat they will keep the conning tower well below surface.

Roth stays in a corner, leaning back with arms folded. The boat has two periscopes, the observation scope and the attack periscope – a scope that on a boat without armaments serves as a second pair of eyes. Lookouts sit at both and search the sea and sky.

The skies are safe. The man on the observation scope steps aside for Theo, who swivels to see a coastline, far away. The slow-moving dots he sees are steam coasters with wispy black smoke, hugging the land, hoping they won't be seen.

As Theo steps away from the scope Roth shoves himself upright. He intends to take Theo's place on the scope but with a whirr of motors both periscopes drop to their homes beneath the floor. Roth glares around the control room to see who did it but nobody moves.

Theo breaks silence. 'I instructed you to leave the control room, Sturmbannführer. You have no right to be here.'

Crewmen glance sideways then turn back quickly. Roth's neck flushes purple. His voice is quiet but it hisses and splutters.

'Accompany me to my quarters, Kapitänleutnant. Do it now!'

Roth leaves the control room clumsily and hurriedly, Theo following. Once they are through the bow tube room door Theo slams it behind them, anxious to speak the first words. He manages it. Roth, it seems, is still speechless.

'Your presence in the control room jeopardises the safety of my

THE MAN WHO PLAYED TRAINS

boat Sturmbannführer. I instructed you to leave and you chose to ignore me. Either I am in command of this vessel or I am not.'

Words said without thinking. Words that could have prompted a negative response from Roth but he seems to have missed them. His colour has gone and he appears to have calmed. The wooden door to the cabins is closed. The padlock and chain that was once on the watertight door is now wrapped harmlessly around the door handle.

Roth looks Theo up and down, from sea boots to beard.

'I have heard about you naval men,' he says calmly. 'You escape the real war. You know nothing of the bloodshed and slaughter faced by our real fighters.'

Theo stands facing him. There is nothing to say.

'So! You agree with me! I know about you, Volker, I have read your dossier. You are not a real fighter. Your father was a miner. You are merely a miner, like him.'

A mining engineer and now a naval man, a twice-decorated commander of a Kriegsmarine boat. Yes. My father was a miner. Words thought but not spoken.

'You were a miner in Salzgitter. Your people there failed us, Volker, they failed Germany. Under the Reichsmarschall's Four-Year Plan you were to deliver twenty-four million tons of iron ore by last year. And what did you produce? Not even one third of it! That is a failure, Volker!'

The man has done his homework. Theo was there when production geared up. It made no difference how many men and machines they sent, the ore they mined was poor, the grades were low. Theo wonders if Roth knows he, Theo, refused to transfer to the Lorraine.

'Failed us, Volker! Have you nothing to say?'

'I am needed in the control room, Sturmbannführer.'

Roth's colour rises. He turns his head to one side and spits at the floor. Then the sneer: 'Go about your wretched business! I outrank you, Volker! I am a better man than you in every way!'

'He woke, Kapitän,' Lewandowski says excitedly. 'I have told nobody!'

Theo is in the aft tube room. Now there are three men in the bunks, all on the wall opposite Peter's. Two are asleep and one is pretending to be.

'But he sleeps now. He seemed well?'

'He was disturbed and he was pale. Should we not call the medic?'

Theo seems not to hear. 'The Chief Engineer brought him food, scrambled egg. Did he eat it?'

'He ate all of it.'

Theo nods. He stands thoughtfully, stroking his stubble. Then he turns to the steel door he just came through and attempts to open it fully. It jams, won't open wider than it did when he squeezed into the room. A small block of steel, welded to one of the hinges, snags the door when it opens.

'Stoker Fischer has difficulty getting in and out, Kapitän.'

'Then Stoker Fischer is too fat.'

There is a grunt from one of the bunks. Lewandowski smiles.

Theo takes out a small tin, opens it and pinches one of the yellow tablets with his fingernails. It breaks in half and he holds a fragment out on the palm of his hand. 'Here,' he says. 'If Peter wakes before we surface, give him this.'

'With respect, Kapitän, I do not think I should do that.'

Theo stiffens. 'Yes. Very well. But take it. Give it if he becomes disturbed or cries out. For the next few hours we will be silent-running on motors. He must not be heard.'

He knows Lewandowski is right. His son is unlikely to cry. Since Theo first saw him he has shown few signs of emotion.

CHAPTER FORTY-FOUR

THE FIRST CLIFF PATH Spargo ascended from the beach ended at a sheer drop. He balanced on the edge of it, scanning the cliffs from a new vantage point. It was a waste of effort, he was chasing shadows, there seemed to be holes everywhere. Binoculars would have helped. He descended through rubble and returned to Benares. The man pointed to a ledge he had seen while he was waiting.

'There is another place, that hole. Now you go to that one…'

Spargo did as he was told. Went up. Came down.

One hour and several trips later, Benares pointed again. Spargo raised his arms in despair.

'I can't check every bloody one of them! It'll take the rest of the day!'

'We have the rest of the day. You will do it, Mister Spargo.'

Spargo suspected Benares was playing with him, exacting revenge for any number of things. It was clear to him the paths were made by small animals and not one of them went from one side of the collapse to the other. Whenever he investigated a place he had to return to the bay and start over.

'There is another,' Benares said. 'There, do you see it?'

'Another of your shadows. It's rocks sticking out.'

'It is a hole, I think. I have been to the water's edge and from there I can see it clearly. It is a hole in the rock.'

Spargo's body had been working mechanically, fighting tiredness and pain. Ignoring Benares he sat on a boulder and stretched out his legs. There was a limit to what his body could do and he was close to that limit. Also, he still had to get out of the bay. Still had to climb to the top.

'It's time we went back to Bar.'

Benares looked at his watch. 'Mister Bar will be sleeping, it is his time for rest. You will make one more trip.' He pointed. 'Up there, to that place I have seen.'

'I can't get there. I'm not a climber. It needs ropes.'

'That is an excuse. I can see a ledge, you can cross it. Go, Mister Spargo! Do not try my patience!'

Ironically, until now, Spargo had genuinely wanted to find the old adit. Searching the cliffs had rekindled a boyhood interest in exploring. Had it not been for the tiredness and pain, and the fact he was no longer the fit lad who once leapt between boulders, the experience might have been a pleasant one. Now he was past caring. Not for Jez – that was what spurred him on – but for himself.

The overhang Benares had seen was near the very top of the cliffs. Staring up at it, Spargo had the notion that if it were possible to get to that high then it might also be possible to climb right to the top and escape from Benares. Bar would be in the car with the engine running and the heater turned up. Unless he had a gun – unlikely, because he had been on a plane – there would be no resistance.

Spargo set off. Halfway to the overhang he stopped for a rest. Benares, far below, was sitting on a rock at the water's edge, cleaning his shoes in the sea. Spargo continued his climb. Ahead of him was the ledge Benares had seen. It wasn't a true ledge but a thin, vertical slice of rock that had torn away from the cliff. It leaned outwards precariously, as if any additional weight might cause it to fall outwards. When he got closer to it he peered into the crevasse-like gash between the cliff and the slab. It looked bottomless.

The overhang Benares had seen was on the far side of the slice. He could see it properly now and there was something about it, something unnatural. For one thing the overhang was flat underneath whereas those he'd seen so far were irregular. Also, he was sure he could see patterns, parallel lines on the rock. Clouds moved. The light changed. The lines became clear. He knew he was looking at half-barrels – the remains of the drill holes that were charged with explosive for blasting the rock. He had found the old adit. The original entrance had gone but the tunnel was there.

Spurred on by what he was seeing, Spargo knelt down at the end of the ledge and started to crawl. It was madness. Crawling across meant looking down – an abyss on one side of him and a sheer drop to the bay on the other.

An experienced climber might have walked across. A tightrope walker might have run. Spargo was neither of these. Gradually he eased himself forwards until he straddled the slice, one leg in the crevasse and the other outside it.

With sweeps of his arm he cleared stones from his path, stones that smacked and cracked as they bounced to the bay. After ten minutes of shuffling on his backside he stopped and looked back. He was halfway across and he'd had enough. Nothing he had ever done had equipped him to cross something like this.

Aware again of the pain in his side he closed his eyes. It was a mistake because dizziness overtook him, a numbness that started in his feet and spread through his body. Like a child on a horse without reins he slumped forwards and clung to the ledge. His arms turned to rubber. His grip failed.

Spargo didn't know how long he had lain there. Roused by the shrieks of gulls he came round refreshed, his head clear and his pain gone. He knew exactly where he was and why he was there but he no longer cared, no longer felt danger.

A few minutes later he was standing on moss-clad rock, reaching high for firm handholds and heaving himself up. Peering into the adit he saw nothing but blackness. The glare from the sea had been strong, and to get used to the gloom he stepped into the gloom. For a while he could see only a low-roofed, narrow tunnel that sloped gently downwards, but gradually his eyes adjusted. How far could he see, he wondered? Twenty meters? Thirty, perhaps? Though the floor was littered with fallen rocks the adit hadn't collapsed, it wasn't blocked. He remembered Bar's torch, took it out and switched it on. In its light he went further, picking his way around rocks.

John Spargo, walking in Sam Spargo's old mine.

There was no point going further. The mine would be flooded. Sooner or later he would come to drowned workings and the thought of that unnerved him. What would Bar do now, he wondered, would he admit to the consortium he'd found the mine? And if he did, would they bother to fund exploration, bring in pumps the size of trucks, site them on the cliff and pump water for months?

He imagined what it would be like down there. After fifty years under water the workings would be treacherous and knee-deep in mud. Exploration of the mine would be a colossal waste of time, effort and money. Anything stored there, protected or not, would have rotted away.

He turned to leave. Took two or three steps towards the dazzling entrance. Then he changed his mind. Despite his imaginations he had no fears of being alone underground. He knew the dangers. He knew what to look for.

The adit seemed to go on for ever. Because it curved slightly the daylight soon vanished. Its roof was uncomfortably low – painfully low for a man with a hip wound. Apart from a few fallen rocks the floor was clean, there was no ankle-deep mud like in some mines he knew. Once there were rails for small locos that pulled long trains of tubs full of ore and waste rock. His father had told him that before the cliffs collapsed the waste rock was dumped in the bay. The ore came out that way too and was loaded onto coasters at a jetty, destroyed when the cliffs fell. Very small quantities of ore, Spargo guessed. Minute, compared with the amounts from mines he was used to.

Because there had once been rails the floor of the adit was smooth, there was no danger from unseen shafts. He walked on with his head well down, now and again craning his neck vulture-like to peer ahead, checking the way was clear and the roof safe. His breath, and the heat from his body, mixed with the mine's cold air and formed a steamy white mist. It glowed in the torchlight. Obscured his view.

As on the cliffs, his soles gripped the rock well. His footfalls, though light, echoed around him with deep, hollow booms. He felt safer here than on the cliffs – and infinitely safer than he'd felt with Benares. Here he was in his element, a no-go place for his abductors, an underground alley where getting lost wasn't possible. If his torch failed he would simply turn back.

His real concern was the air. He checked through his mental list of bad gases, the odourless poisons that crept up on you gradually, knocked you down before you knew they were there. There might also be another problem, one often overlooked – not the presence of poisons but the absence of air – a simple lack of oxygen. He took deep breaths. The air was fresh, kept clean by winds in the bay. Air that smelled more of seaweed than old mine.

It crossed Spargo's mind that by finding the adit he'd changed everything. If Bar had seriously thought of him as an asset, he was even more of one now. He was no longer expendable and if he played his cards right he might even get to handle the next stage of Bar's project. He would suggest to Bar that he, Spargo, was the best man to plan and manage the dewatering and exploration. The locals knew him and trusted him. He could reassure them – with all honesty – that it was simply exploration. There would be no mining.

He stopped dead. Something had changed. The echoes from his footsteps had been hollow and distant and they were now short and flat – the change you get in a blind alley when you approach the end wall. Spargo, attempting to see under the persistent haze, ducked down and shone the light under the fog. His instincts were right. Ahead of him, blocking the tunnel, was a pyramid of broken, angular rocks.

He could see what had happened. The left hand side of the tunnel had been cut away to provide a safe refuge for miners and more recently its roof had collapsed into the tunnel, filling it from wall to wall with broken rock. He moved cautiously forwards, picking his way over rubble.

Checking the roof for loose rock he shone the torch beam upwards. It was like peering up into an unstable, badly built factory chimney. Rocks bigger than his head hung ready to fall, and trickles of water seeped from fissures and splashed on the pile.

It had been a bad place to widen the tunnel. The rock elsewhere was solid and safe but here it was broken, the natural rock joints all gappy and loose. As if alerting him to the dangers a book-sized slab broke away silently, dropping to the pile with an echoing smack. Rock falls can be hair-triggered, they loosen so gradually that a footfall, a cough or sneeze – even body warmth from an intruder like him – might bring on another collapse.

Spargo shone his torch at the top of the rubble pile. It seemed to light up nothing, it was as if darkness swallowed the beam. Curious, he mounted the pile, dropping to all fours as he neared the top. The broken rock didn't quite touch the roof of the tunnel; over the years it had settled and slumped to leave a narrow void like the slot of a letterbox. By leaning forwards and holding the torch at arm's length he could see over the pile.

He expected his torch beam to light the roof or the walls on the other side of the collapse but there seemed to be nothing. He tried again, slithering forwards with his back against the tunnel roof and directing the torch beam in a different direction. Still he saw nothing. To make the gap bigger he shoved loose rocks through the gap and heard them tumble down the other side. It wasn't long before he realised that if could loosen a few of the largest blocks and shove them through too, the gap would be wide enough to squeeze through.

He tried. Managed to get his head and shoulders into the gap. Managed, also, to drop the torch – his hands were wet and it was smeared with mud. The torch clattered down the rocks and went out.

Spargo told himself he didn't need the torch. His imaginings were triggered not by darkness but by nearness to sleep – the time of night when thoughts ran wild and raised demons. Going back would be simple, he would slide down the pile and retrace his steps, keeping his head well down while he groped the adit sidewalls. On the way in he had seen no side turnings; the trip back to surface would be tedious but safe.

It wasn't the thought of a torchless journey back to the cliff that made Spargo determined to get through the gap, it was simply that curiosity got the better of him. He was a mining man, and what he had seen on the other side of the collapse – or what he hadn't seen, because the torch hadn't lit anything at all – puzzled him. The possibility Bar might employ him made it even more important to see what was there. The more he could tell the man, the better.

If he could get his head and shoulders through the gap then the rest of him would follow and with luck his torch would still work and he would retrieve it. To widen the gap he removed more rocks. This time he pulled them towards him rather than pushed them through. Finally, when he was sure the gap was wide enough for him to slide through, he thrust himself forwards. It was a mistake. A protruding nub of rock in the roof tore against his side and unable to cope with the pain his body gave up. It was, Spargo thought in his last few seconds of consciousness, like lights in a shop at closing time, going off one by one.

The visions came to Spargo the way they always came – white ghosts walking, drifting past him, staring with unseeing eyes. As always he tried to run but his legs wouldn't take him. He tried to hide. Tried to pretend they weren't there.

Though the visions lasted only minutes, to him it was more like hours. Groaning, he came round slowly. Remembering where he was he groaned again. The pain in his side was now a dull throb but there were other pains, pains in his back, his legs and his arms. Exhausted, he lay still. He wanted to sleep. Wanted to lie there for ever.

It was time to get out. Slowly, taking care not to make contact again with the wedge of rock, he eased himself backwards. The gap was tight and his jacket rucked up, he couldn't slip back, nor could he reach back to straighten it because to get through the gap he had stretched out both arms ahead of him. Like a fish on a barbed hook, the more he struggled the tighter he stuck. Reluctantly he realised there was only one way to go and he slithered, snake-like, through the gap and down the other side.

For the first time since he entered the adit he was able to stand upright. He took advantage of the space to stretch his arms, his legs and his back. He groped for his torch and when he found it he thumped it. It came on and its beam lit, albeit dimly, a cavern the size of a small house. He was in one of the mine's old stopes – one of the huge underground voids left by the miners after they'd mined out the ore.

Conscious of the need to check dangers Spargo held the torch high, darting its beam across the stope's roof and walls. The adit he had come down continued in the opposite wall as a much larger, square shaped tunnel, a mine drive twice his height. Returning to the surface without walking on into drive didn't enter his mind. So far, all he could tell Bar was that the way into the mine was blocked by a collapse that could be moved easily. And then what? He needed to know.

He crossed the floor of the stope and entered the drive. Like the adit, it sloped gently downwards. Hoping to get more light from the torch he rubbed its glass with his jacket but the more he rubbed the dirtier it became. The dirt on the glass cast blurred shadows, and what had seemed like a good light in the adit now seemed faint and dim. He was taking risks now; if his torch failed he could well be in trouble; venturing underground with one source of light was a real no-no. He had broken so many rules, he was so unprepared.

He had only taken a few steps into the drive when he paused. Again, the echoes weren't right. His footsteps, instead of sounding hollow and booming, were flat and mute, but in the torch's dim light he saw nothing to trouble him. Then something, he didn't know what, made him stop and he pointed the torch down. Six feet in front of him there was no tunnel floor.

The first miners at Kilcreg mined ore from mineral veins they followed through the rock. Later they learned the mineral they wanted was not just in the veins, it was also throughout the rock in small grains. To recover it they removed huge masses of rock, and in doing so they cut through old workings. Once-safe tunnels then ended unexpectedly, high up in the sides of great underground voids. Spargo, it seemed, had reached one of these subterranean death traps.

This was the end. If the crates had been brought this far into the mine then it was not to hide them, it was to destroy them. He took a shuffling step forwards. Then another and another, moving closer to the edge as drawn by a magnet. Dark underground voids can do that, you get close and you want to look down. To steady himself he moved to one of the side walls, reached out with his free hand and touched it with outstretched fingers. With his other hand he pointed the torch down, and although the weak beam appeared to light nothing at all, it seemed to throw shadows. He wiped the glass on his jacket and pointed the beam upwards. The tunnel roof was there but the walls seemed to continue into the void. It made no sense at all.

Concerned he was hallucinating, he blinked to clear his eyes. Bad air poisons you slowly, it affects your brain, slowing your reasoning. Spargo had been so concerned with the state of the roof and walls he hadn't thought about air. On the other side of the blockage he'd had fresh, clean air. Here it lacked oxygen.

The only clear thought in Spargo's head was that he was too close to the edge. He knew he had to step back but he realised, as his legs crumpled beneath him, that he no longer had control over his movements. Grabbing pointlessly at the wall he toppled forwards, into blackness.

CHAPTER FORTY-FIVE

CONDITIONS IN U-1500 ARE GRIM. In the day it runs submerged and at night it runs on the surface where it is propelled by its diesels, replenishing air in its tanks and recharging its batteries. To do this it runs at schnörkel depth, a clever device that is, perhaps, not so clever. If the boat runs at more than a few knots there is a risk of bending the schnörkel's steel tubes. If the tubes are bent the boat cannot submerge.

Tides run fast through the Pentland Firth. If Theo gets his timing right then deep water currents will carry his boat through. In the control room he sits at the scope with his eyes on the coast. They are not yet near the Firth; they have a long way to go.

'You are submerged, Kapitänleutnant.'

A self-evident truth from Roth. He has come up behind Theo, spook-like. Theo tries to ignore him but the man hovers close. He touches the grey steel of the periscope.

'May I?'

The request is hard to resist. Theo imagines Roth squatting on the pads, his pig-eyes seeing a coast that can only be Scotland. He imagines him checking the charts and that must not happen. Unwinding himself from the column he stands in Roth's way. Someone, like before, hits a switch. The periscope slides down between deck-plates.

'About to submerge, Sturmbannführer. Silent running. Passing through enemy-patrolled waters.'

'And these waters are?'

Unsure what to say Theo hides his anxiety. He wasn't expecting this interest. Hidden in his cabin is a plot of their true course, a clear cellophane overlay that he alone sees – and that he alone updates regularly.

There is another chart on the control room's chart table. Roth goes to it and stands behind navigator Rydel, who crouching over it drawing fine lines in blue Chinagraph pencil. Theo can hardly believe what he is seeing.

'So this is our course, Volker?' Roth asks, touching the fine line on the sheet. 'This is the route in our orders?'

Theo's mind runs in circles. It is almost unbelievable that he, Theodor Volker, has failed to anticipate that Roth might want to inspect the charts. It is even more unbelievable that Rydel has been stupid enough to take the chart from his cabin and expose it to view.

'This place,' Roth asks. 'Where is this?'

Rydel responds. 'Your orders, Sturmbannführer. I cannot comment.'

Roth swivels on his heel and stares hard at Theo. Theo looks at the chart, becomes transfixed by it. It is a new chart, one he's not seen before. And it is a false chart. The course Rydel has plotted on it follows the one in Theo's orders.

'Here,' Theo says quickly, pointing to the end of the short, fine blue line. 'You can see our progress.'

Roth is tapping a finger on the cellophane overlay.

'I asked what is this place, Kapitän, not where we are. I can see where we are.'

'Scotland.' Theo says. 'These are the Shetland Islands. Our course takes us well north of them.'

'I am aware of that.'

Roth's fat finger traces the blue line. At each change of course there are points, each marked with a time. Everything is false; if they were following the correct course it would have been impossible to have travelled that far in such a short time. Roth inspects closely and nods his approval.

'Very good. I shall retire to my quarters. You will call me when you next decide to surface.'

With a dull click of heels the man leaves. Theo stares at the map overlay. It is a complete work of fiction. Then he stares at Rydel. The face looks so young, so innocent. It blushes.

They run deep for an hour. The sound man sits nervously, headphones clamped to his ears and fingers on dials, turning and fine-tuning as he seeks far off sounds. At intervals Chief Engineer Lange stops the motors so the sound man can hear clearly.

Again at periscope depth, Theo scans the scene. They are thirty kilometres from the coast. Though much too far to the north to be seen is the Isle of Orkney and its Scapa Flow base. He is uneasy. He sees no boats, no patrols. Does this mean the waters ahead of him are mined? Have the British have changed their safe channels?

In the aft tube room Peter is awake. The boy is sitting up but looks sickly and pale. Theo sits beside him on the bunk and asks how he feels and if he wants food. The boy says nothing.

'I have not used the tablet,' Lewandowski says. 'He has slept. He has been so quiet that I worry, Kapitän. I know he is sick, his eyes are strange, he does not focus them. I gave him thin oatmeal and he brought it all up.'

Theo shakes his head. The voyage has hardly started. If Peter is like this now, what will he be like in a month? Or in three?

A cook in the galley bundles long loaves in his arms, struggles with them to the Petty Officers' space and dumps them on a makeshift table. Ten places are set, five a side. The cook has already brought fried eggs, fried bacon and sausage – a meal the Bosun calls The Enemy's Breakfast. There is coffee, of sorts, made from god-knows-what. Rumoured to be burnt acorns.

Theo arrives at the table, reaches for a loaf and breaks off a large piece. Chief Engineer Lange is seated there, eating.

'Have you seen Roth, Chief?'

'A couple of hours ago, Kapitän. He was throwing up. He does not like the sea.'

They talk, joking and laughing. Lange speaks some English, as does Theo. Theo makes a joke that is a play on English words and they both laugh. To their surprise, so does Rydel.

Theo says, 'You speak English?'

Rydel hesitates before answering. Laughing was foolish and careless.

'I speak a little.'

Lange laughs again. 'Don't let Herr Roth hear you. He will have you shot as a spy.'

It is a poor joke and there is no more laughter. Theo exchanges glances with Lange and mumbles his oft-made comment that walls have ears. Even the walls of tin fish. After their meal Theo ushers Rydel to his cabin and closes the door. He looks the navigator in the eye and speaks quietly.

'That course you were plotting. It had false entries, false positions. It was wrong of me to confide in you that I am deviating from the set course but you are the navigating officer, I had no choice. The responsibility is mine and mine alone and I cannot allow you to falsify documents, however well-intentioned your actions. From now on I shall navigate, I will update your charts. If Sturmbannführer Roth asks why you are no longer navigating then refer him to me.'

Navigator Rydel saved Theo's skin, Theo knows that. But it was a clear breach of regulations he cannot condone, he dare not collude with juniors, however well-meaning. Nor can he bring himself to ask why the man put himself at such great risk.

As Rydel leaves Theo's cabin, Roth appears. The cooks are clearing away plates and the man barges through the Petty Officer's space like an uncaged gorilla, shoving and cursing.

'The stink!' he yells. 'I will not tolerate such an appalling stench for one moment longer!' He sees Theo. 'Kapitänleutnant, I demand your attention! Do not walk away from me!'

Theo turns and glares.

'Volker, this stench pervades my quarters, it turns my stomach!'

'My cooks are cooking breakfast, Herr Sturmbannführer. My men need their food.'

'I cannot believe you would have allowed such foul air to permeate the quarters had it been occupied by the Reichsmar – '

Roth cuts himself off mid-word. All crewmen within earshot turn and stare. Until now the reasons for the strange configuration of their boat, the absence of armaments and the new cabins in the bow tube room have puzzled them. Now they have new information. Roth has been indiscreet and he knows it.

'You will come at once,' he says to Theo, no longer shouting. 'You will come to my quarters. You will breathe the foul stench.'

Theo obeys. The air everywhere, in the gangway, the tube room and the cabins, is poor. But no worse than normal.

'You see?' Roth says. 'These cabins stink like sewers. The ventilation does not work. You will have it checked and repaired immediately.'

Theo places a hand near the air vent near the bunk and feels a breeze of cool air.

'It is working properly, Sturmbannführer. We are partly submerged so the air is not good. I have more pressing problems to deal with. I have a fault with one of my engines and its repairs must take precedence.'

'Your vessel disgusts me. And your men, Volker! They stink like peasants!'

'There is water for drinking and cooking. There is little to spare for washing.'

'I do not want your excuses, I want actions. There is another thing that disturbs me. I have seen one of your officers fraternising with a common seamen.'

'Fraternising, Sturmbannführer?'

'I have seen them in conversation, talking socially. I have seen your navigating officer, that man Rydel, talking with the man Lewandowski who works on the engines. Talking in Polish, Volker! Is the navy now so weak you recruit immigrant peasants?'

'I believe they are from the same town, from Rostock, which I am sure you know is now in Greater Germany, Sturmbannführer. We are on a small boat and we all have a common enemy to defeat. It is difficult for my men not to… as you say… fraternise.'

'With Polish scum?'

'The Führer has called on all Aryan peoples to help overcome our adversaries, I am sure you are aware of that. You must also be aware the military has many Polish divisions.'

'Of course. But it is the duty of all officers of the Reich to control and correct these lesser races.'

While they talk, Theo takes the opportunity to inspect the cabins. He attempts to distinguish the smells, sniffing vents and gratings the way a winemaster might check wine. Though they are mainly odours from cooking he detects amongst them the smell of the waste tank in the bilges. The bilges are vented to carry away methane – an explosive and dangerous gas – but the smell isn't strong. He wonders how Roth would have coped on Theo's last command, when the discharge pump failed and the sewage tank overflowed into the bilges. Even he, who thought he was used to such things, felt wretched.

Theo turns to leave. 'I will do what I can.'

'The details of this will be entered in my report, this fraternising, this stink, and your lax approach to discipline.'

'You must do what you must do.'

'And you must do something to stop this steel cesspit from rolling from side to side.'

Theo nods sharply and attempts a click of heels, knowing his soft leather boots will remain silent. He walks away, wondering who will read the man's report. Does Roth really believe they will return to Germany? And if they do, does he believe there will be anything of Germany left?'

Theo knows about these things. Back at the dockyard Walter was less than discrete, he spent time with colleagues who confided that key government departments had moved out of Berlin and that the Soviets had reached the River Oder, faced there by divisions commanded by SS Reichsführer Peter Himmler – Hitler's evil spirit – a man with no military training. What was it Walter said when they were standing together in the dockyard?

'Either the man has hidden talents or our country is doomed…'

CHAPTER FORTY-SIX

SPARGO, CONVINCED HE had fallen into hell itself, coughed, choked and flailed his arms. If this was hell then it was an ice-cold, watery one. To him, if he had indeed fallen to his death, then he was condemned to spend eternity even more confused than he'd been when he was alive.

His torch was there, still lit, close by him on dry ground. There was no stope, no huge black void, just an optical illusion fostered by an expanse of flat water and a tired, fuzzy brain. He was, he realised, kneeling in shallow water. Still baffled he stood up, reached for his torch and shone it down. Feint patterns of light danced on the tunnel roof. What had seemed like a void was in reality dark water, its surface now alive with ripples that reflected and twisted the torch light.

Kilcreg mine was indeed flooded. Spargo had reached the water table, the natural level of water in the ground. The tunnel he was in sloped gently downwards. What he'd mistaken for the edge of a void was black water. In the distance, beyond the reach of his torch beam, the roof of the sloping tunnel met the water. In such poor light its flat surface resembled a huge, dark hole.

It didn't matter to Spargo the water here was not deep. In his mind he saw it as deep as the mine itself, a bottomless maze of flooded passages, shafts and cavernous voids. Drowned workings where men once laboured. Things dreams are made of.

Soaked through, Spargo hurried back to the collapse. Taking his time was no longer an option, he had to get back to good air and then back to the surface. If Benares didn't get him, hypothermia would.

Taking care to keep his wound safe he slid over the collapse. In the narrow, low tunnel beyond it he locked himself into a stooping walk and took small, fast steps, keeping count of them to lessen the tedium, crooking his fingers to help remember the hundreds. At close to five hundred he saw a pinpoint of light. On the way in it had helped him but now it was a hindrance. It dazzled him. Cast long shadows.

On his way in he'd passed refuges, shadows in the wall, places of safety slashed out of the rock, places for miners to crouch when the wagons passed by. To guide himself he reached out with his free hand as he walked, grazing one of the sidewalls with his fingertips. With his head down this helped him keep straight. Helped his balance.

For a while all went well. Then, when passing one of the shadows, his fingers didn't connect and he stumbled sideways into thick mud. This space was more than a refuge, it had no back wall and its roof was high. Shining his torch he picked out a vein of white. Not ones for wasting good ore, when the miners came across it they mined it out, creating a winding, tight passage. Spargo twisted sideways. Squeezed awkwardly into it.

Unlike the main tunnel, this one did not slope; water dripping into it had not drained away and what looked to Spargo like a smooth concrete floor was in reality a sea of undisturbed slime that oozed over his feet. Steam rose from his clothing, filling the passage and obscuring his view.

Drives that follow veins often thin down to nothing. This one did not. It widened into a small, cave-like space. Its end had been panelled off with a timber planked wall with a door in the middle that was partly closed and which drooped from its hinges. Spargo waded closer. The bottom of the door had rotted. Its metal fittings had corroded into solid green bubbles of verdigris. A copper latch, Spargo realised. Also copper hinges.

In this place there was no iron or steel. Unlike other miners, the men that came here had no studs in their boots and carried nothing that could, accidentally, make sparks. Spargo knew these places. Knew he had found the mine's explosives store.

Tottering under its weight he lifted the door aside. The room behind it was the size of a small garden shed. Its back walls had been hacked into rock and its floor was flat concrete, raised a few inches to be clear of the mud. His torch beam lit a wooden box, then another and another, whole stacks of them. He stopped breathing. If he'd had any control over his heartbeat he would have stopped that too.

One of the stacks leant against the back wall. The boxes, like others in the store, were rotten, their sides had broken away and their contents – paper-clad sticks of explosives, had spilled out. No longer solid, the sticks flopped obscenely down the front of the pile like tangles of intestines. A garden of delicate crystals grew on what little remained of their paper wrappers.

The clusters of bright yellow needles reminded Spargo of crystals Jez grew years ago from a science kit. Hers were safe. Those he now stared at could not be more deadly. To his right were more boxes that had once been cardboard, their contents a slumped, putty-like mass that exuded a syrupy glue. Here the crystals were dirty brown and quite different, they smothered the pile like fine fur.

Long ago the miners used black powder in the mine, gunpowder that broke the rock softly. If they had continued to use gunpowder then the explosives store Spargo stood in would now be harmless, its contents ruined by damp. The explosives that sat there now, deteriorated with age, were more sensitive and dangerous than they had ever been.

Spargo, still motionless, took stock: the yellow crystals were picric acid, which meant the explosive was probably TNT, a military explosive he knew little about. The brown fur was nitro-glycerine and the explosive it coated had been blasting gelatine. Strange, the way it rotted. Sweating, they called it. This lot had sweated for over fifty years.

Spargo knew that if he dropped his torch he wouldn't hear it hit the floor, wouldn't even hear the bang. He tightened his grip on it as he shone it at his feet. Saw he had planted his shoes on the resinous, brown ooze. His heart didn't stop but it fluttered. He felt it.

It would be more fitting for him, he supposed, to be blown up in his father's old mine than falling to his death from the cliffs – and infinitely more fitting than suffering the indignity and pain of Benares' knife or garrotte.

Bizarrely he worked through figures. Blasting gelatine detonated at three miles per second – over six hundred thousand miles an hour –

and not as the rolling ball of orange fire so beloved of special effects men but as an intense, silver-blue flash. He, Spargo, would suffer the fastest death known to man… though suffer was hardly the word. The brilliance of the flash would probably register in his brain and before any sound could reach his ears he would be vaporised, reduced to molecules in a brilliant gas cloud that roared into the bay like the world's biggest cannon.

This was no time for panic. What he did next would determine his fate. Had his shoe not been stuck he would have walked slowly backwards. What was odd was he had stepped in the stuff and yet he was still there, though that didn't mean he would still be there if he tried to step off it. Why hadn't he triggered it?

The safest thing to do would be to take off his shoes. Still scared he might drop his torch he stuffed it into his deepest pocket. Then, in the dark, moving slowly and forgetting his wound, he crouched down. Pain stabbed at his side and he jerked upright, lost his balance, reached for the doorpost but missed it and hit something else. With gyrating arms he flung himself backwards, out of the room and into the mud. The door came with him. Fell flat on top of him. Except for the sound of his breathing there was silence. Irrationally and pointlessly he waited for the bang. With the heavy door on top of him he sank slowly into soft slime.

His torch still worked. Finally clear of the door he attempted, but again failed, to wipe its glass clean. There was just enough light to see his footprints in the resinous mass, footprints of thick, wet mud that had protected him, saved his life.

He aimed the torch at the thing he had stumbled against. It was large and rectangular and there were more of them, five or six, back in the shadows to one side of the doorway. That they were made of metal was obvious; their corrosion had added blues and greens to the grotto of colours.

Spargo tested the doorpost for firmness and then, taking hold of it with one hand, reached down to the concrete. What had once been a bronze sheet five millimetres thick was now no more than two; acid mine waters had taken their toll; the bottom edge of all of the boxes had collapsed under their own weight to leave jagged, irregular holes.

The hole in the nearest box was the shape of the African continent and, with heart pounding, Spargo bent back its ragged edges. Expecting to find rotted wood from a crate he eased his hand inside but could feel nothing. Puzzled, he knelt on the edge of the concrete and slipped the torch into the box. It was empty.

Bar had said his boxes were coated with rubber. These no longer were, though the dark sludge they stood in could well be the remains of it. Spargo turned his attention to the other boxes, pushing at corroded metal until it gave way. Though he couldn't reach them all he knew they were empty. They had never contained wooden crates.

The nitro-glycerine headache hit Spargo suddenly, jabbing his brow like nails through his skull. Nitro fumes reach the brain quickly. Workers who make such explosives become immune, they keep their immunity when away from their work by secreting small balls of explosive in their pockets or handbags, touching them occasionally to keep headaches away.

No longer able to focus Spargo stepped back from the store, and squelching through mud he aimed for the exit. Every step he took, back to the adit and then up the slope to its entrance, jarred his brain.

It wasn't long before he emerged high on the cliff face, bent double and slit-eyed. After three hours in torchlight the world looked pale pastel and the air like pure oxygen. He lay down on the ledge and took deep draughts of it. Felt it chill his lungs.

He didn't know how long he'd lain on the ledge, only that he was weak, hurting all over and shivering with cold. A squint over the edge of his eagle's lair revealed Benares, no longer pacing the seashore in his smart Spanish shoes but sitting on the beach in the shadow of a huge boulder. It was a spot that gave him a clear view of the overhang. Had he been awake he would have seen Spargo make a slow, painful and unnerving climb to the top of the cliff.

It would have been easy for Spargo to sneak up on Bar. The man was sleeping soundly in the passenger seat of the SUV. He sprang from sleep as Spargo, hardly able to stand, heaved himself into the drivers' seat.

'We had a deal,' Spargo said. 'I found the mine entrance, I went in, I found boxes about this big…' He did the angler thing, holding his hands wide. In one hand he held a jagged, postcard-sized sheet of corroded metal and he thrust it at Bar. 'I broke this off one of them, I'm guessing it was once bronze. All are empty, there are no wooden boxes inside, no rotted wood and no paintings. Even if there had been they would be ruined.'

Bar took the metal and turned it over. He stroked his chin and regarded Spargo thoughtfully.

'Nothing, John Spargo?'

Spargo pressed himself against the back of the seat. Never in his life had he felt like this. He was in another body, another head. The pounding was still there, a regular beat behind his eyes.

'There never were any wooden crates in the bronze boxes. They were empty when they were loaded on to Volker's U-boat.'

Bar stayed thoughtful.

'Is it possible the crates could have been removed from inside them? Perhaps by someone who worked on the mine?'

'All I know is they are not there now.'

'Come now, John Spargo, you are an engineer. Tell me what you think.'

Spargo sighed. 'Our deal, Bar?'

'I will honour it, John Spargo. You need have no fear.'

'The boxes,' he said, then paused and nursed his head. 'All are badly corroded. I'm sure they have not been opened. I could only inspect one properly but I could see the bronze screws. The rubber coating has gone but there is a trace of it in the countersinks.'

'What is a countersink?'

'The screws are recessed into the surface of the lids. There is still black stuff covering the screw heads. If the boxes had been opened this would have been scraped off.'

'Enough, John Spargo, spare me the technicalities. Do I have your word there are no paintings?'

'You have my word.'

'Then I believe you. If the bronze boxes are empty it means the crates were not placed inside them in Monowitz.' He pondered this for a while and then started to laugh quietly, wiping his eyes with the back of his hand. 'John Spargo, I have been outwitted!'

'By Göring?'

'God, no! Had the Reichsmarschall known of my plans I would not be here now. It can only have been my former colleagues.'

'That means you were wrong about the painting. Perhaps your favourite lady was returned to the Louvre after the war.'

Bar chuckled. 'By that I assume you mean the Leonardo? Who knows where that now is? But it is no longer my concern, John Spargo, I have no interest in it, it is no longer within my grasp. Nor is it within the grasp of the consortium and that gives me great pleasure. Now, enough of this. Where is Luis? What have you done to him? You have settled your score with him for hurting you?'

'I'm sure he will turn up. Where is my daughter?'

'The deal, John Spargo, yes. I have been told your daughter is coming to us, she is unharmed. When she arrives you will do one more thing for me, you will drive me to the airport.'

'You and Benares?'

'Luis can make his own arrangements.'

Bar looked Spargo up and down, looked at his clothes, his hands and his face. All were caked with dried mud. It was also in his hair, matting it down.

'You look like a creature that crawled from a swamp,' he said. 'You will attract attention. Clean yourself up.'

Obeying without question Spargo took the car key, opened the door and climbed out. Using handfuls of heather he attempted to wipe himself down but it made little difference. Cold and wet he slid back into the driving seat, replaced the key in the ignition and started the engine. Gripping the wheel for support he turned it sharply and set off, slowly and carefully, back the way they had come. As they passed the abandoned track leading down to the plant yard Spargo noticed something ahead of them, in the far distance, coming towards them.

'Car, up ahead! Is it Jez? Who is bringing her, Murphy?'

Bar leaned forwards, as if being one foot closer would help him see better. 'I cannot see anything, my eyes are not good. I do not know who is bringing your daughter. Luis made the arrangements.'

'You mean you arranged to bring her to me even before I did all this for you? Even before I went into that underground hell-hole?'

'I did not know you would go into anywhere, John Spargo. I was expecting you to return and tell me you had found nothing.'

'And you'd have been happy with that?'

Bar shrugged. 'Happy is an inappropriate word. Let us say I would have accepted your word.'

Spargo stared ahead. 'It's a vehicle, a Land Rover. It's the police, I can see its roof light.'

Bar sat bolt upright. 'That track, the one we passed,' he said, gesturing frantically. 'Where does it lead?'

'Down to Kilcreg, it went to the plant yard, it was a short cut up to the mine. It's impassable, overgrown.'

'Turn around! Drive down it!'

'It's impassable, damn it!'

'Do it! Do it!'

CHAPTER
FORTY-SEVEN

ROTH SPENDS TIME on his bunk, seasick and subdued. He eventually emerges clean-shaven and heads for Theo's cabin, passing the makeshift breakfast table on the way. Seated at the table are the boat's junior officers, including Rydel, who is eating oatmeal, a thick creamy porridge that sticks to his spoon. All stand as Roth approaches, not out of respect but to give him space to pass.

Roth trips, stumbles and falls. Rydel's plate flies up, turns in the air and lands on Roth's back. Men drop their food and turn towards Roth, they help him up and start wiping him down. Mistaking their actions, Roth draws a small automatic pistol and swings it wildly. Rydel crumples silently to the deck plates. A bright slick of blood stains the chequered blanket on a nearby bunk.

'Kapitän, you must come!'

The shout is from Lange, his voice breaking. Men move fast. A first-aid box is passed hand to hand through the boat and the medic, a hydroplane man, elbows others aside. Roth is backing away, gripping the pistol, his finger inside the trigger guard. Theo arrives, ignores the gun and looks down at Rydel. Lange speaks.

'The Sturmbannführer slipped and fell on Franz. He struck him with the barrel of his pistol.'

While Lange speaks he glances at Roth as if scared he'll be next. Men rip paper from packets, pass wound dressings from hand to hand and then to the medic. Not only is the flesh split above Rydel's ear from where the gun struck, there is a gash on his face from when he fell. Within minutes he looks like an Egyptian mummy, his head criss-crossed with bandages that secure thick lint pads. Theo stands clear and feels helpless.

'How is he?'

'Bad, Kapitän. Skull fracture, possibly. He bleeds from his ear.'

'Can he be moved?' His question is stupid. They have no choice, he is blocking the gangway. 'Carry him aft, to the tube room. Just you and the medic, Chief.'

Lange nods. Roth backs away from the scene with his gun in his hand. Lange and the medic move Rydel the way they move dead men, Lange at his head with his hands under the man's armpits, the medic between his legs with his hands under the man's knees. Crew stand aside to let them pass.

When they have gone Theo addresses his men. If there is fear, he must kill it now.

'You two, clean up this mess. The rest of you return to your posts, take your food with you.'

Roth has played into his hands. His mind skips though official procedures and then runs into fantasy. He will seal Roth's cabin door, cut off his air supply. In a few hours he will be senseless and in a day or so he'll be dead. Such thoughts trouble his head fleetingly. To do this kind of thing is not his way. The cabin will provide a good cell. The bulkhead that separates what should have been the forward torpedo room is twenty-millimetre thick steel, part of the boat's pressure hull. Roth's gun will be useless to him there. Unless, of course, he puts it to his own head.

Lange and the medic struggle with Rydel, manoeuvring him through bulkhead doors and between engines. The restricted aft tube room door is a hindrance but they squeeze him through and set him down on a bunk. Blood is soaking the dressings. The medic attends to them and adds more lint pads. Marek Lewandowski, knowing nothing of events, looks on, open-mouthed. Then Theo is there, watching.

'There is nothing more I can do for him, Kapitän,' the medic says, wiping his hands. 'We must hope he recovers.' He looks around the room and sees for the first time the figure in the bunk near Marek and he stares, first at the bunk, then at Lewandowski and then at his captain. Theo holds the man's gaze.

'He is my son,' Theo says. 'I had no choice. Please, not one word…'

Securing Roth is simple. He has returned to his cabins. Theo, armed with the automatic pistol from the drawer in his cabin, jams a long steel bar through the handles of the cabin's wooden door. Roth does not appear. The pistol is not needed.

As Theo passes his own cabin one of the two phones on wall gives a single, short ring. This phone has not rung before. It is a direct line to Roth's cabin.

'Kapitänleutnant, this is an outrage. I demand you free me immediately.'

Roth sounds calm, he speaks quietly. Theo listens to more demands. He is tempted to hang up but instead he responds.

'You struck and injured one of my men.'

'He was insolent and stupid. You command a boatload of fools. How long do you think you can get away with this charade? If you release me now I shall forget the matter. If you do not you will certainly live to regret it.'

Theo slams the phone down. It rings again but he ignores it. In a Kriegsmarine court he would plead Roth jeopardised the safety of his boat. But would he be tried it be a naval court? Unlikely. The SS looks after its own. It executes men, women and children for trivial offences. Justice in Germany has gone to the wall – which is where Theo will go if Roth has his way.

The phone rings again. This time Theo answers.

'Perhaps I was hasty, Kapitänleutnant. Possibly it was not a deliberate act on the man's part. Possibly he stumbled.'

'My witnesses say it was you who stumbled.'

'You must appreciate I reacted in the only way I could. I believed I was being attacked and I defended myself. The Schutzstaffel will not be threatened, Kapitänleutnant.'

'You will remain in my custody.'

'How do I eat? It is a long voyage.'

'How do I navigate? The man you wounded is my navigating officer. Food and drink will be brought to you. First you will surrender your pistol.'

'Very well. I am under arrest?'

'You are under arrest, Herr Sturmbannführer.'

There is a buzz on the line. Roth has hung up on him. Using the other phone Theo pages the bosun. Two or three seconds pass before the man knocks on his door.

'Sturmbannführer Roth is my prisoner, Bosun. He will remain confined to his quarters and has agreed to hand over his gun. It is of course possible he has other weapons. You and I will search his bags.'

'His suitcases, Kapitän.'

Despite the man's smile there is fear. Imprisoning an SS officer and the searching his belongings is courting death.

'As you know, I have no gunnery officer. You are responsible for discipline and will be there when I search. If you are ever called to explain your actions you will say you were under my orders. You need not fear Sturmbannführer Roth, not aboard my boat.' Theo hands him his automatic pistol. 'I want you armed. Take this…'

Soon they are at Roth's door. Theo bangs on it and calls out. There is no response.

'Perhaps he is sleeping, Kapitän.'

'He is not.'

He calls out again. Slowly he slides the steel rod from the handles on the door and the Bosun moves forwards, pistol gripped firmly.

Again and again the Bosun apologises. An hour has passed since Roth kicked open the cabin door and smashed down on the Bosun's gun hand with a long, heavy spanner. For such an overfed man Roth moved surprisingly quickly. He was still armed. Theo was powerless to help.

Roth has gone, again securing the bulkhead door with the padlock and chain. The Bosun is in pain, his wrist hangs limp, there are broken bones. Theo has bound it tight with strips of cloth torn from Roth's spare shirts. Theo suspects that by now Roth will have assumed command of the boat. Chief Engineer Lange, with the muzzle of a pistol in his ribs, will have no option other than to obey. He is a capable officer but he is no U-boat commander and certainly no navigator. Theo fears for Peter. Hopes Roth will see no reason to visit the aft tube room – the gangway between the main engines is narrow and the natives unfriendly.

So far there are no noticeable changes. The boat is still submerged, still running on motors.

The Bosun is sitting on Roth's bunk, nursing his wrist.

'I should have stood further back. I should have anticipated he would pounce.'

'The error was mine.'

Theo is about to say more when he hears footsteps. The chain on the watertight door clatters to the floor and Roth appears, Theo's Mauser in his hand. Behind him is Chief Engineer Lange and behind Lange, holding Roth's small pistol, is the Second Watch Officer, Oberleutnant Ralf Spengler. A loyal Party man, it seems. And a turncoat.

Theo, still staring, nods slowly. In his crew there are rabid anti-Nazis like Stoker Fischer. There are also those whose National Socialist beliefs lie dormant, young men who wait to see how things turn out and then side with the winners. Perhaps, in war, these things are understandable.

The Bosun, standing beside Theo, spits at Spengler. 'You Judas! You gutless bastard!'

'I have taken command of your boat, Volker,' Roth says, tilting his head back and peering along his nose. 'You will be confined to this room for the rest of the voyage which, I can assure you, will not be a long one. The mission is abandoned, we will return to Hamburg and soon you will face the hangman. Others who disobey me will join you.'

Theo nods. 'I have no quarrel with armed men, Sturmbannführer.' Then to Lange: 'Do as he says, Chief.' And again, to Roth: 'You have severely wounded my navigating officer. I am the only other member of the crew capable of returning this boat to Hamburg. What will you do, navigate yourself?'

'That is no longer your concern.' He turns to Lange. 'Engineer! You will navigate!'

'I cannot. I am not competent.'

Roth turns to Spengler. 'So?' he snaps. 'Who else is there?'

Spengler seems unsure.

'Only the Kapitän, I think, Sturmbannführer.'

Roth looks at Theo, at his seaboots, his coveralls, and finally at his face. 'Very well. You will come. Place your hands in your pockets and walk slowly.'

'I will come on the condition you take care of my bosun. You broke his wrist. He needs medical attention.'

'You will come now!'

Roth jabs the pistol in Theo's ribs. Theo winces but stands firm. Roth attempts to outstare Theo. Theo, disinterested in boys' games, attends to the Bosun's wrist.

'Very well,' Roth says. 'He can come. A man with one arm is no trouble.'

Crewmen in the gangway stand and listen. As the small group approaches they vanish into cabins and alcoves. At Theo's cabin Spengler stops and shoves Theo in. The cabin has been ransacked, Theo's things are everywhere. The transparent chart overlays are unrolled on the bunk, one true chart and one false. Roth comes in, picks one up, shakes it in the air and throws it back.

'Explain, Volker!'

'There is nothing to explain.'

The overlays hold no secrets. One shows their true course, the other the course in the orders.

'And this?' Roth asks. 'What is this?'

'It is a tobacco pipe, as I'm sure you realise. I have several. I collect them.'

'It is an English briar.'

'It's a good smoke.'

'You have English friends, enemies of the Reich?'

'Our nations have not always been enemies.'

Roth sniffs. 'And what are these?'

'They are personal documents.'

On the floor is the specimen bronze box Heiss brought to Walter. Roth tries to slide it to one side with his foot but it is heavy and won't move. Its lid lies beside it, drilled with screw holes at close centres around all four edges. On Theo's table are books bound in sealskin, stacked there by Spengler.

'These are diaries, Volker. Lonely men and misfits keep diaries. Pathetic men, men who are weak.' He kicks at the box. 'Why is it so heavy? What is this metal?'

'It is bronze.'

'And this, what is this?'

'A cigarette lighter.'

Roth's right hand moves fast, his knuckles striking Theo high on his cheekbone. The man knows how to cause pain. Theo reels backwards, holding his face.

'I can see it is a lighter, Kapitänleutnant. What is it made of? Where did you get it?'

'It's silver. The eagle is gold.'

'It is the Luftwaffe eagle.'

'It was given to me by Reichsmarschall Hermann Göring. A personal present.'

For a while Roth is speechless. It cannot be. A present from The Führer's deputy to man like Volker is unthinkable.

'You are lying.'

'Walter Wolff was with me. When you see him you must ask him whether or not I am lying.'

Theo watches Roth's face and sees doubt. Then the man snorts, snatches up the overlays and calls out to Lange.

'I shall take over this cabin, Engineer. You will remove the Kapitänleutnant's possessions to the cabins I am vacating. You will do it personally.'

Lange looks anxiously at Theo.

'Do it, Chief. Do as the Sturmbannführer says.'

The cabin moves go smoothly. When it is over, Spengler, pistol in hand, escorts Theo towards the bow tube room. Theo stops at the latrine, Spengler waiting. He takes comfort from knowing no other crew members have gone over to Roth.

'I hope you know what you are doing,' Theo says with his back to the man. 'It is three days back to Hamburg. How long do you think you can keep this up? You and your new SS friend can't stay awake the whole time. What happens when you both fall sleep?'

Spengler jerks the pistol, motioning his captain to move. Back in the gangway they pass a cook in the galley, slicing a fat block of cheese with a long bladed knife. It is hours since Theo has eaten and he reaches for a slice. Spengler jabs the gun barrel hard into his back and the cook glares at the man with clear hatred. Theo gives a slight shake of his head and the man puts the knife down. Such men will take risks for him. That is not what he wants.

Two hours pass and the vessel has not yet changed course. Theo, locked in the forward cabins with all his possessions, takes out his fountain pen. He intends to write in his journal but the ink from the pen is everywhere, expelled from its innards by changes in pressure. Unable to write, he worries again about his crew, hopes they won't move against Roth. A boat like this is no place for such heroics. He has experienced firearms discharged by accident, bullets ricocheting off bulkheads and tearing through flesh.

The phone on the wall gives a barely audible buzz. Theo lifts it, expecting Roth.

'It is Marek Lewandowski, Kapitän.'

'Get out of my cabin! Get back aft!'

'The Sturmbannführer knows I am here, Kapitän. He demands fresher air in here so the Chief Engineer told me to dismantle the vent ducts and check them out. I am working behind the door and I have jammed it closed.'

'Very well. Take care. How is Rydel?'

'Still unconscious. Still pale. Robert is with him.'

'Robert?'

'The medic.'

'Of course. And how is…?'

'He is sleeping. He has eaten bread. I am worried for him.'

'And Oberleutnant Spengler? Has he not inspected the boat? Not the aft tube room?'

'The Oberleutnant has stayed in the control room with the Sturmbannführer. Diesel Stoker Fischer says they've not got the guts to leave it. He says that if we – '

'Do your job and get out of there. Do not pry. Do not take risks.'

It is six in the afternoon and the skies are already dark. The boat has run on its batteries for ten hours, close to their limits. Unless they are recharged soon, all power to the boat will fail.

As if on cue Lange shouts orders. Theo hears the thud of seaboots, hears ballast tanks blow. The boat is surfacing. Soon it will flood with clean air. Theo hears more familiar sounds, the engines starting, first the battery charging sets and then the main diesels. Compressors replenish the air in the tanks, the air the crew will breathe when they next submerge. Through the steel bulkhead he hears twittering Morse Code from the wireless room and then loud music, British or American. He hears Roth shout. The music stops. Then someone is there at Theo's door. It is Spengler, waving a pistol, motioning him out.

'Sturmbannführer Roth wants you in the control room.'

'Sturmbannführer Roth wants you in the control room, Kapitän!'

The result of the reprimand is a dig in the ribs. The control room is silent. Though they are on surface nobody has gone to the bridge. Roth orders Theo to the bridge to take soundings.

'I assume you mean sightings, Sturmbannführer. Yes, they are long overdue. I hope for your sake we are still on course. Also, I assume you have checked the skies? Is it dark up-top? Is it cloud free? If I am to take star sights it helps to be able to see stars.'

At other times such a comment would raise sniggers. Today there are none.

Lange is there, holding the case containing the sextant. 'There is some cloud, Kapitän. But possibly the skies are clear enough?'

Theo dresses for topsides. He shrugs on his thick jacket, then his cap and his sea-boots. With the case in his hand he steps to the ladder.

'What is that, Volker? What is in that box?'

'The sextant. I need it for a star fix.' He looks at Spengler and then at Roth. 'You had better find yourself a new First Watch Officer, Sturmbannführer. My guess is that Spengler here considers such things beneath him.'

Spengler scowls. 'Do your job, Kapitänleutnant.'

Crewmen within earshot hiss through their teeth. Roth glances at the men around him. Demands silence.

Another night passes. To most of the crewmen all light is artificial, time of day has little meaning. Every few hours Spengler escorts Theo from his prison to work on the charts. So far, neither he nor Roth has discovered Peter. Both men fear the engine room crew; to run the gauntlet between the two diesels is an assault course of noise, vibrations, fumes and moving machinery. Also, Spengler is well aware of Stoker Fischer's hatred of Party men.

Theo is in the control room when it happens. Lewandowski comes for the medic and says Franz Rydel is now semi-conscious. Both men leave. Spengler, escorting Theo, listens and watches and then alerts Roth. All three, Spengler at the front, Theo behind him and Roth at the rear, file towards the engine room. It is the moment Theo has been dreading.

Spengler swings back the engine room door and steps over the sill. Theo follows, but Roth is less confident. The engine room is a fug of hot oily air. The noise from the diesels is deafening.

Determined to catch up with Lewandowski and the medic, Spengler strides along the walkway between the great engines. At the end of the walkway the aft tube room door is ajar. Spengler, having expected it to fly open when he put his weight behind it, shoves it a second time. Giving up, he squeezes through the gap between the door and its frame. Once inside he pokes his head and shoulders back through the opening and beckons to Roth. He shouts, making himself heard above the diesels' roar.

'They have blocked it, Sturmbannführer! They have welded it so it cannot open further!'

Roth attempts to squeeze through the gap but he cannot. Theo, behind him, notices Fischer, tucked back in the shadows just an arm's length from Roth. The man is wearing shorts and is stripped to the waist; he has been working on the engines and is smeared with dark oil. In his eyes Theo sees hate and anticipation. The stoker is a predator, ready to pounce.

Theo shakes his head. Fischer scowls.

Roth kicks the door, more from frustration than an attempt to move it.

'This is your doing, Volker! What do you mean by it? What is the point?'

A childlike cry from the other side of the door provides the answer. Spengler is squeezing back through the gap, one arm around the jammed door and the other dragging a child by the arm, a pale boy with rough mousy hair. The boy trips over the sill and sprawls flat on the engine room walkway.

Theo jumps forwards but Roth blocks his way. Peter is crying now, beating Roth's boots with his hands. He grasps a boot and hauls himself up it, but when he is almost on his feet Roth steps back and lets the boy fall. Fischer, still in the shadows, gives a roar and springs out with his outstretched and fingers like claws – claws that fasten around Roth's fat neck.

In the confines of the room the blast from the pistol is deafening. Fischer, hit, spins back into the shadows. Peter clamps his hands to his ears and screams. Theo throws Roth aside and scoops his son.

Men stand aside as the procession moves through the boat. Those that know Theo's secret look on anxiously. Those that do not, stand and stare at their captain and the child in his arms, they hardly believe what they see.

CHAPTER FORTY-EIGHT

SPARGO, IGNORING BAR'S INSTRUCTION to turn down the old route to the plant yard, drove on. The police Land Rover was still far away, travelling slowly towards them on the uneven track. Bar, panicking, grabbed for the steering wheel and yanked it out of Spargo's hands. The SUV lurched sideways, swerved out of the rutted track and jammed tight in deep heather. The engine stalled. Bar waved his arms at Spargo and cursed in English, Spanish and German.

Reconsidering his position, Spargo restarted the car. The chances of Mitchell being in the Land Rover were slim, and the prospect of having to explain his predicament from scratch to a stranger did not appeal to him. He and Bar would be carted off to a police station and he didn't want that to happen, not if Murphy was arriving with Jez. If Murphy teamed up with Benares, then god knows what might happen to her.

Spargo cranked the wheel, bounced through the heather and joined the other track

'That is sensible, John Spargo. I knew you would not let me down.'

Spargo knew the risks he was taking. The old route ran flat for a short distance before plunging through a deep cutting in the valley side. He had walked the route many times when he was young, and years later had taken Jez that way to the old mine buildings, through the old plant yard and up the hillside, through the cutting and up to the moor.

The cutting was different now. Years of rain had eroded the track and carved out deep hollows. With both hands gripping the wheel Spargo rammed his foot on the gas, confident that if he couldn't drive through the hollows then maybe, if he went fast enough, he could fly over them, like Day and his potholes. The SUV lurched, grounded, spun its wheels and dropped so far to one side that Bar grabbed the door as if trying to get out. Jutting rocks bruised the suspension and tore at the bodywork; something underneath snapped, and dragged along underneath them.

'John Spargo, I think you have broken the car.'

Spargo, unfazed, kept going. He emerged from the cutting high above the old plant yard with the SUV dragging its silencer and the remains of a fence. Unsure if the police were following him he roared into the old plant yard and came to a stop on the middle – he had to, he had no choice because Mitchell's car blocked the gateway to the road. Another, a marked police car, had been jammed across the Kilcreg road at the foot of the hill.

'Don't tell me to tell me to try to break through,' Spargo said. 'I won't do it.'

'That man. Is that Detective Inspector Quinn?'

'It's DS Mitchell.'

'Get out and walk to him. Take the car key if you wish, I am in no mood for any more of this nonsense. Tell Mr Mitchell I wish to speak with him. And about yourself – he will ask you, so be careful what you say – tell him you fell down in dirt. Remember that Luis is still here and you do not yet have your daughter.'

Spargo did as he was told. As he stumbled towards Mitchell, Mitchell walked towards him. The two men approaching each other like Wild West gunmen and when they met, Spargo held out his hand and passed over the car key.

'You look like shit,' Mitchell said.

'I feel like it. I fell.'

'Into a concrete mixer? Have you seen yourself?' he reached out, grabbed Spargo's coat and pulled it aside. Spargo yelped with pain.

'That's blood. That's a knife wound, it's bad… in fact it's so bloody bad I'm surprised you can walk. Who's the joker in the car?'

'His name's Bar. He's Spanish.'

'Did he do this to you?'

'It wasn't him. He wants to talk to you.'

The sound of squealing tyres made both men turn. The police car that had been blocking the road was now roaring up the hill pursuing a silver-grey Alfa Romeo that came down the hill, turned in the road and was racing away. By the time Spargo and Mitchell reached the road the police car had returned with the occupants of the Alfa in the back. Spargo hobbled towards it and saw Jez, her face pressed against the car's side window.

'Dad! What have they done to you?'

'That's my daughter!' Spargo yelled. 'Watch that little bastard with her, he abducted her!'

Then Mitchell was there and Jez was out of the car, hugging her father.

'Where's Murphy?' Spargo asked her. 'Who's that in the car?'

'His name's Midge.'

With his daughter safe, Spargo could point fingers and name names. He arm-waved at the car in the plant yard.

'The man in the car is Oscar Bar, he's behind all this, he set all this up. There's another of them down in the bay... but watch him, he's got a knife, he is the moron who stabbed me. The one you've got in your car abducted my daughter.'

'No, Dad, no!' Jez said, her head shaking. 'You've got it all wrong!'

'I have to say that your account of events differs in almost every respect from what I've heard from the others,' Mitchell said to Spargo next day. He had pulled up a chair beside Spargo's hospital bed and was perched uncomfortably on the edge of it. Spargo, propped on pillows, twisted to face the man.

'Does that really surprise you?'

'Mr Bar says he is a client of yours and you are doing consulting work for him. He says this Luis Benares is an agent for a charitable trust that has been funding the diving work.'

'It's not a charitable anything. It's – '

'Spargo, hear me out?' Mitchell scraped the chair closer to the bed, sat on it properly and leaned back. His eyes darted to the lights on the ceiling, the rail for the bed screen and the stand with the drip.

'How's the wound?' he asked, his eyes settling once more on Spargo. 'Any problems?'

'Jabbed up and stitched up. They said I was lucky it wasn't infected. I'm due out after consultant's rounds.'

'I'm glad to hear it. This Mr Bar… he told me he's long suspected Luis Benares has been using the trust's funds for personal gain. He said he's been waiting for an opportunity to catch him at it.'

'That's bullshit! Bar runs the whole game. He's responsible for three murders, including my mother's.'

'Three murders? The man's ninety years old, he can hardly stand up. Your mother was beaten by Ian Letchie.'

'I said he was responsible for them, I didn't say he did them himself. He was an officer in the SS during the war, he's been selling art looted by the Nazis. At the end of the war he smuggled it out of Germany.'

Mitchell raised an eyebrow and gave a faint smile.

'In empty boxes?'

'He's told you about that?'

'He's told me everything.'

'Did he tell you his name isn't Oscar Bar? It's Walter Wolff, the man named in Volker's journals. He knew Volker in the war. They were stealing art from Göring.'

'Are you on anything, Spargo? To kill the pain, I mean.'

'Would you rather believe me or Bar?'

'I'm not sure I have any choice. We have Luis Benares. He has already confessed to hiring Letchie and paying him to find out about you and your mother. He has told us Letchie killed both your mother and Lewis. He has also admitted murdering Letchie in your basement, he described the place to me and to DI Quinn, right down to details of the wire used to garrotte him. And Luis Benares stabbed you, you said that yourself.'

'That's true. But Bar is behind it.'

'According to Benares, Mr Bar had no part in it. Mr Bar has explained that the trust is a charity established to recover lost works of art. He has told us about the work carried out on the U-boat on behalf of the trust. There were supposed to be old masters in the metal boxes you found in the mine.'

'Did he tell you about these old masters? Did he say one was the Mona Lisa?'

Mitchell shook his head. This time he didn't smile.

'Are you sure you're not on anything, Spargo? Last time I heard, the Mona Lisa was hanging on the wall of the Louvre in Paris. Mr Bar did tell me the name of one of the paintings he was hoping to recover, I wrote it down. A portrait of some woman or other, Zandi or something, he said.'

'It's all in Volker's journals. You need to read them.'

'Unlike you I don't have the luxury of spare time. One of my detective constables has read Lewis's translation. He said he found it interesting but hardly relevant to your mother's murder.'

Spargo sighed and slumped back on his pillow. 'Have you let Bar make any phone calls?'

'Why do you ask if I've let him? We have no reason to hold him. He's made several calls. Including one to a London lawyer, one of the best.'

'And that bothers you?'

'It does if he's innocent.'

Mitchell leaned forwards, his voice dropping to a whisper. 'When we arrived at Kilcreg you were driving Mr Bar. Why was that?'

'I was taking him to the airport. He wanted to get out quick.'

'In a vehicle with no silencer?'

'It wasn't like that. We could have taken my Volvo.'

'But you were leaving Luis Benares behind? Don't you think it supports Mr Bar's story?'

'Which is?'

'That the man had been holding both of you in an old mine building. That you were escaping from him.'

'He would say that, wouldn't he?'

'You were taking him to the airport willingly?'

'No. He threatened me.'

'Threatened you? He had no weapons. He's got a heart condition. What did he threaten you with, a Zimmer?'

'He had my daughter.'

'According to your daughter she was held by a man named Grant

Murphy. We believe he flew out of Heathrow yesterday on a flight to Seattle. We have no idea where he is now.'

'She was held by that little creep with the Alfa. He's been watching her for weeks. And perhaps also by Murphy,' he added, reluctantly.

'Only by Murphy, according to your daughter. The young man's name is Rollo. He insists he was paid to keep an eye on your daughter, even Luis Benares agrees with that. According to Rollo, he soon realised something wasn't right about Murphy. He played along with him until he had opportunity to get your Jessica away. He even drove her to Kilcreg to find you. You were there, Spargo. You saw them arrive.'

Spargo was shaking his head. 'Murphy and that yob abducted her. She's suffering from that empathy thing you get when you spend too long with your abductors. She's been through a lot. She needs proper care.'

'She seems remarkably resilient to me. She said this Murphy once worked for you, is that right?'

'We were partners.'

'Seems to me you have some very strange friends, Spargo. And while I'm on the subject, there's something that's been niggling at me since the start of this business. You had Volker's journals. If Letchie and Benares wanted them, why didn't they just kill you and be done with it? They seem to have killed everyone else who stood in their way. You know what I'm thinking, Spargo? I'm thinking you know much more about this than you're admitting.'

'You're wrong.'

'Then let me spell it out to you. According to DI Quinn you've been trying to sell pewter in Edinburgh – pewter Kalman recovered from that submarine.'

Spargo looked up at the ceiling. Stared at the lights.

'Who told him that?'

'Quinn pulled in a couple of jokers named Anthony Day and Montgomery Teague.'

'That doesn't surprise me. I asked my daughter to put Quinn's boss Curtis on to them.'

'Oh?'

'She does a bit of forensic work. Geological stuff.'

'So you said.'

'She was analysing samples of soil for the police down there. I suggested to her that one sample might have come from an old builder's yard I just happened to know. Seems I was right.'

'The pewter, Spargo...!'

'It was Kalman's idea. He said he had it legally. He was looking for a buyer.'

'And you found him one?'

'It wasn't like that.'

Mitchell shifted in his seat as if he was about to leave. 'Oh well, that's DI Quinn's business, not mine. I can't sit here all day. As I said, you seem to be in bed with some very strange people.' He pushed back the chair, breaking the silence of their small ward with a jarring scrape of its legs. 'Mr Bar wants to talk to you, he says you and he have unfinished business. I would have thought it was worth keeping in with a man like that, he must be rolling in it, hand-made suits, private plane...'

'Private plane?'

'A charter. Waiting for him at the airport.'

'Where is he now?'

Mitchell was zipping up his jacket. 'Outside. I offered to drive him to the airport. Oh, there's another thing... that neighbour of your late mother's, Mrs Munroe. She's back from her daughter's. She's asked to see you.'

'Has she been told about my mother?'

'She has. As you might expect, she took it badly. I'm going, Spargo, I need to get out of here, I hate these bloody places. Do you want to see Mr Bar or not?'

'If you try to implicate me in anything whatsoever you will be wasting your time, John Spargo,' Bar said, taking the chair Mitchell had vacated. 'I am a respectable businessman, a highly respected entrepreneur. Luis has admitted everything in a signed statement. As his employer I was given time alone with him. My statement to the police does not conflict with his in any way.'

'Why did Benares lie for you?'

'Lie? Luis did not lie. He was responsible for everything that happened here.'

'You were responsible. He was working for you.'

'It was his decision to hire Letchie and therefore he must take responsibility for the results of that man's actions. It is cleaner this way, do you not think? It avoids so many complications. Besides, he has a wife and children in Madrid and he knows I will keep them from harm. I am sure you understand what I am saying.'

'Mitchell thinks I'm involved in this. Because I was left unharmed he is convinced I'm in Benares' pocket. Not in yours of course, Mitchell thinks the sun shines out of your arse.'

'And so it does, John Spargo.'

'Why was I not harmed?'

'I must leave. Your policeman friend Mr Mitchell has been good enough to offer to drive me to the airport so I must not delay him. And do not forget to honour our contract, John Spargo. I expect to hear from you shortly.'

'You'll cancel the contract. You don't need me now. The Canadian mine is nothing to do with you, it's already sold. You used it as a hook to hold me.'

'That, of course, is true. But you are wrong about the contract, I shall honour it and so will you. From what I have seen you are in need of the money. Before I go there is another thing I wish to say. I own several legitimate and very profitable businesses, John Spargo. The departure of Luis is most inconvenient and I am in need of another loyal employee. Is it possible you might consider learning Spanish?'

'Just go, Bar! And tell me why I wasn't harmed.'

'Harm you? I could never harm you, John Spargo. Nor any child of yours.'

CHAPTER FORTY-NINE

THE PROCESSION OF MEN, Roth, Spengler, and Theo carrying Peter, passes through the U-boat from stern to stem. When they reach the bow tube room Roth dismisses Spengler and gestures, calmly, for Theo to enter the cabins. Once inside, Theo sits down on a bunk with his son on his lap, the boy snuggling close and sucking his thumb. Theo has no wish to fight, he knows he is beaten.

'Is this child yours, Kapitän?'

'My crewman, Fischer. How badly hurt is he?'

'He will soon regret Oberleutnant Spengler's bullet did not kill him.'

'I am in command of this vessel, Sturmbannführer. You will ensure Stoker Fischer receives medical attention.'

'You are mistaken. I am in command of this vessel. The boy, tell me, explain everything to me.'

'He is my son.'

Roth nods, slowly. 'You are a fool. Never, in my service for the Reich, have I seen such incompetence. You have betrayed the German nation. You have betrayed your crew and betrayed Oberführer Wolff.' He gestures with his pistol to Peter. 'Against his knowledge you brought this on board.'

'Oberführer Wolff knows I have the child on board.'

'You are a liar! An officer of the Schutzstaffel would not countenance such a breach of discipline.'

Theo says quiet, stroking the boy's head. Roth's neck colours quickly.

'Tell me why you brought him!' Then, more quietly, 'For my own enlightenment please, Kapitän, it will make no difference one way or the other because what you have done is punishable by death. But of course you know that.'

Still Theo still does not answer.

'Very well. You will remain here. The boy will come with me.'

'The boy will stay.'

Roth comes forward, raises his pistol and touches the tip of its barrel against Theo's temple. Changing his mind he points the gun at Peter's head.

'We can resolve this little problem here and now, Kapitänleutnant. The decision is yours. Either the boy comes with me or you no longer have a son.'

Peter understands. He presses closer to his father, gripping the top pocket of Theo's coveralls with his free hand.

Theo didn't see the gun move, didn't feel the blow. He comes round on the floor, staring up at a light he cannot see clearly. He moves his fingertips over his head and feels his nose, his mouth and his ears. He tries to stand, but cannot. When he finally manages it he trips against the bunk and falls flat.

The room is hot and airless. The cabin door is open but the watertight door to the bow tube room is not. Intent on opening it he releases the side clamps but the locking wheel will not turn. He returns to the cabin and gropes for the phone. Roth answers it.

'Where is my son, Roth? What have you done with him?'

'He is with me.'

'You harm him, Roth, and…' he stops short. He is wasting words. 'Tell me how you will navigate. The safety of this vessel is my responsibility.'

'The Chief Engineer is well able to handle this vessel.'

'He is no navigator. We will never get to Hamburg. The River Elbe is a nightmare. If you damage this vessel you will answer to a naval court.'

'I think not.'

The phone goes dead. Theo paces the floor then returns to the bunk. He tries to decide what his next move should be but he cannot think clearly. Unintentionally he sleeps again, and when he wakes the air in the cabin is worse than before, it is stale and lacks oxygen. It is also dark; the bulkhead light is out, as are those in the tube room, as are the ubiquitous, ghostly blue lights that bathe every part of the vessel.

All is quiet in the boat. There is no gentle hiss from the vents, no hum from the motors. In his head he runs through the electrical circuits, the switches, the breakers and fuses. It cannot fail like this, not all at once. Not accidentally.

The shot and the screams come together, a weapon discharging and high pitched shrieks that can only be Peter. Powerless and wretched Theo beats on the bulkhead door. He was a fool, he should have let Fischer and his men have a go at Roth, he should have taken that risk for the sake of his son. Distraught, he leans on the door, his forehead pressed to the cold steel. He is the author of this nightmare. He should have left Peter at the farm.

Theo doesn't need instruments to tell him the boat is submerged. It is rising, slowly; the hydroplane servo controls have lost electrical power and the men trim the boat manually. It tilts steeply, bow first, and then levels off. The lights return unexpectedly, as do the familiar sounds of pumps and motors. Fresh, cold air blasts from the vents.

Theo puts his ear to the door and hears the pulse of the boat, the mechanical noises. Missing are the familiar sounds of boots on gangways, the walking and talking, the slam of lockers and the clatter of pans. The boat sounds dead.

Then, suddenly, the only sound is Peter, crying loudly, shouting and protesting. The shouts turn to coughs, long and loud. The boy is close, in the crew's quarters. Roth's padlock and chain clatter and fall. The locking wheel turns. The bulkhead door opens.

Chief Engineer Lange is carrying Peter. The boy is shouting, protesting. When he sees Theo he twists round and reaches for him. Theo grabs him and hugs him.

'No armed escort, Chief? No Roth? No Spengler? Are they getting careless?' Lange looks grim. 'What is it, Chief? What is happening?'

'I have to report the death of a member of the crew, Kapitän.'

'It shouldn't have happened. He should have stayed – '

'Not Fischer, Kapitän. Fischer is very much alive, the bullet passed through his shoulder. It is the First Watch, Oberleutnant Ralf Spengler.'

'Spengler? My god! Where is Roth?'

Theo steps through the doorway. He doesn't have to hold Peter because Peter is holding him, clinging crab-like with his arms, legs, feet and hands.

Apart from the drone of motors the boat remains quiet. Crewmen off-watch lay slumped on bunks. Others lay in hammocks, slung up beside them. All appear to be sleeping. Cooks in the galley are preparing meals. When Theo approaches there is a clatter of pans, as if on cue.

Theo speaks quietly to Lange, asks him again where Roth is, where Spengler is, and how this thing happened. Lange remains quiet, as do the cooks. Quiet, because they are listening.

Outside Theo's cabin Lange takes Peter from Theo's arms and walks away quickly. Theo opens his cabin door and winces at the slaughterhouse of pillow feathers, blood and bone. He goes to the lifeless figure sprawled flat on his bunk. It is a clumsy, nasty death. The man's one remaining eye glares up at him. Intending to close it Theo reaches down but takes a quick step back. Can't bring himself to do it.

He returns to the bunk slowly. Reaching down he retrieves his pistol from Spengler's still-warm hand and wipes it in the bedclothes. To make it safe he releases the magazine, pulls back the slide, and catches a live round as it flies from the breech. Fingers working deliberately he presses the round back into the top of the magazine. He does these things slowly and deliberately, without thinking. His mind is elsewhere.

Lange returns without Peter and stands in the doorway.

'I hardly need to ask why, Chief,' Theo mumbles. 'I need to know who.'

Lange shakes his head. His eyes are on the bunk. On Spengler.

'He was an officer under my command,' Theo continues. 'I was responsible for him.'

'Shot himself, Kapitän?'

Theo glares angrily. He grabs the blood-soaked pillow from the bed and waves it at Lange. Feathers flutter down, red and white.

'Through a pillow, Chief? Shot himself through a pillow?'

He calms himself. With eyes not quite focussing he looks down at the dead man. He doesn't want the detail. Doesn't want to dwell.

'Where is Roth?' he asks. 'I am surprised he hasn't rounded everyone up and shot them.'

'Not enough bullets in his Walther?'

Again Theo glares. 'Where is he, Chief?'

'Kapitän, I have not seen him. I was in the latrines and somebody tied the door shut, I could not get out. I have asked the men but they say nothing.'

'Where is Peter?'

'He is safe. I left him with the bosun in the aft tube room.'

'And Rydel?'

'Unconscious again. He was delirious. We think he is worse.'

'And Fischer?'

'He has been patched up by the medic. He should be resting but he's still working.'

Theo shoves Lange into the gangway, steps out himself and closes the cabin door.

'Come with me. Stay with me.'

The control room is strangely normal. Theo is aware of Roth's absence, there is so much more space. It was as if the man had always been there – a design fault – an oversize, unwanted fixture that came with the boat.

The men are at their posts – the hydroplane operators, a lookout on the observation scope and another on the attack periscope. There is also the bosun, an engine room mechanic and two young ratings. All have their backs to Theo. He mutters his thoughts. In the quiet of the room they are easily heard.

'Roth as well as Spengler, is that it?' He raises his voice and addresses the men in the room. 'Am I to hunt for the Sturmbannführer's body as if we are playing a children's game? Chief, in my absence you were the most senior officer. Tell me you had nothing to do with this madness!'

He gets no such assurance. The control room crew sit minding their gauges and dials, far more attentively than is necessary. Nobody turns, nobody speaks. Theo, frustrated, storms down the gangway to the engine room with Lange at his heels. Theo is thinking of places and spaces. Places where Roth might be.

Roth cannot have been dumped overboard because they were submerged. The bilges, then? He hopes not. Surely every other scrap of space on the boat is packed tight with provisions and spares, there is nowhere on the boat to hide a body.

'Chief, why my bunk?'

'He and Roth took turns to sleep in your cabin.'

On Roth's orders the weld on the aft tube room door has been cut off and the door now opens fully. Rydel hasn't been moved. Face ashen, he lies on his back on the bunk. The bosun is there and Fischer too, his left arm strapped tight to his chest. Peter is sitting on a bunk and when he sees his father he slips down and runs to him. Theo looks hard at Fischer.

'Where is Sturmbannführer Roth?'

Fischer shrugs. 'Kapitän, I do not know.'

'Stand up straight when you talk to me!'

Lewandowski looks down at the deck plates. It is a deliberate, unfaltering gaze. Beneath them, like in the bow tube room, there is space for torpedoes, torpedoes they do not have. The bosun frowns. Lifts Peter up and carries him from the room.

'Lift the decking. Lift it, Fischer!'

Fischer tries, but with only one good arm he does not succeed. Lewandowski stoops to help but the steel plates are too heavy, even for two men, designed to be lifted by torpedo hoists and this boat has none. Theo kneels beside Fischer and with help from Lewandowski and Lange they heave the plate up on its hinges, tip it right back.

Three of the four torpedo bays beneath the deck are filled with sacks of potatoes. Taking up a large part of the fourth bay is what remains of Sturmbannführer Roth, a figure more hideous in death than in life. Theo stares down at the mess that was once the man's head, shattered by the long wrench now lying beside it.

Theo's voice is a whisper. 'Stoker Fischer... is this your work?'

Though Lewandowski turns his face away Theo is sure the grisly scene is not new to him. One blow from the wrench would have killed the man but there have been many more, an appalling act of violence done with great hatred. The side of the man's head is missing. The skull and scalp lie in pieces.

'I asked you a question, Fischer.'

'I did it, Kapitän.'

Theo looks pointedly at the man's strapped-up arm. Fischer could have wielded the wrench. He could not have moved the body, nor lifted the deck plates.

'They will hang you for this, Fischer.'

'Soon there will be nobody left in our country to hang me, Herr Kapitän.'

Theo turns on the man, but words fail him. He knows he should call the Bosun and have Fischer arrested, but chances are the bosun was part of this. Maybe Lange too, and Fischer's engine room colleagues. Theo knows that to protect Peter he might have done the same thing, perhaps not so violently but who can say? He looks down at the body and fixes his gaze on the bloody mess. A trivial penance for letting it happen.

'When we act in this way we become like them. Like them, we set ourselves above laws of decency.'

Fischer and Lewandowski hang their heads. Scolded schoolboys.

'Where is his pistol?'

Fischer gropes under a mattress. Passes Roth's Walther to Theo and again hangs his head.

Despite Theo's disquiet he cannot bring himself to despatch the dead men with honours, which is what he should do. At dusk the remains of Spengler and Roth are lifted to the deck through the torpedo loading hatch and slid wordlessly from the deck by Lange and the bosun. Theo watches from the bridge as the bodies float away, arms and legs splayed like cloth dolls. It is not the way these things should be done.

Theo's cabin has been scrubbed clean and his belongings are again in their places. Peter, back in the aft tube room with Lewandowski, is coughing constantly and holding his head with both hands. Theo, alone in his cabin, opens the boat's logbook and is relieved to see Roth made no entries. The entry Theo makes now is brief: 'Sturmbannführer Ludwig Roth and Oberleutnant zur See Ralf

Spengler lost overboard, believed drowned'.

Theo spends time with Peter. Lewandowski says there is recurring mucus that makes the boy vomit. The medic has attended to Rydel and changing his dressings. He repeats to Theo there is nothing he can do for Peter, he is trained for first aid, he is not a physician.

Theo, again in his cabin and alone with his thoughts, vows he will never return to mining. Mines are too dangerous for a man with a son. When this war is over he will return with Peter to his father-in-law's farm. Together they will make the farm live again. He reaches for a telephone and calls Lange to his cabin.

'This war will soon be over,' he says when Lange comes. 'The Soviets are closing on Berlin.'

'Is that not enemy propaganda, Kapitän?'

'That may be so, but it does not mean it is untrue. When Berlin falls it will be the end of Germany.'

'And if that happens, what will become of us?'

'When it happens, Chief. You know the procedure.'

Lange shakes his head and smiles. 'Operation Rainbow. What moron thought up that name? What if we are in mid-Atlantic when we get the message? Do we invoke Rainbow, open the sea cocks and scuttle her? Are we expected to swim home? And what if instead we decide to make for an enemy port? Who is to say we won't be picked off by the bomb-happy British?'

'What are our alternatives, Chief?'

'Will you tell me our destination, Kapitän?

'It was to be Buenos Aires, Argentina. Now, it seems, we are making for Hamburg. With these changes of course I doubt we have sufficient fuel to reach South America, which means I have decisions to make. Also, I have other problems.'

'Peter?'

Theo nods. 'Stoker Fischer has two children of his own. He suspects Peter has bronchitis and fears it will develop into pneumonia. But my concern is not just for Peter, Chief. There is Rydel. His condition is worsening.'

He has been sitting on the edge of his bunk. Now he stands up and brushes himself down with his hand as if shifting crumbs. It is a

THE MAN WHO PLAYED TRAINS

dismissive, topic-changing gesture.

'However, Chief! Gamblers and guesswork! Pneumonia? Who knows? I have never known so many self-styled experts in such a small space. They thought we were going to Norway. They also thought we were to be carrying Göring, taking him somewhere safe and sunny.'

Theo's forced flippancy doesn't fool Lange.

'So Roth's remark was right? We were to carry the Reichsmarschall?'

'No, that was never going to happen, it is what I was supposed to think. Have you ever seen the Reichsmarschall?'

'I have seen photographs.'

Theo sits down again. Lange has been standing, leaning back on the closed door. Theo waves him down into the desk chair.

'I have seen Göring, Chief, I stood beside him. He is the fattest man I have ever seen. There is as much chance of getting an elephant into a matchbox as getting him into this boat – except perhaps by lowering him by crane through the torpedo loading hatches. I have been to his mansion, I have seen his specially designed lavatory seats. There is one on his personal train, it is three times the width of the one in the forward cabin, he would not even be able to get through the lavatory door. It was something you said to me on the Elbe, something about Roth's size, about him getting stuck in the hatch and trapping us inside. That is when I realised I had been fooled about Göring.'

Lange is frowning, struggling to understand. Theo knows he must confide in the man. Soon there will be things he will want him to do. Unorthodox things.

'How much do you know, Chief? Do you know we are carrying valuable paintings?'

'The cargo in the bow tube room? There have been rumours.'

'There should have been more, enough to fill the whole of the space. I was led to believe the design of this vessel was changed to convey Göring and his treasures to Buenos Aires. No doubt our Kriegsmarine admirals were told the same story.'

'And they believed it?'

'Evidently. I was told the SS has made plans to get our leaders out of Germany, against their will if necessary. The changes to this boat were commissioned by the SS, not the Kriegsmarine.'

Lange shakes his head. His frown is fixed in place as if drawn in dark pencil. Theo continues.

'I believe the true purpose of this boat was to take art treasures out of Germany. We were never meant to take Göring.'

It wasn't just Göring's size that raised doubts in Theo's mind. It was Walter, deciding at the last minute not to come – and having arranged, presumably a long time in advance, for Roth to take his place. There was no way Walter would have come aboard a U-boat, not with his fear of water.

It is too much for Lange.

'These are political matters, Kapitän, I do not understand them. There are decisions we must make. Are we to continue to Hamburg?'

'Back into the fire, Chief? I think not. Either we take our chances with the British or we will make for Portugal. I understand the natives are friendly there.'

'What will become of the paintings?'

'Does that bother you? The sea is deep.'

'I am a simple man. I wonder why people should go to such trouble with old pictures when our country and people are threatened.'

'When this war is over there will be some very wealthy men.'

'Or there would have been.'

'No, my friend, there will be. I have been told that treasures such as these have been transported from our country for many years. Our shipment is but one small part.'

Both men sit quietly. Finally, Theo speaks his mind.

'Chief, I want to put Peter ashore. And Franz Rydel of course. I want you to speak to the officers and find their reaction, will you do that for me? And send Lewandowski to me.'

'You will put it to the vote?'

'This is a naval vessel, not a democracy. I said find their reaction, not take notice of it.'

'Shall I tell them Portugal?'

'You can. But I have another destination in mind for Peter and Rydel. Perhaps Lewandowski also.'

'And perhaps others?'

'I think not. I am sure the men will prefer Portugal to Scotland.'

Throughout the night they ride on the surface. A new course has been set. Theo has moved Peter to his cabin and he sits through the night with him, cradling him in his arms, listening to his shallow, difficult breaths. Soon the boy will be in good hands. As will Franz Rydel.

As Theo had hoped, Marek Lewandowski has agreed to be put ashore too. It makes so much sense. Peter knows him and trusts him. The war will soon end, and when it does Theo will return to Scotland for Peter, perhaps stay a while with Morag and Sam – stay until his own countrymen's resistance to the occupying forces has died down. And what then? Return to the farm? At least it is something to aim for.

He considers Lange's question about Walter's paintings. Throwing them overboard would be an appropriate end for them – a kick up the arse for Walter for involving him in his crimes.

He unbuttons his jacket, takes out his pipe, packs it tight with tobacco but does not light it. Not yet. Not in the boat.

Peter stirs in his sleep and sits up. Trapped mucus blocks his lungs and he coughs it up while Theo looks on helplessly. He has made the right decision. Sam and Morag are good people, they will make him well.

The pipe in his mouth is a temptation. The door is closed, they are running on the surface and the air in his cabin is good. The lighter Göring gave him still works, Lange found fuel for it. He goes to strike it but then sees sense. His son is ill. A smoke-filled cabin will not help him. In the dim cabin light the lighter is shiny, and as he is returning it to his pocket Peter reaches out and takes it from him, turns it over in his hands and fondles it. Strokes the gold eagle with the tip of his thumb. Feels the contours of its sharp-pointed wings…

CHAPTER FIFTY

KILCREG LAY IN THE GLOOM of a silvery sea mist. Visibility was so poor that Spargo, conscious of being close to the edge of the road and not being able to see it, took the bend on the hill at little more than walking pace. This would be his last trip, a visit driven not by emotion – lately he'd had his fill of that – but by a sense of duty. Rosie had asked to see him. It was a request he could not refuse.

Further down the valley, the mist thinned. As he approached the cottage that had once been his mother's he swung in the road and stopped on the grass verge where Mitchell parked his car on that first, dark day. He stepped out onto damp grass, slammed shut the car door and then checked his wallet to see if he had enough to pay Rosie for the damage he'd done to her garage when he took her stepladder.

Rosie heard the car arrive. Before Spargo reached her gate she was out in the road and running towards him.

Running, at eighty-seven years old.

'John…? Oh John, I hoped you would come!'

She met him in the road with a motherly hug. She was dumpy and round-faced with a shock of white hair, wispy cotton wool that had once been dark, neat and permed. Her rose-red face beamed. Then, as a switch had been thrown, it turned solemn.

'Morag…' she said, suddenly close to tears. 'Such a terrible thing to happen, I'm so sorry. She was good to you and a good wife to Sam. Do you have time for a cup of tea, or do you have to go? I've baked some scones.'

Her voice sang, a trace of the Nordic lilt that the old ones still had. He listened to it fondly, picking out the odd smattering of dialect words heard so rarely now.

THE MAN WHO PLAYED TRAINS

'I've got all the time in the world, Aunt Rosie.'

He had been inside Rosie's house so many times. He had helped her redecorate it. He could remember hanging, at least thirty years ago, the flowery wallpaper lining the living room walls. He waited in that room while she made tea, refreshing his memory with the same old photographs in the same old places. Unlike Rydel's room in Edinburgh the room was spotless.

She came from the kitchen with her best china teapot, two cups and two plates packed tight on a tray. She set it down on a side table and then moved it, table and all, until it stood between two armchairs. The scones came with butter and jam. He was about to complement her on her ability to conjure up such a spread when she cut him short.

'Sit down, John. There is something I know about Morag and Sam...' she paused while she poured milk into the cups '...something I shouldn't tell you. I promised them I would not.'

Spargo sat quietly, smiling inwardly. What little gem did she have for him? That his mum and dad weren't actually married? That would have been a real sin back then – also most unlikely in a place like Kilcreg. Nor could it be true, because he had his original birth certificate and it said Morag and Samuel Spargo. No excitement there, then.

Rosie passed him a cup and saucer and he took it. He reached for a scone from the plate, broke it in half and spread jam on it.

Rosie sat down. She seemed to be taking her time. Slowly she placed her teacup by her side and then laid both hands in her lap.

'The things that have happened here,' she said quietly. 'I think I know why.'

'It's no secret, Aunt Rosie, not now.'

'Do you know about the Germans?'

'I know about the U-boat.'

'The Germans,' she repeated.

'You mean Franz Rydel and Mark Lewis? Yes, I know about them. Actually they were Polish. I also know Mark Lewis changed his name from Marek Lewandowski.'

She nodded. 'That is so.'

'Do you know about the boxes?' he asked. 'The one on the roof?

The ones in the mine?'

'Boxes, John?' Her frown said she didn't. 'The men came in the night. They brought Franz and Mark ashore in a small boat. There had been an accident or something and he was unconscious. I didn't see them arrive, of course, I saw the next day. Franz was hurt very badly, he had bandages around his head. When he returned he stayed at the mine house. He lost the use of his arm, poor man.'

'Returned? What do you mean? Was he in a prisoner of war camp?'

'Prisoner of war? No, when he returned from hospital, I mean. Do you remember them, Marek and Franz? When they were not working they used to play games with you. You were a quiet wee boy, you kept yourself to yourself. Marek taught you, he spent months with you. Later he became a teacher.'

Spargo nodded. Sipped his tea. 'They lived in the extension in the mine house, I remember them vaguely. I think they were miners.'

'Only Franz Rydel worked at the mine. He didn't work underground, because of his arm. When the mine closed he moved to Edinburgh. I don't know what he did there, I never saw him again. As I told you, Marek became a teacher, he taught languages, English and German. He went to live in Inverness and married a local girl.'

'And before that?'

'What do you mean?'

'You said after they were landed they went away.'

The question seemed to puzzle her. 'No, only Franz, he went to hospital. Marek didn't go into hospital. Before Franz went there Sam gave him different clothes… gave them both different clothes. He could hardly have them going around in German uniforms, could he? He burnt everything. Their papers too.'

'Burnt them? You mean they weren't handed over as prisoners of war?'

'They weren't prisoners, were they? Nobody arrested them or anything.'

Spargo shook his head. Rosie was old. He was beginning to wonder if she was losing the plot.

'Sam told the authorities that Marek and Franz were Polish seamen from a merchant ship that had been torpedoed. They were questioned of course. They said they had been in a small boat for days and it had been wrecked on the rocks. The police and army searched along the coast but of course they didn't find anything. Nobody worried, not really, the war was nearly over and people were starting to celebrate. Franz was in hospital for nearly a month. For a short time he went to a refugee camp with Marek, and then they came back here to work. They couldn't go home, could they? Not with what happened to Poland after the war.'

'Are you saying everyone here knew they were from the U-boat? Yet they all kept quiet?'

'You know what it was like here, John.'

He knew very well what it was like. Except at the mine, Kilcreg had no electricity, and only the mine and the doctor's house had a telephone. There were no televisions, only two or three cars, and no regular bus. The place wasn't nearly as quiet as it was now but it was much more cut off. A very different world.

'I met Franz Rydel,' Spargo said, sitting back as if nothing he'd heard had surprised him. 'Recently, I mean. He still lives in Edinburgh. Mark moved there from Inverness after his wife died, but he died too.'

It sounded blunter than he'd meant it to sound but there was no way he was going to explain what really happened to the man who became Mark Lewis. She nodded knowingly.

'I'm not surprised he died. He wasn't a very healthy young man. He was always so scared. He thought the authorities would find who he really was and send him back.'

She reached for a scone, snagged her sleeve on her cup and it went over, dumping its contents on the rug – déjà vu for Spargo – not a dead arm this time but a hand that had started to shake. Rosie jumped up, dashed to the kitchen, returned with a cloth and knelt down to wipe.

'Did you know Morag and Sam had a daughter who died?' she asked.

It was said as an aside, slipped into events as if she hoped it wouldn't be noticed. Spargo bit his lip.

'I do know that,' he admitted. 'Nobody ever said. But when I was ten I found a birth certificate in a drawer, hidden under the lining paper. I asked my mother what it was and she snatched it from me. It upset her so much I never mentioned it again.'

'Janet Mary Spargo, born in May nineteen-thirty-eight,' Rosie said. 'She died of influenza when she was two.'

'Why are you telling me this?'

'Because their little boy also died from the same disease. It was a terrible time. She – '

'Their boy?'

'He was taken to hospital in Thurso. He was around your age. Perhaps a month or two older.'

'I had a sister and a brother?'

'I don't know, John. I don't think so. I don't think you had any brothers or sisters.'

She stood up quickly and scurried to the kitchen. She didn't come back to the room but instead she pulled out a chair from under the kitchen table, sat down on it and stared out of the window at the hillside. Spargo walked to her and put his hand on her shoulder. Spoke softly.

'What are you trying to tell me, Rose?'

She stood up suddenly as if shaking him off. Went to the drainer and moved dishes, putting them in some kind of order. She didn't speak again until she finished doing it.

'They brought you off the submarine with Marek and Franz,' she said. 'You were sick with pneumonia and they thought you would die. Your father didn't think you would survive the journey he was about to make and so he brought you here. The reason they let Marek come ashore was that on the submarine he had taken care of you and Franz. Morag and Sam nursed you back to health and kept you as their own. I don't suppose you remember any of it, you were only a wee slip of a boy. The captain was a man named Volker and you were his son.' Her eyes darted to his and then back to the window. 'I don't remember Mr Volker's first name. I never met him, of course.'

Spargo knew it couldn't be true, he wondered how to respond without hurting her feelings, but when he opened his mouth to reply he couldn't find the right words. He turned away from her, returned to the living room and slumped into a chair.

No, it couldn't be true, not something like this. But in the silence, things slipped into place in his mind, Bar's remarks that he could do him – Spargo – no harm, nor harm any child of his. And there were other things, things like Bar's knowledge of his father, Sam Spargo, the things said in Spain. Had Bar guessed from the start that Volker had been here, landed his sick child here? And, if he had done that, he might well have offloaded the crates here. It made sense, horrible sense.

Rosie interrupted his thoughts, came in from her kitchen and rearranged tea things. Keeping her back to Spargo she spoke to him as if commenting on the weather, or the state of her garden.

'A long time ago Morag told me Sam meant to tell you these things when you were old enough. But he died, of course.'

'It can't be true,' Spargo said. 'The boy was German. I hardly know a word of the language.'

'I don't remember you saying anything at all for many months. Morag and Sam only spoke to you in English, Marek and Franz too. They were educated boys, they spoke English well.'

'Someone in the village would have said something. You can't just substitute one child for another. There are death certificates and papers.'

Spargo was in denial; either Rosie was getting senile or she'd got hold of some cock and bull tale from her neighbours. He would be able to disprove it easily by getting hold of old records. Compare DNA tests if necessary – though he wasn't sure who with.

'Back then we had a doctor here,' Rosie said. 'He took care of things. Sam and Morag were well-liked. We all knew what happened, we all colluded. We were saddened enough by the death of their daughter. And then for John to die too…'

John? Spargo jumped up and went to the window. The mist was clearing, whipped into nervous swirls by a sharp breeze. Fine drizzle clung to the pane and refused to run down it. He fidgeted with his fingers. A man his age, frightened by knowledge. He waited silently for more from Rosie. Like him, she stayed quiet.

'I'm so glad I told you,' she said at last. 'You're old enough to know it now.'

Old enough? How old do you have to be to hear something like this, the secret of a lifetime passed from one to another for safe keeping. He was close to tears but he wasn't sure why. It felt as if someone was rearranging his innards.

'What did they do with the body? Of their boy, I mean.'

'What people always did with bodies,' Rose said, matter of fact. 'They buried him.'

'In Thurso?'

'Why in Thurso? They brought him home from hospital. We buried him at the Crag.'

'I thought the Crag was disused?'

'It wasn't back then.'

She came over and stood beside him, staring out to the road. The drizzle turned to hard rain. It was what happened at Kilcreg. Things changed unexpectedly.

'If you don't like the weather, just wait a while,' Spargo said in an attempt at humour that Rosie ignored. 'They didn't make it,' he added, serious again. Rosie turned and looked at him, puzzled. 'The U-boat,' he said. 'Volker's submarine. They were going to South America. They didn't make it.'

'I'm not surprised,' she said. 'All that sea.'

Spargo needed air and outside he got plenty. He got rain too, rain that soaked his hair and ran down his neck. Unsure what to do he walked aimlessly towards where the mine house had been and then changed his mind, turned in the road and walked purposefully back. When he reached the remains of his old school he turned onto the path beside it and kept up the brisk walk, slowing when the path steepened and taking short-cuts over rocks, scrambling like an ape on all fours.

High on the hilltop the ragged grass made way for dark heather that swamped the old path. Making for the cliffs he ploughed through it. Rain drifted from the sea in soft, drenching gusts, rain that drained off his jacket and soaked his trousers, his socks and his shoes. Shivering now, he gazed out to the bay. If he was indeed Volker's boy it would be ironic if he succumbed to the very same illness that brought him to this place.

The Crag was tucked in a sheltered hollow overlooking the sea. Once a simple overhanging rock that provided shelter for ancient man – over two thousand years ago, he'd been told at school – it became the site for a small graveyard and then a stone chapel.

All that remained of the chapel were four high walls. Such were the superstitions of the locals that, unlike the old school, and more recently the mine house, the chapel walls had never been robbed of their stone.

He reached the graveyard wall and its tall iron gate. He had been there before, long ago when he'd explored the place for a dare. He was seen by Mrs Kennedy who ran the post office and shop, and she told his teacher. The Crag was a holy place, he was told next day. It held spirits. He had never been back there. He had never taken Theresa and Jez.

Had the residents of Kilcreg conspired to keep their children away from the place for a more sinister reason, he wondered? Were they scared they might discover the grave of their very-much-alive school friend John Spargo?

He was weeping now and he wasn't sure why. Stopping at the gate, he gave it a shove. It opened half way before it jammed against weeds. Once, people from the village kept the place neat. Now, within the shelter of the walls, lush undergrowth swallowed the gravestones.

Hampered by greenery he skirted the wall, spiralling inwards as he inspected inscriptions on flat slabs and headstones. Amongst weatherworn stone stumps, tall obelisks poked through the undergrowth like masts on a green sea, the tallest of them carved with a skull. The ancients were like that, they hedged their bets, mixed their old beliefs with the new Christian teachings.

His visit to the place years ago had scared him. Could it be the cause of his nightmares, his imaginings? Had the ghosts he'd imagined back then stayed with him?

But pagan skulls were not part of his nightmare. There was something else, something deep in his memory that struggled to surface. He moved to a place where the wall had toppled and sat down on wet stones. Placed his elbows on his knees and his head in his hands.

Jez was right, his dreams were muddled, they didn't fit together in time. His mother had taken him to the doctor about his visions long before he came to this place, long before he went underground with his father and long before he heard tales of man-engines and dead miners.

Bar said Volker's boy was taken from the farm in the truck with the crates, crates to be sealed in the bronze boxes and then coated with rubber. Buna rubber, Jez had said. Rubber made from chemicals rather than imported latex.

Bar had mentioned Monowitz. At the time it hadn't rung bells but they were ringing now. He knew what the Nazis had done, he had read the books, seen the documentaries. He knew the slave labour camp for the workers at Monowitz in Poland had another name – Auschwitz Three.

He, John Spargo, had been there, he'd been driven through Poland in a truck, concealed between crates in a rat's nest of blankets. Aware for the first time where his dreams – his imaginings – really came from, he buried his face in his hands. The white ghosts, the men, women and children that turned to him. Stared with those unseeing eyes.

Bar had said January, nineteen forty-five. This was the month the Nazis, fearing their death camps would be being discovered by advancing troops, emptied Auschwitz, the month prisoners not transported by train were force-marched through Poland. Most fell dead on bleak, snow-swept roads.

Rosie is right. He is Volker's boy. He has seen hell.

John Spargo is a lost boy, one of Peter Pan's children. He has lost not just two parents, but four. What would Oscar Wilde have made of that, he wonders? Misfortune? Carelessness? Behind his cupped hands he manages a cold, wet smile.

Morag knew about the box in the roof, he is sure of that. She didn't give in to Letchie, she gave her life to protect her surrogate son from the truth. Truth he struggles with now.

He has abandoned his search for the grave. It is hidden here somewhere, somewhere safe. He stands up, makes his way to the iron gate and tugs it closed behind him. Again he walks to the cliffs. Again he looks down to the bay.

This time he closes his eyes and sees his father, wading through surf with a child in his arms.

But which father? He can't remember a thing, not a damn thing. He dips a hand into his pocket, takes out the shell of the lighter and strokes the gold eagle with the tip of his thumb. Feels the contours of its sharp-pointed wings...

THE MAN WHO PLAYED TRAINS

AUTHOR'S NOTE

BEFORE THE START OF THE SECOND WORLD WAR, German Reichsmarschall Hermann Göring amassed an art collection sourced from within Germany and Occupied Europe. Almost exclusively this comprised works confiscated or 'bought at gunpoint' from Jewish owners, galleries, museums, and private collections. He traded items with other collectors and his network of agents successfully exported paintings to Switzerland where they were stored before being sold to private collectors.

According to officials at the Musée du Louvre in Paris, in August 1939 the portrait of Lisa di Antonio Maria Gherardini, the wife of prominent Florentine citizen Francesco del Giocondo di Zandi (better known as the Mona Lisa) was placed in a crate and taken to safety. Official papers from other European nations place it in the Altaussee salt mine in Austria.

There was never a U-boat numbered U-1500. During the war the German Navy converted a number of its Type IX submarines to carry cargo, removing all six torpedo tubes and designating them Type IXD2 boats. Official records show the Nazi regime did not allocate the number 1500 to any U-boat, leaving a gap between U-1407 and U-2321.

Escape by U-boat at the end of the war was not unknown. When Germany surrendered to the Allies, Kapitänleutnant Heinz Schaeffer put ashore all married men and sailed from a Norwegian Fjord in U-977 in defiance of Kriegsmarine supremo Admiral Dönitz's radio instructions for U-boats to surrender. The boat arrived in the Rio del Plata in South America in August, no doubt unaware that in the meantime, Argentina had declared war on Germany. He and his crew were arrested and sent to Washington, where they were interrogated about the whereabouts of Adolf Hitler who was rumoured to have escaped from Berlin. They were eventually shipped back to Germany.

Throughout the war the SS built an industrial empire based on slave labour. Forced labour and prisoners of war built the Monowitz industrial complex and others just like it. Those Jews, and other minority groups abhorred by the Nazi State, who were considered fit enough to work, were selected for slave labour. The remaining six million were destroyed inhumanely.

On 15th January 1945 an aircraft of the US 15th Reconnaissance Squadron photographed the camps at Auschwitz. The aerial photographs show a covering of deep snow. The crematoria had been dismantled, though they were intact when photographed by a Mosquito aircraft of the South African Air Force the previous June. Photos from this aircraft also show the massive Buna synthetic rubber and benzene plant at Monowitz, at that time still under construction.

On 18th January, fearful of discovery by the advancing Allied troops, the camps around Auschwitz despatched more than 5,000 children, women and men to Germany on foot in sub-zero conditions without food, proper footwear or clothing. 2,720 died on the journey, many beaten or shot. 1,300 died during the first 100km of the forced walk.

On 28th April 1945 Göring's mansion, cleared of its treasures, was blown up by Göring's personal troops to prevent it falling into the hands of the advancing Russian Army. Today, its location is marked by a block of rough stone on which is carved the name 'Carinhall'.

THE MAN WHO PLAYED TRAINS

THE MAN WHO PLAYED TRAINS

THE MAN WHO PLAYED TRAINS

ACKNOWLEDGEMENTS

This novel could not have been written had it not been for the patience of my family, the tolerance of staff in various coffee shops in and around Edinburgh (you know who you are!) and my mentors over the years, especially Stan Cox, Dr Gwyn Thomas, Don Cooper, Pat O'Connell and John Beswick.

I would like to express my sincere thanks to Matthew and his team at Urbane Publications for having confidence in me as a writer and for publishing and promoting my work.

Richard Whittle believes that he discovered the power of the novel and his love of writing at the age of eleven when he read Paul Gallico's *The Snow Goose and Jenny*. On his overseas trips many years later he armed himself with an excess-baggage mix of paperbacks that did not include crime novels – as an ex-policeman he had vowed never to read them, let alone write them. Now, years later, he no longer feels that way. His central characters, people like you and me, find that they have been dragged into situations beyond their control and from which there seems little chance of escape. For them, crimes are most definitely involved.

Richard has been a policeman, a police marksman and police motorcyclist, a diesel engine tester, professional engineering geologist and Chartered Engineer. He has worked in civil engineering, geothermal energy, nuclear and mining industries in seventeen countries in Europe, Africa and the Americas and is able to draw on a wealth of personal experiences. Well known in his field as a technical writer, he spent time as a book reviewer for technical journals and regularly contributed to professional publications.

As a spare-time novelist he had several short stories published. In 2002, writing as Alan Frost, he was shortlisted for the Crime Writers Association's Debut Dagger Award. More recently, his self-published novel, *Playpits Park*, has been downloaded as an eBook more than 4000 times.

Richard has been a trustee of a Scottish Charitable Organisation, acting first as its project manager and then its technical advisor. He now writes full time. He currently lives in the Scottish Borders, not too far away from Edinburgh.

URBANE

Urbane Publications is dedicated to
developing new author voices, and publishing
fiction and non-fiction that challenges, thrills and
fascinates.

From page-turning novels to innovative
reference books, our goal is to publish what
YOU want to read.

Find out more at
urbanepublications.com